Copyright © 2013 S. J. Wolff
Dagger of Aita: Retribution
First Edition, Paperback – Published 2013

Cover designed by Wolff Paw Studios - WolffPawStudios.com

EarthShine Press

Printed in the United States of America.

This book is a work of fiction. Names, characters, places, and incidents either are products of the author's imagination or are used fictitiously. Any resemblance to actual persons, living or dead, events, or locales is entirely coinci-dental.

ISBN: 0615840426
ISBN-13: 978-0615840420 (EarthShine Press)

THE DAGGER OF AITA

RETRIBUTION

S. J. WOLFF

DEDICATION

This book is dedicated to those in my life who've been there throughout this process. To those who believed I could do it even when I doubted myself.

To my beloved, you are my heartbeat. Without you, I would have given up a long time ago and life would be dull indeed.

To my children, you've watched me struggle, get knocked down and get back up again. Learn from my mistakes but also my triumphs. And always know, this book is proof that dreams really can come true.

To my dearest friend and kin sister, you know who you are. Without having known you, there would be no Nix. You are an inspiration.

To a mentor, teacher, and friend - My high school English teacher, Mrs. Karen Owens. You may not know how important you were to a young would-be writer. Yours was the first voice of encouragement in my life. Your wise and ever-positive words of encouragement squashed the negative voice in my head and made me believe.

Tнe WATCHERS

From
The Book of Enoch
Section 1 Chapter 6

[1]*And it came to pass when the children of men had multiplied that in those days were born unto [2]them beautiful and comely daughters. And the Watchers, the children of the heavens, saw and lusted after them, and said to one another: 'Come, let us choose wives from among the children of men [3]and beget us children.' And Sêmîazâz, who was their leader, said unto them: 'I fear ye will not [4]indeed agree to do this deed, and I alone shall have to pay the penalty of a great sin.' And they all answered him and said: 'Let us all swear an oath, and all bind ourselves by mutual imprecations [5]not to abandon this plan but to do this thing.' Then swear they all together and bound themselves [6]by mutual imprecations upon it. And they were in all two hundred...*

[7]*...And these are the names of their leaders: Sêmîazâz, their leader, Arâkîba, Râmêêl, Kôkabîêl, Tâmîêl, Râmîêl, Dânêl, Êzêqêêl, Barâqîjâl, Asâêl, Armârôs, Batârêl, Anânêl, Zaqîêl, Samsâpêêl, Satarêl, Tûrêl, Jômjâêl, Sariêl. 8 These are their chiefs of tens.*

Born, to the Daughters of Men were a hybrid race known in biblical times as the Nephilim. Pleased with their offspring, the Watchers doted on them, teaching them the forbidden knowledge of weapons, jewelry, and the secrets of the natural magics.

Today, their preternatural progeny walks the Earth and are known as the Alimentatori.

Chapter One

Along the shores of Lake Champlain

Her musky scent hung in the air, igniting my desires.

Red hot thirst grew within me, threatening to tear apart my self-control. I swallowed, fighting back my natural urges. Closing my eyes, a whispered breath escaped in an erotic sigh.

As my Angel neared her climax, my senses sang in anticipation. I bared my teeth, preparing for the ultimate in ecstasy. The human body produced adrenaline only long enough to get it through whatever excitement, fear, or stressful situation it might encounter. It was short lived in the system and had to be harvested at a precise moment to be effective. Some of us preferred to use fear as the catalyst. Not me. I liked my Adrena raw, primal…loaded with sexual energy.

My tongue eased over a small area of her neck, preparing her for what was to come. Within seconds the skin would numb. She would not even realize what I was doing.

When the moment came, she writhed beneath me, her breath coming in short gasping bursts as razor sharp teeth slipped easily into her flesh, straight to the vein.

I moaned, covering the area with my mouth. Anticipation of

the moment carried me on a wave of pleasure. The metallic taste of blood followed by the slightest aftertaste, a sweet nectar-like liquid touched my tongue, sending a shudder through me. As the Adrena entered my system, the high was immediate, the drug like no other. The rising climax built to a deafening crescendo within me, causing the tightfisted control I usually exhibit to slip loose.

My senses reeled.

A pleasure-full moan escaped my lips followed by the breath catching in my throat.

The world was filled with rushing sounds, bursting stars, the euphoria intense and beautiful. I hovered just between reality and pure unadulterated ecstasy. When I was unable to hold back any longer, I plunged deep within her recesses, finishing with one loud ferocious growl. Several moments passed as the world settled around me. Collapsing beside her on the bed, the room seemed to waver. I heaved a sigh in contentment.

A synthetic rush would never match the taste of a human at the precise moment of orgasm. No wonder some Alimentatori had trouble controlling themselves. Releasing one's partner, when one wanted to continue the high for as long as possible could be difficult. But, like all good things it always ended much too soon.

As I rose from the bed, I rubbed a hand over my face. Stretching my arms upward, I twinged. The skin stretched across the tightening muscles of my chest, stinging where the little human had raked her nails across it. I brushed my fingers over the marks she'd left. My mouth twisted into a half smile. *She had her moments. Almost drew blood this time.*

I turned, glancing down at the nubile young red-head I'd taken two years ago as my *il Scelto,* my chosen one.

Unique Evangelique, I liked to call her. Most people just called her Angel. Sweet, sassy, a bit of an attitude when she didn't get her way. But more important, the girl was a wild cat in the bedroom.

Thus far our relationship had been mutually beneficial, though *not* mutually exclusive. It would never be so. Angel was my *devotee*. As such, she was given all the considerations of my chosen human companion. However, because she was human, I would never take her to wife.

Alimentatori did not wed humans. Ever.

Okay, that was not completely true. Our first ancestors, the Grigori, had engaged in marriage. From what I understood, the practice continued for one or two generations. When the two diametrically opposed species combined, it resulted in mixed blood nestlings, infant creatures with long lives, an addiction to the adrenaline produced in the human body, and no desire to be thought of as human, the first generation of my kind. As our numbers grew, there was no longer a need to seek a spouse from the ranks of short-lived humans. So over time, the practice ceased entirely.

Which was fine by me.

We lived seven times longer than the average human. Who needed the pain associated with knowing one's time with someone was fleeting?

Evangelique rolled away from me and buried her face in the pillow. Under normal circumstances I wouldn't allow a She-hume to stay the night. However, it was not unusual for Angel to stay. She knew the score, never assuming it meant more to me than I could give.

Turning over, I inhaled. Alas, tonight I needed my space. "I'm going to go take a shower. Do you mind showing yourself out?" I heard her turn and sit up. Her whispered response broke with the subtlest hint of surprise. She trailed her fingers down my back in an obvious effort to illicit a physical response. "Jace? The night's still young. Aren't you're good for another round or two." Her voice was husky, full of allure. I steeled myself against her charms. When it was obvious, I was not responding to her cajoling, she pouted. "What gives?"

Ignoring her question, I rose and walked toward the en suite bathroom. Before closing the door, I turned and gave her a look I hoped would assuage her. I paused long enough to speak over my shoulder, "Thanks, Angel. You're the best."

A half hour later when I emerged from the confines of the steam filled bathroom, she had disappeared. Rubbing my hair with a plush, burgundy towel, I crossed the room to the window. I wrapped the towel about my lower half. Crossing my arms over my chest, I stared out into the night. A frown crinkled my brow.

Over the last week, an odd sense of foreboding had grown within me.

I had not heard from Julian since just after his arrival in Italy almost two weeks ago, and my elder brother wasn't one to go so long without a word. Ever since our parents died, we kept close tabs on each other, and his current lack of communication worried me.

What was even more disturbing was the absence of any contact with Julian's Second, Adrien. Julian might be out of touch, but

Adrien shouldn't be. He should have responded to the voicemail I left hours ago asking him about Julian's lack of communication.

I walked to the nightstand where I'd left my cell phone and picked it up.

Still nothing.

Setting down the phone, I tossed the towel over a nearby chair and then climbed between the Egyptian cotton sheets. Switching off the bedside lamp, I settled back onto the pillows and stared into the darkness of the room. It was almost four a.m. in Italy. The ascension would have completed. There was no reason for my calls to go unanswered. So, why were they?

I pondered the various reasons and then came to a conclusion. The only reason Julian would not have made contact was because something or someone was keeping him from making a phone call. If Julian was in trouble, I would be damned if I would lie around waiting for the phone to ring. Never in my life did I sit around waiting for something to happen when I could be out there making it happen. It just wasn't in my nature to be that patient.

Tossing back the top sheet, I turned to plant my feet on the ground. I crossed the room to grab pants out of the drawer. As I donned a pair of royal blue sleep pants, the silken material slipped against my skin scarcely registering. I made my way to the bedroom door.

When I reached the top of the large staircase at the center of the house, I place my hand on the dark mahogany banister. Within seconds I reached the bottom step. I paused for a moment, unsure of what to do next.

Maybe I was being paranoid. He'd never ascended before. I didn't know anyone who had. Being out of touch could just be part of the process.

Glancing around the darkened foyer, my toes curled away from the cool Spanish tiles of the floor. I mulled the possibility over in my mind. If this was part of the process, then he would call me once it was complete. Of that I was sure. *Besides, just what was I going to do?* Rush to Julian's side and ruin everything for him? An Aliment leader needed to be self-sufficient, strong willed, and without fear. If I showed up, it would make Julian look weak, as if his own brother didn't trust him to be on his own in a foreign country. This couldn't be further from the truth.

Julian was everything to me.

He was my elder brother, father-figure, mentor, and the one person in the world who knew me for who I was and loved me anyway. I would do anything for him, and I had regular proof that he would do the same for me.

At one time I considered Julian's determination to ascend and sit on the Great Council his downfall. I didn't understand his desire to sit amongst the leaders of the Kin, to demand the respect that had been for so long denied us. For me, prostrating ourselves in front of the very same people who shunned us as children seemed demoralizing. I didn't believe we had to sit on the Council to have our house recognized by self-aggrandizing members of traditional society. However, when Julian set out to do something, nothing could stop him, not even me.

I admired that about him.

His drive was what had kept us alive after the brutal slaying of our parents. To this day I had no recollection of what happened. From what I understood they died saving my life, a truth that was at times hard to bear. All I knew was that Julian had found me unconscious, beneath the bloodied bodies of our parents.

I smiled as I remembered waking to find Julian sitting by my bed awaiting some sign that I would survive. He'd never given up on me. That was the remarkable thing about Julian. Despite losing our parents at such a young age he never faltered. He took charge that day and gave me something to live for.

Several years later, he turned his attention to restoring the house of Samsaveel to its former glory and built a Clan. Once those tasks were completed, Julian petitioned for House acceptance, but the Great

Council rejected us time and again.

Ironic really, considering the family seat should have been our birthright. Had our parents lived past our youngling years, they would have placed the sacred tattoo of our well-respected house upon the left breast of each of us, denoting our rank as nobility within the House of Samsaveel. Regrettably, the tattooing of the young could only be done by the hand of an immediate relative and under the scrutiny of a designated Council representative, of which, we had neither.

It wasn't until Nathanial Briggs came into our lives, that things changed. The elder took us under his wing and guided Julian's hand until our Clan was strong and Julian our Padrone. As our leader, he petitioned the Council once again, and this time, well, that was what this trip to Italy was all about. After years of struggling Julian had earned the right to take the family seat. He'd proven his worth and was now embarking on the final step.

I shook off the somber thoughts of moments ago. Pride spread through me, lifting my shoulders, and raising my chin a little higher. Julian was the best man, Aliment or otherwise, I had ever known, and he *would* call me. I just had to find a way to do something I was no good at. Be patient.

*****

For three days the worry gnawed at my gut like a termite embedded in an ancient oak. Every worry, fear, concern for Julian's safety and his lack of response compounded. Eager for one moment of peace, I sought solace with a beautiful stranger. In the bliss of that moment, exhaustion pulled me down into a restless slumber.

The loud pounding on the front door of my home startled me awake.

Squinting at the bedside clock, I glared at the angry red numbers.

Just after two o'clock. I growled. *Someone has a death wish.*

Pushing the willowy sweat-drenched leg of my companion from across my middle, I sat up. Inhaling deeply, I moved to rise. An unpleasant odor wrinkled my nose. I paused. Turning away from the foul smell, my lip curled in disgust. My crisp, clean sheets stunk of flowery perfume mixed with human sweat. I shook my head and hoisted myself onto my feet. *This is why you never invite a vessel to stay the night. Downright, nasty.* Maybe I should have sought out Angel, instead of settling for whatever her name was. She would have been good for a moment of bliss and forgotten worries without the inevitable after party regrets.

The pounding on the door commenced again, reminding me of the reason I was awake at this god forsaken hour. In an instant I was off the bed and across the room.

Whoever it was better have a damn good reason for using my door as tympani.

I bent over and picked up the red silk robe I'd tossed to the ground a few short hours before. Shrugging into it, I crossed the room.

My passage down the grand staircase of our ancestral home was swift and silent. I sensed the presence of another Aliment before I touched the door. I yanked it open expecting to see one of my kinsmen, but not this one.

A moment of surprise registered before I was able to recover. *Adrien?* My heart raced. I knew it. Something was wrong. Adrien would never leave Julian's side, in unfamiliar territory surrounded by strangers. It was his job to protect him. My gaze sought his, my stomach in knots. All those feeling I'd sought to squelch with the vessel upstairs came rushing back. Sadness, worry, fear echoed in his familiar dark eyes.

"Jace, I'm sorry to wake you but."

Moving aside, I beckoned him in. Speaking in a hushed tone, I studied his worried features. "Adrien? Why aren't you with Julian?" My eyes narrowed as I remembered the human guest upstairs. ""Never mind. You can explain yourself in a moment." I motioned him to silence and led him into the study. If I was going to have to take Adrien to task for failing in his duties, I wasn't going to do it front of a human.

After he entered, I explained, "I have a guest upstairs. Wait here while I extract myself from that situation. I will be back in a moment."

I closed the door and crossed to the stairs. A few moments later, I burst through the door of my room. Worry spurred an urgent, almost angry outburst. "Get up and get out."

The woman's peaceful slumber shattered, and she started. I shuffled around the room, picking up her clothes as she stretched unhurried on the bed, my urgency not registering. "What's wrong? Didn't I please you?"

The muscles in my jaw ticked. Losing patience, I crossed to her, grabbed her arm, and dragged her out of bed. "This isn't about you. I just need you to go." Shoving her clothes at her, I pushed her toward the door, "Now."

She stumbled but recovered as she clasped her bunched up clothing to her chest. "Fine. You don't have to be so pushy." As the girl struggled to shimmy into her panties, while balancing on one foot and holding on to the clothes I'd forced into her arms, I noticed tears well up in her eyes, causing the green orbs to glisten like twin emeralds.

Fuck! I scowled. "Don't cry. I told you, this isn't about you." Just another reason to wish I had not allowed her to stay. If I had sought out Angel instead, I wouldn't have had to waste precious minutes tossing the girl out before dealing with Adrien. "I have more pressing matters to deal with than soothing hurt feelings. Please, get dressed and meet me downstairs. I will call you a cab."

After what seemed like endless minutes of waiting, she appeared at the top of the stairs. I mumbled under my breath, "Bout fucking time."

She sniffled but refused to meet my glare. When she reached my side, I escorted her to the front door. Pulling some money out of my wallet, I handed it to her. "Here, take this. It's for the cab."

The young girl nodded and clutched the money to her chest with a white knuckled fist.

She was frightened. *No matter.* If she expected to play in the twisted world of the Vessels, then she should expect far worse. The abrupt end to the evening and my little outburst were tame in comparison to what some other Aliments did for pleasure.

As the cab pulled away, I closed the door and then turned the dead bolt lock. The resounding clicks echoed through the foyer like a death knell.

Though the moment was upon me, I hesitated. Did I want to hear what Adrien had to say? No, but I had little choice. I owed it to Julian to hear his Second out.

A moment later I faced Adrien in the confines of the study. I turned on him, my voice taking on a hard edge, "Now, tell me what's wrong? Why aren't you with Julian?"

He glanced away from me, almost like he was afraid of what my reaction would be. He was right to be afraid. If he allowed any harm to come to Julian, I would make sure he felt the full measure of my displeasure, and then he would be compelled to look for a new Clan.

"I'm sorry, Jacen." Adrien fidgeted with a drink he'd poured for himself while I was upstairs. "I don't know how to tell you this."

My eyes bored into him as a pained frown pinched my lips. "Adrien, where's Julian?"

"Julian..." his gaze met mine for the first time as if trying to impress upon me his deep regret, "Julian is dead. He was murdered."

Murdered? The horrific news hit me like a shock wave pushing the breath from my lungs. My knees gave way causing me to sink down on the arm of the wing back chair. I stared at my brother's Second. Shaking my head in silent denial, I turned from Adrien's sympathetic gaze. I'd expected him to say Julian was in the hospital or some other mundane thing that would blow over with time. But this? How could this be? No, there had to be some mistake. The muscle in my jaw tightened as my gaze returned to Adrien's. His devastated look said it all. He spoke truth. Fury welled up within me, and my voice came out in a menacing whisper. "What happened?"

He cast his gaze downward, unwilling to meet my anger head on. "Everything was going well, just as it was planned," he swallowed as he met my stare, his brown eyes carrying the weight of his own guilt, "he'd been drinking."

A grim frown turned the corners of my mouth downward. ""RUSh?"

"No, he'd sworn off the stuff that morning. I think his impending Ascension made him rethink his penchant for that shit. Anyway, he was into the hard liquors that night. Well, you know your brother, a little goes a long way with him."

I crossed my arms and nodded, acknowledging Julian's Achilles heel, but didn't interrupt.

"As was my duty, I was with him from the moment he left the Ascension ceremony until the moment he was ready to call it quits on the booze. Then I went to get him a cup of coffee to take the edge off his buzz. When I returned, I saw him leaving the room with a woman."

Taking a deep breath, he pushed his fingers through his shock of blond hair and then looked back at me. His warm brown eyes reflected his shame. "I swear, if I thought anything was wrong, I would have followed them." His voice sounded choked as he continued, "I figured he was just taking the party upstairs with the girl, you know?"

"And, he didn't?" My eyes narrowed in accusation.

"No. He didn't. An hour later when I went up to the suite,

I knocked on his door. He didn't answer, so I went in."

I closed my eyes, my breathing purposeful, attempting to calm the rage within me. "He wasn't there?"

He shook his head.

"What are you saying? That this woman not only disappeared from beneath your nose with my brother in tow but was also responsible for his death?" The thought was absurd. No Aliment would kill another. It was against every law by which we lived. So, if she wasn't an Aliment, then what was she? A human vessel? That was slightly more plausible. The idea of a vessel revolting against one of us? Every instinct in me screamed, 'never in a million years,' but logic prevailed. Ridiculous as it may be, what else was there?

Adrien nodded.

My eruption was immediate, rivaling the explosive force of an angry volcano, spewing ashen embers to the highest realms of the heavens to fall to earth with burning, caustic ferocity. Flying off the chair, I was in his face before he had time to mount a defense. "What the fuck? How could you let some human kill my brother?"

"Whoa, whoa, whoa, Jace!" He held up his hands, palms toward me as if fending off me, my anger, and the ludicrous statement. "I never said she was human."

What? "She was Alimentatori?" My anger boiled, though tempered now by shocked disbelief.

"No fucking way." Adrien came down hard on the side of our people. "You know as well as I do that no Aliment would ever harm another, let alone the newly Ascended."

His response both cooled my anger and confused the hell out of me. "If it wasn't an Aliment and it wasn't a human, then what the hell was it?"

"I can't be sure. I believe she was what they call a Cambiare." Stunned, I shifted backward. *A what? What the hell was a Cambiare?* As if he read my thoughts, Adrien continued.

"They're something I have never seen before, Jace. Over there, they're like some kind of urban legend. People who turn into things, animals. I don't know, creatures. Strong. Real strong. All I know is that we were told to stay the hell away from Assisi. It's the heart of Cambiare territory."

"And, what makes you think this woman was one of these creatures?"

"I don't know. A hunch, I guess." He paced the room a few feet away from me, as if he were trying to figure it all out. "We'd been searching for hours when his car was found. It was abandoned outside of Assisi. In it we found blood, lots of blood. The trail led away from the vehicle as if something yanked him out of the car by force and then dragged him away." A shiver shook his body as a memory seemed to capture his mind, and his eyes took on a hard gleam. "We found him several yards away, tossed in the bushes. He was lying there decapitated, his head next to him. His entire body was covered in deep gashes like something had taken great pleasure in tearing him apart." He shook himself out of the daze and glanced up to meet my stare.

Swallowing the bile rising in my throat, I rose and walked to the window. My thoughts heavy, I studied the darkness beyond the paned glass. Shuffling behind me alerted me to Adrien's intent to join me. As he paused next to me, I refrained from looking at him. "The whole scene was like something out of a horror movie." His whisper would have been inaudible to anyone who was not of our kind. "I've never seen anything like it. Julian was not able to fight it off, yet the woman survived. This is what leads me to believe she is more than meets the eye. But, why would a Cambiare kill your brother? What would they have had to gain?"

A chill crept up my spine. My shoulders rose as I inhaled, then expelled it in a sorrow-filled sigh. I focused my eyes, filtering the existing light to allow me to see into even the darkest reaches of the tree line. "Does a beast need a reason to do what is in its nature?"

"I suppose not, but Jacen, I don't think you quite understand. no normal animal could have done that to him."

I felt his gaze on me, but I remained unmoved. "Mark my words, the beast will look into my eyes and understand the consequences of having taking Julian's life."

His avid stare was upon me, studying my profile as if assessing my outer calm. "From what I've heard, they have the reflexes and predatory nature of a large wild cat. And, their strength is reportedly superior to any Aliment."

I glanced in Adrien's direction, my brow arching in sarcasm. "Is it now?"

He nodded, his features somber. "Whether their minds are more human or beast, I haven't a clue." At a loss, he stuffed his hands into the pockets of his khaki slacks. "Either way, they will be formidable."

Turning back to the window, my own grim determination reflected back at me from the spotless glass. "Then the hunt shall be challenging."

Chapter Two

As the sun crept over the horizon, I tossed clothes into the suitcase lying open on my bed. Adrien had insisted on accompanying me to my room, hesitant to leave me alone for any length of time. Was he afraid I would disappear, withdrawing into my sorrow, leaving him alone to deal with the Clan on his own?

My jaw set, the muscles in my cheek jumping as teeth ground together.

My brother, the only family I had left, was gone. Adrien, who had bound himself by sacred oath to the service and protection of Julian, sat in the corner of my room, guilty eyes pleading for understanding.

I didn't care.

Maybe one day I would look at him without wondering why he still lived while Julian lay cold and unbreathing. His mere presence made me want to strike out at him. However, I had far more important matters to which to attend, like retrieving my brother's body, seeing his soul released, and then hunting down the Cambiare whore responsible for his death.

My gaze wandered to the clock on the bedside table.

Seven hours until I'll be in the air, headed to Rome.

A shiver of dread coursed through me as nervous tension churned my stomach. I dreaded the wait ahead of me. It gave me far too much time to think. By the time I boarded the plane, I would be as strung out as a RUSh addict in the throes of a violent withdrawal.

Sweet Aita, I hate flying.

Ironic since if not for an in-utero procedure, I, like my ancient ancestors, would have been born with wings.

Until the fourteenth century, our ancestors reveled in flight. They walked like demi-gods among humans, their wings bearing proud witness to our direct descent from the Grigori. That all came to a screeching halt when we went from being works of wonder to works of the devil.

Then when those sent by the church to capture, torture, and kill our kind, went on their rampage through Europe, it became clear. To save our race from total annihilation we had to sever our tie to the ancestors.

At first the practice of removing the wings of our children was brutal. Just after birth, the wings were surgically removed; much like a dog's tail was cropped as a pup. An elder Aliment once told me the procedure was necessary to hide what we are. As I listened to the tale and then touched the scars on the old man's back, even as a child I recognized the haunted look in his eyes. Desperate times called for desperate measures, I suppose, but I couldn't imagine surviving such a barbaric practice.

We lost so many children during The Rending. Thankfully that dark period in our history had been short lived, but it left far more than the physical scars. The devastating heartache which followed rippled throughout our community.

In the end, that is what drove our best scientists, some of the most brilliant men in the world, to set about finding a less barbarous way to deal with the issue. Finally, after many years of experimentation, they perfected a procedure that allowed the scientist to isolate and destroy the genes connected to the growth of wings in utero.

Of course, as in any political battle, the vocal minority, in this case the proponents of allowing nature to take its course, shouted the loudest. *Like the birds, we were meant to fly, wings make us unique, wings give us dominion over man, blah, blah, blah.* You name it; someone had spouted it. Unbeknownst to humans, this movement was what catapulted the world into the era of human flight.

The corners of my mouth lifted into a wry smirk.

I remembered the history lessons I studied as a boy. Two young, idealist Aliment brothers believed if they could give our human cousins the ability to fly, then perhaps we would be afforded the right to cease the in-utero modification of our children. They of course were wrong, and it appeared probable that their efforts and those of others like them were too little too late. The scientists tasked with performing the procedure found an increasingly number of cases where the gene no longer existed in our offspring.

Wings were being bred out of existence, which was fine by me. It was hard enough fitting into the human world without giving ourselves away, to do so sporting a pair of wings would be near impossible.

Which brought me right back to my present situation, mere hours from boarding a plane, and I *hate* flying. Very little in this world would ever induce me to board a circular tube that defies the laws of gravity and is, relatively speaking, a new mode of transportation. I shivered again. I wouldn't do it for anyone other than Julian.

My hands shook as I zipped the bag closed. Picking it up by the handle, I then set the wheels on the ground and glanced up at Adrien.

"I'm ready."

He stood and crossed the room. "Good. We need to meet with the Clan before heading to the airport."

I nodded, knowing it had to be done. "Call a meeting. Have everyone meet at Corridoio Sovrano in one hour."

By all rights, this meeting should have been called as soon as Adrien brought news of Julian's death. I hesitated, unwilling to share my private pain with the others. Now, I was out of time. They had to prepare for receiving Julian and needed to choose a new leader.

Twenty minutes later, I was the first to arrive at the hall which stood on the back acreage of our land. A very long time ago our parents purchased the property with the intent of building a place for their future Clan. Unfortunately, just after they had the house built, they were killed. They left the property to us. When Julian received a stack of papers from the executor of their estate, he placed them in an intricately carved box our mother had given him when he came of age and then tucked the box away in our father's desk. There, the papers languished for a hundred years. Then, one day he received an offer to buy the antique desk. Intent on accepting the offer, Julian began the process of cleaning it out. As he pulled out parchment and dusty quills the long-forgotten box re-emerged. Opening the box for the first time, he found the plans for what they'd called "il Corridoio Sovrano", the Sovereign Hall. It was then that Julian had picked up the reigns and fulfilled the long dead parental dream. Though I was little more than a preteen at the time, I remembered the moment clearly. His drive to see the structure finished was something I had never seen in him before, and it was quite a mystery to me then. Now, standing in front of the large domed hall he built, I understood. He was honoring the memory of our parents, putting aside his own dreams, to breathe life into the ones our parents left behind. My throat closed around the sorrow, filling every space within me. I swallowed, attempting to dislodge the sudden lump in my throat. I choked back the sadness, unwilling to allow it a resting place.

I moved forward to unlock the outer doors of our sacred space. The cool confines of the darkness within beckoned me to enter. Doing just that, the doors closed behind me with a quiet swoosh, blocking out the sounds from without and leaving me alone in the silence of the space. Flipping on the foyer lights, I paused a moment to lean against the panels and stare straight ahead at the double doors which led to the meeting hall. Within a few short minutes the space would be full of Clan members unaware of the dire news I was about to rain down upon their heads. There was no stopping the impending storm, and no use hiding from it either. I crossed the narrow hall to the double doors. Once in front of them, I stopped to prop the doors open. The interior of the sacred space, dark and cool in the summer heat, beckoned to me. My fingers found the light switch on the wall to the right of the doors. Artificial light spilled over the octagonal room bathing the room with a soft glow.

The Sovereign Hall, though smaller than most church halls, was a room large enough to accommodate full meetings of the Clan. *All thirty-seven of us—well, thirty-six with the loss of Julian.*

The architectural lines of the domed room were clean and crisp. Gun-metal grey walls came together each attached to the other by dark cherry wood joists, which rose up from the wooden floor and joined braces at the top of the eight-foot walls. From there the mosaic-tiled roof curved upwards into the sky, depicting images from our people's history. A large candelabra, which we'd converted to electricity, hung from the direct center of the room.

Three rows of overstuffed, deep red chairs alternated with small round cherry wood tables followed the curved lines of the walls and radiated outwards from the center in three waves. Located furthest from the center were identical smaller chairs for the children of the Clan. The corners of my lips turned downward. Good in theory, not so much in practice, as these seats were rarely occupied. The children seemed to prefer playing behind them rather than sitting in them. The next row was for the younger adult people, both married and single. We currently had nine children, seven married couples, and a few single stragglers, which is where I fit in, though as Julian's brother I always took a place of honor to his right along with the six eldest members of the Clan. That would change now that he was gone, but that was the least of my worries. Glancing at the seat at the far side of the circle, a memory of Julian sitting there kicked me in the gut. *Who would occupy the high seat now? Who was worthy of taking on the role of Padrone?* I sighed heavily. I could simply hope whoever it was would live up to the memory of

Julian.

As I took my place, I gazed at the empty seats. Though it had been less than three weeks, it seemed like ages had passed since the last time I sat here. We gathered as a Clan the night before Julian was due to leave for Italy. We celebrated well into the night, and all with the world was right. This hall had known such happiness and joy, it was hard to bring myself to sully those memories with tragedy. Unfortunately, it could not be helped. Today, the walls of this hallowed place would know sadness the depth of which they had never experienced. Grief would fill the air, suffocating the memories, leaving behind a kind of emptiness. Our Padrone was dead, and it was up to me to bring our people through this as best I could. Laying my head back against the soft leather of the chair, I closed my eyes and mentally prepared myself for the task ahead.

Less than an hour later the room was full, and I had not moved from my spot. I wiped away the tracks of the few tears shed while alone with my thoughts and concentrated on the task at hand. All curious eyes were on me, and I had no idea what I was going to say. No amount of mental preparation would have made this task any easier.

To delay a moment, I reached for the glass of water someone, perhaps Adrien, had placed on the table next to me. I sipped it slowly, wishing for this all to be over. But, to no avail. When I placed the glass back on the table, the Clan still sat watching me, and my mouth was still dry. Running out of reasons to keep from addressing the group, I sat back and uncrossed my legs.

I breathed deeply as I pushed back the pain of what I had to say. "I...," stumbling over how to begin, I looked above the heads of my Kin and sought out inspiration. It came in little waves of conversation, little bits of a whole. "Thank you for coming on such short notice." *Was it just me, or did my voice sound unusually hollow?* "I'm not sure..." I awaited a stroke of genius from above. When nothing followed, I brought my gaze back to the others in the room. Easing into the news would just prolong my own agony. Being blunt would be like stabbing each one present in the heart with a sharp knife, messy and painful. *Who am I kidding?* The news was painful no matter how one found out. The best I could hope for was to ease my own plight by being forthright. "Two days ago, Julian was murdered."

The loud outcry of disbelief filled the room, echoing against the curvature of the roofline and reverberating along the walls. I held up a hand to stem the flow of questions, knowing it did no good to ask. "It happened shortly after his Ascension to the Great Council. I don't know all the details yet. I merely know what Adrien was able to relay."

A sobbing came from nearby and I glanced over my left shoulder. *Damn it! I am such an ass.*

Amidst my own pain, I'd forgotten about Magda. No woman should ever have to find out in the company of so many that her intended would not be coming home to her. I should have taken her aside and told her personally.

Catching her eye, I held out my hand. She reached for mine and slipped her cold fingers into the warmth of my grasp. I squeezed her hand in gentle consolation and drew her to sit next to me. She took Julian's seat and leaned over our clasped hands sobbing. Rubbing her back awkwardly, I leaned over and whispered, "I'm so sorry, Magda. I didn't think."

It was all I could do to comfort the grieving woman.

Placing a gentle kiss upon the back of her head, I closed my eyes fighting back the emotion within. There was no time to show weakness, not when I had the eyes of the Clan upon me. I needed to be strong and show them I was capable of exacting Retribution delle Parentele—Kin Retribution. It was my right as his only surviving family and I was not about to let anyone take that away from me.

Straightening, I cleared my throat and met the stares of those who'd known Julian so well. They'd all loved and supported us as the family we'd missed having as children. They'd given him a sense of purpose and me a place to call home. He'd fought for them and for me. Now it was my turn to return the favor.

"I will be leaving this afternoon to retrieve my brother's body. I will make arrangements from that end to have him returned home. I will expect you to make the arrangements on this end."

Several murmurs in the affirmative echoed in the space as most nodded in agreement. Magda's soft voice rose above the rest as she drew my attention. "When you return we will hold the rites."

The lump in my throat returned as I gazed down into her grief-stricken eyes. "No, you will hold the rites without me present. I will do what I can in Italy. I will not be returning home until I've found the creature responsible for Julian's death."

One of the elders spoke up, "There is no need for that. He was our Padrone. We will send a delegation to the Council and petition to have his killer turned over to us."

My steely gaze found the eyes of Eustis Fowler. "With all due respect Eustis, he was indeed our leader, but first and foremost, he was my brother. I will not give up my right to Kin Retribution."

Eustis seemed to shrink back into his seat, avoiding my direct glare. Once I was sure there would be no more suggestions of anyone else going after Julian, I continued, "Now, as I was saying, I will retrieve Julian's body. What I need from you is to prepare for his arrival." I glanced around the room taking in the familiar faces. "Also, you will need to choose a new Padrone. Julian would not want the Clan to move forward without leadership—"

Adrien interrupted, standing up. "Jacen."

I glanced up at him unsure of why he would interrupt me. "Yes, Adrien?"

His eyes sought mine from where he sat across the room. "May I have the floor for a moment?"

Sitting back in the chair, I crossed my legs and motioned for him to address the group.

He stood and spoke, "As you all know, it was my duty to keep Julian safe. I failed in this effort and wish to offer my sincere apologies to all of you. I ask forgiveness and for the opportunity to make things right." His gaze locked with mine as he continued, "If the new Padrone accepts my petition, I will pledge myself in service to him."

My eyes narrowed as I considered Adrien for a moment. His meaning was subtle, unexpected, and completely sincere. He expected me to be the new Padrone. Glancing around the circle, I realized perhaps he wasn't alone in this thought as all eyes looked to me for guidance.

Me? The next Padrone? The thought was absurd. I was not my brother nor had I any desire to be. To head off any suggestions of the kind, I rose and countered his declaration with one of my own. "I know Julian wouldn't want anyone to blame Adrien. Adrien was a loyal and devoted protector. Any one of *you* would be lucky to have him watch your back. Now, if you will excuse me, I have a plane to catch."

I strode across the room, determined to escape the uncomfortable silence. My fingers brushed the nickeled surface of the door's handle when a familiar, well-loved voice rang above the rest. "Jacen."

The breath froze in my lungs. If it was anyone else, I would already be through the door. But Nathanial Briggs took us in, guided us as best he could through our early adult years, and was like a father to us.

A frustrated growl threatened to wheedle its way out. Squashing it, I allowed my hand to drop down next to me. *Damn it.*

Next to Julian, Nathanial was the only one in the world I would lay down my life for. To disrespect him by leaving would dishonor all he had done for us. Nothing under the sun would cause me to treat him so. I turned on my heel and met his steady gaze with my own.

He walked toward me, his gait awkward as he maneuvered his cane between the seats. As was his habit, he was dressed to the nines. But now, through the myriad of years his body transformed until coats he'd worn perfectly in youth, now fit like burlap sacks. Along with his bygone physique, Nathanial had lost a good amount of hair, at least up top. The rest of it hung like long grey tendrils to his shoulders. As he approached, I noticed how pale and drawn he appeared. My brows drew together as I realized he was not doing well. When he stumbled, I stepped forward and took his arm.

"Yes, Nathanial? What can I do for you?"

Nathanial's aged blue eyes looked up at me with determination. "It's not what you can do for me, Jacen. It's what you can do for your brother."

Confused, I stared at him. Was his mind so addled by age that he hadn't understood what I'd said? "There's nothing more I can do for Julian, Nathanial. He's dead."

The older man drew himself up to his full height. Looking me straight in the eye, he screwed up his mouth in anger and raised his cane as if contemplating its use against my unsuspecting head. Then recovering himself, he growled, "I know that, you buffoon. I'm old not stupid. What I meant was Julian would want you to take his place."

Three steps away from freedom and there it was. I glanced up at the expectant faces around me.

Backing up as if attempting to retreat, I shook my head. "As flattered as I am, I don't think so."

Magda stood up. "And just why not?"

I glared at her willing her to sit back down. Instead others rose around her. Her left eyebrow arched as if posing the question, a second time.

I swallowed hard as I looked around the room. Nearly half the clan was on their feet expecting an answer from me; the other half watched with interest awaiting the reason for my objection.

My mind went blank. I had lots of good reasons. *Why couldn't I think of even one of them?*

Chapter Three

I gazed out the little porthole the airlines liked to call a window as we began our descent. One minute above the clouds, the next amidst the swirling, misty white mass. The plane bumped, and my fingers tightened on the arm of the seat.

As the ground came into view, I rolled the possibilities over in my mind for the umpteenth time. His loss haunted me, and not a moment passed that I hadn't asked myself, why? Why would someone want him dead? Why had he left the party with that…thing? None of it made any sense.

The plane jerked and bumped as we touched down at Roma Fiumicino Airport. As we taxied to the gate, the pretty blond flight attendant, who smelled of jasmine and chocolate, rose and picked up the handset at her station.

"Please remain seated with seat belts securely fastened until the aircraft has come to a complete and total stop. At this time, we would like to welcome you to Italy. The local time is seven twenty-five a.m., and it is absolutely beautiful seventy-six degrees outside. We hope you enjoy your stay in Italy's historic capital. We know you have a choice in airlines, and we thank you for flying with Eleganza."

The intercom clicked off as the flight attendant replaced the handset.

Finally, able to release my death grip on the arms of the business class seat which had been my torture chamber for the past eight and a half hours, I turned to Adrien. "Enjoy our stay? Huh, not likely."

Adrien's glance met mine briefly, long enough to sympathize with my plight, but then shied away like that of a hound that had been reprimanded by its heavy-handed master. Perhaps my brother's death weighed as heavily on his shoulders as it did on mine.

As soon as the plane jerked to a stop, Adrien was on his feet. Before I even had a chance to unbuckle my seat belt, he had unloaded our bags from the overhead bin and placed them in the seat next to me. I wondered at his intense, urgent manner. *Maybe he hated flying even more than I did.* Shrugging it off, I removed my seat belt in preparation for disembarkation.

It took several minutes for the door to open. Once it had, I rose as well. Adrien maintained his place in the middle of the aisle, holding back the stampede of other passengers who were anxious to be on their way and allowed me to pass in front of him. For a moment, I dwelled on the knowledge that a few short weeks ago, he would have done the same for Julian. A pang of regret stabbed at my heart. If only he had been able to stave off Julian's death the way he held the other travelers at bay.

Leading the way through the throng of humans, Adrien turned toward customs. "The Council will have sent a car for us, so we should be able to go straight to headquarters."

"Great. I want answers."

*****

If someone had told her a few weeks ago that she'd care one way or another about the arrival of another Alimentatori to Italy, she would have laughed. After all, what sane Cambiare cared whether a Feeder lived or died?

Yet here she was awaiting his arrival just the same.

Having never met the man she sought; she had no real way

of identifying him. Would she be able to recognize him from his resemblance to his brother? Julian had light, sandy blond hair. Did Jace as well? One thing was certain: siblings, whether human or otherwise, always had a similar scent trail. So, if all else failed, she would literally sniff him out.

She reached into her pocket. A moment later she withdrew her cell phone and checked the time. *Seven twenty-seven.* According to the board his flight was on time and had arrived at the gate, so at any moment he should stroll into the baggage claim area.

Looking around the terminal for somewhere a little less obvious to blend in, she noticed a few tables open at Chef Express. Meandering her way through the slowly increasing crowd, she scanned the area for a place to wait. When the sliding glass exit doors to her right *swooshed* open an all too familiar scent wafted in on the spring breeze. Eyes narrowing as her hackles rose; she turned to face the oncoming threat. To her surprise, the Aliment who just entered the terminal didn't seem to have taken notice of her at all. He rushed past, still several feet away, oblivious to her presence. Breathing a sigh of relief, she thanked all that was holy that though quite advanced, the Alimentatori sense of smell wasn't quite as refined as the Cambiare's. Quickening her pace, she crossed the terminal to join the others in relative anonymity at the coffee bar. Truthfully, the likelihood of the Aliment scenting her out amidst the throng of humans was slim, but it was best not to push her luck just the same. Blending in as much as possible, she crossed to the counter and ordered a cappuccino and then took a seat facing the oncoming travelers. Moving the paper cup to her lips, she sipped the hot liquid and watched the Aliment over the rim of the cup. If her hunch was correct, he was there for the same reason she was. As if in confirmation of her suspicions, the man removed a small cardboard sign from his coat pocket and held it in front of his chest. When he turned, the name scrawled on the paper in black ink drew her immediate attention. The corners of her naturally plump lips turned upward. *Mr. Jacen Trudeau.* Nope, she wasn't going to have to sniff him out at all.

Letting her gaze drift past the driver and to the mass of approaching travelers, she frowned. Unfortunately, that also meant he wouldn't be alone. She would have to find another way to get to him. At least the sign would make it infinitely easier to spot her mark.

All she needed to do now was sit and wait.

Several minutes later two men stopped a few steps away from the waiting driver. She immediately recognized the blond mountain of a man as the companion of the dead Aliment. She had seen him numerous times when tracking his master. The other man, though taller than his friend, had a muscular build and swarthy good looks. His black hair brushed the collar of a white business shirt. His solid muscular body encased in a white business shirt which he had tucked into an expensive looking pair of navy-blue dress pants. When he glanced around the terminal his gaze met her for a brief second. The breath caught in her throat. Even from this distance she could tell he had the most phenomenal ice-like, silvery blue eyes which seemed to hold an unmistakable air of superiority. Heat rose to her cheeks as she looked away breaking their momentary connection. He was not Julian's brother. His looks were far too unusual, even for an Alimentatori, though his attitude spoke clearly of being in charge. *But, then an air of entitlement often accompanies the beasts of Bracciano.*

Could he be the one then, this Jace for whom she was dispatched? She lifted her nose to sniff the air to isolate his scent. Everything from an overwhelming woman's perfume to the numerous blends of coffee permeated the stale climate-controlled air bombarding her senses. Picking out an unknown scent amidst this environment was going to be impossible. Frowning, she returned to watching the pair. She was just going to have to wait until she could get closer to confirm that he was the one for whom she came.

*****

A driver dressed in a black suit, driver's cap, and sunglasses stood near the baggage carousel holding a sign with my name on it. I moved to acknowledge him. Adrien's hand on my shoulder stopped me. I looked at him, my confusion evident.

Dropping the bags, he leaned forward and shook his head. "Wait here. Let me check him out first."

I frowned but did as he requested.

Having a Second was going to take a lot of getting used to.

A few moments later, Adrien returned to my side. "Sorry about that. We can't be too careful." He paused and glanced around the airport. Then, as if he found nothing amiss, he bent over and picked up the bags. Motioning for me to move forward, he said, "The driver checked out. His name is Sergio. There will be time for formal introductions later. Best to keep moving. It's not safe for you to be out in the open like this."

Adrien's whole cloak and dagger manner bothered me. If this supposed urban legend killed my brother, why would I be in danger when I'd just set foot in the country? *The only ones who knew of my arrival sat on the Great Council, unless...*

My eyes narrowed as a niggling suspicion grew within me. Perhaps he didn't trust someone on the Council. I would have to be sure to ask when we were alone and well out of earshot of any other Aliment. To question a member of the Great Council's loyalty to the crown or to each other was tantamount to treason, and I wasn't about to get myself killed over an unsubstantiated suspicion.

Following the other two men, I exited the terminal.

The ride to Bracciano took nearly an hour and was uneventful. So much so, that Adrien's snoring could be heard above the satellite radio, which piped classical music into the back compartment of the limo.

The tinted glass divider between the front and back slowly descended to reveal the back of Sergio's head.

I glanced up.

"Signore, siamo quasi là." Italian rolled off his tongue as easily as English rolled off mine. I struggled with the translation.

"I'm sorry?"

He pointed ahead of us. A large, closed gate sat at the end of the dead-end road. "We are almost there."

"Ah, okay. Very good." I folded the copy of Corriere della Sera, an English local daily newspaper, with which I occupied my time, and then sat forward anxious to get my first glimpse of our Seat of Power. From what Julian told me Casa Sede di Alimentazione, sat atop a cliff face overlooking the exquisite *Lago di Bracciano*. Lake Bracciano had been the home of the Alimentatori since we arrived on its shores before Rome was well, Rome.

Though I had never been to Alimentatori headquarters myself, my brother had been back and forth for several months prior to his Ascension. He once tried to get me to come along, but well, did I mention I hate to fly? Besides, one didn't just show up on the doorstep of an Aliment leader without an invitation.

As the gate opened, it revealed a pristine, long, twisting driveway lined with massive olive trees. They had to be at least thirty-five feet in height, their silvery gray-green leaves filtering the sunlight. The shadows swayed and shifted with the breeze, casting a kaleidoscope of patterns before us. As we made the final turn on our journey, the trees gave way to a thick blanket of well groomed, emerald colored grass. At the far end of the property an impressive modern-looking villa jutted upward out of the sea of green and into the brilliant blue sky. Ivy topiaries, fashioned into winged men, stood at either end of the grand veranda, paying homage to our origins. They seemed to stand guard over the entrance to the home, featureless faces staring blankly ahead. Their wing tips extended up to nearly brush the bottoms of two large identical balconies projecting out from the second floor.

The property surely did not disappoint. Even still, it was hardly what I expected.

For some reason I imagined the headquarters to be a little more, I don't know, business and a lot less pleasure. Concerned that we might not have been taken directly to headquarters, but instead to a private residence or perhaps a hotel, I addressed Sergio, "This is the Sede di Alimentazione?" I hoped he understood what I asked, and that I had pronounced the name right. Julian had mentioned it no more than once, and my Italian was rusty.

He waved his arm toward the house in a grand gesture and grinned. "Sì, questa è la Sede di Alimentazione."

No matter the spoken language, one could not mistake the immense pride, which radiated from the other man. One would think he, himself, owned the monolithic estate.

Moments later, the car pulled to a stop in front of the massive, tiled veranda. The driver got out and walked around to open my door. Emerging from the limo and into the sunlight, I squinted. So, this was it. The moment for which I'd waited two days. I was finally going to find out exactly what had happened to my brother.

Walking toward the curved marble steps, I left the others to deal with the bags.

Nothing more was going to stand in the way of finding the underlying cause of Julian's murder.

Chapter Four

The double French doors seemed to magically open as I neared. Glancing up, I found a stern-faced human behind the magic. He wore a well starched black jacket with a pristine white cotton shirt beneath it. He spoke not a word as he stepped aside to allow me entrance.

"Jace Trudeau. I'm here to see the Council." I said with authority as I moved through the doors.

"Yes, I know," was his simple response. He led me through a maze of hallways toward the back of the property. When we reached another set of double doors, he opened them. Standing aside, he motioned me into the room.

My gaze travelled through the doors to survey the room on the other side. I scowled. If this was the Council room, I was the walking dead. Turning, I glared at him. "I said, I am here to see the Council."

Without skipping a beat, he replied, his voice tinged with an indignant Italian flare, as if I'd offended him in some way, "You will wait in the library until *they* are ready for you."

My gaze returned to the room. The "library" as he called it, was less like a library and more like a private lounge. Yes, it had bookshelves lining all four walls, most of which had books on them, but that was where any resemblance to a library ended. The walls were painted dark forest green with all the woodwork painted stark white. Paisley curtains of green and blue were drawn back from large tinted, plate glass windows. I supposed the tint was necessary to allow light in yet protect the room's occupants from prying eyes. Made me wonder what private things happened in this room that needed protecting. If the large bar in the corner of the room was any indication, it was probably a kind of recreation that could get certain types of Alimentatori into trouble with the outside world. "How long will I have to wait?"

"I will return for you when you are summoned," the butler said with little emotion in his tone. Immediately after I exited the doorway, he shut the double doors, effectively cutting me off from asking any more questions.

Left with little choice, I made my way to the bar where a human bartender was currently in attendance. Perhaps he could be of some use to me in whiling away the minutes while I awaited an audience with the Great Council.

As I approached, he beamed. "Che cosa posso ottenere per voi?"

What can you get for me? How about a one-way ticket in to see the Council?

Eying the frosted glass bottles with scrolling deep

blue lettering which lined one of the bookshelves behind the bar, my eyes narrowed. *RUSh* - privately produced synthetic adrenaline. It was potent but didn't have the same kick as live Adrena. Another shelf held a variety of hard liquors which stood like good little soldiers awaiting orders. I doubted those got used much at all in this place. "A shot of RUSh."

Without a second's hesitation he answered in English, "You've got it."

The liquid was smooth going down. The punch came when it hit the system. A shudder rushed through me as it burned its way through like quick silver, igniting an intense burst of energy. My eyes widened in surprise. The euphoria was like nothing I'd ever experienced, even from a vessel. Glancing at the bartender, I turned puzzled eyes on the man. "What the fuck is this?"

He looked confused, as if he didn't understand the question. "It's what you asked for, sir, RUSh"

I shook my head in disbelief. It wasn't at all what I remembered the synthetic to be.

A hand came down on my shoulder. Turning to see who'd joined me, I realized Adrien had managed to find me. He chuckled. "I see you've found the bar."

I nodded. "Yeah." I held up the empty shot glass for him to see. "And I tried a shot of the RUSh they've got over here, and wow, is it amazingly strong."

Adrien took the open bottle from where the bartender had left it and raised it. "Want another?"

I shook my head. "No thank you. I need a clear head when I meet the Council for the first time."

"Suit yourself." He responded, pouring himself a shot. "From what I understand, they've intensified the effects of the synthetic through a new process of maturation. At one point, Julian couldn't get enough of it." I could tell he immediately regretted his words as he shook his head and then met my eyes. "I'm so sorry, Jace. I didn't mean to—"

I held up my hand to stop the apology before it went any further. "You don't need to apologize every time you bring him up. I loved my brother. I know he had his weaknesses." I glanced at the bottle sitting in front of me and shrugged. "And to be honest, at least now I can see why. It's much improved since I last tasted it." *If I could get my hands on a bottle or two of the new and improved synthetic,* "I might just be able to wean myself off the one-night stands."

He chuckled, as if doubting my sincerity. "Even the ones with Angel?"

The memory of a night we spent together not too long ago surfaced, and I let myself get lost in it for a moment. A satisfied grin transformed my face. She was the perfect woman. Passion, lust, and no strings all rolled into one. "Okay, maybe not completely off *her.*"

The good-natured ribbing came to a quick end as the double doors swept open and a beautiful woman with dark auburn hair sailed. All eyes in the room turned to watch as she strode forward as if she owned the place. She was obviously an Aliment. No human could ever hope to command the attention of every red blooded Alimentatori within a room like she did.

I leaned over without looking away from her and whispered into Adrien's ear. "Who the hell is that?"

He shrugged and turned to watch the scene unfold.

She moved across the room as if her every action was a practice in seduction. Long delicate fingers trailed along the back side of the couch mimicking a lover's gentle touch, all the while her big brown doe eyes, assessed her surroundings. She turned to me, her teeth tugging gently on her bottom lip adding the smallest hint of hesitation to her otherwise confident appearance. But in the next moment she cocked her chin an arrogant degree and any hesitation disappear. Her calculating eyes warmed as she scrutinized me. Her gaze seemed to stroke my body with an invisible touch. A shudder ran through me as my body reacted of its in accord. An ember of desire burned just below the surface as her gaze raked my frame. When she completed her appraisal, our eyes met briefly. An elegant auburn brow pulled upward in a superior arch. Her lips twisted, the left corner of her mouth slightly higher than the right, and then she winked. In that moment, I realized what she had just done. As a cat played with a mouse before devouring it, she had toyed with me. What was worse, I had allowed it.

Adrien chuckled, drawing my attention. As he turned back to the bar, my brows dipped in a dark scowl.

"What's so funny?"

He simply shook his head and sipped on his drink. Though his amusement rankled me, I chose to ignore it in favor of keeping the peace.

Moments later, the doors to the Library opened again. I glanced over my shoulder. The stern-faced butler entered. His gaze sought mine. His head dipped indicating it was time. I nodded in understanding. I pushed myself off the bar stool and clapped Adrien on the back. "Let's go."

Adrien and I followed the butler through a labyrinth of twists and turns just to end our trek in an empty hallway. Glancing around, I frowned. No doors. No Windows. Nothing but a dead end. *What the hell?* This made no sense. Just as I was going to address the issue, the human moved to allow us to pass. Confused, I stopped. Adrien brushed past me and proceeded further into the hall. He came to a stop directly in front of the far wall. Moving to join him, I whispered, "Obviously, you know something I don't."

With a wry turn of the lips, Adrien pointed to the corner above our heads. "Smile, you're on camera."

Directing my gaze to where he'd pointed, I immediately understood. Hidden amidst the shadows of the corner was a hole no bigger than the size of a pencil tip. A micro-lens viewed all who approached. Most wouldn't even notice it was there.

"I see. Wonder how many of those are planted around the grounds." I responded, feeling strangely violated by its presence.

"Let's just say, don't assume you have privacy anywhere on the grounds. Hell, for that matter, don't assume you'll have privacy anywhere in Italy. The Council sees everything." He whispered; his voice strained with irritation.

As he finished speaking, the slightest sound of gears churning somewhere within the walls filled the air. To my amazement the wall in front of us shifted backward about an inch and then slipped slowly to the right revealing a hidden passage behind it. Once all movement had stopped, lights flickered on, illuminating uneven, rough, hewn stone stairs, which stretched well into the earth. I glanced over my shoulder. The butler hadn't moved, so the door and lights were controlled by whoever was watching, not by him. That made things interesting. No getting in or out without someone being aware of our movements. Which also meant someone besides Adrien had seen Julian leave that night. There would probably be footage somewhere of the woman he had been with. The thought cheered me, though not enough to ease the sorrow of his loss.

As Adrien followed me down into the stairwell, I realized the butler made no effort to join us. "Aren't you going to show us the rest of the way?"

Ignoring my question, he retreated down the hall. A moment later the sound of grinding gears filled the narrow passage. Just as the door eased to a close, a sudden realization hit me. Stopping in my tracks, I watched helplessly as the space behind us disappeared and the last remnants of freedom evaporated. Apprehension stole through me, tripping its way up my spine warning every little hair along the way.

We were trapped, and there was nowhere to go but down.

When we reached a bend in the stairs, I could see

the passage opened into another hallway. "Where does this lead?"

Adrien's calm voice seemed to echo in the empty space surrounding us. "Don't worry. There's a short hall at the end and then several rooms off it. We are going to the third door on the left."

My tension eased with his words.

A few steps from the bottom, I realized Adrien was correct. Most of the doors were closed to prying eyes. However, the one Adrien had mentioned stood open, awaiting our arrival.

Drawn by two large well-armed Aliments standing guard further down, my gaze lingered on the closed door behind them. My curiosity getting the better of me, I stopped. "What's in there?"

"Don't know and don't care. What the Council keeps hidden down here is none of my fucking business, and I want to keep it that way." He paused as he pushed past me and lowered his voice as if sharing a confidence, "So should you."

Taking his advice, I shrugged. "Just curious."

"Those types of curiosities are better left unexplored, especially here."

Content to let it go, I followed.

Seconds later we entered through the open door, and I knew we were still not quite there. The room was too small to be used for anything of any consequence and was pretty much empty. The single piece of furniture, a solid oaken desk with matching chair, sat in the center of the room. Though the chair was empty, it was obvious by the quiet hum of the computer, the mess of paperwork, and assorted paraphernalia strewn across the desks surface, it wasn't always so.

"What the hell is going on? They send for me and then direct me to a secretary's office?" I glared at Adrien, my patience at an end.

"She's not a secretary. She's the personal assistant to the Great Council. She deals with everything that comes through the Council and is disseminated to the general public. Nothing happens here without going through her." He made a quick motion to silence me, and the act grated on my nerves. A sudden overwhelming urge to punch something reared its ugly head. Adrien would be lucky if it wasn't him. I knotted my fists at my sides and resisted the urge.

We stood for several minutes waiting, my patience straining with every passing moment. Then, finally the door behind the desk opened, and a cheery-looking mousy blonde walked in. Her rumpled business skirt looked as though it had seen better days, and her thick glasses seemed too big for her face as they slipped down her nose while she read from the file at the top of her stack. The door closed behind her, and she glanced up, her big blue eyes wide as she realized for the first time she was not alone. An odd, strangled sound escaped her as she jumped forward and threw the files onto the desk. Moving around the edge of the desk, she held out her hand and crossed to greet us. "Oh, I'm so sorry. I didn't know you were down here already. My name's Alcie. You must be poor Julian's brother, Jacen, isn't it? I'm so sorry for your loss. He was a good man."

"Yes, he was a *great* man." Her chipper manner nicked my already frayed nerves and I unintentionally ignored her proffered hand.

In what appeared to be a sudden onset of embarrassment, she dropped her hand back to her side. Her gaze sought Adrien as if looking for an ally but then dropped to the floor. Her face reddened a touch as she wiped the palm of her refused hand on her skirt as if by doing so it would erase the sting of rejection. Turning on her heel, she spoke over her shoulder, her tone flat and uneasy, "Yes, well…um, if you'll just follow me." She fled to the door and hastily entered the code into the key pad next to it.

I hadn't meant to frighten her. She'd just irritated me by being late and then had the nerve to greet me with a cheery exuberant grin. *What kind of person gives condolences while wearing a smile anyway?* Even still, she had given me no cause for discourtesy. I made a mental note to apologize when I was done with the task at hand.

Turning my mind to the moments ahead, I realized for the first time I really had no idea what I was going to say to the Council. Going in guns blazing and demanding answers wouldn't work. Not with these Aliments and certainly not in their territory.

As Alcie escorted us into the adjoining room, I considered what I knew of my brother's death. He was killed by the Cambiare. Of that we were certain. My knowledge of the creatures was severely limited, and Adrien was of little help. He had neither the knowledge nor the experience to guide me through this. What I really needed, only the Council could give me, an understanding of my enemy and permission to start a war.

But what, I wonder, would they ask in return?

Chapter Five

Setting my jaw, I mentally prepared for the coming encounter. With resolve I stepped through the door and into the inner sanctum.

My gaze traveled the expansive room, and I finally found satisfaction in my surroundings. This was what I had looked for since I had arrived, some sense of the old. Where the halls and outer office had been lit with modern lighting, this room glowed beneath the flickering light of two grand chandeliers each holding dozens of glass votive candles. The floor of the large room glistened with reflected light, its slick black marble adding elegance to the underground chamber.

The walls were dark stone like the stairs we'd descended. Ornate Persian tapestries depicting ancient war scenes hung throughout the room adding warmth to the otherwise bare walls. Without a doubt the most impressive and eye-catching thing in the room was the oversized curved table, which sat at the far end of the chamber. Made of rich mahogany, it was intricately carved with the symbols and histories of our people. I wondered at the secrets it held. Never in my life had I longed for knowledge of my own history as much as I did in that moment. Its well-worn surface had been privy to it all. The secrets it held must be riveting.

Pulling my gaze away from its surface, I took in the presence of the Great Council. Though I couldn't see their faces, I knew they watched me as I assessed my surroundings. My gaze traveled to each one in turn. Each wore deep, blood-red velvet robes with the hood pulled down far enough to sink their features into shadow. Gold embroidered symbols adorned each hood denoting the Great House the member represented. Black embroidery flowed around each symbol and was carried up the center of the hood to wrap around the neck and down each side of the robe's opening. My gaze stopped on the one unoccupied seat. By the gold engraved symbol, I knew it was for the House of Samsaveel, where Julian should have sat.

Drawing my eyes away from the empty seat I carried on with my observations. When I finished taking in the remaining, red-robed individuals I had a count of sixteen great houses in attendance.

That left...

I zeroed in on the only uniquely adorned individual at the table.

Our High King, Morbius of the House of Armaros. He sat at the exact center of the curve, his black velvet robe intricately embroidered with gold. Like the others, he bore the symbol of his house prominently displayed on his hood.

The woman who escorted us in instructed me to take my place at the center of the room, directly in front of our King. Once I'd done as instructed, Morbius spoke.

"It is with great regret that we meet you today, Jacen of Samsaveel. Your brother was our brother. Your pain is ours." His voice whispered from within the reaches of the hood. His tone seemed sympathetic yet there was a strange undefinable edge to it.

My eyes narrowed as I tried to make out the features of the man who ruled our people. "Thank you, Your Highness. I, too, wish we could have met under less dire circumstances."

"It is our understanding you have questions about the death of your brother. Did your brother's Second not explain the circumstances of Julian's death sufficiently?" They knew of my questions already? How could they have known when I, myself, had been unsure of what I'd needed from them?

Returning my gaze to the featureless faces before me, I responded, the strength of my voice disguising the sudden anxiety I harbored. "Adrien explained well enough. I have a great understanding of how my brother died. Yet questions remain."

"Then ask if you must. We will answer if we are able."

A wave of uncertainty flowed through me, shaking me to my core. The time had come. It was now or never. Clenching my fists in front of me to calm my nerves, I straightened and spoke, "I've been told an urban legend killed my brother." Not a single sound was uttered from anyone in the room. "I've been told that this creature walked into our seat of power and walked out with Julian. What I do not understand is how." I let the information sink in. My gaze traveled to each of the members in turn just to return to Morbius. "Am I to believe that this lone Cambiare managed to find her way past the security gate, through the maze of hallways, and into the party without so much as being noticed? Please, tell me, how that was possible. Was he not under the protection of this Council?

The question hung in the air between us as time seemed to stand still. Then an eruption of indignant voices rose.

"How dare you…"

"You doubt our protection?"

"Who do you think…?"

A fist slammed against the table, and silence cut through the room. My gaze found the empty hood of our king. "You forget yourself, Jacen. You come here, question us, the Elders of your Kin, in a tone dripping with disrespect and expect what? To shame us?"

I knew it was a dangerous game I played, but I needed answers. Dipping my head, I choose my words carefully. "I meant no disrespect, sire. I only meant to question the safety of the members of this Council, and your own safety as well, my lord. If one of these creatures can spirit away a member of this

Council from beneath your very noses, then there must be a breach in security somewhere. Someone helped them, and I would like to know who."

My declaration was met with a rumble of whispered comments. When Morbius held up his hand, the room fell silent. "We cannot tell you who betrayed us as we do not know." He sat back, crossing his hands over his middle. "When we locate the person responsible, you will be informed. For now, you need only to retrieve your brother and return home."

The muscle in my jaw worked as I replaced bitter sorrow with thoughts of vengeance. "I claim my right of Retribution delle Parentele. I'm not leaving Italy until I do so with the beast's head as my trophy."

My statement met an uncomfortable silence. I swallowed but refused to look away. To do so would be to admit defeat.

When Morbius finally stirred in his seat, his voice hissed out from the darkness of his hood, obviously angered by my declaration. "You are not sensible like your brother."

I remained steadfast in my resolve. "No, sire. I am not."

"Then we are at an impasse."

Taking a deep breath, I suddenly knew what I must do. "Not necessarily."

He shifted forward in his seat, resting his arms on the table before him. "What is it that you propose?"

I watched him intently. My features relaxed, as the knowledge that I had his full attention sunk in. Without a doubt, he'd be unable to resist my offer. "I propose we work together. If you will tell me everything you know about the Cambiare and give me permission to hunt it within your territory, I will find the Aliment who betrayed all of us."

Once again easing himself back against the well cushioned seat, he seemed to consider my offer. The Aliment to his right leaned over and whispered to the king. The intricate symbol on his hood, an impressive flourish of embroidery with an embellished gold Ђ, stood for *the house of Jomjael*. As the king nodded in agreement with whatever the other said, my eyes narrowed.

Finally, Morbius straightened and redirected his attention to me. He motioned to the Council members around him. "We require time to consider your offer. Alcie will show you to your room where you may await our decision."

As he rose to leave, the door behind us opened, and Alcie called to us. "This way if you please, gentlemen."

I frowned and made no move to depart. "Sire, if you please, when will you have an answer for me?"

He ignored my request, waving a dismissive hand in my direction. My shoulders sagged as I realized my audience with the Council was at an end and I had yet to resolve anything.

Sighing heavily, I turned on my heel and exited the room.

*****

Several minutes later, Alcie led us to a room on the second floor.

Adrien walked ahead of me. A second later he stopped short. His skin turned ashen his eyes haunted by some unknown demon.

Concerned, I joined him. "What's wrong?"

He frowned and shook his head, "Just a bit of deja vu, I guess." He shrugged. "This is the same suite they put Julian and me in."

An involuntary shiver travelled down my spine. I understood his momentary hesitation. Clapping him on the back I whispered, "Don't worry. I doubt my brother's ghost is going to come back to haunt you."

Unlocking the dead bolt, Alcie pushed open the door and breezed into the darkened great room. Placing the key card on the small table next to the door, she turned toward me. "This will be your suite while you're here. Adrien, you know where your room is." She crossed the expansive floor and threw open the curtains. "And Mr. Trudeau, if you don't mind, you can take the larger room on the right."

"No problem. Thanks, Alcie. I appreciate the hospitality." I stood in the room, assessing my new surroundings. The deep blue carpeting, plush and inviting, matched the color of the throw pillows on the couches. The same rich color, though less pervasive, appeared in an alternating pattern of yellow and blue pin stripes on the pristine white curtains. The walls, painted a light yellow and accented with stark white baseboards, contrasted beautifully with the cerulean hues. Doors on either end of the main sitting room stood open, and I saw that our bags had already been delivered to our respective rooms. An eyebrow rose as I realized they had always intended for me to stay on the grounds. Convenient for them I supposed but not so much for me. There were far too many prying eyes here for my taste. I preferred a little more privacy than what the villa offered. I guess this would have to do, for now. However, if this became an extended stay, I had no intention of making this room my temporary home.

Alcie's voice interrupted my wandering thoughts and drew my attention. "Well, I guess I better get back downstairs." She breezed her way back toward the door. Before closing it behind her, she gave me a look which I suppose was meant to reassure. Unfortunately, she seemed to lack the confidence to pull it off. Instead, she appeared a timid mouse shivering beneath the avid glare of a hungry feline. "If you need anything else, you may use the phone by the couch to call on Orsino. He's the human who showed you in when you first arrived."

"Wait, Alcie." I called but was too late to stop her as the door clicked into place. "Damn."

Adrien's eyebrows rose as he plopped down onto the dust-colored couch. "Well, I guess we're pretty well stuck until they make a decision."

I blew out a breath, relaxing for the first time since I arrived. In the next moment I crossed the room. I took the seat opposite him on the other couch. "Yeah, great. Just what I need, to sit around and wait some more."

He shifted on the couch to lay his head back against a pillow. "Gods I'm tired. Back and forth to the U.S. twice in one week. This jet lag is killin' me. "

I thought about the moments before we were ushered out of

the inner sanctum and shook my head in frustration. "I thought for sure they would go for the trade of services angle."

"They still might. You just got to be patient, Jace. Things don't happen quickly over here."

Taking a breath, I ran a hand through my hair. He was right. Once again, I had to find a way to be patient. But, how? I needed them to agree. I bounced my foot impatiently on the carpeted floor.

Before long, the silence of the room was broken by a quiet snore emanating from my Second. I expelled a frustrated breath. At least one of us knew how to efficiently pass the time. Thinking to explore my surroundings, I rose and walked into the bedroom to which Alcie directed me. Of course, the color scheme matched the outer room. The luxurious bed's headboard sat against the opposite wall. An elegant down comforter draped over the edges of the mattress. It looked cozy enough. I glanced around the large space and realized a balcony like the ones overlooking the front yard jutted off this room as well. Crossing to the double French doors, I opened them wide and moved into the sunlight. The view was breathtaking. The lazuline lake gleamed in the sunlight, cool and inviting. One didn't need enhanced hearing to appreciate the sound of the surf, its rhythmic ebb and flow soothing to frayed nerves. Opposite me the sand-colored buildings of the village of Bracciano peppered the shoreline. From what Julian had told me, the village thrived during the summer months as the streets and beaches writhed with tourists of all shapes and sizes. Our kind could easily slip in amongst them unnoticed.

Walking past a small white café table and chairs set up in the middle of the balcony, I crossed to peer over the edge of the sturdy white bannister. Frowning, I stepped back again and shook my head. Any hope of slipping out of the villa via the balcony was lost. It was a sheer drop to the beach below, too far even for the likes of an Aliment.

Resigning myself to the reality of my situation, I returned to the room. Reaching for the door to my left, I stopped short, my heart plummeting to my feet. Swallowing hard against the sudden lump of emotion wedged in my throat, I reached out tentatively. My fingers brushed the shiny, dark wood of Julian's ebony walking stick. I plucked it out from behind the curtains hanging next to the door. My fingers ran along its smooth surface in reverence. He'd loved this piece and hardly ever went anywhere without it. The stone on the top glistened in the sunlight, catching my eye, and I rotated the staff until I grasped the palm sized round-cut sapphire in one hand and the staff in the other. Holding the jewel fast, I twisted the other end until it clicked and then gently pulled. A thin, four-inch, double-edged blade emerged, and with it came the memory of Julian sharpening the blade with the utmost care and polishing the wood on the sheath until it gleamed. Reflected light winked at me as if sharing a wicked secret. He had always loved the idea of a weapon within a weapon. In the end it had done him little good. I slipped the blade back into place. If only the memories could be banished so easily.

*****

Her eyes narrowed as confusion ignited within her. The dark-haired man with the unusual eyes stood on the same balcony where Julian had taken his morning coffee for weeks.

She frowned. Figures they gave him the same rooms they gave Julian previously. Of course, how better to convince someone who might be watching that he truly was Julian's brother. She lifted her nose and scented the air in the hopes of identifying him. The wind was strong off the lake, and it filled her nostrils with the distinctive smell of fish. The only way she was going to be able to scent him at this distance was if the wind shifted directions, which seemed unlikely. She would just have to find a way to get closer. Glancing around the surrounding area, she froze as an Aliment guard walked toward the trees among which she had chosen to hide. There was no way she would risk getting caught just to find out whether it was him or not. She would have to come back after dark, when her presence would be less likely to attract unwanted attention.

After the guard passed several feet away from her, she dropped to the ground in silence, and then crouched to listen. Assured that they had not heard her dismount; she turned and darted toward the boundary wall of the property. Within seconds, the seven-foot brick wall loomed ahead of her. She paused. As the camera mounted at the corner where the two walls met made a sweep of the area just ahead of her, she ducked behind a tree, counted out the well-memorized timing, and then peered cautiously around the base of the tree. Her lips twisted sideways; the tension broken briefly by the knowledge she would once again succeed. In a flurry of fluid movement, she left the relative safety of the tree line and was across the open expanse before the wall. With one controlled leap, she was on the wall. Dropping off the edge, she descended with ease. Glancing back once before disappearing into the brush of the neighboring property, she smirked.

Piece of cake. They'd have to do a little better than a wall, a few guards, and a strategically placed camera to keep her from getting to Jacen.

Chapter Six

Two excruciating hours had ticked away. My irritation with the Council, for being forced to wait on an answer, was growing.

"How long does it take to make a Gods damn decision?"

Adrien exhaled, obviously as exasperated with me as I was with the situation. "It's the Council. They move in their own time, and nothing you say or do will change that. So, you might as well calm down—"

"I *am* calm." I snapped; aware the sharpness of my tone might suggest otherwise.

"Yeah, right," Adrien responded, the sarcasm rich in his voice. "Dealing with the Council is a delicate you can't go in guns blazing, kick ass, and take names." He paused as his gaze met mine. "That tactic will only get you thrown into the streets. You need to employ patience and most of all respect for their authority. You'd do well to remember they are the law here. In the States it's easy to ignore them and go about your business without much interference, but here?" He shook his head and whistled a long-drawn-out tone. "I wouldn't recommend it."

"So, what? I'm just supposed to jump through their hoops like a trained dog and hope for the best?" As he nodded, I scowled. Everything in me rebelled at the thought. "You know

I'm no good at playing nice. That's why Julian was far better suited for this life."

He chuckled. "Yes, I know. However, if you want something from them, then you must play nice. That's all there is to it." He stretched his long legs and placed his booted feet on the coffee table. "Listen, suck it up, and before you know it, you're back in New York and ignoring the Council to your heart's content."

I fully understood that sometimes to get what you want you have to swallow a bit of pride and bow to another. But the taste of humility was unappetizing and bitter on the tongue. The mere thought was enough to trigger my gag reflex. Swallowing, as if in proof, my lips pinched into a severe frown. I knew he was right. In the end I would have to play the game by their rules. *Afterward, the Council could kiss my—*

A loud penetrating knock interrupted my internal rant. Momentarily distracted, I crossed to the door, hedged it open, and glanced out. Recognizing Orsino, I opened it wide and frowned. "It's about fucking time."

He looked down his nose at me as if I'd once again said something to offend his delicate sense of propriety. I didn't give a shit. He seemed like he could stand a little upheaval in his well-ordered world. "Sir, the Council will see you now.

I glanced at Adrien and mimicked the butler's grandiose manner. "Shall we?"

The corners of Adrien's mouth lifted in suppressed humor. "Indeed."

By the stiffening of the human's back and the sudden flush of his cheeks, I knew we finally managed to ruffle his feathers. He turned on his heel and stood aside.

"I trust you...*gentlemen,* can find your own way back to the Council chambers?"

As I moved through the door I took a moment to pause in front of the rigid man. When he refused to meet my eye, I laughed and slapped him on the back. "Don't worry, Belvedere. We'll be out of your hair before you know it."

I passed him still chuckling at the man's expense. When I gained the stairs and began my descent, I heard him question my lineage. He wasn't the first and he would not be the last.

Several moments later we once again stood in the outer office of the chamber facing Alcie.

"Welcome back, Gentlemen." She rose and walked to the keypad next to the door. "The Great Council is awaiting your arrival."

She punched in her code and swung the door open, this time allowing us to enter alone. The door closed behind us, and I moved to take my place. I waited, the silence of the room unnerving me with each passing moment. Though unseen, I could feel the eyes of everyone in the room resting on me. Were they waiting on me to speak? No, it had to be part of the game, something to keep me off balance. I strangled the sound which attempted to escape and bit down on my resolve. If it was a game we were playing, then I would certainly not be the first one to speak.

After what seemed an eternity, our king's voice whispered from the confines of his darkened hood, "Jacen of Samsaveel. We have come to a decision."

I held fast, unwilling to give up my position of power and waited for him to continue, though impatience nipped at my nerves.

"We agree to your proposal."

I let out a breath I hadn't even realized I had been holding. The next instant I was plunged back into the depths of uncertainty.

"However, there is one stipulation. As you have seen, your house seat sits empty. As such, we require your allegiance to this Council. You must sign the Contratto di Servizio. in exchange for our help."

Stunned into silence, I could do little more than blink. The tension in the room grew as I struggled with the unexpected conditions they laid at my feet. *A contract of service?* It was the last thing I had expected to hear and the one thing I would not willingly give to avenge my brother. How could they ask that of me? Pledge my life to the Council? Sign away all my rights and live as one of them for the next three hundred years in exchange for a bit of information and permission to hunt the one who'd killed my brother? It hardly seemed a fair trade, but what choice did I have? I couldn't hunt the beast without their approval, at least not legally. To do so could mean my own death and the disbanding of my clan if anyone found out. The muscles in my jaw ticked. Nothing in this world would induce me to do something that would cause my clansmen harm. But neither could I give up on attaining vengeance for my brother.

I straightened, my decision made, I spoke with resolve. "I will agree to your terms, with a few small stipulations of my own."

"And they are?" Morbius's voice rose, his suspicion adding a dangerous edge to his already menacing tone.

"I must be allowed to hunt on my own. The killing of the beast is my right, and I will not give up that right to anyone. One other thing: I will not Ascend until after I have extracted my vengeance. When the beast is dead, my life will belong to the Council."

Morbius's confidence oozed from his every pore. His deceptively pleasant tone snaked out from the recesses of his hood. "And with these additions, the terms are acceptable to you?"

In that moment, I wanted nothing more than to tell the leader of our people to fuck off. Instead, I swallowed my pride and nodded. "Yes."

Chapter Seven

$\mathcal{A}$drien's stiff-lipped whisper hissed next to my ear as we passed into the outer office of the Council's chamber. "All I want to know is, what the hell were you thinking? With your inability to conform, signing the Contratto might as well be a death sentence."

"You think I don't know that?" My anger boiled over. "I didn't have a fucking choice!"

"There's always a choice, Jacen. Always. You *chose* to give up your own freedom in favor of revenge." Disbelief, anger, maybe even a little disgust, radiated off him in waves.

Not trusting myself to hold my temper, I *chose* to ignore him and stomped off in the direction of the outer door.

My dash for freedom came to a quick end when Alcie's voice halted me. "Mr. Trudeau, I need a word please."

As I turned, I noticed the brilliant, almost child-like grin she wore the first time I saw her had disappeared and had been replaced by a pinched frown.

"Certainly. What can I do for you?"

"I have some documentation you need to sign before leaving."

Crossing the short distance between us, I came to a stop in

front of the petite woman's desk. She looked up at me, her deep-set hazel brown eyes wary as she slid a small stack of papers across the desk toward me. Placing a pen on top of the papers, she continued. "I've marked the areas that need your signature."

Accepting the paper-clipped stack, I looked over the six-page document. It was the service agreement I had agreed to verbally just seconds before. My brows furrowed. *No wonder they'd kept me waiting for two hours. It had given them time to prepare my life sentence.*

I perused the documents, reading each area carefully before affixing my signature upon the bottom of each page. When I came to the section about the Ascension, I read it over to assure I fully understood the consequences of signing the document. Looking up, I frowned. "Alcie, I can't sign this section."

I placed the pages down on the desk and showed her the entry. "It states I will take my oath in one week's time."

"Yes, that is correct." Alcie said, sitting back in her chair. "That is what I was told to include."

"Well, I renegotiated that point a few moments ago. I will not sign it until it reads Jacen of Samsaveel will take his Oath of Service only when the beast that killed his brother is dead."

She studied the documentation and then pulled out a sticky pad. Jotting a note, she placed the pink sticky next to the passage I'd pointed out. "Very well, Mr. Trudeau. I will speak to the Council and make the necessary changes to the contract. Once it is done I will send it to your suite for signature.

"Excellent. Then I better get going. Thanks, Alcie." Turning away from her, I remembered there was one more thing I needed from her. Something far more important than mere paperwork. Turning back to her, my face held a grim expression. "Oh, one more thing, whom do I talk to about having Julian's body sent home?"

She hesitated a moment, gnawing on her bottom lip as if in indecision. "Um, I guess I can make the necessary arrangements." Opening the bottom right drawer of her desk, she leafed through several files. Finally, she withdrew three travel requisition forms. Turning, she presented them to me. "As this is an emergency, I can request to have your travel thus far reimbursed and we will pay for the costs of Julian's return flight. I'll make all the travel arrangements. You'll just need to fill out all of these."

I looked at the identical forms she handed me and frowned. I guess to them it was just a matter of mere paperwork after-all. My stomach churned with the thought. Concentrating on the task at hand, I asked, "Why do I need three of the same form?

"One for you. One for Julian. One for your Second. Three travel requests, three forms." A thought seemed to occur to her as her frown grew more intense. "You will, of course, be accompanying him home."

"No." Her surprised gaze found mine as I handed two forms back to her. In the next moment, I took up the pen I used previously. Jotting down the required information, I heard her stammer as if trying to broach a difficult subject. Ignoring her, I handed the paperwork back to her. "I've made all the arrangements at the other end. Our clan will be awaiting his arrival and will deal with things there."

"You're not going to be present for il Rilascio?" She seemed to have finally found her voice and her opinion on the matter was clear. She disapproved.

It was to be expected, I supposed. As Julian's last bit of family, I should really be present for the Release. Unfortunately, I now had to direct my attention to the hunting of the beast instead. Bitterness crept into my tone as I responded tersely, "As I said, I've made arrangements. I won't be leaving Italy until the beast has breathed its last."

Seeming to accept my decision, she nodded in understanding. "What about his personal effects? Do you want them sent home as well?"

I considered it for a long moment. It would behoove me to go through his effects myself before sending them home. There might be something the others would have missed, something to indicate why he'd met with the Cambiare. "Not yet. I want everything delivered to my room by the end of the day. Can you do that for me?"

The phone next to her rang interrupting our conversation before she was able to respond.

She motioned for me to wait a moment and picked up the receiver. "Yes?"

"Yes, sir, he has."

"Okay. I will tell him." She hung up the phone a puzzled look on her face. "That's odd."

My brow furrowed in concern. "What's wrong?"

"Apparently you're to report to Security. The Council would like you to take over as Chief of Security."

Pleasantly surprised by the news, I nodded. Before long I would have access to all the video files from the night of Julian's death. Smug confidence tainted my expression. The beast would finally have a face. "Excellent."

My response was met with a quiet, almost disgruntled, snort. Glancing at Alcie, I realized I might very well be the only one in the room who was pleased with the news. Her scowl spoke clearly. She was downright pissed off. "They're waiting to give you a guided tour of the grounds and explain how their systems work."

My eyes narrowed. "Do you have a problem with me assuming control of the security office?"

"No, of course not. Why should I?" She glanced at the paperwork still on her desk, and I could almost see the wheels turning in her head. "It's just...," Her mouth twisted as she appeared to chew on the inside of her cheek. "I haven't even filed your official contract yet. Most of the time it takes a few days before the newly contracted is granted access to the vital systems." She looked up at me, as though assessing a new threat, then shrugged. "There must be extenuating circumstances to which I am not privy. Anyway, I'll get your paperwork filed immediately, Mr. Trudeau. In the meantime, you need to go to the second-floor security office."

Having been effectively dismissed, I nodded my understanding. Smart, efficient, and obviously hiding something. I guess, it was now officially my job to find out what. But, not now. I couldn't risk tipping anyone off. No one could know what I was really looking for. Until I knew who to trust in this Gods forsaken place, I would trust no one. To be honest, I hoped she *was* innocent. I could use a friend in her position. "Call me Jace. All my friends do. Also, I wanted to apologize for my earlier behavior. I'm sure you can understand. My brother's passing has me out of sorts."

I didn't think it was possible. Her formerly stern aspect cracked to some extent. The corners of her mouth rose, though the straight tight line her lips made suggested she resisted the urge. She rose and presented her hand. "Si. I do understand, Jacen, but thank you for saying so. Ciao."

This time, I clasped her warm hand in mine. "Ciao, Alcie."

After dropping the handshake, I turned to Adrien. "Let's go."

As he joined me in the hall, I paused. Preferring to ignore the tension developing between us, I glanced down the hall, my gaze once again landing on the set of armed guards several doors down. "Think Security knows what's in there?"

Adrien didn't even seem to think about it, just shook his head, and answered, "I doubt it."

"Well, I guess we'll just have to do a little digging on our own, then. There are far too many secrets in this place. It would be helpful to know which ones I need to worry about." I took a few steps toward the stairwell. Adrien's hand on my arm stopped me.

"Jace..." He stumbled over how to say whatever he was looking to say. "I know you don't want my constant companionship, but you could be in real danger. You don't seem to take that seriously."

"What danger?" My left eyebrow rose. "According to all accounts, my brother was mauled to death by a mindless, crazed she-beast. If that's the case, then I'm not in any danger, at least not until I start hunting it." I chuckled. "Trust me, I'll take it seriously when there is reason to. Until then, relax. I've got this."

Adrien's look told me in no uncertain terms he was not satisfied with my answer. "Trust you? Tell me, Jace, just how am

I supposed to do that when you leave me out of decisions like pledging your services to the Council?" Scowling, he shook his head in disagreement. As an angry growl rumbled deep in my chest, it was silenced as his steely-eyed gaze found mine. "I know I wouldn't have been your choice for a Second..." He shrugged as if searching for the right thing to say. "That you kind of *inherited* me along with the position, but you accepted my petition. I knew then you weren't ready for the changes losing Julian threw your way. However, I thought we at least had each other's trust. Now? I'm not so sure." His voice softened as he continued, "There is no going back, Jace. He's dead. No amount of self-sacrifice or prostration before the Council will fix that. You're alive, and it's my job to assure you stay that way. I've already failed at it once with Julian. I wasn't there when your brother needed me most, and the guilt eats at me every time I think about it." He turned his back on me, but not before I had seen the truth of his words reflected within the depths of his somber dark eyes. It took several minutes for him to regain his composure. When he was able to face me again, I could see that he recovered his strength of conviction. "Believe me when I tell you, I will do whatever it takes to avoid a similar outcome with you. If that means babysitting you to keep you out of trouble, then I'll do it. If it means following you around, at your beck and call like some kind of lap dog, then so be it. Don't even think about making my job harder by keeping me out of the loop when it comes to planning or trying to ditch me somewhere along the way. Trust *me*," he pointed to his chest, his voice full of outraged belligerence, "in the end it will be easier to work with me rather than against me. So, the ball's in your court, Jace. How do you want to play this?"

I stared at the older man in dumb silence.

Wow. Who knew he had it in him? Of course, the obvious answer to that question was, Julian. He believed Adrien would make an outstanding Second. Over the years I'd had my doubts, preferring to believe Julian had chosen him because of their deep friendship rather than out of good business sense. At least now I could honestly say I understood what he must have seen in Adrien. There was a quiet strength, an unshakable loyalty, he exhibited that many would be hard pressed to match. Just to whom he would prove loyal still wasn't quite clear. I guess he deserved a fair chance to prove himself. "You're right. I accepted your services as my Second when you offered them to me. As such, it is no more than right, I allow you the opportunity to do your job. But, Adrien, you can't protect me from everything. There will be times when I need to go it alone. It's just in my nature." Holding up a hand to stem any protest, I continued, "You earned Julian's trust over many years of service and friendship. All I can ask is for you to give me the same consideration. He willingly trusted you with his life." I let the words hang in the air. "I'm not yet ready to do so."

The reminder of his failure obviously hitting home, he heaved a heavy sigh. "I can accept that."

"Then we have an understanding?" He nodded, accepting my decision without further argument. "Good." I chuckled as his stance relaxed. "Don't worry; when I figure out where the beast is hiding, you'll be the first to know."

Apparently satisfied with the outcome of the conversation, Adrien's big hand slapped me on the back. "I'd better be."

Chapter Eight

Fifteen minutes and two flights of stairs later, we knocked on the door of a suite off the second-floor landing. The metal door opened with an audible squeak.

A young Aliment male with short cropped blond hair and dark brown eyes poked his head out. Blocking the opening with his large body, he eyed us with suspicion. "Sì?"

"Jacen Trudeau." I waved a hand toward my friend then continued, "Secondo il mio, Adrien. Eh, um…Ci hanno…detto di incont…I'm sorry. Do you speak English?"

At the man's subtle nod, I rewarded him with a quick smile. If I was going to stay in Italy for any length of time, I was going to have to brush up on my Italian. "We were told to meet someone up here for a tour."

The man's eyes narrowed as he sifted through my impatient English. Within seconds he had translated my words, and his lips spread into a wide grin. "Sì. Sì, Mr. Trudeau. We were told you were coming. Un momento per favore. "

The door closed again. Looking at Adrien, my eyebrows rose.

He shrugged, but refrained from speaking as the door creaked open, this time enough to allow us in.

"So sorry to make you wait. Few visitors are allowed up here.

We're off limits to most guests. For you, sir, siamo un libro aperto."

The corners of my lips turned upward half-heartedly. *An open book, really? Well, we will just have to see how open they truly are, especially when they find out why I am actually here.*

As I stepped through the door, I took in the immense suite.

Numerous Aliments manned desks, each with a half a dozen mounted monitors sitting before them. They wore specialized glasses made to protect sensitive Aliment eyes from the refresh rate of the screens. To humans the flickering was hardly perceptible. To our kind it caused severe headaches, especially after extended use. I had a high-end pair tucked into my laptop bag back in my room for use with my own personal computer.

As we stepped further into the room, the redhead from the Library came out of a glassed-in office a few feet away. Sauntering forward in the same seductive manner we'd witnessed previously, her ruby red lips luscious against her pale porcelain-like skin parted in anticipation of speaking. "Gentlemen, it is a pleasure to meet you." Her voice was what I imagined it would be: husky, sexy, with a deep Italian accent. "I'm Karina Mariucci, head of security for the Council. I will be your guide for the afternoon."

Grasping her hand in mine, the strength of her handshake surprised me. The first time I had seen her she'd seemed like a formidable woman. Finding out she was the head of security? Well, that would just make life interesting. "I do believe the pleasure is all mine."

We followed Karina through the obligatory tour, asking questions along the way. As the tour concluded several minutes later, she motioned for us to follow her into her office. "Gentlemen, if you would please..." She walked to her oversized mahogany desk and rolled out a large map of the grounds over its spotless surface. "This is a map of the all the locations of cameras we have on the grounds." She pointed to the one that appeared to be just outside the door to the Security office. "As you can see by all the monitors in the adjoining room, each one correlates with a location on this map. There isn't a place here that isn't being constantly monitored." She said, obvious pride creeping into her voice.

Security that was unseen, but ever present. It's exactly what I'd been hoping for. They had to have footage of Julian and the woman somewhere in these offices. "It's good to know that in this at least your security team has done excellent work, Ms. Mariucci."

She bristled at the implication that her team had perhaps not performed so admirably elsewhere. "My team is well equipped and very good at their jobs,

I chuckled at her response. "I'm sure they are. I, of course, meant no offense."

Giving me a tight-lipped nod, she busied herself by rolling up the maps. "Are there any more questions I can answer for you before you go?"

Ah, all was not forgiven. Oh well. I guess it was time anyway. "Yes, where do you keep the security recordings?"

Her features seemed to freeze, as her eyebrow rose. She motioned to the man who'd let us into the security office and as he made his way t to the door, she ended all pretense of civility. "I'm sorry, sir. That information is only available to authorized personnel. Now, if you would please," she motioned for us to exit the office, "I have work to do."

"As of an hour or so ago, I *am* authorized personnel." Brushing passed her I whispered close to her ear, "Feel free to check my credentials."

Pulling out the chair behind the desk, I sat down.

"What the hell do you think you're doing?" Her shrill screech echoed in the small glass encased room.

Amused by her perplexed outrage, I kicked back in the chair. Casting her a look of challenge, I responded, "My job. Which would be a lot easier if you'd bring me everything you have from the night of Julian's Ascension."

Obviously stunned by my response, she just stood there and blinked at me. When she refused to move, I looked passed her and pointed to the man whom she'd called just moments ago to escort us out of the office. "You there, what's your name?"

The man popped to attention and behaved as though freshly out of boot camp. "Vincenzo, signore."

"Vinny, I'm Jacen of Samsaveel, the new head of security. I need everything you've got on the night of the last Ascension." He cast a surreptitious look toward Karina, unsure of what to do. My right eyebrow rose, and my voice took on a tone of authority. "Will that be a problem?"

He swallowed and looked away from his former boss. With his next words, he betrayed the woman's trust. "No, sir. That won't be a problem."

"Thank you, Vinny. I'll be waiting." Obviously glad to be dismissed from the room, he turned and darted out the door.

"I'm sorry, but who authorized this? And why was I not informed?" Karina's voice was hard and unyielding. Yep, she would be formidable.

"By agreement and authorization of the Great Council." I eyed her closely, my eyes narrowing. Realizing her anger was moments from exploding, the right corner of my mouth rose. To add insult to injury I propped my feet up on her pristine desk. "Listen, this wasn't personal, and I can assure you, it's temporary. I'll be gone before you know it."

She snapped her jaw closed and turned on her heel. "This is outrageous."

"Karina," I called after her. As she paused in the doorway, I continued, "Leave your key card with Vinny on the way out."

Chapter Nine

"**D**amn it." I took off the specialized glasses Vinny had loaned me and tossed them onto the desk. I rubbed my tired burning eyes and then rested my forehead in my hand.

How could there be nothing?

Somehow, she managed to get onto the grounds, into the villa, and slip out of the party without being seen by the cameras. I knew it was impossible, though the empirical evidence seemed to suggest otherwise.

Leaning back in the chair, I glanced at the unrolled maps I'd strewn all over the table across the room as I'd compared camera angles with locations trying to get a grasp on how she'd done it. From what I could tell, every inch of the compound had cameras trained on it at one point or another. To get onto the grounds, she'd have to have studied the movements of the guards and know exactly where each camera was. It would have taken weeks, maybe even months to gain that kind of knowledge. Even then, the odds of not being seen by at least one camera were miniscule. It all seemed to confirm my first suspicions.

She had help.

Glancing at my watch, I realized it was already late into the evening. Right about now, I could use a good night's sleep. I would start fresh in the morning, maybe get Vinny going through activity logs.

Rising, I stretched and groaned as my muscles rebelled against the long sedentary day. I cringed as a muscle tweaked in my back. This was not a lifestyle I wanted to get used to.

Exiting the office, I glanced over to where Adrien lounged., leg propped up on a young Aliment woman's desk. For all intents and purposes, he appeared to be engrossed in whatever story the woman was weaving for him.

"Hey boss, find anything useful?" Vinny's voice boomed across the room.

I turned my head in time to see his eyes crinkled in amusement as his leathery cheeks pulled up in what could only be called a smirk.

Was he hoping I would fail? If so, I would be happy to disappoint him. "Not yet, but soon."

I crossed to Adrien and lowered my voice. "I think the travel is catching up to me. I'm heading back to our rooms."

"Do you want me to come with?"

Unlike me, Adrien looked well-rested and ready to take on the night, or at least the woman. Seeing no reason to interrupt his evening, I shook my head. "Nah. The night's still young, and I'm just going to crash. I'll see you in the morning."

Adrien gave a curt nod. "Alright, Jace. Get some well-deserved rest. I'll see you in the morning."

Several minutes later I entered the dark interior of our living room. Closing the door softly behind me, I sighed and leaned against the wooden panel. Had it really been just a few days since Adrien had shown up on my doorstep and my whole world had come crashing down around my ears? It seemed a lifetime ago, and the weight of it all fell heavy on my shoulders. Pushing myself off the door, I made my way across the darkened room and entered the bedroom. A cool breeze came in from the opened doors of the balcony, and I breathed deeply. One good night's rest and I'd be ready for the hunt.

*****

My eyes snapped open. I regulated my breathing keeping it slow and rhythmic. The moon shone through the balcony doors as a shadow moved silently within the confines of the room. Maybe it was the hint of a strange musky spice floating in on a cool damp breeze which had alerted me to the intruder's presence. I didn't know, but my muscles tensed in anticipation. Whoever it was edged their way to the bed and stood above me. Eyes glowing with reflected light peered down at me through the darkness.

Coming out of the bed in an instant, I lunged for the shadow. To my surprise, my hands came up empty as the night wraith avoided my grasp. With a quick movement, the shadow became a silhouette illuminated by the moonlight and the figure was clearly defined.

Disbelief stunned me for a moment. *A woman?*

My mind screamed out, *not just any woman, THE woman.* As she darted out onto the balcony, the corners of my mouth turned upward. She had made a grave mistake. There was no way off the balcony. I charged after her, assured of success.

When I darted out into the moonlight, a flash of golden eyes and a wicked grin greeted me. With the grace of a large cat, she ran along the narrow railing and leapt onto the roof above my head.

In one fluid movement I was on the railing, fully prepared to follow. Before I could move, a large hand grabbed my arm and yanked me down. I landed unceremoniously on the ground.

"What in the hell did you think you were doing?" Adrien's angry voice broke the silence of the night as he loomed over me. "I know things look pretty bleak right now, Jace, but that's no reason to off yourself."

Frustration rumbled out in a low growl. "I wasn't trying to off myself, you stupid ass. She was here."

"Wait, what?" Adrien seemed less certain he'd done the right thing. "Who was here?"

"Julian's killer." I raked a hand through my hair. "I woke up, and she was standing over me. I chased her out here. She went up on the roof, which is exactly where I was going when you intervened."

"So, you actually saw her? We know what she looks like now?"

"Yes, I mean, no." Rising, I glanced up at where the woman disappeared and frowned. "It was dark, and she was fast. She had golden eyes…" I realized how ridiculous that sounded. "What are you doing here anyway? I thought for sure you would have made a night of it."

"Nah, the girl was a temporary distraction. I had just come in when I heard something from your room. When I opened the door to investigate, I saw you walking out onto the balcony. Figuring you might need some company I followed. Imagine my surprise to find you standing on the railing looking for the entire world like you were preparing to end it all. How was I supposed to know you were chasing something?"

"Fair enough, but for future knowledge, I'm not suicidal. If you see me teetering on a ledge, figure there must be a good reason for it, and leave me the hell alone."

"Got it. No more whisking you off precarious perches, no matter how crazy I think you might be."

"Good, now you go get some sleep. I'm going to the Security office. I think we might have caught her on video this time."

*****

The night breeze rushed passed as she breached the perimeter wall. Landing with a soft thump on the other side, she darted into the brush.

That was too damn close. A second slower and….

She shivered. She needed to stay as invisible as possible, and tonight she nearly blew everything out of the water. It didn't pay to mess with an Aliment in his own territory, and from all the Intel she gathered thus far, this one was especially dangerous. In minutes he could have brought the wrath of Morbius down on her head, and then where would she have been? She shivered again. She knew full well what happened to a Cambiare who messed with Morbius.

Picking her way to the road she frowned. Pulling out her cell she pressed a speed dial button and waited for the call to connect.

"Ciao." She paused as the voice on the other end spoke. "Well, it is, but it isn't. Hold on a second…" Arriving at her little Fiat, she dropped to one knee next to the right front tire. Reaching up into the wheel-well she plucked a key from its hiding place. When she gained her feet again, she continued to the driver's side. "Si, I'm back. Had to get my key. To answer your question, I'm not sure. I can tell you he appears to be the one we are looking for, but, I don't know. Things just don't smell right, ya know?" She unlocked the car door then slid into the seat behind the wheel. "Listen, can we talk about this when I get there?" Turning the key in the ignition, she relaxed back against the leather seat as the engine roared to life. "Si, I'm on my way now. Ciao a presto." Pushing the end call button, she glared down at the blank screen for a moment. What did she have to tell him anyway? She couldn't lie and say mission accomplished when it wasn't. She tossed the phone onto the passenger seat. Biting down on the corner of her lip she guided the vehicle onto the paved road and mulled over her dilemma.

Things had just become a tad more confusing. At first she'd been sure she had the wrong Aliment, but then the big oaf had shown up and called him Jace. It had to be him. But, how could he be the one? It made no sense. After a few minutes, she slammed her hand against the steering wheel as a thought occurred to her. Was it possible they were trying to draw her out by using a decoy? It seemed the solitary explanation for the discrepancies. *Porca vacca, she'd fallen for it and nearly been caught.*

*****

A few minutes later, I pounded on the door of the Security

office. My teeth ground together in complete vexation. *The cameras had to have caught her this time.*

When the door opened a cautious two inches, I shoved against it.

Though taken by surprise, the older night guard stood his ground in the doorway.

"Get the hell out of my way." When he refused to move, I scowled. "Do you have any idea who I am?"

"Non mi preoccupo chi siete. Non va la spinta il vostro senso dentro qui senza identificazione."

He didn't care who I was? I wasn't getting in without identification? What the fuck? Didn't these people talk to each other at all? Every member of the staff should have known what had transpired this afternoon. In truth, at any other time I would have admired his single-mindedness. However, tonight I was in no mood to play games. "I don't have identification on me. It's in the room." I leaned forward trying to see who else might be hanging around by the door. "Is Vinny around?"

The man closed the door further to block my view. "Look, I'm Jacen of Samsaveel. You might know me as the new Head of Security."

The blood seemed to drain from the older man's face, leaving him pale and apparently shocked by my declaration. Obviously, he recognized the name. Good. So maybe they did communicate with each other.

"Oh, scusilo, signore. Non ho realizzato…" He took a hesitant step back as if unsure of what to do. "I didn't know you were coming."

I waved my hand, dismissing his excuses and pushed past him. I stomped passed a group of shocked onlookers as all activity in the large room came to a halt. "I want the footage from all of the cameras on the roof in my office!" When no one moved to do my bidding I shouted, "Rapidamente!"

Before I'd had the opportunity to gain the solitude of my office, a timid voice stopped me in mid-stride. "Signore, the cameras on the roof are no longer in service."

I jerked around, my utter disbelief evident. "What do you mean they are no longer in service?"

The tiny Aliment woman stood her ground, despite the withering look I cast her way. "Elemosino il vostro perdono, signore. The cameras have been out of commission since a severe lightning storm four weeks ago. It damaged the entire sistema del tetto…"

She stammered to a stop as I directed my full attention to her.

"The entire roof system?" At her hesitant nod, I scowled. "Are you telling me we have no eyes on the roof at all?" I jammed my finger toward the ceiling emphasizing my point. "That we are completely blind up there?" When no one dared answer and everyone I looked at cast their eyes in another direction, I fully understood. My fingers balled into fists as I blew out an angry breath.

"And no one thought to have it repaired?" What kind of dog and pony show were these people running?

The spindly man who'd first spoke up hastened to answer. "No, signore. I mean, yes, signore. Karina placed a requisition for repairs immediately, but it has not happened. I guess it's lower on the priority list than other things." He shrugged his shoulders as if at a loss for anything else to say.

Well, fuck me. I couldn't catch a break.

What could possibly be of higher priority than the security of the villa? Something didn't add up. At least now I knew how she had slipped in unseen. All she'd needed to do was get to the roof and slip in a window like she did tonight. That didn't, however, explain how she had avoided the cameras inside.

Chapter Ten

A knock on the door woke me from a fitful sleep. Squinting against the sunlight streaming through the curtains of the balcony doors, I glanced at the bedside clock. *Ten already?* It was nearly five in the morning when I finally gave up on finding any sign of my would-be attacker's presence on last night's footage. *The woman was a freaking ghost.* I rubbed my weary eyes and sat up as the knock came again this time louder and more persistent.

"Just a minute." Crossing to the bedroom door, I swung it open and glanced around the living room area. It was empty. Adrien must have gone out. Grabbing my robe, I slipped it over my shoulders leaving it hanging open as I walked toward the suite entry. Before I'd had an opportunity to tie the belt at the waist the door swung inward to reveal Alcie balancing a tray of food with one hand against her hip and opening the door with the other.

When she saw me, her face lit into a genuine beacon of joy. "Buon giorno, Jace. How was your night? I heard—" She must have realized I stood naked a few feet from the doorway as her blush spread to the very tips of her ears and she spun around to present her back to me. "I'm so sorry. I…thought you were still asleep. I figured I would leave the tray on the table for you…for later."

"No problem, Alcie. Come on in." When she peered over her shoulder as if afraid to turn around, I couldn't help but chuckle. She was a strange one indeed. I had always been secure in the knowledge that women, human or otherwise, found me attractive, so it was no surprise Alcie might as well. To become so embarrassed by my nakedness? It was downright amusing. I couldn't image any other Aliment woman who would react in such a manner. It was really kind of endearing. Deciding to let her off the hook, I slowly wrapped the edges of the robe around my waist and belted them into place.

"Everything's covered, I promise."

"Are you certain? I wouldn't want you to think I was taking advantage of the situation."

"Quite certain." Stepping forward as she turned around, I extended my hands. "Can I take that for you?"

"Si, please do." She handed me the tray and peered up at me, her sparkling blue eyes large and trusting. "Again, I'm sorry to burst in on you. I really did think you were still sleeping. Adrien had said you were up late last night working."

I took the tray and turned away from her. Pausing to place the tray on the table next to the door, I spoke in an effort to reassure her. "Forget about it. No harm done." I continued toward the bedroom. "Give me a second to put on some clothes. I'll be right back."

By her hurried nod, she seemed a little relieved that I had volunteered to get dressed. I shook my head. She was definitely a strange one.

Several minutes later I returned to the living room fully dressed. "So, what is it that really brought you here, Alcie?"

She tittered nervously and perched herself on the edge of the couch. "Can't a girl bring a gentleman breakfast without there being some ulterior motive?"

My eyes narrowed as I studied her fidgeting figure. "Sure, if it's the woman's job to do so. But, Alcie, you and I both know that bringing me breakfast is not in your job description. So, why are you here?"

She looked away as if trying to find a way to broach a difficult subject. "I...I needed to talk to you about a couple of things."

"Alright. I'm listening." My brow furrowed. As I took a seat on the arm of the couch across from her, I studied her.

"Jace, I'm sorry. Your brother's things have...well, they've been misplaced."

Tightness in my chest worked its way into my throat as a niggling suspicion rose within me. "What do you mean they've been misplaced?"

She rose and paced the length of the couch. "I mean, I can't find them anywhere. I left them in the storeroom outside my office after we cleaned out the suite, and now...they're gone."

I stood and stuck my hands in the pockets of my blue jeans. Turning away from her, I shook my head. This was ridiculous. Things didn't just disappear. Either she moved the suitcase and forgot, which she seemed far too organized to do, or someone took them. "What would someone want with Julian's stuff?"

She shrugged and shook her head. "I don't know. Maybe the same thing you wanted with it?"

"Possibly." I conceded the point, though it didn't sit well with me. No one would have the same interest in Julian's personal belongings as I did, and they certainly didn't have any right to them. The muscle in my jaw flexed. Justified outrage sprang to life. "It doesn't matter why they took them. I want them found and returned to me."

She looked at a loss for how she was going to accomplish such a feat. "I'll do what I can, Jace, though I'm not sure where to start."

I mulled over the possibilities in my mind and frowned. "Is it at all possible you had the luggage sent home with Julian?"

"Impossible." Her response was adamant. "I would have had to file a special customs form, which I did not do. And his body is scheduled for a flight this afternoon, so even if I had done so, I wouldn't have forgotten about it." She paused for a moment as if thinking about things. "I'll figure out something."

Realizing there was little she could do right now, I backed off the topic. "I'm sure you will. When you find the suitcase, have it delivered here."

She nodded in understanding. "I will. Do you want to see him before he leaves?"

Stunned by the abrupt change of subject, I stared at her.

"I know you will be unable to participate in the Release, I just thought you might want to see him before..." She shrugged her shoulders as if nudging me to finish the sentence on my own.

Did I want to see Julian? My stomach sank with the thought. What Adrien told me about how Julian had been found sent a shiver down my back. I didn't want to see the brother I loved my whole life lying in a ceremonial burning box and certainly not in that horrible condition. But, he deserved to be sent off with the proper rites, and I was his sole family. Besides, I needed to say goodbye. Swallowing against sudden sadness, I nodded. "Yes, I do."

Wanting to change the subject, I walked over to where I'd placed the breakfast tray. Picking up a cold piece of toast, I munched on it. "Alcie, who would a work order for maintenance on security cameras go through?"

"Anything that has to do with building security or the electronic systems goes through special services. They're located off property in Bracciano."

"I'll need their phone number."

Alcie furrowed her brow in consideration. "Why do you need it?"

It was obvious there were problems with security but after her initial reaction to my appointment, I debated over how much to tell her. Erring on the side of caution, I answered. "I need to confirm some information I'd received from one of the security officers last night. It was about a work order sent out a few weeks ago. I want to check on the status of the service."

"You could also check with Karina. From what I understand all security orders would have gone through her."

I took a sip of hot black coffee and nodded. "I plan to."

"Well, in the meantime, I'll get you the number. Also, I'll have a car pick you up in an hour to take you to Julian." She turned to leave. "I should get back to work. Is there anything else you need from me before I go?"

"I can't think of anything else." I walked with her to the door. "Thanks, Alcie."

"I'm glad I could help. Ciao, Jace."

*****

"Are you sure about this?"

Adrien's question caused a pang of unease to course through me. What the hell did I expect to find in there? That it wasn't really Julian in that box?

Shrugging off the notion, my resolve quickened. "Yes, I'm sure."

As the driver opened the door and stood to the side, Adrien responded, "Fine, then let's do this."

Let's do this. His words echoed in my mind as I sat alone in the car. For the first time since landing in Italy, it occurred to me that this was what I dreaded all along. I spent every spare minute focusing my attention on my need for vengeance and wrapping myself in a cocoon of busy work, anything to keep myself from dwelling on his loss. But now, it was time to rip off the bandage and stare straight into the gaping, festering wound, and I wasn't sure I was strong enough to survive it. It would have been so much easier to send him off to our clan without saying goodbye. But Julian deserved more than that.

Climbing out of the car, I took in our surroundings. The large hanger before us sat with doors open and a large private jet nestled within.

Glancing around, I noted a long, well-kept airstrip lined with blinking lights and a few smaller buildings peppered around the area.

I looked over at Adrien in question. "I thought we were going to the airport in Rome."

"This is the Council's private airfield." Adrien answered.

"They have their own plane?" I couldn't stop the astonishment from creeping into my voice.

"Of course. You didn't think the Council members flew coach, did you?"

I guess it made sense. If you're going to be the leaders of an entire race, you might as well travel in style. "Huh, and they made us fly commercial."

Adrien chuckled, leading the way into the hanger. "I guess you didn't rate, but Julian does."

He said the last with a poignant sense of pride I truly appreciated. Finally, my brother had risen above our lowly beginnings and earned the respect in death he'd so longed for in life.

As we entered, one could hardly miss the pristine jet liner bathed in artificial light as if on display at a museum, rather than sitting in a hanger waiting to travel. From the looks of its glistening white exterior, it could very well have been fresh off the line at the factory. Twin blue stripes ran along its side and up to the tail. "A Gulfstream. I'm impressed."

Adrien's jaw dropped open as he mocked me, "I'm impressed you even knew what it was."

"Hey, just because I don't fly, doesn't mean I can't admire a fine piece of avionics. Besides, how hard was it to figure out with G650 emblazoned on the tail?"

Walking past the airliner, the good humor I had managed to maintain for the past few minutes disappeared entirely. An intricately carved rosewood ceremonial casket sat on a wheeled cart ready to be placed in the cargo hold.

Taking a calming breath, I walked over to it. Before reaching it, I heard a familiar voice call out to me. Turning, I recognized Alcie crossing the hanger toward me.

When she came to a stop beside me, she spoke in hushed tones, "I hope you don't mind me showing up like this. I didn't want you to have to go through this alone."

Adrien moved forward, asserting his presence. "He isn't alone."

Under his intense scrutiny, Alcie faltered. "I'm sorry. I didn't mean to intrude." She held out a satchel as if in explanation. "I can go if you'd like. I just thought you might need these."

My brows furrowed into a bunch at the center as I cast Adrien a withering look. I reached out to take the satchel.

Allowing my features to relax into a mask of polite civility, I peered down at Alcie. "You can stay if you'd like. I'm actually glad you came." To my astonishment, it was the truth. Her presence was a welcome distraction. Dropping to one knee, I placed the bag she'd handed me onto the smooth pavement of the hanger floor. Opening the bag, I perused the contents. On top a deep blue robe was folded neatly and tucked around the other objects in the bag. Removing it, I placed it gently across my raised knee, being careful not to allow it to brush the ground. Once I was sure it was secure, I continued my investigation. Withdrawing a beautifully etched crystal cruet, I held it up before me. The thick amber oil rolled against the sides of the oval shaped bottle leaving a thin layer behind. Looking up at Alcie, I questioned, "Vita Eterna? "

"Sì. It's for the blessing."

Nodding, I placed the bottle on the ground in front of me and then reached in to remove another object. My fingers brushed a cool metal article. Clasping it, I withdrew my hand. The glint of silver and blood red jewels caught my eye and my heart dropped to the floor. I knew immediately what I held.

The Dagger of Aita.

This was one of the most sacred artifacts of the kin. Carved with the ancient symbols of my people's power, the three inch rosewood hilt was dotted with small rubies, each stone reminiscent of a tiny droplet of blood embedded into the rich dark wood. Used strictly for the burials of those highest within our ranks, the gleaming silver blade caught the light from above and winked at me. Mesmerized by the incredible beauty of the ceremonial knife, I rubbed a thumb along its sleek shining surface. I'd heard about it but never actually seen it. And now, as I knelt on the cool dirty floor of a hanger in the middle of nowhere, preparing to send my brother off into the afterlife, it rested in *my* hand.

My jaw tightened. It somehow seemed wrong. Yes, my

brother had earned the respect of the Council. But, had he been elevated so greatly in these few short weeks that it made the use of the dagger his right? I wished it were true. No matter how I tried, I couldn't quite get my mind around that possibility. Placing the dagger back into the bag, I made to move on.

"What are you doing?" Alcie's strained tone made me look up.

"I appreciate the gesture, but I can't use the dagger. It would be sacrilege." A thought occurred to me as I withdrew three candles and a gold coin from the interior of the bag and placed them with the oil. "How did you get the Dagger of Aita? Shouldn't it be in a well-guarded place?"

"It was. I signed it out for you. And before you ask, the Council is aware and approved its use."

My brows rose in surprise. "Then, Julian is to be treated as a royal?" That really made no sense. "Why?"

Alcie shrugged. "I don't know. All they said was that Julian had to be released properly. The Council was adamant the dagger be used, and Morbius himself entrusted me with its safe passage."

"And you didn't think to ask why?"

She laughed at that. "It's not my job to ask why, Jacen. I just do as I'm told and trust the Council knows more than I."

Adrien fidgeted beside me and I glanced up at him. He wore a worried frown, and when my eyes met his, he shook his head slowly as if to say, *don't push it, Jace.*

Believing I understood his concerns, I eased up on the objections.

"Fine, I'll do as they ask. But if we are going to do this then we better do it right."

Grabbing me by the elbow, Adrien dragged me away from Alcie. When he felt we had put enough distance between us, he spoke through gritted teeth. "I can't let you do this, Jace. You can't just take her word for it and perform the Rite of Aita. It's strictly forbidden for anyone but the royal family to perform the rite. Last time I checked, neither you nor Julian had a drop of royal blood coursing through your veins. Going through with this would make a complete mockery of everything the Rite stands for." Adrien's angry tone conveyed the same concerns I'd given up moments ago.

Confused, I glared at him. "I thought…"

He interrupted my response. "If you choose to do this against my advice, then I will not be party to it."

I stared blankly at my Second in utter disbelief. How had I so misunderstood his signals? If he felt so strongly about the situation, then I had no choice.

I took a few steps backward, meeting Adrien's gaze the whole time and spoke loud enough so both could hear, "I believe it is best to perform the ceremony without the Rite of Aita." Adrien relaxed. I turned back to Alcie and handed the dagger back to her. "I won't need this. Please see it safely back into the hands of the Council and thank them for their generosity."

She cast an accusatory look over my shoulder. *Poor Adrien. If looks could kill, I had no doubt he'd be swinging from the gallows by now.* "Are you sure, Jacen? Throwing an honor like this back into the face of the Great Council could be…upsetting."

"Regardless of how the Council reacts, I have to do what I believe Julian would want me to do. After taking in the wise Council of the one person who knew him best, it is my conclusion that Julian would not have accepted such an honor, knowing it was not his birth rite. So, I must decline on his behalf."

Though she didn't seem to like my decision, she accepted it. Reaching out, she took the dagger from my hand and grasped it in both of hers. Ringing it in a nervous gesture, much like one would a wet towel, her eyes took on a shiny, watery appearance. Was she about to cry? Gods I hope not. A woman's tears were one thing I had trouble staying strong against. Instead, she gazed up at me with a look of admiration. "You know, Jacen of Samsaveel, I do believe your brother would have been proud of you for standing up to the Council. Not everyone is strong enough to do so."

With that, she turned and walked out of the hanger. I

couldn't help wondering if her last words were meant for someone specific.

"I don't trust her." I hadn't even realized Adrien had joined me until he had spoken.

I watched as Alcie made her way to the exit door on the other side of the hanger. "Why? Are you seeing something I'm not seeing?"

"She's way too *sweet* to be an Aliment."

My eyes narrowed as I peered at him. I watched him as her stared at Alcie's retreating backside. He watched her with an unusual interest, one which would seem to indicate a true depth of feeling. Just what that feeling was I was less certain. However, I somehow doubted it was merely distrust. Raising an eyebrow, I gave him a sideways glance. "Really? Funny you don't like her then. Julian always said you have quite a sweet tooth."

To my amazement, a rosy tint spread up Adrien's neck. Not meeting my eye, he walked toward my brother's casket. "Less talk, more ritual."

Slipping the robe over my clothes, I bent to pick up the rest of the ritual items. "So, she's sweet and quiet and totally reserved. What's the harm?"

"Sweet, quiet, reserved and totally not my type. If you knew me at all, you'd know that." Adrien's irritated tone declared in no uncertain terms that I'd touched a nerve.

"If you say so. But, hey at least one of us would have something to distract him from the reasons we're here."

"I don't need a distraction. And neither do you." He lifted the top section of the lid and stepped back. "Now, can you please do what needs to be done so we can get the hell out of here?"

I swallowed a cheeky response and moved to take my place beside the casket. When my gaze fell to where Julian rested, a sharp intake of breath was all I could manage. One thing was for sure, once the ritual was complete, I was going to find a way to seal the casket. I wasn't about to allow anyone else to see him like this.

Though a mortician had done what he could to make him

look peaceful and all in one piece, it was a futile effort. To me his pale skin no longer looked real. Heavy makeup caked over the areas to cover up the slashed, torn skin beneath. An ugly, cable knit turtle-neck sweater, something he never would have worn, covered the rips at his throat.

He'd been posed with his hands folded over his stomach and my heart sunk. He looked as if he were lying on our lawn daydreaming, just as we'd done numerous times as children. The memory stole through me, an unwanted reminder of what I'd lost and would never have again.

Reaching out, I touched his hand. It was so cold, so lifeless. I bit back the sadness and straightened. If I was going to get through this, I had to remain focused. Memories and mourning would come later. Right now, I had family obligations to deal with. *Family obligations*...something inside me seemed to taunt. *You have no more family, no more obligations to them. You are alone.* I pushed the thought deep into the recesses of my mind as I prepared myself for the coming ritual.

The first thing I need to do is take the...

My brow furrowed as I studied his right hand. Lifting it, I checked his other hand. "Where are they?"

"Where's what?" Adrien asked.

"His rings are gone."

"Which ring?"

I scowled. "Both of them."

Adrien frowned. "I know he had one of them on the night of the Ascension. I'm just not sure which one. Refresh my memory again, the family crest and what was the other one?"

"The old one our parents gave him right before they died.

Adrien thought for a moment and then recognition dawned. "Oh, that's right. It had that weird symbol on it, looks like a number three sitting on a fancy fence."

At another time his description of the ring would have been funny, but today with the task at hand and concern for the ring's any good humor was lost to me. "Yes exactly. He's not wearing it either."

Adrien moved to the casket and jammed his hands into the side of it, exploring the interior. "Maybe it fell off."

"Both of them?" There was no way both rings had magically fallen off Julian's fingers in transit.

"No, I told you he was only wearing one of the rings the night he died. The other is probably with his personal belongings."

I moved to the bottom half of the coffin and opened it up to mimic Adrien's efforts. "You mean the personal belongings that have mysteriously vanished?"

"Those would be the ones."

My lips clamped together in grim determination. I slid my hands along Julian's unmoving legs. After a thorough search of the casket, I had to concede, neither ring was with Julian.

First his personal items disappeared, and then his ring was stolen right off his finger. *What the hell is going on here?*

Of course, I had no way of knowing which one he had been wearing. I did at least know where to start my search. "I think we'll have to make a call to our coroner and see if he remembers the ring. He would have been responsible for logging anything that came in with Julian."

"Sounds like a plan. I can do that while you perform the rites." Adrien put his hands on his hips, a look of deep thought on his face. "I'll go see if I can catch Alcie. If not, I'll give her a call to see if she can give me the information. I'll be waiting outside when you're done."

*****

A half hour later I folded the blue robe carefully and placed it back in the bag. Straightening, I stood staring down at my brother's lifeless features. A face I'd known as well as my own and would never see again.

"It's time, Jace." Adrien's words interrupted my quiet contemplation. "They're ready for him."

Sighing heavily, I glanced over to where the flight crew waited. Nodding, I spoke. "Give me a minute."

He acknowledged my request with a nod and moved back several paces.

Turning back to Julian I placed a hand on his shoulder and leaned forward. "I promise I'll find whoever did this. They'll join you in death before I'm through."

Squeezing his shoulder, I reiterated. "I promise."

Chapter Eleven

Walking to the car, I struggled to remain stoic. Releasing him into the hands of strangers was perhaps the hardest thing I ever had to do. Settling in the backseat of the vehicle, I waited for Adrien to join me.

A few minutes later we were back on the road. As the distance between Julian and I grew, the emptiness within me did as well. It would be hard coming to terms with his loss. At least I had a chance to say goodbye. "Were you able to talk to the coroner?"

Adrien glanced over at me as I stared, glassy eyed straight ahead. "Yes."

"And?"

I could hear him as he inhaled and exhaled. "He swears Julian wasn't wearing any jewelry when they found him. He verified it with his notes. The ring had to have disappeared before he got there."

"So, I was right. It's been stolen." Even I could hear the sadness in my own voice.

Adrien shrugged, unable to contradict my assumption. "I guess so."

I swallowed. The lump in my throat made it difficult to

breathe. I turned to the window, unseeing, my mind overwhelmed.

"I'm so sorry, Jacen…about everything."

Maybe it was the intense loss permeating every fiber of my being, or maybe it was my need to blame someone, anyone, for Julian's death. Either way, Adrien's apology sounded hollow in the cool interior of our limousine.

But dwelling on the loss was neither going to bring him back nor would it give me any solace. Drawing my mind away from where it was want to wander, I concentrated on our next move.

"We need to go to Bracciano."

Adrien glanced over at me. "Okay. Mind telling me why?"

"Last night one of the security personnel told me Karina had sent off a request for new cameras to be installed over a month ago and the work has yet to be completed. I want to find out why."

"You've got it. Happen to have an address?"

I withdrew my cell phone. "Yep, Alcie sent me a text earlier with the address and phone number of the company which handles all of our security maintenance needs."

Handing the phone to Adrien, he glanced at the text and then leaned forward to give the driver instructions.

Sitting back, he screwed up his mouth in consideration. "So, what exactly are you hoping to find? Do you think Karina had something to do with Julian's death?"

I watched the passing scenery speed by. "I don't know."

A half hour later, we pulled over in front of a small electronics store. Climbing out, I squinted at the well-worn sign hanging above the door. *Gesep Elettronica.*

Following Adrien through the door, I couldn't help feeling let down by the dusty, dark interior. For a company that handles all the security for the Aliment stronghold, it sure didn't look like much. A bell attached to the door tinkled to alert the shop owner to our arrival, and part of me wondered about the wisdom of handing over our security needs to a company so ridiculously out of touch. Shelves lined with ancient looking electronics, wiring, monitors, and surveillance equipment made at least ten years ago concerned me. Why in the name of the Gods would the Kin deal with these people? What could they offer that a better stocked company couldn't?

The answer to that question seemed even more allusive when the door to the back swung open and a decrepit old human shuffled in.

"Ciao, signori. Che cosa posso fare oggi per voi?"

I acknowledge the man with a nod and smiled pleasantly. "Hello. Do you speak English?"

The man nodded and gestured, rocking his hand from side to side. "Sì, little bit."

Not sure how to broach the subject of Karina's request, without befuddling the man with English, I fumbled with where to start. Expecting Adrien to be just to my right, I gave a quick sideways glace but realized he'd left me to fend for myself at the counter while he stared out the front window. What good was having a Second if he wasn't around when you needed him?

"Do you know Sede di Alimentazione? Are you the security expert Karina has dealt with previously?"

The man's face paled. He looked furtively around as if nervous about talking with me. He appeared to check the room, scanning every nook and cranny—for what I had no clue. But then, when he had completed his peculiar ritual he leaned in and met my eye. "You," he pointed to me and then to the counter, "wait here."

I nodded. When the old man tottered away, I turned and watched Adrien who was still studying something outside. "What's wrong?"

He didn't answer at first. Then a moment later, he spoke. "I keep getting the feeling someone is watching us."

Walking to where he stood, I looked out the window. I scanned the rooftops and the visible corners of the street and could find nothing. "I don't see anything."

Adrien tensed. "Neither do I. But from the moment we got out of the car, my short hairs stood on end." He looked over at me. His broad lips turned downward in a stern grimace.

"Someone or something is out there. I just don't know where."

I shrugged. "All right, we can check out the neighborhood when we're done here if you like. In the meantime, mind helping me understand what the hell this guy is saying?"

He chuckled. "You really are going to need to learn Italian."

"Maybe in my next lifetime. For now, that's what I've got you for."

Several minutes later the door swung open again. It wasn't the old man who entered the room.

The younger man's rich timber seemed to convey hidden meaning as he spoke. "Hello. I'm Luca Gesep. My uncle says you two are in need of some specialized help?"

Surprised and somewhat relieved that he spoke English, I returned to the counter with renewed hope for answers. "Yes, I guess you could say that. I'm the new Head of Security at Sede di Alimentazione. I need you to check on a service order submitted about a month ago. It was for new roof cameras."

He eyed me suspiciously. "I mean no disrespect, but I don't know you. How do I know you are telling me the truth about who you are? It would be my head if I talked with anyone who walked into my store and claimed to be the head of Aliment security."

I thought on it for a second. "I got your address from Alcie. Call her. She'll vouch for me."

Flipping open his cell phone, he dialed what I assumed was Alcie's number. After several minutes of back and forth with whoever was on the other end, he snapped it shut. "Okay, so you checked out. What happened to Karina?"

"She's taking a little vacation." My answer was intentionally cryptic. No need to let it get back to her that I'd been here. "She'll be back in a couple of weeks."

The man motioned me to silence as the door behind me opened. "Ciao, bellezza. Che cosa posso fare per voi?"

From the first moment she entered, an unusual scent emanated from her. Not unpleasant really, just different. My eyes narrowed as I breathed deeply trying to place the scent.

Spicy, cinnamon-like…musky? Knowing I'd smelled it before, I cast a surreptitious look over my shoulder. I didn't recognize her. Perhaps a common perfume the women of this country used. She approached the counter with a map of the area spread out before her. Stylish sunglasses and a white floppy hat obscured much of her face. Placing the map on the counter next to me, she studied it in earnest, her long black hair draping the side of her face. As she looked up to speak with the shopkeeper, I noticed brilliant white teeth and a smile to warm the hardest hearts. "Ciao. Potete aiutare? Devo ottenere a Assisi."

Ah, she was a tourist looking for directions to Assisi. I leaned forward on the counter next to the map and studied the directions the shop keeper was giving her. *Huh, I could think of some directions I wouldn't mind giving her.*

I bit my lip as her scent washed over me causing a flutter in my stomach. Adopting my best, seductive tone, I glanced up at her. "You're going to Assisi?"

I couldn't help myself. Something about the perfume she was wearing made my blood boil. Never in my life had such a scent driven me so quickly past the point of distraction.

She glanced over at me briefly and nodded. "I am trying to. Do you know how to get there? I'm hopelessly lost."

"No, I'm sorry. Always wanted to visit though." I'd lied through my teeth on that one. No way was I going to Assisi, even for her. Not until I knew more about the Cambiare. Going there now would be akin to suicide. "So, I'd better leave the direction giving to this fine Italian gentleman."

She went back to her perusal of the map, dismissing me as easily as she changed from Italian to English. The shopkeeper bent over the map and showed her the streets to take to Assisi. I listened carefully to the conversation and watched as his finger slid over the map showing her the quickest route.

When he was done, she gave him one of her brilliant, toothy grins and folded up the map. "Grazie. Apprezzo l'aiuto." Turning to leave, she hesitated a moment. When she turned to look at me, a lump formed in my throat. "Signore? Do you believe in destiny?"

I gave her a puzzled look. "That's a rather odd question. If I have to be honest, no. No, I don't."

She gave me a sly, knowing look and then continued. "That's too bad. Destiny has a plan for all of us; it's just whether or not we choose to see the signs." As she walked toward the door, my gaze followed her. Leaning casually against the counter, I watched as she turned briefly to smile back at me. "If you make it to Assisi, look me up. I'll be staying there a while."

As our gazes met a flash of desire seared my body. "It would help if I had a name to go with the face."

She laughed. "Well, if you listen to destiny, maybe she'll whisper it to you." And with that she walked out the door and disappeared.

Amused, I stared after her.

Adrien joined me and laughed. "Wow. That was one strange woman."

I chuckled and turned back to the shopkeeper. "You get many like her in here?"

His tone was flat and not at all amused. "On occasion but that one I've never seen personally before." He looked at me with a look of earnest disapproval. "Signore, I would be very careful if I were you. It wouldn't do to go messing around with the likes of them. The Cambiare are more dangerous than they appear."

"Cambiare—what?" I stared in shocked horror as the realization hit. Somehow, I had imagined the Cambiare as vile rabid beasts roaming the night, taking victims indiscriminately. But, she was far from unintelligent. She proved herself fluent in at least two languages, which was more than I could say for myself, passed herself off as human as easily as I did, and most of all she seemed to be self-aware and had an exceptionally quick wit. Which meant one thing: Julian's attack wasn't random. His murderer had targeted him.

"You didn't know?" The salesclerk seemed surprised. "I thought for sure you would have recognized her scent."

"I've never met one before. I didn't even know they had a

scent." I frowned, remembering the night I was attacked in my bedroom. Had there been a scent then? Was I just too out of it to notice or perhaps my assailant was not who I believed her to be?

The thought bothered me.

I didn't like the vulnerability of not knowing who my enemy was. This was going to take a lot more time to sort out.

"Well, they do. I can't smell it, but then I'm human. I was told your kind has enhanced senses. That's why I figured you'd know the moment she walked in."

"Ah, I see. Well, like I said, I've never met one before."

Extending his hand over the counter, he waited for me to take his hand. "I never got a chance to introduce myself. I'm Luca Gesep. Sorry about not trusting you right off. Can't be too careful in my line of work." He lifted the counter and motioned for us to enter the back area with him. "My uncle owns this shop. I do a little side business out of it as well."

"What kind of side business?" I studied his features wondering what sort of trouble I might be getting into.

"The kind people pay to keep quiet."

As he led us into a tiny back office, I noticed his uncle scurry out another door like a rat abandoning a sinking ship. "It's obvious your uncle is afraid of us. Why aren't you?"

He chuckled. "My uncle is an old man. He's lived a long life and has done so by staying out of other people's business." He paused in front of the desk and pulled out the chair.

"You don't mind getting involved with us?" Something bothered me, but I couldn't put my finger on it.

"Let's just say I'm an equal opportunity capitalist. I don't discriminate because of species. Your money is as good as any humans, and as long as I do the job you need, I'm fairly certain I'm safe."

I reevaluated Luca. He didn't seem to care which side he was on as long as someone paid him. Another human who valued money over common sense. Good to know. I would watch my back with this one. "How did you come to be involved with the Alimentatori?"

He shrugged and leafed through a log on his desk. "I guess it's been about six years now." Stopping to think, he glanced up and nodded. "Yeah, six and half, I think. I met Karina at one of the local bars. We hit it off, had a brief fling, and then a few months later she approached me about setting up a full-fledged security perimeter for where she worked. Something about having trouble with break-ins or trespassers. I don't remember exactly. Been a long time." He eased back in his seat and eyed me speculatively. "What's the deal with the replacement cameras for the roof? What happened to the old set up?"

My brow furrowed. "Lightning took them out about a month ago, which is what brought me here today. I need to know why they haven't been replaced yet."

Luca flipped a few more pages in the log and then scowled. "Probably because I never received anything requesting work."

"Are you sure? I was told Karina personally sent off a service order requesting new cameras."

"Well, if she did, I never received it. I log all work requests into this book as soon as I get them. Keeps me clear on what came in first and what takes priority, and it's safer. It isn't easy to hack a logbook kept in a safe, unlike keeping it on a computer hard drive." He pointed to the book and turned it around, so I could see the entries for the previous month. "See, nothing here."

"Is it possible someone else received it and it didn't get logged?"

"Nope. I open everything that comes addressed to this store. If it arrived, I would have seen it and logged it." He shrugged. "Don't know what to tell you. No log. No receipt."

Frustrated, I exhaled. So, Karina either put in the request as her staff said she did and it was intercepted, or her staff was lying to cover for her. Either was possible, and at this point I had no clue which was the right assumption.

Chapter Twelve

Sipping the coffee, I brought up, I stared out at the lake as the sun set to the west.

Absent video footage, a misplaced suitcase, missing rings and now a service request that was never filed. This whole situation was getting more bizarre by the minute.

Everywhere I turn there is nothing but questions. I went through the hours I spent looking at footage in my mind. So much of the time I had looked specifically for Julian's attacker. Maybe I'd not seen the whole picture.

I swallowed the last of my drink and stood up. There had to be something there I was missing, some clue as to what was really going on.

Exiting my room, I found the outer lounge empty. "Adrien?"

When no one answered, I walked to his room and knocked. "Adrien? Are you there?"

Still no answer. He must have gone out. I would call him later if I came across anything interesting.

A few minutes later I sat at Karina's desk scouring the footage I previously decided was worthless.

Three hours passed before something caught my eye. Sitting forward, I ran the section over again, this time slower.

As I sat back a confident smile parted my lips. "Gotcha, you son of a bitch."

Grabbing my phone, I dialed Adrien's number.

"Yeah, it's me."

"Where the hell are you?" He sounded angry.

"I'm in the Security office."

"You should have waited for me. For all I knew you were dragged off just like your brother." Yep. He's angry.

"Calm down. I'm fine. I need you to find Karina and bring her to me as soon as possible."

"Okay, why? Did you find something else?"

"I'll explain when you get here."

*****

I didn't have to wait long. Barely fifteen minutes later. Adrien barreled through the door with a livid redhead in tow. He wrestled with her flailing arms, trying to keep them away from his face. A crack echoed through the outer office as her palm made contact with his cheek, and his howl of pain was drowned out by her screech. "Bastardo! Get your filthy hands off me."

Enraged by the slap and Karina's continued defiance, Adrien let loose with an indignant barrage of foul language. Grabbing her by the wrist, he twisted her arm wedging it up behind her back and inched her toward the door to my office.

Surprised and somewhat amused by her outrageous behavior, I stood up and waited for them to arrive.

As they entered, Adrien kicked closed the door and shoved her toward me. "You wanted me to bring her to you. Well, she's here, and you owe me a shirt."

Glancing down at his chest, I realized he had several buttons missing from the front of it. "Yeah, well, I thought I could trust you to bring her to me without causing a scene and alerting the whole freaking villa."

She stomped around the edge of the desk and met me, nose to nose. "You think I'm causing a scene? Just you wait. You haven't seen anything yet. The moment I am done here, I'm going to the Council. They need to know about the way I've been treated." She leaned in to emphasize every word. "I'll have your head on a silver platter."

Towering over the woman I didn't falter. Meeting her steely eyed gaze head on, I spoke slowly to assure she didn't misunderstand me. "Don't ever threaten me, you mewling little bitch. You'll find my bite is a lot worse than my bark." Grabbing her by the shoulders, I shoved her back toward the front of the desk. "Now, sit down, and shut up."

Crossing to join me, my Second rubbed the bright red spot on his cheek and moved his jaw as if checking to make sure it still worked properly.

Directing my attention to Adrien, I frowned. "You okay?"

"Yeah, it's fine." He chuckled and shot Karina a cocky smile. "I've had women do far worse."

Karina bristled. "Touch me again and see what happens."

I chuckled. "Careful, Adrien, I think she likes you."

She cast a disdainful eye my way and sneered. "Careful Trudeau, or you're really going to piss me off."

"Oh, see and here I thought I already succeeded." Sitting on the edge of the desk, I looked over at Adrien and continued in a mocking tone, "Note to self, try harder next time."

Ignoring my humor, Karina sat down and glared up at me. Raising an eyebrow, she sat back in the chair. "I know you didn't drag my ass in here just to annoy the shit out of me. So, what is it? What do you want?"

"You're right. I do have something we need to discuss." I walked back around to the other side of the desk and I took my seat. Rolling forward I clicked the mouse. Turning the monitor around so Karina could view it, I said, "So, it took me a long time, but I finally figured out why I couldn't find her on any of the video footage of that night." I paused as I looked up. "Someone altered the video. Watch the time stamp at the bottom right-hand portion of the screen." Clicking play, I watched her.

The footage played, and her brow furrowed. Sitting forward,

she studied the video. A short time later genuine surprise etched her features. "Che diavolo, run that back."

Clicking the mouse, I moved the cursor on the screen to just before the time stamp jumped by forty-five seconds and pushed play.

"How is this possible?" Shocked disbelief and then anger crossed her face.

I stopped the video and sat back. "You tell me. There are at least four more files with missing footage."

"You can't think..." She shook her head in adamant denial. "Anyone could have..."

"No," I interrupted her, angered by her outright denial, "not just anyone, Karina. You. You had the means, the skill, and access to all of the footage."

"That's ridiculous. A number of people have access to these files. Anyone with a security badge and access code could have logged in and tampered with the files." She looked directly into my eyes as if it would somehow help convince me of her honesty.

I nodded in agreement. "Yes, you're right. An access code and ID are needed to access the system. In fact, that is exactly what led me to you."

I watched as the blood drained from her face and I knew she was caught.

"That's not possible," she whispered in a strained voice.

"Not possible? Your access code was the solitary one used to access each of the damaged files."

She fidgeted in her chair as I picked up the phone. "Who are you calling?"

Ignoring her, I dialed the security extension. "Yeah, you can come in now."

A panicked look came over her face as she shot out of her seat. "What are you doing?"

"If you won't talk to me, then you'll talk to the Council."

"I'm telling you, I had nothing to do with this." Her voice shook as fear finally grabbed hold of her. "It wasn't me.

Someone had to have used my code."

I eyed her knowingly and shook my head, "I'm not buying it."

She thought for a moment and then frowned. "I don't know what or who you would believe, but I didn't do this."

As the door opened two officers of the Paladini della Guardia marched into the outer office. They were dressed identically in black, form-fitting, high-necked, short jackets which stood open at the throat. The symbol of the House of Armaros dominated their deep red ascots, tucked neatly into place as well as the matching berets perched upon their short-cropped hair. Thick gold embroidery, reminiscent of the intricate pattern found on Morbius's robes, wove its way around the stiff collar and was repeated at the wrists. Bright gold buttons adorned the front and ran in two rows, giving the jacket a double-breasted look. Black pants with matching embroidery running down each leg disappeared into the tops of sleek, tall, black leather boots adorned with gold buttons on their sides. At their hips, a holstered sidearm warned others off. To complete the look, each wore stern-faced hard expressions, stating without words 'don't fuck with us.'

On the whole, they were regal, intimidating, and completely badass, as the king's guard should be.

Dragging my gaze back to Karina, every ounce of my self-satisfied, superiority shone through the cool glance I threw her. "And I'm supposed to just take your word for it?" I rose and waved the men into my office. "Sorry. Not going to happen. Now, if you don't mind, I've got a hunt to begin."

Realizing that the royal guards had arrived, she sat forward and whispered urgently, "There are things going on here you do *not* understand."

My eyes narrowed. "Oh, I see things quite clearly. Only you know what's truly going on, right?" Placing my fingertips on the smooth surface of the desk, I leaned over and looked directly into her eyes. "You would say anything to cast suspicion elsewhere. Now, get out of my office."

As the guards came to either side of her, she rose. Her lip

curled in disgusted anger. "Look at you, so sure you know what's going on." She mimicked my stance, her face a mere hairbreadth away from mine. "Let me tell you something: you know nothing."

With that she pushed off the desk and brushed passed the Guardians who in turn fell into step behind her. I dismissed her with barely a thought, feeling confident the Council would now be willing to give me what I needed to find Julian's killer.

"Take her to holding. The Council will want to speak with her."

One guard turned at the door to acknowledge my request, and a second later, all hell broke loose. Karina struck the other guard in the throat and made a break for the door. In a quick, agile movement she opened the door and darted into the hallway. Before the stunned guards had a chance to react, I jumped the desk and was in pursuit. "Don't just stand there, you idiots. Go after her."

I reached the door in time to see her disappearing down the stairs. Bursting through the opening with the guards and Adrien hot on my heels I hit the stairs and took them two at a time. By the time we reached the bottom she had vanished, leaving the front door open in her wake.

Following her, I made a mad dash to the opening and yelled to the men with me, "Alert the guards! If she leaves this compound, I want them in pursuit. Tell them I need her alive."

Just before darting through the open portal, I heard one of the guards shout instructions into his radio. Coming to a stop in the middle of the grassy lawn, I scanned the grounds allowing my enhanced sight to travel over every blade of grass around me but to no avail. I growled in frustration letting it erupt from me like spurting magma from an angry volcano. Nothing indicated which direction she had gone. No blade of compressed grass, no overturned rock, no crushed foliage of any kind. The bitch had left no trail. I was at a loss.

Turning back to the villa, I joined Adrien and the other men. The guard who'd been struck in the throat glared at me, angry I supposed over his personal injury. "Mi dispiace, signore. She came at me so suddenly—"

I held up my hand to stem the flow of excuses. "Don't say a word. Adrien, you're with me. You two, do something useful."

As Adrien fell into pace next to me, I growled. "Gods damn it. We had her."

My Second shrugged. "Did we?"

I stopped my furious pace and glared at him. "Yes, we did."

Adrien pursed his lips and shook his head. "I'm not so sure."

Turning away from him, I took the stairs to the front porch two at a time to put some distance between us. "It had to be her. Her code was used on all of the files, and she was the only one with the opportunity to edit the files."

Adrien kept pace with me, refusing to give up. "Was she? For all we know she was telling the truth. Someone could have learned her code and used it to throw us off."

"Karina didn't have prior knowledge of the changes that were coming. She didn't hide her tracks initially because she was Head of Security. Who was going to take a second look at that footage? Then, by the time she knew about her replacement, she had no time to fix her error."

The firm hand on my shoulder stopped me in midstride.

"Jace. I know that all sounds logical to you and perhaps it is. However, you need to be more careful. You can't go around accusing other Aliments of traitorous behavior without being completely beyond-a-shadow-of-a-doubt sure that they are the guilty party. And to have her sent to holding before she was given a chance to prove her innocence? That's not how things are done here." He put his hands on his hips and glared at me as if I'd committed a grievous error in judgment. "Frankly, if you'd pulled something like that on me, I'd have run too. It was obvious from the minute we walked through the door you were gunning for her. I saw it in your eyes. She never stood a chance. I don't think it would have mattered if she could have proven she hadn't altered the files. I think you would have found a reason to serve her up to the Great Council."

The muscle in my jaw worked as I restrained the building

anger. "Suddenly I'm the bad guy in this scenario while you take the side of someone who aided in the murder of my brother?"

Adrien sucked in a breath. "Gods. You still don't trust me, do you?" He raked an agitated hand through his disheveled blond hair and growled aloud. "I'm not taking sides against you, Jace. My oath to you prevents me from doing so. What you need to realize is that there are forces at play here you may not like or even understand. They are real, and they are dangerous. Someone is lying daily to us, and we can't be sure who it is or what they are trying to keep us from finding out. And today, my friend, you played right into their hands. You tied up your investigation in a nice, neat little bow without asking yourself why. Why would Karina leave herself wide open to scrutiny by utilizing her *own* code to access those files? What would she have to gain? Not to mention the obvious discrepancies between what security officer told you and what Luca Gesep told us earlier today. Who was lying in that equation? What we really need to do is sort through the lies until the truth emerges. Not go off half-cocked and accuse people of aiding the killer of a newly Ascended Council member."

I considered what he said for a moment. Looking back toward the front door, I stood undecided. Was it possible I'd jumped the gun with my accusations and subsequent actions against Karina? Maybe, though a part of me rebelled against the thought.

"Okay, so going for the jugular might not have been the most prudent or elegant of moves. I can admit that. However, I've never been one to pull my punches, and I certainly won't allow someone off the hook simply because they *said* they didn't do it. I suppose the missing requisites were circumstantial and that it is completely possible that Luca was lying the whole time. Even so, when you add the info he gave us to the use of her code to access the files, I still believe my case is pretty air tight." I paused to allow him an opportunity to respond. When he didn't, I continued. "She may have fooled you with her pleas of innocence. I'm not buying the magic beans she's selling. It's obvious that you've got a thing for a pretty face. You don't trust Alcie, whose been nothing but helpful, and you want me to let the pretty redhead walk. Makes me wonder how well you actually know her." He made a strangled noise as if to deny my accusation. I barreled ahead without stopping. He had had his opportunity to speak. Now it was my turn. "She's a predator, plain and simple. I recognized that the first moment our paths crossed. She uses men to get what she wants and isn't above swaying her hips and bedroom-eying her way to the top. Well, it won't work on me. If that ill-tempered redheaded she-witch wants me to believe in her, she's going to have to try a whole lot harder. Unlike some I could mention, I'm not an easy kill. In fact, I devoured her kind on a daily basis back home. No woman, Aliment or otherwise, has ever brought me to heel, and I'm not about to let it start now." I paused again to take a breath and held up a finger to silence his retort. "You want me to respect you? Then stop thinking with your dick and get your fucking head on straight. Despite her pretty face and professed innocence, she's guilty as sin, and I'm taking her down."

"My turn now?" He looked at me in question then continued when I gave a nod. "Good, because I have something to say. When I pledged my services to you as the brother of my dearest friend, I hoped to find the same kind of friendship with you that I had found with Julian. It is becoming readily apparent I was sorely mistaken. You habitually speak and act without thinking. When I offer advice, you rarely heed it. In fact, it would seem you take great pleasure in doing the exact opposite of whatever I advise. You put yourself in jeopardy daily, expecting me to just shut up and take it. And now you've insulted me on a level that in ancient days would have ended in bloodshed, not that I'm *not* contemplating beating the shit out of you right here and now. Believe me, I am, but I respect Julian's memory too much to let his piss ant little brother push my buttons. If we can't be friends, so be it. But by the Gods I'm not going to let you ride roughshod over me when it comes to acting in your best interest. I am sworn to protect you, and even if it means protecting you from yourself, that's exactly what I'm going to do. So, you can either get with the program, or find someone else to take my place. But until then, *I* am your Second, and you *will* respect me as such."

Turning, he paused perhaps attempting to get a handle on his anger and then looked in the direction of the Library. "Now, I find myself in need of a good stiff drink. You can join me if you wish or go back to our suite. Either way, think about what I've said and let me know your decision. If you choose to take another Second, then I will pack my shit and head home tomorrow." He stomped a few feet away turned around and shouted, while jabbing a finger at me, "Oh, and by the way, good luck finding anyone who doesn't feel the urge to kill you after working for you for twenty minutes. I know it only took me fifteen."

Stunned I watched him walk away. *Wow.* That was like watching a tornado rip through the heart of a Midwestern town, painful yet awe inspiring. "Huh." I was impressed. The corner of my mouth lifted in a half-smile. "I think I'm going to have myself a drink."

Chapter Thirteen

I found Adrien drowning his sorrows at the bar. As I walked up behind him, I heard him speaking to the bartender.

"The kid drives me fucking nuts. If it weren't for his brother, I'd let him go off all crazy and get himself killed."

The bartender laughed as he wiped the bar. "Sounds like you both need a bit of a break from each other. You should try going into Anguillara Sabazia. There's a private little club named Eros that sits on the beach. It's an invitation-only kind of thing. They charge a fortune at the door, but the place is well worth the price. I tend bar there on occasion. It's loud enough to keep a man from thinking on his own troubles and filled to the brim with hot women."

I took the seat next to my Second. "Sounds great." I looked over at Adrien. "What do you say? Up for getting good and sloshing drunk among a bunch of people we don't know and a few we would like to get to know?" He eyed me with suspicion and downed a shot of tequila. "Come on. I promise not to do anything that drives you fucking nuts." His head dipped in embarrassment as he realized I had heard his complaints. "What do you say?"

He slammed the shot glass down on the bar and glared at

me. "Fine, but you're paying all night, and if you do one thing to disrespect me, even in the slightest, I'm going to drag your sorry ass outside and kick it twelve ways to Sunday."

I laughed then glance toward the bartender. "Invitation only? Is there some special code word or something to get in the door?"

The man chuckled. "No, just tell the man at the door Anthony sent you over."

"Got it. Thanks a lot, Anthony." I placed a hefty tip in his jar and then turned my attention back to my Second. "Let's go blow off some steam, and tomorrow we'll get back to work."

*****

Having made it past a hulking bouncer who took his job seriously, we entered the cool interior of the night club.

Eros was a far cry from just a bar.

Like any other high-end nightclub, the atmosphere was electric. Alcohol flowed freely as men and women congregated together gyrating to thump, thump, thumping of rhythmic dance music, pumping its way through hidden speakers and into the blood of everyone in the crowd.

But, that was where the similarity ended.

This was a *Covo di Iniquità*.

It might have had something to do with being in the heart of Alimentatori territory, but this Covo, or den as we called them in America, had more than its fair share of humans in attendance. So much so, that the distinct odor of Alimentatori seduction hormones flowed like wine through the aisles eliciting a powerful erotic response in their human counterparts.

Furrowing my brow, I glanced over at my Second. Leaning over, I spoke loudly to assure he heard me, "A bit more than I'd expected."

Adrien nodded. "You should see it on a weekend."

"You've been here before?"

He nodded his head. "I've been here a couple of times, but

Julian only came with me once. Not his kind of party."

Nodding, I pointed to a couple of seats at the bar and then led the way through the throng of people. Reaching the bar, I took one of the empty stools and turned to survey our surroundings a little more thoroughly. Colorful lights illuminated the area of the dance floor. I watched for several minutes as Aliments mingled with humans. Aliments paired themselves with human men and women, dancing, leading them into seduction as easily as eliciting devotion from a loving pet. The sexual tension within the club was undeniably hedonistic. The place was a fucking Aliment orgy waiting to happen.

Before the night was through, many humans would be more than satisfied by their Aliment lovers and vice versa.

I smirked as I thought about the times I'd coupled the hormone with another hidden talent: entering the mind of my human companion through erotic visions. Angel quite enjoyed the use of that talent. I could drive her to the edge of orgasm without ever touching her.

I know. It was not the intended use of our ability and certainly not for what it was originally, but times had changed. Our ancestors may have used that ability in a far more altruistic way. Giving visions to humans, alternatively guiding and inspiring greatness or punishing and causing madness, just wasn't done anymore. Thankfully, our kind no longer had an obligation to straighten out the mortal world. Now, we could just stand back and watch it rise or fall of its own accord.

Personally, I believed it was better this way. They did their own thing, and I did mine. I used my, uhm…*powers of persuasion*, whenever and however I saw fit. And tonight, would be no different. If I happened across someone, I would like to get to know a little more intimately, then she and I would enjoy the night and part in the morning, regretting nothing.

"You owe me a drink." Adrien's shout broke my train of thought, and I glanced in his direction.

"Order what you want. I've got you covered."

A broad smile spread across his lips, and he turned to the bartender. Raising his voice to be heard clearly over the music,

Adrien placed an order, "Hey, can I get a shot of ouzo and a beer?"

I clapped him on the back. "Thanks, but I'm not in the mood for a beer."

He glared at me in stubborn defiance. "Those are for me. You order your own shit."

"Fine." Turning the seat around, I placed an order, "Limoncello." I didn't really know what it was. I'd heard some people taking about it on the plane. They'd said it was hugely popular over here, so I figured I might as well give it a shot. At Adrien's questioning look, I shrugged. "When in Rome…"

He snorted and downed the shot of Ouzo. "Yeah, though we're not in Rome."

I chuckled. "Technicalities…"

Glancing at my watch, I realized several hours had passed since we first arrived at Eros and thus far the night had been a bust. Though there were several hot Italian numbers in the place, none had caught my interest yet. Put out by my body's lack of response to any of the numerous women who propositioned me thus far, I nursed my fourth Limoncello my mood turning as sour.

Must be jet lag.

Adrien ordered his fifth shot, and I chuckled. "Careful, Adrien or I'll have to carry you home."

"Scusi." A sultry voice purred close to my ear.

My back stiffened. She stood behind, somewhat to the left over my shoulder. I didn't turn. I didn't need to.

A Cambiare brazen enough to walk into a nightclub filled with Alimentatori? *What were the odds?* I toyed with my glass, resisting the urge to spin around and face her down.

Then spicy cinnamon filled my senses, overwhelmingly and inexplicitly seductive. Though similar to that of the woman in the electronics store, this woman's scent held me captivated. A shudder ran down my back, as every hair on my body rose in anticipation of her touch. The incomprehensible attraction set fire to my previously sagging libido.

When she leaned over next to me, the side of her breast grazed my upper arm. Her touch coupled with the overwhelming scent was too much.

What in the hell was wrong with me? Was I so caught up in the spell of this place that I'd find anything on two legs attractive? Another shudder ran through me, reminding me that it was not the environment which was to blame.

Disgusted with myself and my body's betrayal over a fucking Cambiare, I downed the remaining liquid in my glass and slammed it down on the bar. Rising, I scowled at Adrien. "I need some air."

I turned, bumping into her as I shoved my way to the exit.

I heard Adrien's shout as I opened the door. Ignoring his concern, I continued out into the warm, breezy night and headed for the beach. When I reached the shoreline, I gazed out over the water, my thoughts in turmoil.

Why had I reacted so strongly to the woman at the bar without once looking at her? It could have been the lemon liquor making me more susceptible to her influence. In combination with the erotic environment, it *could* have caused my control to slip. Even as I thought it, I knew the liquor and environment had nothing to do with it. I did not respond to anyone else. Why her?

Another far more alarming reason occurred to me.

What if they, like the Alimentatori had a scent which allowed them to seduce, maybe even manipulate others easily? The thought didn't sit well. Though, it somehow seemed to make sense.

The musky, cinnamon sweetness could be a siren's song designed to lure in unsuspecting individuals. It could be the very reason Julian hadn't fought her. She used the pheromone to weave a spell over him to keep him from escaping. He had been a willing participant in his own death.

*****

She scowled at Jacen's quickly retreating back. Glancing down at the growing purplish spot on her white suede jacket, she growled.

Cazzo! The *figlio di puttana* ruined her new jacket.

The bartender handed her a couple of cocktail napkins. Her brow rose skeptically. As if those tiny little squares would do much to help. Leaning over, she spoke to the man across the bar. "Do you have any salt?"

His face turned from polite confidence to confusion. Instead of asking, he shrugged. "Sì, naturalmente."

As he turned to retrieve what she'd asked for, she slipped off the jacket and spread it on the bar.

As the bartender slid a small bowl of course granulated salt across the counter toward her, she dabbed gingerly at the stain. "This is all I've got back here."

She looked down at the bowl. *Sea salt.* It would do. "Thanks, Sal."

As she poured the salt over the spot, she groaned. *So much for a chance encounter.*

Thus far, today had been a complete and utter bust. Angry frustration knit her brow. He dropped his guard, and she seized the opportunity to establish contact just as she'd been instructed to do. How could she have known he would go running off at the slightest touch?

The disappointment she was sure to see echoed in Dante's eyes would haunt her to the grave. She dabbed harder at the stain as if attempting to blot out the image of the elder's disapproval. Of course, it wouldn't be the first time he looked at her that way. It seemed to happen far too often of late.

Dabbing at the salt granules, she was so intent on her own thoughts, she failed to realize the lapdog had risen.

"Have we met?"

Startled, she glanced up at him. Her contact-clad brown eyes met his avid stare. *Yes.* She fervently hoped he didn't remember their brief encounter. "No."

The man's brow furrowed as he studied her face intently.

She arched a well-groomed brow and ignored him as though she had no interest in further conversation.

"I'm sorry about that."

Good Gods, why wouldn't he just go away? She brushed at the now purple-tinted granules hoping her continued rudeness would motivate him to leave.

As she lifted the jacket, the salt fell away from the suede, and a severe frown deepened the corners of her mouth. *Cazzo*. The home remedy had managed to take the barest amount of liquid out of the fabric, but the purple stain remained.

"We can pay for the cleaning." He persisted still awaiting her attention.

Instead of acknowledging him, she slipped her arms into the sleeves of the jacket and picked up her wine glass. Without looking at him, she spoke, "That won't be necessary."

He shrugged then threw a couple of bills onto the bar. "If you choose to go that route, have the invoice sent to the Sede di Alimentazione, care of Jacen Trudeau."

Of course, she knew this already, but, if he was in a talkative mood, she'd indulge him. "You live at the Sede?"

"We are guests there." He eyed her as if still attempting to take her measure.

She averted her eyes to stare into the rich red liquid in her glass. "Ah, I see. And you're American by the accent."

He nodded.

Now the decisive moment. "So, tell me Jacen, how do you find my country?"

His smile warmed. "I'm Adrien. The man who spilled your drink is Jacen."

She gave a curt nod and then hid a knowing look behind the lip of her glass as she took a sip of merlot. Confirmation from the lapdog himself. How gratifying. "Does your Padrone know you offer up his money as if it were your own?"

His chuckle was warm, almost seductive as he leaned toward her. "Nope. But, it doesn't matter. He owes me. He was supposed to buy the drinks tonight. Besides, he's the reason you have a damaged jacket."

The stink of Alimentatori pheromone emanated from his being like a bad cologne. She almost gagged but stopped it with a shudder. Why did Aliments have to stink up the place just because they wanted to get laid? It was disgusting. "Then I would say he still owes you, because no amount of cleaning is going to fix my giacca."

"Be that as it may, the offer stands."

Saccharine sweet and equally distasteful. She plastered on her best fake smile and lifted her glass in mock toast to the man. "Well noted." She took another draught, her gaze never leaving the Aliment's. "Now, if you don't mind…"

His face fell in disappointment as the message was delivered loud and clear. He glanced down at his watch as if time was suddenly of the essence. "Yes, of course. I probably shouldn't leave him wandering the city alone anyway. It was a pleasure meeting you."

With that, he turned and trailed after his master.

A wicked smirk crossed her lips. *That's a good little Aliment. Maybe if you ask nicely, he'll give you a bone.*

She chuckled at her own wit as her gaze followed him.

Seconds later he disappeared out the double doors, and she leaned against the bar. She glanced around the club taking in the debauchery surrounding her. With a wrinkle of the nose, she shuddered. There were far too many Aliments in here for her comfort.

She was just about to call it a night when she spied Alegra and Dante in the corner. *Great.* Her jaw clamped down and she rolled her eyes. That was all she needed.

Alegra was already plenty angry over Nix's earlier jaunt into Anguillara Sebazia alone. Finding her at Eros had probably topped off her foul mood.

As far as Nix was concerned, she was the one who should be pissed. When Alegra had shown up unexpectedly outside of Gesep's then demanded Nix report to Dante immediately, she'd been madder than a hornet shoved out of its nest. What right did her older sister have to order her around as if she were a kit?

Dante had taken her side, of course. Who would blame him? Even if he was the head of their Glaring, hell, the leader of the entire Cambiare nation, he was Alegra's mate, and he was nothing if not loyal.

She swirled the wine around the glass absently. *Gives pussy-whipped a whole new meaning.* Not that she'd ever say so aloud.

Nix took another swig of wine as her gaze met Dante's over the edge of the glass. His dark eyebrow arched with knowing superiority. She swallowed. *Porca troia.* The night just kept going from bad to worse. Had he heard her last thought? She certainly hoped not.

As the bartender approached, she turned to him, presenting her back to Dante, and slid her glass over to the human behind the counter. "Do you mind? I suddenly feel the need to drink, heavily."

He poured a second glass, as his gaze caressed her features lingering a bit too long on her full lips. "No problem, Nix. If you feel the need for anything else, don't hesitate to ask."

Oh Gods. Not him, too. Most nights she would have endured his attention as he was genuinely a nice young man, but tonight she'd had just about enough of being tolerant. "Thanks. I'll keep that in mind."

She wouldn't, but he didn't need to know that.

Picking up the glass, Nix drank a goodly amount to steel herself against the upcoming encounter. Several seconds later, she crossed the room and stopped next to her sister's table. Leaning down, she kissed her sibling on both cheeks. "Ciao Alegra." After she placed her glass on the table, Nix slid into the seat opposite her sister. "I thought you had to work tonight."

"I did. Then Dante called and said you were coming here." Alegra sat forward, her eyes intense in her rebuke of her baby sister. "What were you thinking, coming here alone?"

Meeting her angry glare head on, the younger woman shrugged. "I called Dante to let him know where I was headed. I kind of figured he might show up." She winked at the older gentleman sitting leisurely at Alegra's side.

"Basta! You were foolish, and you know it, Nix." Alegra's

white-knuckled grip on her beer glass was the single indication of how truly angry she was. "You know what happened the last time you ventured here alone." She sat back and glanced around the room as if checking to ensure that no one was taking a particular interest in their conversation.

Dante's golden eyes glowed as he gripped Alegra's hand and stroked a thumb over her knuckles. "Calm down, my love. No harm was done. Nix is in one piece. Might I suggest we continue this discussion once we find our way back into our own territory?"

Dante Provenza. Always the rational one. He could calm a glaring of unruly Cambiare with the wave of a hand. Of course, it wasn't very often one met up with a direct descendent of the original line. Most of the originals were hunted to extinction in the fourteenth century when the rabid, marauding witch hunters of the Catholic Church came upon their settlement in France. The Franciscan monks, disagreeing with the killing of innocents in the name of the church, followed the precepts of their patron saint and opened their doors to the remaining Cambiare. They built specially designed catacombs to house the families who came from all over Europe to escape slaughter. Buried deep in the hill of the Basilica di San Francesco the Cambiare's numbers returned, and eventually they were able to rejoin society, though to find an original line, one had to know where to look.

Nix sipped her wine and eased against the back of the booth. "No worries, Dante. My sister just mothers me. She sometimes forgets that I'm not a kit anymore. I've grown up and am perfectly capable of taking care of myself."

Alegra snorted in response.

"You are capable of many things, Mia Bella, the smallest of which is taking care of yourself. Like a young kitten you pounce and play, dashing in and out of trouble as quickly as your mood changes. Your sister merely wishes to keep the trouble to a minimum and you out of danger."

He took her sister's side, yet again. What did she really expect? Nix placed her right fist on her heart, inclined her head to the left, and bowed in the customary sign of respect. "Of course, Dante. I meant no disrespect."

Dante nodded in acceptance of her show of obedience and then rushed to remind her of their current circumstance. "Not here. There are too many curious eyes upon us. We will discuss what is to happen next once we are away from here."

Chapter Fourteen

As the first rays of the sun touched the pristine beauty of Lake Bracciano, I sipped the cappuccino Belvedere had brought to my room. The day had finally arrived. I was to meet the Kin's historian in the Library at seven, and he was going to show me all they gathered over the years about the Cambiare. By the end of the day, I'd be well-prepared for the upcoming hunt.

Downing the last of the drink, I rose. Extending my arms toward the sky, I stretched each muscle in my body to relieve the tightness which had grown from a restless sleep. It was going to be a long day, perhaps an even longer night. No matter. I was ready for it.

As I turned to go into my room, a glint of silver caught my eye. Glancing upward, I saw that it was a small chain hanging precariously off the concrete edge of the roofline. Hopping up on to the railing, I deftly walked the narrow surface until I was within reach of the object. Wrapping my fingers around it, I tugged gently until it pulled loose from its mooring. I clasped it securely in the palm of my hand then jumped down onto the balcony. My fingers spread to reveal the found treasure. A tiny oval locket on a small delicate silver chain about the size of a bracelet shimmered in the early morning light. Opening the tiny object, I found a picture of a smiling dark-haired man on one side and a beautiful golden eyed woman on the other. She had to be the woman who was in my room. With eyes like that, how could she not be?

Snapping the treasure closed, I stuffed it into my jeans pocket and padded my way into the bedroom. I would find out soon enough when I returned the locket to her, personally.

The minutes ticked by as I waited in the Library for whoever was to meet me. Adrien relaxed on the couch, reading the local paper, unworried about the lateness of our guide.

"How can you be so calm? He was supposed to be here a half hour ago."

"It does no good to pace like a caged lion. I prefer to occupy my mind, so I don't dwell on other things. You should try it. Maybe it would teach you how to deal with your impatience." He folded the newspaper, concentrating on an article written in Italian.

Chomping at the bit, like a race horse anxious to start the run, I knew nothing would stem the flow of nervous energy pouring through me. I was minutes away from getting what I needed. Moments away from understanding the beast.

As I turned to make another round of the room, the door opened. An unassuming older gentleman entered the room. He wore an expensive gray pinstripe jacket and matching pants. He surveyed the room, his gray-blue eyes landing on me.

"Jacen of Samsaveel?"

I nodded.

"Good." He crossed the floor and extended his hand to me as he neared. "I'm Leo. I work for the Council." I shook his hand and returned his greeting. "If you'll please," he removed a key from his pocket as he pushed past, "follow me." Proceeding across the room, he gave a nod to the bartender, and the man in turn reached under the bar. When one of the bookshelves on the far wall moved,   I knew the bartender had pushed a release of some kind. *Interesting.* Even as head of security, there were still things, hidden things, I didn't know about this villa.

Sensing my surprise, he shot me a wry smile. "What? You thought we called this the Library because of the impressive number of books?" I fell into step behind him, and Adrien joined me moments later. "You've been granted limited access to our archives."

"Limited access?"

"Yes. Limited access." Reaching out he yanked on the bookshelf, and it opened on silent hinges revealing a door.

Stopping behind him, I studied the portal over his shoulder. The black paint gleamed, though from a small chip near the lock, it looked as if the under lying panel was reinforced metal, not wood. If the dead bolt and keypad were any indication, whatever was behind that door they wanted secure. It seemed odd. Who locked up historical records?

Curious as to how forbidden things were, I pushed the limits just a bit. "I was promised unlimited access to whatever I need."

Leo paused as he pushed the key into the dead bolt lock. "Unlimited access to whatever you need to investigate your brother's death is not the same as unlimited access. You will have full access to any records I feel directly impact the investigation of the murder."

I tried to protest. "What you feel directly—"

He interrupted me. "This is not negotiable. These archives contain every bit of knowledge, history, and information on our family lines. It is valuable beyond your understanding. I am one of only a few who have keys." He paused to punch in a number in the key pad next to the door before turning the knob. The door cracked open just enough to reveal the flickering of a dim motion activated light. However, instead of continuing through, Leo turned to me. His eyes held a hardness I wouldn't have guessed him capable of. "Now, either you respect the Council's wishes, or I lock this door and you fend for yourself."

Understanding his concerns, I put my hands up in defeat. "Got it. Nothing but what you give me."

He nodded and twisted the knob. The door swung inward, the old hinges squealing in protest. Proceeding into the dim room, Leo reached out and stopped me from going too far. I waited while he located the wall switch. A moment later, recessed lights flickered to life illuminating the hidden room, bathing it in bright white light. I sucked in a breath, the sheer grandeur of the room momentarily stunning me to silence. From the outside, I'd thought it might be the size of a walk-in closet. But this, this was incredible. The square landing on which I stood overlooked a two-story circular room. Specially designed Rosewood built-in bookshelves lined the rounded walls from floor to ceiling, giving an air of regal importance to the room. Each shelf housed stacked books, papers, rolled maps, and various other documents and ancient objects. The only place in the whole room devoid of shelves was where the matching staircase jutted out from and followed the lines of the wall until it reached the sleek, black-tiled floor below. Placing a hand on the railing, I stepped off the landing and carried on down the stairs in wonder.

Reaching the bottom, I took a moment to look up and was rewarded with a stunning sight. The domed ceiling was divided into four sections, each painted with an ancient fresco. One scene was of our creator, the great winged God, Svutaf. I'd seen representations of him in other places but nothing like this. In this painting he had his great black, raptor-like wings extended out behind him. It was the first time I ever saw his wings extended, showing off their true magnificence. He seemed to hover overhead, watching our every move. Beautiful, yet unnerving, all at the same time.

Was that what our wings would have looked like if our ancestors hadn't been forced to hide our true identities?

The thought whirled around in my mind like a breeze ruffling the leaf of a memory. The pain I saw in Nathanial's eyes as he spoke of The Rending. He would have been a child when they came for him. He spent the rest of his life physically and emotionally scarred. I always empathized with those who went through the barbarity of The Rending. Until now I scarcely understood the majesty of what they gave up.

Something Nathanial always said when asked about that time

echoed through my mind. *History does not apologize*

That was a theory I'd become all too familiar with. First my parents and now Julian. All well-loved. All dead. It was a lesson I would not soon forget.

I swallowed the bitterness and turned my attention to the rest of the ceiling.

The space directly opposite was home to Aita, the God of the Underworld and his wife Queen Phersipnei. Taking in the artwork, I was suddenly struck by Aita's dark mysterious eyes, which seemed to follow my movements. In Aita's right hand he held the sacred dagger aloft. Moving on to his queen, I noticed her traditional robes, the same color red as the Council's. *Coincidence? Probably not.*

Sandwiched between the murals of our most important Gods were ancient scenes of creation and historical battles.

Where the murals met, at the very center of the ceiling, there was a depiction of two crossed axes, the bronze blades turned outward jutting from ribbon-bound birch rods.

Pointing to the arched ceiling, I nudged Adrien. "Check that out."

Adrien looked up and whistled. "Wow."

"No kidding." I turned toward Leo as he joined us. "I had no idea. This is incredible."

"Isn't it? My family has been responsible for keeping the records safe since the beginning of time." The pride Leo held for his job and family responsibility showed in the straightening of his back and the confidence of his voice. "This room is my church. If you listen carefully, you can almost hear the spirits of our ancestors whispering their secrets to you."

"Intriguing frescos. They're very Giotto-esque."

It was Leo's turn to look surprised. "You know Giotto?"

I laughed. "Well, obviously, not personally." Shrugging, I jammed my hands into the pockets of my blue jeans. "Let's just say, I'm a student of the arts."

Adrien addressed Leo, as he stared up at the murals. "What are the axes for?"

He glanced up at the ceiling. "They are called Fasces. Our ancestors created them a very long time ago. Then our ancient Roman cousins corrupted them. They became a symbol of the lictors, bodyguards of the Magistrates of Rome, who carried them as a symbol of their power and authority." He shrugged and glanced back at me. "For us they've always been a sign of the strength of our unity. Like the birch in its handle, we are bound together many, yet one, stronger together than apart. At one time each of the royal houses was given a Fasce to remind them of this unity. Over time most of them were lost."

I nodded, impressed with the man's knowledge and passion for his job. He obviously knew his shit. Unfortunately, I needed information that was actually relevant to my current crisis. "Where are the records I'm allowed to handle?"

"Over here. I've already laid them out on the table."

I followed him to the large table in the center of the room where two ancient-looking books sat. Though the age of the books was impressive, I glanced up at Leo, confused. "That's it? Just these two books?"

Leo seemed offended. "Just? These books are filled with the observations of my father and grandfather. They did extensive studies of the Cambiare when they arrived in Italy in the fourteenth century.

"I didn't mean to demean your family's efforts. I was just hoping for something more recent."

A red flush rushed to the man's face and he seemed to be searching for a reason not to clock me. I almost chuckled. He was half my size and older than me by at least a hundred years.

Adrien stepped forward, effectively putting himself between me and the angry elder. "I'm sorry. He didn't mean to disrespect you or your family. He's young and brash." My Second gave me a stern disapproving look before continuing, "He often speaks before thinking things through."

Taking a cue from Adrien, I had the good sense to look chagrined. Perhaps I could have been more so, but my disappointment was hard to get over. "Adrien's correct. I truly meant no offense."

Leo seemed to doubt the sincerity of my pseudo apology. Choosing to accept it anyway, he moved away from Adrien. "Fine." He motioned to a cluttered desk under the metal stair case. "I'll be over there if you need me.

Pulling out one of the rosewood chairs with one hand, I pulled the first book toward the edge of the matching table. Taking a seat, I opened the age-hardened, leather cover. To say it was old would have been a severe understatement. Flipping through the thick yellowed pages, I noticed detailed sketches woven throughout. Its script, obviously handwritten in a time when people took a great deal of pride in penmanship. Beautiful, flowing cursive flourishes scrolling their way across the page in fluent...*Italian.*

"Fuck me." The whispered vulgarity seemed overloud in the tall room.

Adrien came up beside me and placed a hand on the table next to the book. He peered over my shoulder to see what had caused my outburst.

"How the hell are you supposed to read that?" he whispered.

I sat back in the chair once again frustrated by my own inability to communicate in the mother language. "I don't know. Do you know enough to translate it for me?"

He snorted in amusement and stood up straight. "Hell no. I'm lucky to string a sentence together, let alone an entire book of antiquated terminology."

I shook my head, anger and frustration working together to make me agitated. Glancing to where Leo sat, deftly ignoring us, I realized I had only one option.

"Excuse me?" His back stiffened, though he gave no other indication of having heard me. "Leo?"

The stern archivist turned his head to peer over his shoulder. "Si, what is it?"

By the tone of his voice, it was obvious he didn't like me very much. Probably because of what I said earlier. I didn't care. We needed help if we were going to be able to understand anything his father and grandfather had recorded so many years ago. "I'm sorry to disturb you, but would you be able to help us with this? We can't read Italian."

He sat for a moment, as if contemplating my request. Then, without warning he slid back his chair and rose. Looking down his nose at me, he frowned. "Wait here, and don't touch anything."

Leo walked up the stairs and exited the room in silence. Several minutes later he entered again with a young Aliment boy in tow. Bringing the boy to the table, where we sat waiting, he presented him to us. "This is Gino. He's my youngest. He can translate his grandfather and great grandfather's writings for you."

I glanced up at the boy, who was no more than a babe in Aliment years. My cheeks burned in embarrassment. To have a young boy translate his mother tongue into the English language, when I could only understand one language...

Looking over at Leo, I recognized the smirk on his face for what it was...satisfaction. He hoped to embarrass me with his actions and had done so easily.

Deciding to accept defeat gracefully, I stood up and held out my hand to the young man. "Gino, it is a pleasure to meet you. I can't tell you how much I appreciate you helping me out. Maybe if you have time, you can teach me Italian as well."

Leo snorted in humor. "The book is written in Latin, not Italian. I'm sure if you'd like, Gino can teach you both."

Adrien choked on a laugh, quickly turning away to avoid my glare.

Swallowing a snide comment, I gave a stiff nod. "Ah, yes, Latin. Fantastic. I look forward to it."

The child grinned ear to ear and extended his hand gripping my larger one in an exuberant handshake. "I will do my best."

"That's all I can ask, Gino." Releasing the boy's hand, I sat back down and motioned for him to do the same.

When we were seated, he grabbed the book Adrien and I had been looking at. "Papa?" He cast Leo a questioning look. "This is the wrong..."

Leo commanded the boy's attention with a rush of stern,

Italian. "Silenzio! Tu farai come ti ho detto."

I eased back in the chair and gave Adrien a skeptical look. Speaking under my breath, I leaned over so my Second could hear me. "Ready for story time? Do you think we'll get nap time too?"

He chuckled and took the seat beside me. "Wonder if there'll be milk and cookies afterward."

I laughed then turned my attention back to Gino. "We're ready whenever you are."

He nodded and opened the book on the table. "Where do you want me to start?"

I shrugged. "At the beginning."

Following the text with his little pudgy finger, the boy's crisp, clear voice rang out with family pride. "Thirtieth day of the fifth month in the four hundred and sixteenth year of our king, Gustav Semjaza the Good. These are the annals of Giovanni of Tamiel, Honorable Archivist of the King."

"Wait," I interrupted the boy for a moment, "What do you mean the four hundred and sixteenth year of our king? What year is that?"

To my surprise, the boy looked at me as if I'd grown two heads. He glanced over at his father, who rolled his eyes and shook his head. Leo answered for him, "Back in my grandfather's day, years were counted by a king's years, not on an annual basis like it is now. If you want a modern take on the year, it would have been the year fourteen thirty-one."

I nodded and glanced back at the child. "You may continue."

Taking a deep breath, he began again. "How do I explain what the past hours have wrought? I sit here in my room, a safe haven amidst a gathering storm, and can't help but wonder how this knowledge will affect our lives. Everything we know of the world changed in an instant, and it falls to me to carry the tale. How the story will end, I know not. But, it must be told, as the fate of a people depends upon the telling.

It was with a heavy heart I set out this morning to flee the scene of the girl's execution. So fraught with anger over the outcome was I, that I hardly realized how far, how long, or even which way I flew. I realized too late a storm gathered overhead. When the lightning flashed, I knew it was no more than prudent to land and seek temporary shelter until the storm passed. I landed in a small clearing near a lake. Perhaps, sixty-four kilometers from Rouen. As the rain began to pelt the ground, I rushed to an outcropping of rock, hoping to find a small crevice or hole in which to tuck myself. To no avail until I noticed what appeared to be smoke coming from beneath my very feet. Knowing this could only mean a hidden entrance to a cave or dwelling of some kind. I began my search for the entrance.

Chapter Fifteen

1431 A.D. - Outside Rouen, France

As the rain soaked his cloak, Giovanni pushed back the leafy branches which had been used to hide the opening. He bent down to peer into the dark interior of the crevice and frowned in concern. The hole seemed big enough for a normal sized man. One of his kind might find it a tight squeeze. Turning sideways, he tucked his wings tightly against his back and eased his way into the opening. He moved slowly, inching his way forward into the darkness. A brief fluttering thought whispered through his mind as his wings brushed lightly against the wall, and the ceiling dropped until he had to crouch to avoid bumping his head.

Well, this was foolish. It would be quite the humiliation to die wedged between two rocks like fungus. Fortunately, he had not once thought to tell anyone where he was going, so even if someone came looking, it was unlikely they would witness this particular humiliation. Over the years, he had found himself in quite a few scrapes due to his impulsive nature. *So, what the hell. Why should today be any different?*

A few feet farther the smell of smoke mingled with a distinct

Far Eastern spice. Pausing, he contemplated the familiar scent for a moment.

He encountered a similar smell a few years earlier whilst traversing the shores of Taprobane. It had been attributed to a dried bark the locals produced. Puzzled, he continued through the passageway. *Hmm, the French countryside was a far cry from the tiny Island nation and a very odd place to find someone cooking with such a decadent spice.* A moment later the thought fled his mind as the passage widened and his attention was drawn back to the task at hand. Within a few meters he could stand at full height again and breathe without scraping either chest or wings. Then, suddenly, the walls were gone, and he was standing at the edge of an inner chamber. A warm glowing fire, within the confines of a large stone ring, lit most of the recesses of the room, though darkness at the opposite end seemed to indicate that the chamber was larger than it appeared. The smoke rose up and disappeared between two plates of rock where they came together to form the ceiling. He crossed to the fire and looked up through the crack. It was obvious the cave dweller intentionally located the fire so that the smoke would be sucked out the small opening. It was truly a miracle he found the chamber at all. He could have missed the wisps of smoke coming up through that hole and been left to fend for himself amidst the raging spring storm.

Glancing back down at the fire, an involuntary shudder ran through him as the last of damp bone-chilling cold fled before the gift of warmth he had received. Giovanni held his chilled hands out over the heat. "Thank Svutaf for the little things!"

Several minutes later, he rubbed his palms together. "Much better."

His voice echoed through the sparsely furnished room, making him cringe with the overloud sound. As he cast a glance around the cavernous chamber, his eyes alighted on the well-used bed of straw, far enough from the fire to not be a danger, but close enough to still garner some warmth. If the two threadbare blankets were any indication, the inhabitant would have need of that warmth. His gaze traveled to the creative structure a few meters from the bed. A clever sort of table had been fashioned out of several large stones, he presumed, to give the cave's occupant a sense of civilized culture. On its rough, uneven surface a clean wooden plate, horn cup, and various eating utensils sat awaiting the evening's meal. The few food stores in the place were piled up against the far wall.

Giovanni crossed the room and perused the supplies. Small sack of flour, a bit of oats, a few odds and ends. *Not much.* Then a thought occurred to him. *Not a stick of Ceylon among it.* The spice he'd smelled had come from something else.

Curious, Gio continued his exploring of the cave, this time intent on finding the source of the strange scent. As his gaze alighted on a large rock jutting out from the wall, his brow crinkled, the first pinpricks of concern travelling up his spine warning him to use caution.

Ignoring the inner voice telling him to let it be, he walked over to examine the sacred objects. He reached out a hand and ran a finger over the most striking thing to catch his eye. The deep purple cloth draped down the sides of the stone altar, its intricate silver embroidery and beading looked like rivulets of water glistening against the dark surface. The expert artisanship, intricate details, and material were such that only the richest of men would have owned such an item. Yet, it lay unguarded within a cave in the French countryside? Surrounded by meagerness and squalor?

Toward the back of the stone's surface, two natural beeswax candles stood warding off the darkness, the flickering of their tiny flames causing shadows to dance along the wall. At their base, sitting regally between them was a carved statue. Never having seen the like, Giovanni picked it up. Though rough-hewn, the representation appeared to have been lovingly carved out of bone. He could make out the image of a goddess with two large cats sitting at her side. Though he didn't recognize her from any studies he had done of other pantheons, she was reminiscent of the Norse goddess, Freyja, who was known for her chariot pulled by two large cats. Yet, somehow, he knew it wasn't her. At a loss he set the statue back down and moved on to the remaining artifacts.

The wooden bowl at the center of the cloth looked damp from recent use. Giovanni slid two fingertips across its inner surface and brought them to his nose in an attempt to identify the bowl's use. He inhaled the scent and his head shot back, his eyes wide.

Blood tinged with cinnamon. A blood rite with spiced blood? Could be. Not that it mattered. The Alimentatori had their own variations of blood rites. The thought of a human blood rite did little to capture his imagination.

In between the candles and the wooden bowl, the blade of a ceremonial dagger winked at him in the dancing candle light. He picked up the blade and turned it over in his hands. The intricate threading and bead pattern wrapping around the handle was an obvious match to that of the altar cloth. Not really practical for defense. He suspected that was not the intended use of this blade.

His suspicions were confirmed when he angled the dagger just enough to see an inscription scrolling down the knife blade. The flickering candles did little to help with reading the inscription. Frustrated in his efforts, he turned to allow light from the fire pit to reach the blade. He froze in mid-movement, sensing more than hearing anything. The hairs on the back of his neck rose.

He was not alone.

The scent of cinnamon floated to him in the air. He remembered the bowl, the blood, and wondered how such a sent could permeate the air around him like pollen on a breeze. Had he been human, perhaps he would have felt fear or the need to flee. Instead, his mind worked silently and swiftly through his options.

It would serve no purpose to have the tale of a winged man carried to the king of France.

He supposed the easiest way to avoid this was to kill the human. Unfortunately, Giovanni was not a murderer. He'd spent his years in study and recording history. To kill a human went against everything he believed in.

Finally, his thoughts settled on something a little more palatable.

Collegamento di mente.

Entering the thoughts or dreams of a human could be tricky especially from a distance. To do so without the aid of hormone secretion could be dangerous. Unfortunately, doing so was probably his best and only option. He would fuse his thoughts into the human's mind, plant an image…something…anything to cover up what he truly was.

It could work, at least temporarily. Long enough to make it out of the cave and disappear. By the time the human had any inkling something was off Giovanni would be safely on his way.

Deciding it was the most prudent course of action, Gio reached out with his mind to make contact with whoever watched him. His brow furrowed as the tendrils of his thoughts came back empty. Closing his eyes, he allowed his body to secrete the hormone which normally aided in the intrusion. Whether he was close enough for it to work he did not know, but he had to try. He concentrated harder and attempted the connection again.

Once again it was unsuccessful.

There was a dark curtain hanging over the mind of the other, impossible to part, impossible to penetrate, protecting its mind from intrusion. How could that be? No human had the power to keep him out.

A soft, feminine voice lightly accented with French spoke. *It will not work. One cannot enter the mind of the Cath Boblogi unbidden.*

Cath Boblogi? Giovanni's eyes shot open as he realized the person had not spoken aloud; yet, he heard her clearly. Her soft voice came to him in the same way he imagined his voice would be heard within the mind of a human, as a mere whisper.

He swallowed, astounded by the realization. Aliments were always the ones to give not the ones to receive. Never had he experienced the other end of the spectrum, which meant one thing: this was no mere human with whom he was dealing. This was something else.

Turning slowly on his heel, he scanned the room for the creature who had spoken. Locating the presence deep within the shadows, he spoke, "Why do you hide and whisper from the shadows? Are you so hideous you are afraid to be seen?"

In answer a low growl emanated from the darkness. *To see my face is to die. No man will carry the tale home. However, if you leave now, I will allow you to go. Stay and you shall wish you had heeded my warning.*

The truth within her words sent a shiver coursing down his back. By rights he should listen. The idea of leaving without ever knowing who or what she was made him stay. "What is Cath Boblogi? How do I know you even have the ability to harm me? For all I know you're merely a frightened young woman who wishes to scare away someone who's invaded her sanctuary."

By your very words I know you are not familiar with my people. Woman, I am. Frightened, I am not, and I am more than capable of defending my sanctuary.

"And what if I refuse to leave? What then, Cath Boblogi? Shall you rend me limb from limb?" Giovanni knew it was foolish to taunt the entity. However, he was not about to run screaming into the rain without first understanding with what he was dealing. No creature had ever held dominion over the Alimentatori, not even a human. So why should a voice from the shadows?

You are wrong. You may think the Humans have no dominion over your kind but, they are an infestation. When one tries to live in peace as their equals, it takes little time before the infection grows. Eventually it will choke the life from all other beings and leave destruction in its wake.

Gio edged forward believing he might have found some common ground with the creature. "I presume you have experienced such destruction? Is that what has brought you to live hidden away in a cave, far from the hub of humanity?"

That is neither here nor there. I spoke simply to warn you. Trusting the humans will bring you pain. But then, if you choose to stay, I guess I shall be the one to bring you pain.

Damn it. As a scholar, he had hoped to avoid a confrontation and possibly learn something from this creature. Unfortunately, it appeared she was insistent on his leaving.

"I am not here to hurt you or cause you any trouble. I merely entered here to get out of the rain. I beg your indulgence and will be on my way once the storm has passed."

You are neither welcome here nor were you invited. Leave now. The last demand ended on another growl.

"I am not human and will not be frightened away with words. Surely you do not expect me to give up the warmth of a fire based on whispered threats."

I can, and I do. The answer brooked no disagreement as the mass in the shadows shifted forward, crouching as if readying to pounce. As it moved, the firelight caught a reflection and Gio froze intrigued by eyes the color of rich honeyed amber. It had to be a trick of the light. The only beings with eyes like that were the large cats of Africa.

A deep growl echoed through the chamber, sending a rivulet of shivers racing down his spine. He stood his ground, the need to know what the darkness held overpowering his sense of self-preservation. "I will leave if you allow me to see what you are." He paused a moment, knowing his next words could be his last. "Reveal yourself to me, and I shall leave your sanctuary, never to return."

Several moments passed as Giovanni awaited her decision. Then, just when he'd thought she would not respond at all, her whisper hissed through his mind. *Your choice has been made. As I am not without mercy, I shall grant your request before sending you to the Underworld. You shall know what I am...*

Giovanni blinked several times unsure if what he saw was real or imagined as a rush of excitement whirled around in his mind.

He'd been right?

The golden eyes belonged to a beast, but not like the giant cats of the plains of the African continent. No. This she-cat's ebony coat gleamed where the light from the fire touched her. Her eyes sparkled with knowing intelligence and watched his every move. The sheer beauty of the thing took his breath away.

And for a moment he forgot she was something to fear. In wonder he stared at her, his curiosity overriding any sense of self-preservation. *What manner of creature has the sweet whispers of a woman and the body of a beast?*

In response, her hackles rose. *What manner of creature has the features of a man and the wings of a bird but smells like neither?*

She'd heard his thoughts? Another thought occurred to him. *Was she alone?* One he could probably handle. Any more than that and the odds shifted drastically into her favor. He peeled his gaze away from her momentarily to check the darkness surrounding him. From what he could see, there were no others lying in wait. Relieved, he turned his attention back to the she-cat. "I am Giovanni of Tamiel, Archivist of the King of the Alimentatori. My kind has been in existence since the beginning of time, and we have never recorded encounters with your ilk before. What…" As the creature moved closer, the now familiar scent of her cinnamon musk washed over him, fogging his brain, making thought difficult. He swayed on his feet, unable to clear his mind. "You are…unlike any other…beast."

Beast? You dare call me beast? I am descended from an ancient line of kings.

Her angry words penetrated the fog of his mind, and Gio frowned. Had he called her such a thing? It had happened only moments before, yet he could not fathom why he would have done so. Then his thoughts cleared briefly as he remembered what he'd been trying to say. No, she was not like any other beast. He suspected there was so much more waiting to be discovered. Like a reasonable explanation for her existence. Nothing but the most ridiculous origins infiltrated his foggy thoughts. *A gypsy curse? A spell gone wrong? An abomination resulting from a pact with a demon?*

Another growl filled the room. Their connection had once again worked against him.

The spicy, cinnamon musk thickened in the air. He breathed deeply, enjoying the strangely addictive scent. As she moved toward him, his gaze locked with hers. Her eyes flashed with an unearthly glow, as she stared deep into him.

As if in answer to his unspoken question, the cat's body twisted, and the beast cried out. Her labored breathing came out in short gasps as the sound of cracking bone and wrenching muscle filled the silence of the chamber. Each leg snapped backward, causing her to fall under the enormous weight of her own body. For a moment he thought perhaps she had an unseen attacker. Then she rose to her feet and pitched her head back to glare directly at him.

Several moments passed as Gio held his breath for what was to come.

With one final roar and a shake of her body the fur fell away, revealing bare skin beneath. She closed her eyes and ignored his presence. Her face narrowed and elongated, then seemed to sink into itself. A moment more and any semblance of the beast was gone. In its place was a beautiful woman with short cropped black hair and a fair complexion. She pitched her head back and glared up at him just as the beast had seconds before. The same golden eyes delved into him with a knowing glint.

Rising, she brushed her hands together to remove the dirt. Her naked, sweat-drenched body gleamed in the firelight just as her fur coat had before she changed. This time she spoke aloud as she sauntered toward him. "You think me a beast now, Monsieur? Cursed by the gypsies? Or a demon spawn?"

As the movement of her hips drew his gaze, he watched helplessly as they swayed invitingly. He sucked in a breath as his mouth went dry. The overwhelming musk oozed from her every pore, sending his senses reeling and causing a chain reaction within him. The blood pounded through his veins like the hooves a thousand horses running wild. Her silky skin and little patch of dark curls begged for his touch.

No indeed. She was no beast. However, if she were reading his lust-filled thoughts right now, he was sure she'd no longer be able to say the same for him.

The Aliments kept detailed records for centuries on every known creature; yet, never could he have imagined a creature who could so thoroughly and so easily entice him. He shook himself trying to break free from the spell which wrapped around his resistance as surely as metal chains.

"I am Adara of Aberffraw, priestess of the Cath Boblogi." Her fingers stroked up the side of his face and through his damp hair startling a sudden exhale from him. His voice caught in a moan as she leaned in, her breasts brushing the damp, rough material of his cloak. "You seem tongue tied? What's the matter? Cat got your tongue?"

With what could almost be termed humor, she took his mouth with her own. In the midst of the sheer ecstasy of her kiss, something in the back of his mind warned caution, and then her scent washed over him again, and his reason was lost. Nothing could stop the rush of desire as he brought her to him.

Nothing but the excruciating pain of a woman's claws that is.

Where moments ago, her fingers had caressed, the she-beast sunk her claws deep into the back of his head. Giovanni jerked away in pained surprise, the spell of desire broken at last.

Confused, his gaze sought hers only to realize he stared into the eyes of death. The sadistic twist of her lips said it all. How easily she had manipulated him, bringing him within her grasp. Her golden eyes mocked him with glittering humor as if to say, "how easily you've fallen." Perhaps she was right. He allowed himself to be taken all too easily. He deserved that first blow.

But he was not one to hand himself over to death.

Remembering the dagger within his grasp, he jabbed it into her. Sharp blade found soft flesh, causing her to cry out in pain. Stumbling back, she grabbed at the blade lodged just above her left hip. Leaning in he whispered, "Did your mother never tell you it is not polite to play with your food?"

Her golden eyes sought his. Instead of fear he found a fury like he had never seen before reflected in their depths. She growled, drawing the dagger from her hip, and baring wicked looking teeth. "I'm a cat, Monsieur. Playing with my food comes naturally."

Dropping the dagger to the ground, she turned on him with a vengeance. He scrambled to move out of her grasp. Too quickly, she was upon him ripping at his face, arms, chest…anywhere her claws could reach. Turning, he ran toward the door. She descended on him with the agility of a proficient predator, knocking him to the ground. Pain shot through him as his right wing took the brunt of the attack. Her claws tore at his clothes piercing the skin beneath, and he screamed in agony. This couldn't be happening. He was about to die at the hands of a woman…cat…demon spawn all because he'd sought shelter from a storm.

The attack stopped as suddenly as it had begun. The air became heavy with the scent of her change, and he knew he was in the eye of the storm. In moments she would finish him off this time as the cat. Chancing a glance over his shoulder, his fears were confirmed. Death was about to find him lying on the dirt floor of a cave in the middle of nowhere.

He would be damned if he would allow that to happen.

Pushing himself up from the ground, he made a mad dash toward the exit. A few steps in, he forgot to duck and slammed into the low ceiling. Pain exploded within his head, and his vision blurred for a second. There was no time to nurse wounds. Instead, remembering the passageway narrowed as well, he attempted to tuck his wings as he had when he entered, only to cry out in pain. His right wing refused to fold properly. He angled his body and tried to push his way through. His injured wing slammed against the side of the opening sending shards of excruciating pain through him. He had no choice. He could either force the wing through or stay there and die, but there was no way was he making it out alive if the wing was useless at the other end. He needed to be in the air to escape the huntress. The sudden irony of his situation almost made him laugh, a man with wings being chased down by a woman who was a cat. If he made it back to Bracciano, the Council would never believe it.

If? No, when.

Decision made, he grasped the wing and pulled it in front of him, wrapping it as tightly to him as he could manage. Ignoring the pain which radiated through him, he inched his way into the opening. With each movement forward, the wing twitched and resisted restraint. The unnatural position caused a cramp in his shoulder. He pushed himself ever forward, unwilling to give up. Where it had taken him minutes to pass through the crevice while entering, the time now seemed to stretch out into ageless eons as he navigated through the passageway. With each moment he expected to be pulled back and ripped to shreds. Curiously, the she-devil had yet to come for him. Finally, he burst through the opening and into the late afternoon air. The rain he'd hoped to escape pummeled him as he fell to his knees, the urge to vomit overwhelming. Nausea washed over him in waves as he fought to keep the pain at bay. The places she'd scratched burned like fire, and his wing blade screamed in agony.

The knowledge that at any moment she could emerge from the cave to finish what she started pushed him to his feet. Time was a luxury he could not give to his battered and beaten body.

To have any hope of survival, he needed to be in the air and as far away from her as physically possible.

In an act of total desperation, he spread his wings ignoring the signs of intense trauma. The torrent of pain it caused nearly sent him to his knees again. With all the strength he could muster, he pumped his wing blades. He heard her approach and knew it was merely a matter of seconds. Just as the beast sprang from the opening, the wind caught his wings lifting him up and out of her grasp. Every updraft took him closer to freedom yet with each, pain wracked his body. He fought for control as he struggled to maintain forward momentum. The injuries he sustained made breathing, moving, everything hard. Pointing himself back to Rouen was his only chance. He had trusted friends there who would help him if he could make it back.

Several minutes of intense concentration passed before Giovanni realized there was something wrong. His vision blurred time and again. He shook his head attempting to clear the fog only to be awash with nausea. The deep burning which had started at the locations of her assault had strangely numbed and the numbness was slowly, meticulously creeping through his body. Alarmed by the paralyzing sensation, he realized he had little time before he would drop from the sky like a stone.

What had she done to him? Had she envenomed her claws? A sudden realization dawned as darkness closed in around him as his breathing slowed. She allowed him to escape, knowing full well she had already done him in.

*****

Gino paused in his reading. He studied the book before him as if having trouble with translating what he was reading. Finally, he glanced up at me and frowned. "She didn't kill my grandfather."

I started as Leo forcefully pushed back his chair, causing a loud screech to echo throughout the room. His gaze shot passed mine straight to his son. "Of course, she didn't. If she had, you and I wouldn't be here." Though his phrasing made it seem as if he was humoring the boy, his tight-lipped response made me wonder. Leo glanced at me and shrugged. "He was found by a local farmer's wife and given aid."

"Ah, I see." My response was more for his sake than mine.

Leo directed his attention back to the boy. "Now, I think that is quite enough for one day, Gino. Why don't you go to your mother and see if she needs anything?"

Casting a glance toward the child, I could tell by his furrowed brow and downcast eyes that the dismissal didn't sit well with him. Yet, he did as he was told, closing the book and mumbling, "Si, Papa."

After rising, he slid his chair under the table and then looked at me as if longing to speak. Instead, he walked away.

Before I knew it, my own voice rose in the stilted quiet of the room. "Thank you, Gino. You did well. I would love to have you read more for me at another time."

His gaze found mine. Though his lips spread in a wide grin, the emotion didn't quite reach his eyes. "Gods, and father willing, I would like that." Casting a furtive glance toward his father, he leaned in across the table. "But next time we read the good stories."

I chuckled, wondering absently what constituted a "good story" by the boy's standard.

Leo interrupted my musing to shoo the boy toward the stairs. "Go now. Your mother is waiting."

"How can she be waiting, Papa, when she doesn't even know I'm coming?" The boy's impertinent remark garnered a stern look from his father and a chuckle from me.

Adrien leaned over. "So, did you learn any valuable lessons from any of that?"

He seemed dubious. As far as I was concerned, the reading had done exactly what I'd hoped. "Yep. I now have a better understanding of what I am dealing with. Don't let her into my mind. Don't let her scent take me for a joy ride. And by all that is holy, stay the hell away from her lips."

Chapter Sixteen

As we re-emerged from the archive room and back into the library, I thought over Giovanni's story. The tale confirmed one thing: the Cambiare were capable of horrible acts of violence against those they believed were a threat. *Was that why Julian had died? Had he somehow posed a threat to the woman he left with?*

Like a praying mantis, she probably seduced him and then killed him. Julian probably didn't know how dangerous she was. He left here unarmed and became a victim, just like Giovanni. Fortunately, I know what she was capable of and I won't be so easy to kill.

"Adrien, I need to go to the suite before we head out. I want to pick up a few things for tonight."

He shrugged and fell into step next to me as we headed for the stairs. "That's fine. I could use a change of clothes as well."

Glancing to my right, I noticed Adrien wore his usual tan slacks and white button-down oxford shirt. To me he always looked like a desk jockey who just left a nine-to-five in a tiny little cubicle somewhere. "You can borrow a shirt from me if you like."

He paused next to me on the first riser, hand on the railing, and turned toward me. "What's wrong with what I brought with me?"

I paused unwilling to offend my Second's sense of style. "Nothing. Nothing at all. It's just…well…do you own anything that's not white? I want to go to Eros again and see if that woman is there. The one who—"

"Sent you running away like a little girl?" Adrien's smug attitude and raised eyebrow irritated me. Regrettably, he was right. I turned tail and ran the moment I felt my control slipping. I would have to be far more resilient if I was going to be able to maintain my distance from the she-cat who killed my brother, I couldn't fall prey to her seduction juju.

"Yeah, well, I know she was Cambiare, so running might just have saved my life." I continued up the stairs. "I just don't want to call attention to ourselves. I'd rather hang back, watch from the shadows, see if she shows, and then follow her until she's alone. Makes it hard to stick to the shadows when you're wearing white."

"Alright, I'll see what I can do." Adrien followed just behind me as we turned the corner of the landing. "Do you really think the one in Eros was Jul's killer? I mean, it doesn't make much sense for her to saunter right up to you in a bar after killing your brother."

"If she is the one, she probably doesn't even know I exist. Gives me a slight advantage when it comes down to the element of surprise."

"How do you explain her being in your room then?"

I screwed up my mouth as I thought things through. "Julian stayed in the same room. Maybe she was looking for something he left behind." It seemed logical. "And was just as surprised to find me sleeping in the bed as I was to find her standing over me."

Adrien seemed to consider this for a moment, then spoke, "If that's the case, what do you think she was looking for?"

I shrugged. "I won't know that until I find it. Whatever it is has to be with Julian's things."

Our conversation halted as we neared the top of the stairs and the door to security swung inward. Vinny peered into the hall, his gaze landing on me as if he knew exactly where I was. He crossed to the top of the stairs, and his voice rang with authority as he stood two steps above me. "Jacen, we've been waiting for you to emerge from the vaults."

Of course, he knew exactly where to find me. The place was monitored from top to bottom. I could almost smell the scent of Cambiare as the memory of her standing over my bed resurfaced once again, and I realized I had undisputable evidence to the contrary. Irritated, I squashed the memory back into its dirty little hole like a spring snake being crammed into a fake can of peanut brittle. *Okay, fine, nearly top to bottom.* I frowned, more from the internal dialogue than from any real concern over what had motivated Vinny's approach.

Bringing my thoughts back to the current situation, I took in the troubled pinch of Vinny's stern features and realized there was more to worry about than whether or not they had me watched. "Why? What's wrong?"

Vinny shook his head, and his tone dropped to a conspiratorial whisper. "There's been a breach."

My brow furrowed as I attempted to interpret Vinny's concerned tone. My mind raced through the possibilities and landed solidly on the one which was top priority. *She returned while I was in the archive room? But why? What was she trying to find?* The image of a shiny silver locket emerged, and suddenly I knew. Perhaps she did not leave the locket the night she entered my room as I initially thought. Maybe, just maybe, that is what she's been looking for all along. I turned to race down the hall toward my room shouting instructions after me. "Come with me. I know where she's headed. I want her captured, not killed."

Adrien made to follow me. Vinny's arm shot out, and his hand gripped my arm, keeping me from going any further. "Who, sir?"

I looked at him dumbfounded by his ignorance. "The she-cat. If you saw her on the monitors, then I know where she's going, and if we don't hurry, she'll be gone before we get there."

Vinny brows scrunched downward, as his eyes narrowed.

One corner of his mouth turned upward, as he studied me as if trying to understand a newly discovered life form. "What the hell are you talking about? We didn't see anyone on the monitors."

"But you said there had been a breach." My hopes fell as I realized I jumped to the wrong conclusion. If Vinny hadn't been talking about a reappearance of the Cambiare woman, then what did *breach* mean?

"Not that kind of breach, sir. If you'll follow me, I'll explain everything." Vinny released my arm and redirected us into the security office.

Still confused, I did as he requested. Once the door shut behind us, I glanced around the normally quiet office. Every corner of the room buzzed with activity.

"Track it through London. Figure out where the hell it came from." Glancing toward the man who shouted to the room-at-large, my gaze followed his frantic actions. The man was obviously in charge and expected everyone around him to do exactly as told.

"Sir, I can't get through the firewalls. I'm having no success with the codes we were given, and the old codes aren't working either. Someone's locked us out of our network."

"Work around them. That's what you're paid to do." The supervisor strode across the floor, headed straight for the technician who spoke. Rounding the end of the man's workstation, he peered over the technician's shoulder. "Find a way. I don't care how you do it. Just get me into that system."

The seated man pounded out keystrokes on his keyboard while the other pointed to the computer screen and gave instructions. The combined efforts of the men seemed to work magic. Typing with lightning quick speed, code shot across the main screen in the room.

I watched in amazement. What system were they trying to break into?

Then as if in answer to my unspoken question, his next attempt triggered a response. Numerous lines of unrecognizable code scrolled upward faster than I could read it. I caught the word "accepted." The rest was all a blur.

"Yes! Now *that's* what you get paid for." The supervisor clapped the technician on the shoulders with both hands and laughed. "I knew you could do it."

I glanced to where Adrien and Vinny waited for me just inside the door to the inner office. It was obvious Vinny wanted this conversation held privately. I joined them and closed the door behind us. Leaning against the door, I looked to the Security officer for explanation. "What the hell is going on here?"

The man paused, uncomfortable with what he had to say. He shifted on his feet. "At twelve twenty-three this afternoon someone broke into our Security mainframe."

My hardened glare narrowed on Vinny. There had to be more to it than that. "Okay, and? People, companies…hell, even countries are hacked every day, and I daresay we have less to hide than most of them. What's the big deal? I can't imagine the hacker found much of interest in our files and moved on empty handed. Beef up security, and—"

Vinny came up alongside of me and responded in a low voice "It's not the trolling around in the files that's got everyone in a tizzy, sir. It's what they took while they were in there."

What could possibly have been on our servers that warranted all of this? It seemed a bit excessive. My gaze found his. "What did they take?"

His frown deepened as his gaze intensified. "They took several maps to the lower floors, including the floor plans for the Chamber level."

And suddenly I understood.

With grim determination I straightened, meeting his intensity with some of my own. "You think the Council's in danger."

His nod confirmed my correct assumption. "Why wasn't I informed immediately?"

"Sir, you were in the vaults. No one is permitted in there without authorization. Besides, we shut down the feed and were locked out. So, unless you have an innate ability to hack computers, there would have been nothing you could have done to help the situation."

I didn't appreciate being thought of as useless; however, in this particular case I had to concede the truth in his words. I didn't know the first thing about computer hacking and even less about tracking a hacker's online activity. Better to stay out of the way and let the professionals do what they are good at.

Ignoring the uncomfortable sense of being in over my head, I crossed to the desk and took a seat on its edge. Adrien and Vinny followed suit taking the seats in front of me. As they stared up at me awaiting a plan of action, I searched my mind for something to say. "Then I guess the biggest questions are who and why." I stared at Vinny. "Any idea of who it is? Have the Alimentatori pissed off any super hackers recently."

Vinny shook his head. "Not that I know of. There is of course one obvious choice."

I raised my brows. "Such as?

"Karina." He looked between Adrien and me, as if looking for agreement. "I mean, she did work in this office for years and I'd say she was pretty pissed off when you nearly took her in…" Vinny trailed off as his statement was greeted with stale silence.

Karina. I should have seen that coming. It could be her. Though her knowledge of the villa made it difficult to believe she would hack the system just to steal floor plans when she could just as easily sketch the details room by room for anyone who wanted them. I looked over the heads of the two men and watched the activity in the other room through the large plate glass windows. "They're tracking the location of the hacker with satellites?"

Vinny glanced over his shoulder taking in the controlled chaos in the other room. "Well, yes and no." He looked back to me. "We tracked the signal to a part of London. What they are working on right now is isolating the exact location of the computer used to hack the system. What you see on the screen out there is real-time London. We will overlay the tracking information with the satellite imagery and hopefully be able to find a camera or something in the area that might have captured him or her on video."

"You think Karina made it to London and is now hacking our systems? To what end?" It seemed farfetched. From what I knew of Karina, she seemed far more direct than that. "Is Karina even computer savvy enough to hack the system?"

Vinny shook his head. "No. You're misunderstanding me. I don't think Karina is the one who hacked the system. I believe she may be passing along information to Le Anime Vuote, which is known to be in London. I know for a fact they are more than capable of such a feat."

"Whoa, wait a minute." *What the hell was he talking about?* I stared down at Vinny. "Le Anime Vuote?"

Vinny frowned and glanced between Adrien and me. He seemed to be searching for any small flicker of understanding. I was sorry to disappoint him. I hadn't a clue what or who Le Anime Vuote was and I doubted Adrien had ever heard of them either.

When it became obvious, we were in the dark on the topic, he nudged, "Le Anime Vuote, the empty souls?" His surprise was evident. "You're joking. I didn't figure there was an Aliment alive that hadn't heard of the Vuote. For as long as there have been Alimentatori, there have been those who hunt them. We call them the Empty Souls. They're the reason we no longer have wings and are the reason the Cambiare are in Italy to begin with."

"Let me guess, humans." Adrien responded in a knowing tone.

"You've got it. Though, they are not your average every day humans. These humans are trained assassins, disciples to their own cause. They've dedicated countless man hours to ridding the world of the abominations, namely us and the Cambiare."

So, the Cambiare and the Aliment shared a common enemy. Interesting. However, in this case the enemy of my enemy was still my enemy. No way was I going to side with the Cambiare…even against human extremists.

I rose from my perch on the desk. "Ok, well as soon as you have anything, I want to know about it." I held out a hand to

Vinny and waited for him to stand. Once his hand gripped mine, I gave a firm handshake. "You did well. I'm confident you will be able to find the culprit."

Letting his hand drop from my grasp, I glanced toward Adrien. "We should be heading out. We've got some tracking of our own to do."

Adrien nodded and stood, ready to accompany me out of the office.

Vinny followed us and then moving in front of me, he pushed open the door. "Adrien, if you could stay for a moment, I'd like to give you what we have on the Vuote. You need to be aware of who they are and what they stand for in order to protect Jacen."

My Second looked to me obviously not wanting to leave me to my own devices. "Do you mind waiting for a few minutes, Jace?"

I frowned. Why did I suddenly feel like a child asked to sit in a corner while the adults talked about things he didn't understand? "Don't worry about me. I'll go on to the suite and get things ready for tonight's hunt." I opened the door to the office and glanced toward Vinny. "Let me know when you find whoever is responsible for the breach."

Chapter Seventeen

I neared the door to my suite and glanced down at my wristwatch. It was nearly two-thirty in the afternoon, and I had done little to further my own agenda except listen to a child tell fairy tales. The muscles in my jaw ticked. That wasn't quite what I had in mind when I boarded the plane in Albany. I figured locating the beast responsible would be quick, easy, and extremely satisfying. Instead, I seemed to be stuck in limbo, waiting. I was waiting for my brother's things to be found, waiting for Karina to be captured, and waiting for some understanding as to why the Cambiare had killed Julian. I should have been well within reach of capturing the beast responsible. As it stood now, I was no better off than when I was standing barefoot in the living room of my home looking into Adrien's grief-stricken eyes.

I thought about that for a second and frowned. That wasn't completely true. I had seen her...once. Also, in a matter of a few days, I found the breach in security, which had allowed the woman into the villa to begin with. In reality, none of that mattered. It didn't ease the heartache and loneliness Julian's absence brought. Only one thing would.

I paused in my thoughts long enough to unlock the door of

the suite. Crossing the threshold, I moved through the living room area in silence mulling over what was to come.

What did I really expect to find at Eros tonight?

Granted, it was Friday night, so the place should be packed with people. Would she be there? Would I recognize her if I saw her? Was she even the one I was looking for?

Thinking on that, I realized Adrien was right. It made no sense that the woman who approached me in the bar would be the same woman who stood over me in my own bedroom. If she killed Julian, what would drive her to risk capture by revisiting the villa and flaunting herself in front of me at a bar? What would she have to gain either way other than a one-way ticket to hell, courtesy of me?

It somehow made sense that she was looking for something in the room. But no matter how I tried I couldn't reconcile the why of approaching me in a crowded bar. The only explanation had to be that she had no idea who I was. Maybe she liked to pick up Alimentatori on their own turf. She could be in it for the thrill and maybe even the kill. I don't know. Whatever the explanation, if she returned, I would be waiting for her.

A scraping sound emanated from the direction of my room, capturing my undivided attention. I froze in mid-stride. It couldn't be Adrien, as I just left him with Vinny, and no one else had any reason to be poking around in my room.

Except…

Edging my way to the bedroom door, I noticed it was slightly ajar, not how I'd left it. I leaned forward and peered through the crack created between door and frame. Unable to see clearly into the room, I nudged the door open. It swung inward on silent hinges.

Within the recesses of the dark room a woman, her black pant-clad backside facing me, bent over at the waist. My brow crinkled as I followed her movements with my gaze.

What is she doing?

Light from the double doors across the room glinted off a small bit of metal drawing my gaze to the hardwood floor at her feet. Alarm rushed through me.

She was retrieving her locket and almost got away with it.

Before her fingers had a chance to make contact with the delicate silver chain, I rushed forward, arms outstretched, hands grasping. Our bodies connected with the full force of my rage. Together we flew through the air, her wild, angry screams echoing in the confines of the room. As we landed with a hard bounce on the mattress of my bed, her screams ended abruptly when she landed face down in a mound of pillows. Her body bucked beneath me as she fought and squirmed. I threw her to her back and trapped her body with mine. As she screamed, her hands came at me, whether to push at my shoulders or scratch my eyes out, I didn't care. Either way, it could be fatal. Her pointed heel caught my shin, and I sucked in a breath as pain shot up my leg. I wasn't waiting to find out. With lightning-fast reflexes, I grasped her wrists and pinned them to the bed. Finally, gaining control of the situation, I gazed down into her frightened bright...*blue* eyes?

"Mio dio, Jace!" A frightened female voice shook as she peered up at me. "Mi hai spaventato a morte!"

"Alcie?" I stared down at her in confusion. *What the hell?* The young woman's body trembled beneath mine contradicting her forceful statement. I might have frightened her, but from the throbbing in my shin she was still alive and definitely still kicking. I loosened my grip on her wrists. "What are you doing in my room?"

Tears formed in her eyes as she stared up at me. "I brought your brother's personal effects."

Easing away from her, my brow furrowed. "What were you doing with the locket?"

"I...," she choked back a sob and looked away from me. "I wasn't going to steal it."

My teeth ground together as I glared down at her, my patience wearing thin. "You didn't answer my question. What were you doing with the locket?"

"When I slid the suitcase across the desk, it knocked it onto the floor. I was picking it up."

She stared up at me with wide innocent eyes. I pushed myself away from her and stood beside the bed. A sudden rush of embarrassment at my overreaction caused my words to be overly harsh. "Well, next time, wait for us to get back before poking around in our rooms." I stepped away from her, allowing her an opportunity to rise. Holding out a hand, I helped her to her feet. "Did I hurt you?"

She shook her head looking down at her feet. "No, I'm fine."

Reaching out, I placed a crooked finger under her chin and forced her to look up at me. "Listen. I'm sorry. I didn't mean to frighten you. I thought the Cambiare woman had come back. And when I saw you bending over to pick up her necklace, I thought you were her."

She gazed up at me, tears slipping down her cheeks. "It's all right. I understand."

Though she spoke words of acceptance, her voice trembled. She was still unsure whether or not to trust me. I leaned forward, my lips brushing her mousy brown hair as I whispered, "If I wanted you on your back, there are far more pleasurable ways to get you there."

A shiver ran down her spine which I could feel in my fingertips. I bit the inside of my cheek to keep from chuckling. Forgiveness was a mere hair's breadth away and was so easily won it hardly seemed fair.

She gave a nervous laugh and leaned into me. Her breath rushed out in a lust-filled sigh. "If you want me on my back, all you have to do is ask."

I drew back and gazed down at her. Her eyes closed in pleasure, her body leaning into me, waiting, waiting for a kiss that would never come. I chuckled and set her away from me. "I'll keep that in mind."

A loud cough sounded from the open doorway. "Am I interrupting something?"

Startled, Alcie's eyes flew open. By the pink flush, which spread rapidly up her neck and into her cheeks, I could tell she was embarrassed.

I stepped back to put some distance between us. "Nope,

Alcie was just leaving."

Her gaze found mine in confusion. "But—"

I nodded toward the door and raised an eyebrow. "Thank you for dropping off my brother's things. I really do appreciate it. Now, if you don't mind, I have a lot to do."

Her blush deepened as she realized she was being dismissed. Moving away, she cast her gaze to the floor. "Of course, I do as well."

She crossed the room. Just before passing Adrien, she turned and glanced toward me. "If you need me, for anything, I'm just a phone call away."

I nodded. "Thanks, Alcie. I'm sure I'll be fine." I paused a moment and then thought of something she could do for me. "On second thought, would you ask Belvedere to send up some food for Adrien and me? We haven't had a chance to eat since breakfast."

She nodded. Turning back toward the door, she pushed passed Adrien. A few moments later, he flinched as the outer door slammed behind her. Adrien's angry gaze bored into me from the entrance, though his tone was even and held no hint of his true feelings. "What the hell was that all about?"

Rather than explain the details of the misunderstanding, I chose to leave him in the dark. "Don't know."

"Yeah, right." By Adrien's exasperated tone, I could tell he expected more of an answer.

I shrugged. "She found Julian's things."

I nodded and walked to where she dropped the necklace. Bending over, I scooped up the locket and placed it back on the desk. Then I grabbed the navy-blue bag.

When I reached the bed, I unzipped the suitcase and upended the contents onto the comforter and then tossed the suitcase on the floor. Perching on the edge of the mattress, I began the painful task of picking through what was left of my brother's life. His clothes sprawled out next to me still carried his scent. My mouth went dry as I picked up item after item then set them aside. Shirts, underwear, socks, pants, his watch.

Several miscellaneous items all joined the growing pile. Still nothing jumped out at me. Nothing gave any indication of being out of the norm. As I picked up a pair of rolled socks, a hard object fell from within its folds. The glint of gold caught my eye as it bounced softly on the bed. I stared down at it as it gleamed in the sunlight almost afraid to touch its ancient, pock-marked surface. It was one of the rings for which I was looking, but which one? I reached out and plucked it from amidst his belongings and turned it over. A blood red representation of our house symbol stood out in stark contrast against the white and dark blue background of our ancient family crest. At its center one small ruby glistened. For as far back as I could remember my brother had worn it on his right hand. Now, I guess it was my turn to honor our house in the same way. I extended the fingers of my right hand and slipped the ring into place. I gazed down at it, swallowing the unexpected sorrow the sight brought. Bitterness twisted my gut in knots. The two most important men in my life had worn that ring, and both had died tragic violent deaths.

Taking a deep breath, I forced my attention away from the reminder of my brother's absence and returned to picking through his things. As Adrien joined me, I groaned in frustration.

"I see you found his ring."

I didn't answer, just stared down at what was left of Julian's life.

"Did you find the other one? The one you were looking for at the hanger?"

I shook my head sadly. "No, it's not here."

Adrien's confused gaze searched the articles of clothing and various odds and ends on the bed, then returned to me. "If it's not with his things, and it's not with his body, then where is it?"

My gaze found his for a moment. My teeth ground together as the muscles flexed in my cheeks. "I don't know." I looked toward the balcony and remembered a night not too long ago and striking golden eyes staring down at me. "But I think I know who does."

Chapter Eighteen

It was hardly what I expected.

I rifled through the paperwork Adrien had brought from Security as I swallowed a bite of turkey sandwich. "So, these *Vuote*," I paused to take a sip of water, "seems they've been busy."

Adrien leaned forward to hand me a sheet he had been looking over. "Check this out." Taking the paper, I turned it over as he continued, "Says last year they hit one of us outside Paris."

I read through the details of the report, looking for anything that might indicate a connection to Julian's murder. "I see that. There are no similarities. Whoever did this was a professional. One shot to the head from a high-powered sniper rifle, no witnesses. Cold and calculating." I tossed the report on top of the file and sat back. "Julian's murder was personal. The thing that went after him wanted him to suffer."

Adrien snorted. "When did you become a forensic profiler?"

I motioned for him to hand over the file. "Let me see the rest of the reports."

Once I had them in hand, I leafed through the remaining pages. "Two years ago, Prague, car bomb. Three years ago,

Berlin, sniper rifle. Next, sniper rifle, sniper rifle, car bomb. Not once did they do a job up close and personal. From all appearances the Vuote send messages loud and clear without actually getting their hands dirty." Closing the file, I tossed it on the table in frustration. "It doesn't take a scientist to see that Julian's murder was messy, chaotic, and angry. Someone wanted *him* dead and wasn't above getting their hands dirty in the process."

"Okay, I get it, which brings us back to square one. The Cambiare."

"Yep. So, we need to find us a Cambiare and make it talk."

*****

A few hours later we arrived at the only location I knew a Cambiare would frequent.

As I climbed out of the back of the car, I stood aside for Adrien to join me and took in the spectacle greeting us at Eros night club.

Women and men of the human persuasion jockeyed for position in a queue which snaked along the side of the club and disappeared around the corner of the building. Their excited voices filled the night as they chatted together, exchanging exuberant laughter. Each one of the humans standing in that line could trace their lineage to an ancestor who, at one time or another, had been *il Scelto*, the chosen one of an Alimentatori. However, as their presence in the cue could attest, none of them currently held a rank equal to their ancestors.

They were merely *Vessels*. Most enjoyed the party lifestyle. The promise of becoming *il Scelto* and devoting themselves to one Aliment was a carrot on the stick which brought them out in droves. Once chosen as a companion of an Alimentatori, their secret life became real. It elevated them in rank. They would never again be just a human Vessel. They crossed over into the realm of *Devotee,* which brought with it certain perks, not the least of which was skipping the queue for places like this.

My gaze travelled along the writhing mass of people

searching for one particular face. The throng was too thick to be able to see all who lurked within their ranks, and a good portion of them stood in shadows. Could *she* be hidden among them?

I turned to speak to Adrien. "What's the likelihood of her showing up here on a night like tonight?"

He stepped up next to me and shrugged. "Don't know. If she doesn't show, then what?"

I frowned. "Not sure. I guess we'll have to cross that bridge when we get to it."

Keeping pace with Adrien, we walked toward the cordoned off entrance of the club. "You don't have a Plan B?"

"I do, but it's not pretty." As we neared the velvet rope, which blocked the entrance, I pulled out my identification card.

Adrien did the same. "Mind sharing?"

As I handed the card to the same bouncer who was on duty the night I saw the Cambiare woman in the club, my hopes rose. If she made it past him once, maybe she would be able to do so again.

"Not yet. Like I said, if the need arises, there is another option, but it won't be pretty."

I took the card back from the man and waited for him to finish inspecting Adrien's ID. Once he completed his check, he handed the card back to my Second and stepped to the side, unhooking the velvet rope in the process.

A moment later we stood just inside the doors of the club and paused to survey the scene. It was much like it was the afternoon we first came by, dark, teaming with sexual energy, and a haven where Alimentatori could be themselves. Tonight, the club was already filling to capacity with patrons. PopnoTech dance music poured from hidden speakers, electrifying the air around us. The humans in the room responded to the amped up music as it sent waves of excitement and adrenalin coursing through their bodies. The smell of human sweat and Aliment mojo intermingled as they raved together on the dance floor, gyrating with the heavy bass as it thumped through the blood like a heavy heartbeat. Thump, thump, thump, the pull of the rhythm drew them in like moths to a campfire. Thump, thump, thump, before they knew it, they were caught up, reeling within the euphoria of the moment they'd offer themselves up for a night's pleasure without so much as thinking twice about it.

A similar scene would play out in Aliment night clubs on every continent from coast to coast. Rarely was a human able to resist the pull of an Aliment. Could the same be said of the Cambiare?

It occurred to me there was still so much I did not know about the beast I hunted. Hopefully, by the end of the evening that would change. For now, caution would be the play of the day.

Pointing to a table on the other side of the room, Adrien leaned toward me and shouted, "There's a table in the back corner. Should give us a decent vantage point."

Looking toward where he pointed, I agreed with his assessment. The table was a perfect choice, far enough out of the way to not be noticed and with a view of most everything in the room. "Let's get settled in. It's going to be a long-assed night."

He nodded in understanding. "I know. It's hard to be in here, when you're not interested in hooking up."

"Exactly. Let's hope for a quick end to our vigil. The sooner we can get out of here, the better."

I followed him to the table, squeezing passed animated customers and busy waitstaff. As we neared a couple who stood in the middle of the aisle, we had no choice but to part them in order to get to our waiting table. As Adrien passed between them, the man leaned behind him and shouted at the woman.

"Aliment voi ripugnanti piccolo meretrice!"

The woman's shock was evident by her intake of breath. I had no idea what the man had said to her. Figuring she'd respond with equal vehemence, I walked between them. To my surprise, the woman didn't respond at all, at least not verbally. She flew at him with a screech. Attempting to get to her intended target, she threw herself against me commencing a barrage of swings around me. Surprised by the attack, I could do little more than hold her off.

As quickly as the attack began, Adrien finished it with lightning speed. The decibel of the furious woman's shriek could shatter one's ear drums. As Adrien caught her flailing arms. She cried out in anger, a bombardment of Italian spewing from her as she fought his hold.

"Whoa there. Watch where you're throwing punches." He wrenched harder, the action forcing her to arch away from me to minimize her pain. His angry whisper hissed into her ear, "Had you struck my Padrone, you'd be unconscious right now."

Calming, she paled as her eyes grew wide. In fluent English she rushed to apologize, "I'm so sorry. I had no idea.," Her fearful gaze pleaded with me.

I motioned for Adrien to release her. "No harm done. Just be more careful next time." I glanced over at the human male who had been her intended target. "What did he say to cause you to be so reckless?"

Her gaze lowered and an angry flush spread over her cheeks. "He called me a filthy little Aliment whore."

My gaze narrowed in on the man. "If she's an Aliment whore, then what does that make you?"

Though he didn't respond, I smelled the anger on him. I closed the gap between us in a heartbeat, my hand flying to the man's throat. My fingers tightened as I lifted him a few inches from the ground. "I asked you a question."

"I'd rather die than belong to an abomination like you."

I brought his face close to mine. "Careful what you wish for, little boy."

I pushed him backward, releasing my hold on his throat. People scrambled out of the way as he tumbled over a chair and toppled a nearby table, sending drinks flying into the air. I straightened my black leather jacket, settling it back into place around my hips, and then glared down at the man. "Now, make yourself scarce before I really get angry."

The man clambered to his feet and stared me down. Oddly,

he didn't seem to be the least bit afraid. A rising sense of apprehension grew in the pit of my stomach as he brushed at the remains of an icy drink on his shirt. He glanced around, seeming to have realized we had the attention of most of the people around us. Through gritted teeth, he spoke as he inclined his head in a meager show of belated respect. "I meant no disrespect to you, sir."

I didn't buy it for an instant. My eyes narrowed. "Your intentions were clear."

Not interested in further apologies I motioned for security. Within an instant, a bouncer materialized next to me. "Ah…" I spied his name tag and continued, "Nico. I'm Jacen of Samsaveel, the new head of Aliment security. This man has worn out his welcome within our community. Could you please escort him to the door and see he no longer has access to any Aliment clubs?"

The bouncer hesitated for a moment, unsure of whether or not to follow my orders. He was saved from further discussion when a willowy older gentleman dressed in Armani intervened. "Jacen of Samsaveel, yes, of course. You're the American Aliment." He waved his hand toward the human who caused the trouble. "Nico, do as he asks. And call the Polizia. I don't want him within a hundred meters of my patrons."

The bouncer waited no longer. He grabbed the man by the arm and dragged him away. Once everyone around us went back to doing whatever they had been before the disruption, the little Italian man rounded to face me and held out his hand. "I am Alrigo Gattoli, owner of this fine establishment. It is my pleasure to serve you."

Accepting his handshake, I arched an eyebrow and said nothing.

He chuckled as he pushed us toward the empty table we initially intended to claim. "Come. Come. Sit."

As we took our seats, Alrigo motioned for a nearby waitress. "This is Dani. She'll take very good care of you." Addressing the woman, his hands flew into rapid movement. "Dani, rapidamente. Bevande per i signori." He beamed at me and held his arms outstretched for a moment. "On the house, eh?" He paused long enough to take a breath. "You need something, you ask for me, eh?"

Though I was grateful for the man's attention, I'd had enough of being the center of attention. "Thank you, Signore Gattoli, but I'm sure we'll be fine."

He clapped Adrien on the back as he stepped away from the table. Waving and calling out to someone across the club he meandered over to where the other person sat.

"So much for keeping a low profile," Adrien scoffed as we watched the man disappear into the throng. "Thanks to the irate woman, the incensed man, and the gushing owner, the entire population of Eros knows exactly who we are."

I shrugged. "Can't be helped. Let's just hope she wasn't around to witness it. Last thing we want to do is spook her."

As Dani returned with our drinks, I leaned forward and took one of the glasses from her hand.

"Dani, is it?" At her nod, I continued, "Does this establishment cater to any other lifestyle...types?"

The waitress looked confused for a moment, glancing between Adrien and me and then her lips spread broadly, and her white teeth gleamed in the dimness of the club. "Thursday nights."

Now it was my turn to be confused. "Thursday nights what?"

"That's omosessuale night."

My eyes widened as I realized she'd misunderstood my question. "No, no. we're not gay."

"Oh Scusi..." She seemed flustered and hastened to apologize. "I meant no offense."

"It's all right, none taken. What I meant was are the Cambiare welcome here?"

"Oh no, signori. Eros is esclusivo. No animals allowed."

I chuckled. She obviously felt the same way I did about shifters. "I see." Perhaps, she'd bribed her way in the night he'd seen her here. "Are there any who work here who feel differently?"

The woman shook her head. "No, Signori. All here are loyal to the Alimentatori."

Why did she seem like she was spewing the party line? "Be that as it may, the other night a Cambiare woman approached me at the bar."

As she stepped back from the table, the friendly expression she wore moments ago was replaced by a cold, emotionless mask. "No, forgive me, Signori, but you must be mistaken."

My eyes narrowed. *Who or what was she hiding?*

Before I had a chance to ask, she spoke in clipped tones, "If there is nothing else I can help you gentlemen with, I will go tend to my other customers."

When neither Adrien nor I spoke, she left, weaving, and pushing her way through the crowd.

"What the hell?"

I glanced over at Adrien and shrugged. Leaning forward, I placed my glass on the table. "She's hiding something."

"Well, yeah. That was obvious." He took a sip of his drink as he sat back. "We both know there were Cambiare in here the other night. Is it possible the humans realize they are catering to them and are hiding the fact from the Alimentatori?"

I thought about it for a moment. "I suppose it's possible, though it seems unlikely. I guarantee they are aware of what would happen if such a lie were discovered. However," I glanced to where Dani stood taking an order several tables away, "that doesn't mean that a few of them aren't Cambiare sympathizers."

"True. How do you think they are getting by the bouncers?"

I shrugged, considering the question. "Maybe they're forging Aliment badges or pretending to be human vessels and slipping through. It's not that hard to get a human I.D. and pass yourself off as human. We do it all the time."

"Yeah, but to what end? Why would they bother with that just to slip past a bouncer at a bar?" He shook his head not convinced. "I don't see the point."

I sighed in frustration. He was right. It didn't really matter how they were getting past the front doors, when doing so seemed ridiculously dangerous and stupid. They had to have had a reason for showing up at Eros two nights ago. They wouldn't risk being caught in enemy territory, especially after killing a newly ascended Council member without a damned good reason.

"Besides, wouldn't the Alimentatori who frequent the club say something to Alrigo?"

Adrien's question interrupted my train of thought as I glanced up at him. "What?"

"Humans may not be able to smell a Cambiare, but we sure can. So, why wouldn't the Alimentatori have raised the alarm the moment one walked through the door?"

That was not something I had even considered. The bar hadn't been packed, like it was tonight, but there had been a fair amount of Alimentatori present. Why hadn't they scented her out?

As I breathed in the answer came to me in a rush of human sweat unsuccessfully masked by sweet perfumes and musky colognes. My gaze flew around the room in a moment of clarity. "What if they can mask their scent somehow?"

"You could smell her."

My lips screwed into a discouraged frown. *Once again, he was right.* "True." I thought for a moment and then remembered why I left so suddenly that night. "But she was practically on top of me. Maybe whatever they use covers up their scent as long as they keep their distance. Up close though—"

Understanding spread through Adrien's features. "They are vulnerable."

A cat-who-ate-the-canary grin crossed my face. "Which means we can sit back and play 'Spot the Cambiare' by simply looking for someone who steers clear of the Aliments in the club."

Something that was easier said than done.

Over the next several hours the crowd grew with no sign of anyone who avoided our kind.

Leaning over the table, I shouted to Adrien. "This might be a lost cause."

He nodded; his eyes trained on the other side of the room.

"Eros is too crowded. Maybe we should call it a night and go to Plan B in the morning."

"You're the boss. Whatever you want to do I'll do." Even though he spoke to me, his gaze remained locked on something at the other side of the room.

Irritated by his lack of concentration, I turned in my chair, hoping that what had trapped his gaze was the woman for whom we were looking. Unfortunately, it was indeed a woman, just not the one I expected to see.

"She just pops up everywhere, doesn't she?"

I heard Adrien's glass tip and the few remaining pieces of ice slide across the table.

"Oh shit," he mumbled as he rushed to clean up the mess

I chuckled. "Why don't you go over and talk to her?"

He looked back to where Alcie sat alone at a table sipping an umbrella drink. "I'm not here for that."

"Oh, come on. I was just saying we could call it a night. Why don't you stay and talk to her?" By the look on his face he wanted to approach Alcie. Something was stopping him. "You know you want to."

He swallowed and cast his gaze to the wet surface, dabbing at the streaks left behind by the spilled drink. "As I said, I am not here for that. I will see you home."

Realizing he was not going to give in, I frowned. "Fine, but when this is all over, no more excuses. You are going after her."

I rose and placed several bills on the table for Dani and crossed into the aisle. "I'll be right back. Going to hit the bathroom before we head home."

He nodded. "I'll meet you at the front door."

Several minutes later, I exited the back hall which led to the bathrooms and glanced around looking for Adrien. He stood several feet to the right of the doors.

I chuckled to myself as I realized he was no longer alone.

Apparently Alcie wasn't opposed to making the first move as they stood close together absorbed in deep conversation. I stood watching them for a few moments, as I decided on a plan of action.

Now what? Go home and start again tomorrow like I told Adrien? Or commence Plan B?

Sleep was definitely on the agenda for tonight and so was finding a Cambiare.

At this point I would be satisfied with any Cambiare.

Even as I thought it, I knew I lied.

Nothing less than doling out a beating to the right Cambiare would satisfy the bloodlust burning within me. However, I wasn't opposed to torturing a few along the way if it led me to the one responsible. The only way that was going to happen was to enter the lioness's den.

Assisi it is then.

Chapter Nineteen

Emerging from the club into the cool night air, I breathed deeply, cleansing my lungs of the stuffy hormone filled air.

I flagged our car, anxious to get away before Adrien realized I was gone. When the driver pulled up next to me, I automatically reached for the door handle. Before I could grasp it, the door opened.

"Planning on going somewhere without me, Jacen?" *Danger.* That was what the tone of Adrien's voice threatened. Unfortunately, he knew exactly what I was doing and wasn't about to let me get away with it.

Fuck. "Nope, just calling the car and waiting for you."

"Yeah, right." He held the door open, allowing me to climb into the back seat.

Once in, I slid to the opposite side and waited for him to join me. A moment later he settled onto the seat next to me. I sensed his gaze on me, though I tried to ignore it.

He was angrier than I had ever seen him. I could almost hear the air around him sizzle. What held off the eruption I didn't know, but whatever it was I hoped it would last long enough for me to convince him that going to Assisi was our best option.

Fury dripped from his tone like droplets of acid. "We aren't going home, are we?"

The driver's gaze found mine in the rearview mirror, and I could tell he was waiting for instructions. Leaning forward, I spoke in a confident, determined tone. "Take us to Assisi."

"Are you fucking nuts?" There it went. The last tendril of restraint Adrien had. "The one thing they told us: stay the fuck away from Assisi. And you want to go prancing in there in the middle of the night like you fucking own the place? No way." Balling up a fist, he struck out at the only thing he could reach. A solid thud echoed through the car's interior as his knuckles met the ceiling of the car. "Boy, I swear by all that is holy if you get yourself killed tonight, I will leave your soul stuck in your carcass for all eternity. You can fucking forget The Release and any hope of an afterlife."

I stifled a laugh at his outburst. The man was in need of a little good-natured ribbing. "Really? For eternity?"

He glared at me but seemed to be struggling to hide the crack of a smile as he turned back to the window. "Yes, fucking eternity. Let's go."

I chuckled knowing I'd won the battle, but I wondered who would win the war. "Sure thing. Hate to be late for my own funeral."

"Shut up, Jace." He turned to look out the window, and I saw his shoulders bounce with suppressed laughter and knew I had won the war too.

A second later our car leapt into traffic. The scenery passed quickly as we sped away from Eros. As we moved from the busy nightlife onto empty country roads, my fingers ran absently around the jeweled top of Julian's walking stick. Knowing where we were headed, I was suddenly glad I remembered to grab the weapon on my way out of the villa.

I trained my eyes on the darkness beyond the window and went over what I knew of the Cambiare.

Stay away from their claws. If I allowed her to scratch me it was all over.

Be careful of their ability to manipulate thoughts. Of anyone, the

Alimentatori knew just how powerful a weapon entering the mind could be.

But most of all don't fall prey to their pheromones. That one I hadn't a clue how I was going to avoid. I couldn't simply stop breathing while around them.

Turning away from the window, I leaned my head back against the seat. Their scent couldn't be that powerful. Even if it was, I'd just have to figure out something. Maybe it was as simple as staying downwind. Probably not a bad idea anyway, since most animals had an impeccable sense of smell.

My eyelids drooped as the rhythmic sound of tires against pavement and the constant motion lulled me. It seemed like weeks since I slept peacefully through the night.

*****

Startled by something, my eyes flew open. I glanced around the dark interior of the car in an attempt to get my bearings. We had stopped moving. We must have arrived.

A soft snore emanated from where Adrien laid, his cheek smashed up against the window. Like me he seemed to have fallen prey to lack of sleep and monotonous car ride.

Jabbing him with the end of the walking stick, I whispered, "Hey, Adrien, we're here."

He snorted and batted at the stick, then settled back in obvious exhaustion.

A wicked thought drifted through my mind as I stifled a chuckle. *If he wanted to sleep, who was I to wake him?*

Handing the driver several Euros, I whispered, "See that you don't disturb him. He's very tired."

The man's flat lips spread into a toothy grin as he pocketed the money. "Si, signori. He will sleep like baby."

"Good. Wait here for me. I shouldn't be long." As I climbed out my side of the car, I was careful to close the door without waking him.

The streets, similar to Bracciano in so many ways, held the same old world feel. The buildings, aging gracefully, had thus far withstood the test of time. Where Bracciano had been bustling with tourists, Assisi seemed...small town quiet.

What did I expect in the middle of the night? The streets teaming with crazed wild beasts lusting for Alimentatori blood?

I almost chuckled at that. That was exactly what I expected to find.

Great. Now what? I glanced back to where I left Adrien sleeping. Whatever I did, it had to be away from him. He was going to be one raging bull when he woke up.

I meandered through the streets aimlessly for several minutes before coming to terms with the fact that other than going to Assisi I'd had no real plan on how to find the Cambiare. What made me think they roamed the streets in packs just waiting for some unlucky Aliment to wander into their territory?

I paused for a moment to stare up at what had to be the basilica de San Francesco. Floodlights bathed the structure in soft white light. Sandy blond walls seemed to grow directly from the hill, tall and straight with great arches and a beautiful rose window glowing like a beacon in the night.

"Bello, non è?" The feminine voice whispered on a breeze.

Beautiful, is it not? Indeed. Without looking, I nodded. "Yes. Yes, it is."

"Did you come to Assisi to see her?" My brow furrowed as she spoke, a vague memory tickling my brain. "Or to see me?"

The first tingle of warning coursed down my spine. I froze not daring to breathe. I drew my gaze from the basilica and turned my full attention to the woman who had appeared beside me as easily as a wraith.

"I came to see you." I jerked my head toward the basilica. "She was just a stop on the tour."

A wicked look stole across her face as a well-sculpted dark brow rose knowingly above glistening golden eyes. "How unfortunate for her."

She fairly purred as she spoke. The seductive tone accompanied by her delicious scent transmitted a ripple of desire through me. She was the one, the one who stood over my bed then approached me at Eros, the one whose scent had caused me to tumble out of control, and sweet Aita, it was happening again. Swallowing, I shook myself mentally. *No! Stay away from her claws, don't let her play with your mind, resist her…charms.* The mantra ran through my head as I stared into her eyes. I stepped back in an attempt to break away from her spell. Steeling myself against the onslaught of her pheromones igniting the air around me, I fought for control. I needed to do something, anything to distract my mind from her efforts to control my responses. "Who are you?"

She inched closer. "It does not matter, Jacen of Samsaveel. What matters is who you are, and who you are not."

"If you know my name and my house, why would you question who I am?" Slowly, without drawing her attention to what I was doing, I shifted my right hand to the palm hold of the walking stick. With my thumb, I pushed down on the catch and heard a faint click which indicated the release of the weapon. I waited for the right opportunity to draw the dagger from within the confines of the hidden scabbard.

She leaned in, and her breath brushed my neck as she inhaled. Her whisper touched the nerves along my neck causing them to quiver. "You do not smell like your brother. His smell was not unpleasant. But yours…" she sniffed again as if trying to capture what made my scent so unique, "yours is richer, earthier than his. The difference confuses me."

As she stood close, I shallowed my breathing hoping to avoid the hypnotic effects of her musk. "Don't all Alimentatori smell the same to you?"

She chuckled. "Of course not. All beasts have a different scent trail. However, brothers should be similar. You and Julian are not, so either you are not who you say you are or—"

In one swift fluid motion I drew the dagger. Blade grasped firmly; my hand flew to her throat. As I held it there, I expected to see fear. Instead, she merely smiled. "I see you are not in the mood to talk. More's the pity. We have so much to discuss."

"Why talk when actions speak much louder than words." I pushed the blade to her throat. One small drop of blood, almost black in the darkness, slipped down the glinting silver. "Why did you kill my brother?"

Her gaze found mine as she sighed in exasperation. "I thought we had already established that he was not your brother."

"Shut you're fucking mouth, you lying bitch."

She snarled and moved away so quickly I could almost feel the rush of air fill the space where she used to be. In the next moment, she darted away disappearing into the shadows as quickly as she'd appeared.

Fury burst from me like the roar of a tropical storm. Slamming the dagger back into place, I followed in the direction she disappeared. *Not this time*, my mind screamed as I pushed my feet to move faster.

As I neared the end of the block, she veered to the right and headed down an alleyway. I gained the entrance to the back street just in time to watch her push off a balcony and leap to the roof. Her feet flew with fluid motion along the edge of the building, her ebony hair flowing out behind her with the speed of her movements. When she reached the end of the building, she leapt effortlessly to the next without pausing. I trailed below until I found a place where I could make the leap to the roof. Where she took just two jumps to make the transition, I needed at least three. When I spotted an SUV parked to one side of the alley, I leapt to the roof of the vehicle and from there to a balcony overhanging the alley. Then made the jump over to grab the roof line along which she had just run. The instant my hands made contact I pulled myself up. In a matter of seconds, I was back in pursuit, following her every movement with one of my own.

Suddenly, she dropped out of sight. I glanced down to the darkness below. If she thought to hide in the shadows, she had chosen the wrong alley. This space was a dead end, and I was on the end closest to the opening to the street. My impending triumph, nearly palpable, spread through me like liquid gold radiating confidence from every pore. If I dropped down from where I stood, I would block any attempt she made to get by me.

Without thinking, I leapt off the edge and landed with a small thud on the ground below. As I straightened, I walked forward with confidence, my hand going to the hilt of the hidden dagger. "Come on little beastie. There's nowhere to hide."

With my senses on high alert for any movement in the alley, I sprang forward and drew the dagger, holding it out toward the shadows.

A small inkling of danger paced its way to my brain as more than one shadow moved. I froze. She was no longer alone, and I had dropped right into a trap. One by one Cambiare emerged from the shadows, their gazes trained on my every move. I was woefully outnumbered. With deliberate slowness, I sheathed the dagger and brought the walking stick to my side. In an even, non-threatening voice I addressed the growing group. "I am not here to start a war. I'm just here for the girl."

A tall, dark-haired man emerged from the shadows. His back ramrod straight, his broad shoulders pitched backward at an arrogant angle spoke clearly of who was in charge. His deep-set golden gaze never left me. "You have no authority here." At his signal the girl I had been chasing walked to his side and was joined by another woman who was oddly familiar. It came to me in a flash. The woman in the electronics shop, the one who talked about destiny. I looked between the two stunned by their resemblance to one another. Then the image of the woman in the locket surfaced, and it all came together. She was their mother? Why hadn't I seen it before? Of course, each encounter had been brief. One I had not looked in the eye, and the other had worn a hat and sunglasses when we met.

A vague memory came from somewhere deep in my mind of a woman sitting at the café staring at me as I waited for Adrien at the airport.

That was..., I looked between the sisters again and my gaze came to a halt on the one I'd been chasing, *her.*

A wicked upturn of her lips as she observed me gave every indication that she was well aware of the path my mind walked.

My eyes narrowed. Had they both been in on Julian's murder? Had one lured him out while the other laid in wait?

The anger surfaced again as I glared at one, then the other. It all seemed to make sense. *No wonder Julian had been so easy to kill. If he had two beasts to deal with instead of one...*

The reality of the situation in which I found myself hit home. I had captured everyone's attention. "I want the ones responsible for my brother's death."

The man who was obviously in charge spoke again, "If you have come here to visit harm upon any of my family you will have to go through me."

The woman I first met in the shop placed her hand on the man's arm and spoke softly. "Dante, give the man a chance to speak. He obviously feels strongly enough to risk his life." She turned to look at me. The light of kindness lit her features, yet I found it hard to stomach. "Perhaps we should hear him out."

"Alegra!" The other girl shouted, before the one called Dante could answer. "What are you thinking? This is not the time or place for this."

Dante scowled at the young woman. "Quiet, Nix. I will decide where and when is the right time." He patted Alegra's hand in reassurance. "Mi amore, you know we cannot tolerate the presence of the Alimentatori in our territory. He has disregarded the sanctity of our home."

"I understand. You must see his side as well." She looked toward me in sympathy. "He has lost a brother and has a right to his anger." She glanced over at her sister. "He needs to know the truth."

The younger woman's jaw dropped in shock. "Non possiamo fidare di lui. Dobbiamo mantenere il nostro silenzio."

Something about trust and keeping silent. My eyes narrowed as I studied the sisters.

The older woman responded with just as much force and conviction, "Credo che è il fratello di Giuliano!"

The women glared at each other, neither willing to give an inch to the other. Then, Dante intervened. "Basta! Entrambi voi arrestano... abbastanza del bickering."

The two women silenced immediately as Dante once again took charge of the situation. "You will have to excuse my fiancée and her sister. They have differing opinions about you."

My chin rose a touch as I stared at each of the sisters in turn. "I don't care what their fucking opinions of me are. All I want is the one responsible for Julian's murder."

With a growl, the larger man edged his way forward and captured my attention. "No one here is responsible for the Aliment's death."

Of course, he would defend her. The anger boiled just below the surface as I bit my tongue.

He defends me because I have done nothing wrong. The whisper coursed through my mind like a ghost of a thought. *Julian's death could not be stopped.*

Glancing at the man who was obviously in charge, the muscle in my cheek worked double time. "If no one here is responsible then who whispers in my mind that his death could not be stopped?"

Dante froze, his eyes narrowing. "Someone has entered your mind?"

He glanced around the circle of Cambiare. "Who has dared overstep their bounds?"

The woman he'd called Nix crossed her arms over her chest defensively. "Sono stata io."

"Speak English in his presence." His growl held equal parts anger and impatience.

Nix's brow arched and her strangely beautiful eyes locked with mine. "It was me. I am the one who whispered to him."

"You will not do so again unless he allows it. Is that understood?"

Her gaze dropped from mine, though I somehow got the feeling she wasn't truly remorseful. "Sì, Dante."

Through gritted teeth Dante accepted her contrition and waved her away. Having dealt with the insurrection of the woman, he turned his attention back to me. "As I told you before, no one here is responsible for your brother's death. You may choose to believe me and walk away or call me liar again." His fingers stretched out by his sides. The sudden appearance of his long talon-like claws was not lost on me. "The choice is yours Aliment."

A shiver ran down my spine as the memory surfaced of another Cambiare who uttered similar words before ripping an Aliment to shreds. If nothing else, perhaps the tale had served as a warning for this moment. I met his gaze unafraid of the implied threat. "I will leave when I am ready. I seek justice for my brother and I will not go without what I came for."

"You do not seek justice. You seek vengeance. There is a difference." Dante's well-spoken words refuted my claim. "And you will leave our territory empty handed as neither can be found here."

"There is no difference to me." My gaze shifted to Nix. "And I believe they can."

Dante moved forward placing himself between me and Nix. He growled low in his throat in warning.

Every muscle in my body tensed as I prepared for battle. I inched forward closing the distance between us. Wrapping my fingers around the hilt of my dagger, I eased it out of the sheath.

I startled when a dark shadow dropped down a few feet away from me. Ready to face the new threat, I turned sideways thinking to sidestep him if he rushed me. To my surprise I recognized my Second.

"What the fuck, Adrien?"

He sprang forward, putting himself between me and Dante. Grabbing the hand which held the weapon he forced it downward and pushed me backward away from my quarry. His urgent whisper brooked no disobedience. "Not now, Jace. Not here. They'll kill you, and that will do no one any good."

For a second, I considered shoving him away and tackling Dante anyway. My eyes narrowed as I glanced around. The circle of Cambiare had moved inward to protect their leader from attack. If I moved even a hair closer, I had no doubt they'd be upon me like the rabid beasts they were.

Relaxing, I put the dagger back into place and held out my arms. "You can let me go. I'm fine. I'm not going to do anything."

Adrien's gaze sought mine in the darkness. "Are you sure? You're not going to tell me one thing and do another again?"

"No, I promise. We will walk away and live to fight another day."

Adrien dropped his hands from my arms and then stepped away. "Good."

He turned toward Dante. "I'm sorry. He tends to be rather brash and impulsive. We will go without further incentive."

Dante's body language spoke clearly. He was not about to relax his guard. "Very well. You may leave but know we will not tolerate another incident like this in our territory. If he ventures here again, it better be with the proper respect for my people."

Adrien nodded and pulled at my arm in an attempt to get me to move backward. "I can guarantee if he ventures here again, it will be with the utmost respect." When I refused to move, he shifted until he stood in front of me. Casting a warning look over his shoulder, he moved backward forcing me to retreat. I looked over his shoulder as the Cambiare surrounding Dante disbursed slowly.

My gaze caught Nix's and for a moment I saw her lips twitch in humor.

Nix, can you hear me? Her eyebrow rose and without an exchange of words I knew she could. *Good. I will take down all who stand between us.* I cast a meaningful glare to all the people who stood around her. *If you want your loved ones out of danger, don't make me seek you out again.*

A moment of silence passed and just when I thought she would not answer her voice purred within my mind. *Do you think I should just bow before you and allow you to take my head? I think not Jacen of Samsaveel. I bow to no one. I will fight tooth and nail to keep you from harming my family.* She glanced between Dante and me before continuing. *However, I will come to you.*

Tomorrow night. Meet me on the roof of our villa.

Her gaze narrowed on me suspiciously. *No. Not your territory.*

Not mine. We will meet in a place where neither of us holds sway over the other.

Where then?

The silence within my head seemed to mean she was thinking. Then she spoke, her familiar voice cooing within my mind, *there is a place halfway between Assisi and Lake Bracciano in Bomarzo. Parco dei Mostri? Do you know it?*

Park of the Monsters? No, but I will find it. Where will you be once I get there?

A short silence ensued as her sister spoke to her, interrupting our internal dialogue.

As her sister leaned in to speak to Dante, Nix spoke again. *Meet me at midnight in front of the mouth of Orcus, the large sculpture with a wide-open mouth. He sits at the back of the park.*

I gave a slight nod indicating my agreement. *Come alone, and we will finish this.*

She nodded in return. *It is agreed.*

*****

Nix's gaze followed Jacen as he turned and walked down the alley and out on to the street. A moment later the men disappeared past the end of the building, heading toward where they left their car. She sensed Alegra's approach even before she spoke but refused to make eye contact with her sister. "What?"

Her sister exhaled in frustration. "I know you're angry, but you have to realize there is so much more at stake here than whether or not you killed an Aliment."

"Don't you think I know that, Alegra?" She glanced over to where Dante stood speaking with several of his people. "I'm not a child."

Alegra reached out a hand and stroked Nix's hair. "No. No you are not, il mio amore. That is why you must do as Dante says. He will not accept your disobedience on this."

Nix dropped her gaze and frowned. "I have always done as he has asked."

"Have you?" Her knowing eyes reminded me of one occasion I had not.

"I said I was sorry for that."

"You did. It does not change what happened. But, I digress." She stared into Nix's eyes with an earnest plea. "Please, just do as Dante wishes, and be careful."

"Why would I not, Alegra?"

Alegra glanced down the alley to where the two Aliments had disappeared. "Because guilt can be a dangerous companion, mio caro. It makes us reckless and unpredictable."

"I understand." Stamping down a disquieting sense of injustice, she shrugged off her sister's concern. "Neither you nor Dante need worry. I know what must be done, and nothing will stop me from seeing it through."

Chapter Twenty

Unable to sleep any longer, I watched the sheer curtains dance on the warm breeze, which blew in through the open veranda doors. My thoughts wandered through the early morning meeting with the Cambiare woman.

Why had I let her taunts bother me so much? Did it matter if what she said was true? Would it change how I felt about him or what I was here to do?

As I lay there staring out into the bright sunshine, a vague memory awoke within me of a similar day when I was just a small child, only on that day I awoke in a bed at an Alimentatori clinic. The sunshine streaming through the window hurt my eyes, and I turned my head away to find Julian sleeping in a chair on the opposite side of my bed. He looked haggard and worn out, older than he used to. No one needed to tell me that he had not left my side since the attack on our parents. It was written all over his exhausted features. I drifted back to sleep secure in the knowledge that I was not alone. My brother would be there when I opened my eyes again.

And he was.

For days Julian kept his vigil. He talked to me, read to me, and was there in case I needed him.

It was no more than right that I return the favor. I was not there in his moment of need as he'd been for me. By the Gods, I would be there to see justice done and avenge his death, even if it meant tearing apart every Cambiare hovel in Assisi.

If she hoped her words would stave off my need for Kin Retribution, then she would be sorely mistaken. It didn't matter if we weren't biologically related. It didn't make him any less my brother. He had earned my love and loyalty over and over. A lack of similar DNA would never change that. And it certainly didn't change my desire to put *her* in an early grave.

Tonight, she would find out just how little genetics meant to me.

My gaze sought the bedside clock as I hoped the moment wasn't too far off. Unfortunately, though, it was well into the afternoon, and there were still several hours to waste before I could set out for the Parco dei Mostri.

Damn it. What was I going to do to keep myself occupied between now and then?

Throwing back the crisp white sheets, I stood and stretched tired muscles.

Something I needed to do was check in with security. They may have made some progress in rooting out the hacker or in tracking down Karina. I supposed it was as good a place as any to while away the hours.

Just as I crossed to the bathroom to take a shower, the shrill high pitched double ring of the bedside phone split the air. Doubling back, I grabbed the handset. "Hello?"

"Um, Jace?" The familiar voice of Alcie sounded hesitant.

I dropped back to the edge of the bed. "Yeah, what is it, Alcie?"

There was a long pause, and then she spoke again, even more hesitant than before. "Um...Jacen? The great Council wants you down here right away."

My brow furrowed. "Why?"

"I don't know. I was just told you were to present yourself to them posthaste." Her voice shook in nervousness. Did she know more than she was telling? It didn't really matter if she did.

She worked for the Council. If they instructed her to silence, then she wasn't about to tell me anything.

"Alright. I'll shower and be down within the hour."

Her tone changed to a more relaxed one. "Very good. I will inform them of your imminent arrival."

I hung up the phone and screwed up my mouth in thought.

What could they want now?

One thing came to mind right away. They somehow knew about my sojourn into Assisi. I had permission to hunt in Alimentatori territory, but I had not sought permission to venture into the Cambiare territory.

I rose and then crossed to the dresser, where my suitcase lay open. As I riffled through the bag, I continued mulling over the situation.

How would they have known? My thoughts raced to Adrien's angry silence on the car ride home. He spoke very little and it was obvious he was attempting to control his rage. I did not press the issue as I wasn't in the mood to put up with his ranting and raving over my *reckless* behavior.

After grabbing everything I needed, including a clean pair of dark denims and a dark red polo, I placed them on the dresser and closed the bag.

Had Adrien gone to the Great Council to keep me from venturing to Assisi again? I wouldn't put it past him. He'd resented my independence from the start. I frowned, angered by the mere thought of such a betrayal. Well, if he had, I would make sure he regretted doing so.

*****

Sometime later, freshly showered, and shaven I emerged from my room to find Adrien already waiting in the dining room area.

He glanced up long enough to acknowledge my entrance and then went back to reading the local English language newspaper. His lack of greeting was not lost on me. It was obvious he was still plenty pissed over last night's adventure.

My eyes narrowed in suspicion. Was he angry enough to seek the Great Council's help with an unruly Padrone? Only one way to find out.

I dropped into the chair opposite him. "Morning."

His dry, uninterested voice grumbled from behind the newspaper. "Afternoon."

"Right. Afternoon." My frown grew deeper as I grabbed an apple from the bowl at the table center. Taking a bite, I chewed leisurely. Springing the question on him immediately would seem a bit…over aggressive. Best to attempt a bit of small talk first to see if I could loosen his tongue. "Did you sleep well?"

"Yep."

"I didn't. Had awful dreams." I took another bite and sat back, watching for any indication he might be willing to hold a real conversation.

"Sorry to hear that."

I frowned. Not even the faintest flicker of interest in his voice. This was getting me nowhere. Oh hell, I tried. Time to go in guns a blazing. "Did you go running to the Great Council?"

That did it. Immediately he crumpled the newspaper down in front of him as his furious glare pinned me to my seat. "Did I what?"

There was no going back now, so I charged ahead. "Did you take your issues with me to the Great Council?"

He closed his eyes and breathed deeply as if attempting to gain control of his rage. Finally, he spoke. "Are you questioning my loyalty?"

I thought about it for a moment as I chewed another bite of apple and then raised an eyebrow in response.

He folded the newspaper ripping it in several places as he did so. Then placing the paper down next to his empty plate, his angry gaze found mine. "You are an arrogant, selfish bastard. At every turn you thwart any effort I make to be your friend. You leave me out of important decisions. You go heading off into enemy territory alone, despite my concerns for your safety. Then you dare to question *my* loyalty? How many times do you expect me to forgive your insults? Sweet Aita, Jace! You're making me crazy with all your foolish, reckless antics. Do you truly believe you're invincible? That nothing can harm you because you're on some kind of divine mission to avenge your brother's death? Wake the hell up, Jacen. I'm the only friend you have in this place, and the sooner you realize that, the better off we'll both be." He stood up so quickly his chair toppled over. Not stopping to pick it up, he walked toward the door.

My gaze followed him. "We're not done with this."

"Oh yes we are." He didn't pause as he ripped open the door.

"Where the hell do you think you're going? I'm your Padrone, and *I* get to say when this conversation is over."

That made him pause. He turned just enough to glare at me. "Either you're my Padrone, or you're not, Jacen. You don't get to pick and choose when I get to be your Second and when I don't. You can't have it both ways."

His fingers balled into fists and a moment later he was gone.

Gods damn it. He managed to avoid answering the question entirely. In a flash I was out of my seat and heading after him, just to check myself before going through the doorway. Running after him would be a mistake. It would weaken my position. Not to mention it would stroke his bruised ego to make me chase him through the halls. Biting down viciously on the apple I was still holding, I slammed the door and then turned back to the table. *No, this time he was going to have to come to me.*

*****

Twenty minutes later I entered Alcie's office. To my surprise Adrien leaned against the wall, apparently awaiting my arrival.

I glared at him, while addressing Alcie, "What the hell is he doing here?"

"Um, well...I called him, too?" The tremor in her voice made me believe she was struggling to maintain a brave face.

Glancing at her, my voice softened. "Ah, okay. Are they ready for me?"

"Us?" Adrien pushed himself off the wall and crossed to the

opposite side of her desk.

She looked between us like a frightened rabbit.

"Yes, well if you'll both follow me." She stood up and opened the door to the Council's chamber.

Moments later I took my place in front of the Great Council.

Once Alcie exited the room, without greeting or preamble Morbius addressed me. "Jacen of Samsaveel, is it true that last night while you were at Eros you took part in a conflict between two humans?"

That was the last thing I'd expected. *Why would they bother with such a trifling matter?* "Yes, it is true."

"Are you aware that the man with whom you had a very public altercation has been reported missing and subsequently, local authorities are investigating Eros?"

Stunned by the question, I sucked in a breath. "No, sire. I was not aware of that." Something didn't make sense. "Why are the authorities so concerned over his whereabouts? He's probably just sleeping it off somewhere."

Morbius's hooded head shifted. He watched me like a hawk. "The man is an important financier from England. He was apparently here for a business meeting, which he missed this morning. The human who reported him missing works for the British embassy."

I exhaled as I realized the seriousness of the situation. If the man was important to high placed people within the government, the authorities had no choice but to investigate. No amount of bribery would keep them from storming down the doors of Eros and discovering what truly went on there. "Okay. I understand. You want me to locate him and assure he is returned home safely."

"No." Morbius snapped. "You are to stay away from Eros and the whole situation. Your involvement has already caused much trouble."

My brow furrowed in consternation. "Then why am I here? What do you wish me to do?"

"Nothing." He motioned to the man to his right. At Morbius's bidding, he stood and tossed a piece of paper at my feet. It fluttered to a landing face down. Confused by the proceedings, I bent over and picked it up. Turning the page over, it took me a moment to realize what it was.

What the hell?

The man in the sketch could have been my twin. And above the drawing it read, "Desiderato per l'interrogazione." It took less than a minute to translate the meaning. "Desired for interrogation."

A wanted poster with my face on it.

Stunned I sought confirmation. "They think I did something to him?"

No one spoke, just blank hoods turned my way accusatorily. *What the fuck was going on here?* Alarm bells rang within my head warning me to be careful how I proceeded from here on out, and suddenly I understood. "You believe I had something to do with his disappearance as well."

They didn't need to answer. Their silence said it all.

I crumpled the paper in my hand and tossed it to the floor. A flash of anger roared through me. "Who has accused me of wrongdoing? I demand to know."

Morbius was quick to answer. "You demand? You seem to be under the misguided impression that we are here to serve you."

The warning in his voice was clear. I was within an inch of crossing a line it would be hard for them to ignore. "I have done nothing wrong, sire. If you don't believe me, my Second was with me the entire evening."

Morbius's veiled eyes seemed to look through me. "Second. Step up next to your Padrone." Adrien didn't hesitate.

As Adrien joined me, I immediately regretted calling the Council's attention to him. I'm sure he would be only too eager to confess that we'd been separated on many occasions on the previous night.

As our king addressed him, Adrien's chin rose and his back stiffened, "You can verify your Padrone's claim? He was with you the entire evening?"

"Yes, sire. He did not leave my sight."

I had to bite back my own shock. He just stood up beside me and defended me against their accusations. I had been wrong to accuse him of seeking help from the Great Council. *Fuck.*

Before I could dwell anymore on my error, Morbius's voice cracked like a whip through the air, "You are both lying."

My eyes flew to the darkness within the hood, searching for any sign of who controlled my fate. "My Second and I have no reason to lie."

Even as I said the words I knew it was foolish to challenge the elder.

"You dare lie to us when we have several witnesses who state you were not together on several occasions last night? Our own assistant states she spoke with your Second for several minutes and you were not with him. Then when he left Eros, he did so alone."

"That is partially true, sire." Adrien grabbed my arm to stop me from going any further. I wasn't about to stand there and let them accuse me...us of something we didn't do. "Our driver can confirm Adrien was with me a few minutes later in the car. *We* left Eros together."

"Yes, he has confirmed this." The reassurance gave me a second of reprieve but then his next words made my stomach churn. "However, he also stated you paid him not to wake your Second while he slept. It is his recollection that you disappeared for quite some time." His dark hood turned toward Adrien. "Then when your Second woke to find you gone he too disappeared. The driver states it was at least an hour before the two of you found your way back to the car."

Damn it. Apparently, Adrien was right. He was the only friend I had here, and my headstrong arrogance had nearly cost me his loyalty.

I closed my eyes, took a deep breath, and gritted my teeth to keep myself from saying something I might come to regret.

My only defense against their accusations was the one detail the driver had not revealed. Why hadn't he told them we were almost two hours away, in Assisi at the time? Was the punishment for going into Cambiare territory more frightening than being caught in a lie? The consequences of nearly starting a turf war with the Cambiare were bound to be worse than allowing the Council to believe I had done something to a human. I imagined the Council liked to do things...*traditionally*, which meant they might resort to the more archaic methods of punishments, like those used by our ancestors. A shiver coursed down my spine with the thought.

No, it was better they believed Adrien and I were lying, than to reveal where we were. I would have plenty of time to locate the human and prove my innocence after dealing with Nix tonight. Speaking in my own defense would probably fall on deaf ears. It would have to be my last-ditch effort to convince them of my innocence.

"Sire, I know it will do little good to profess my innocence in this matter. Regardless of this fact, I do so anyway." I took my time before continuing, "I did have an altercation with the human, but I did not harm him in anyway. He was in Eros and I had him escorted out. That was the first and the last time I saw him."

Several excruciatingly long minutes dragged by as the blank hood of our king seemed to assess me. Then finally the silence broke. "As we currently have no proof of your involvement in the disappearance of the human and taking into consideration your recent loss, we are feeling generous and will grant you a reprieve. If the man turns up alive, his state will attest to your innocence and you will be free from punishment. If not, then we will revisit our concerns over this issue at that time. In the meantime, know this, Jacen of Samsaveel, the eyes of the Great Council are upon you. We will not tolerate any potential threat to the veil of secrecy our people live behind and need to survive. Is that understood?"

I let out a breath I'd been holding as events unfolded. This was the best outcome for which I could hope. It allowed me time to do what I needed to do, and hopefully the man would reappear unharmed, and I'd no longer be a suspect. "Yes, sire."

I bent my head in acknowledgement of his authority. "Thank you for your consideration."

Rising, Morbius turned his back, effectively dismissing Adrien and me without a word. A second later he disappeared through a hidden rear entrance of the room, and then the others rose and followed.

As they filed out, I stood stunned by the turn of events. Guilt flooded me as I realized Adrien had not been the culprit in today's debacle. In fact, it had nothing to do with either of us. We were at the wrong place at the wrong time and now were the object of the Great Council's scrutiny. *Shit.* It wasn't bad enough I'd portrayed some very selfish and headstrong ideals. To accuse Adrien of disloyalty? I might as well have stabbed the man in the heart. How was I going to recover from that? I blew out a breath. I really fucked things up this time. How was I going to apologize yet again to the man who had been nothing but loyal since taking his oath?

I turned toward Adrien, our gazes locked for a second before he turned on his heel and walked away. "Adrien?"

He ignored me as he exited the inner sanctum. I shook my head. *Yep, it was going to take more than a simple, I'm sorry to break through that wall.*

A moment later, I followed Adrien back into the outer office. Alcie sat, head down, her nimble fingers flying across the keyboard as she transcribed notes into a computer file. As I walked past her, I noticed a slight pause in her typing as she fidgeted with the paperwork, seemingly unaware of our entrance. She glanced up briefly, saw me, and flushed bright pink and then buried her nose in the file as if by doing so she could avoid any conversation.

Was she afraid of repercussions from Adrien or me? Or was it guilt over her part in my unfortunate circumstances? Either way, she deserved to have her fears put to rest. I moved close to her and then leaned over, to catch her eye. "Alcie?"

When she finally looked up, her eyes were red with wet streaks running down her cheeks, and her nose appeared to have been rubbed raw by an overuse of tissues.

Great. The one thing that softened my heart quicker than anything else. Gods damn tears. "Listen, don't cry. You did what you had to do. I won't hold it against you, and neither will Adrien." She glanced over to where Adrien stood glaring at me. The sour look on his face spoke volumes.

"Are you sure? He looks really angry." Her voice trembled as a shiver caused goose bumps to stand up on her arms.

Reaching out, I rested my palm on her shaking hands. "He is not angry with you. I can assure you *that* look is because of me."

A grim frown creased her features. She pulled her eyes away from those of my angry Second, only to look up at me with wariness. "If you say so."

"I do." I patted her hands, hoping to put her at ease. "Don't worry yourself over it."

Alcie exhaled noisily, blowing out a long weary breath. She gave a timid, hesitant smile, withdrawing her hands from beneath mine. "I am terrified that he'll...you'll never forgive me for speaking to the Council."

"No worries, Alcie. None of this was your fault. We know that. You were put into an awkward position and really had no choice but to give them what they wanted."

"Yes, you must believe me, if I thought for a moment they would use what I told them against you, I never would have said a thing." If I'd had any doubt, the adamancy with which she spoke would have banished it.

"I believe you, Alcie, and I appreciate your willingness to take my side, although I would never have asked you to lie on my behalf. I've done nothing wrong, and the Council will know the truth of it soon enough. I'm not worried, so you shouldn't be either." I paused and then changed the subject. "Now, if you don't mind, I have a small favor to ask of you."

Her brows shot upward in immediate interest, obviously as eager to leave the topic as I was. "Certainly, signore. How can I help you?"

I glanced over my shoulder. Adrien stood with his back to us, leaning a shoulder against the wall as he picked something from beneath his fingernails. From his posture, he appeared to be completely oblivious to anything we were saying. *Good.* I turned my attention back to Alcie. "I'm going out tonight, and I would appreciate it if you could find me a map of the area."

Her eyebrows drew together as she seemed puzzled by the request. "Can you not look it up on your own computer or perhaps in the security office? I'm sure they would be more than pleased to give you directions."

I screwed up my mouth, unsure how much to tell her. Alcie seemed ready and willing to help. Was she someone I could trust with secrets? She might not wear the robes of a Council member, but she knew the inner workings of what went on behind closed doors and she held their ear. I had no doubt she had good intensions. As her actions had proven thus far, her loyalty to the Council would always be paramount. So, the prudent course of action was to proceed with caution. My voice dropped to a conspiratorial whisper, "Well, you see I need this to be discrete. I haven't talked to Adrien about my plans, and I don't want Security getting involved in my personal…*business.*"

Her eyes narrowed as her gaze intensified. "You're going after *him,* aren't you? That's why you can't talk to Security, and Adrien would tell you not to." Her jaw jutted out in a stubborn pout. "Well, I won't help you if that's the case."

By the way she'd stressed 'him' I knew exactly who she was referring to, the human the Council had practically accused me of offing. But, she couldn't be further from the truth. "No, Alcie, I'm not. I have no interest in going against the Great Council in that matter."

Her suspicious gaze pinned me to my spot as she assessed whether I was being truthful. "If you are even considering it I would have to advise against it. The Council would be furious if you disobeyed their direct order to not get involved."

"I know. Believe me, the last thing I need is another session with them." My tone was as flat and humorless as my mood had become.

She accepted my statement and exclaimed, "Ringrazi i Gii," which almost made me laugh aloud.

Thank the Gods? As if they had anything to do with it. It was purely self-preservation and common sense on my part which would keep me from dealing with the situation in the way I longed to. "If it eases your mind, I'm not even meeting a man. I am meeting a woman."

"Ah, an affare clandestino." A brief wistful look crossed her face. "Now I understand."

As a flash of Nix streamed through my mind, a shudder of revulsion rippled its way down my spine. *Not in this lifetime. I'd rather pull the nails from my fingertips with a pair of pliers than have even a flicker of interest in that woman.*

Of course, Alcie didn't know that. She merely assumed I was planning an illicit rendezvous, and who could blame her with the way I behaved toward her the other day. Best to set the record straight on that account as well. "It's not like that either, Alcie. After my meeting tonight, I will know exactly what happened to my brother, and Kin Retribution will finally be mine."

Her eyes widened, and her voice took on a sense of urgency. "You've found a lead then?"

"I have. My source wants to meet me alone, hence my need for secrecy and a map."

That served to remind her of the business at hand. "Of course. I didn't mean to pry." She turned back to her computer, her fingers poised for typing. "What's the address of where you are to meet?"

"I don't have an address. Just a location. Bomarzo. Specifically, the Parco dei Mostri"

She swiveled around until we made eye contact. "Parco dei Mostri? Why would you agree to meet her way up there...alone?"

"I think we've been through that already."

"Si. I understand what you've told me. But perhaps you do not understand. Bomarzo is out of Aliment territory. It is not safe for a Padrone to go there alone." She paused as she leaned in toward me. "The park is closed after dark and will be deserted.

You will be a sitting goose."

I nearly laughed at her misinterpretation of the colloquialism. "Duck."

"What?" Her confusion was even more humorous.

"The saying is a sitting duck, not a goose."

Her brow furrowed. "Duck or goose, what does it matter? Either way you will be in danger."

"Alcie, you worry like an old woman. I will be fine."

She shook her head adamantly. "No. I will not allow it." She glanced over to where Adrien stood. "It's much too dangerous for you to go alone. You *must* take him with you."

My chest expanded as I swallowed my mounting impatience. Why did everyone in my life insist I was incapable of taking care of myself? "Like I said, I'll be fine."

Alcie's face contorted into severe disapproval and shook her head. "Testardo, just like your brother."

It wasn't the first time I'd been called stubborn, and I was sure it wouldn't be the last.

The phone on her desk rang, and she automatically reached for the receiver. She held up a finger to indicate for me to wait a moment as she spoke into the handset.

"Ciao. Ciò è Alcie. Potete tenere prego?" There was a slight pause as she listened to the person on the other end. "Grazie."

Her manner became agitated and clipped as she punched a button on the phone to place the call on hold. She glanced up at me. "Promise me you will not go alone. You must take your Second." She paused, the intensity of her gaze reinforcing her words as she awaited my reply.

"I promise to consider it."

Her frown intensified, if that was even possible. "Jacen. You must promise me, or I will go straight in to the Council the moment you leave my office."

Fuck me. She knew how to hold a man hostage. "Fine. I promise I will make every effort to take someone along."

She gave a curt nod. "Good. Then once I have a moment, I will have a map sent up. You should get going. It's not a good idea to keep him waiting any longer."

I glanced over my shoulder and noted that Adrien was now staring impatiently at me. "Probably not."

She threw me a sympathetic look.

"Thanks, Alcie."

"Benvenuto." She gave a quick wave. "Ciao, Jace."

I moved away from the desk as she punched the button to release the holding call and turned her attention to the person on the phone. "Grazie per attendere."

When I turned my gaze locked with Adrien's. As I crossed the room, anxiety crept up my spine. The uncomfortable silence grew deafening as I walked past him. Instead of taking his customary place beside me, he waited to take a position behind me. As we traversed the hall and up the stairs, I couldn't help but wonder, was he deciding which ribs to stick a knife between?

Chapter Twenty-One

As the secret door slid open, I stepped out and allowed Adrien to take a place next to me in the short back hall of the villa. We walked together, though neither of us was willing to break the uncomfortable silence with any discussion of what had just happened.

Despite standing up for me with the Great Council, it was obvious he had no intention of reconciling our differences any time soon. And who could blame him? I insulted his honor and his loyalty, two things he could hardly be expected to forgive readily.

That was fine. I wasn't in a rush to hash out the details of our tumultuous relationship either. It had been a bizarre couple of hours and dealing with him would only compound the crazy. Besides, we would have plenty of time to discuss what happened last night and then this morning when we got back to the suite.

I stuffed my hands into the pockets of my jeans and dropped back to give him some room to brood. Then when he turned right and headed toward the stairs, I veered off in the direction of the Library.

A few moments later I swung the door inward. To my surprise the room was empty apart from the stalwart bartender who always seemed to be in attendance.

Crossing to the bar I addressed the man, "Anthony, a shot of *RUSh* please."

He wiped a shot glass and placed it down on the counter in front of me and then grabbed a fresh bottle from the shelf behind the counter. He uncorked it and poured a goodly amount into the small glass.

I immediately downed the shot and was once again caught off guard by the bite of the synthetic Adrena.

My vision blurred as the breath caught in my throat. I closed my eyes as my heart pounded as if it was trying to escape the confines of my chest. The skin on my arms tingled, the tiny hairs along their surface rising. A long drawn out shiver rose up my spine and buried itself beneath the hair at the top of my neck. Little involuntary quivers shook my entire being, causing me to grip the edge of the bar to control the tremors. The Adrena tripped every nerve ending and enlivened my senses, as it rocketed through my system at light speed.

With sudden clarity I knew it was quite possibly the most powerful Adrena I'd ever encountered.

Whatever they did to enhance the effects made natural Adrena tame in comparison. Where it took almost no time for the effects of the natural product to wear off, the longevity of *RUSh* seemed endless. It took several minutes for the effects to subside. When they did, an immediate need to experience the high again rushed through me.

I opened my eyes to find the bartender smiling at me. "Good?"

I chuckled. "You have no idea."

Anthony shrugged and wiped at the already spotless bar with a towel. "No, I really don't. We're not allowed to touch the *RUSh*. Can have anything else, just not the good stuff. Don't know why." Tossing the towel over his shoulder, he held up the frosted bottle and motioned with it. "Would you like another?"

"That's odd." Not odd at all really. If the synthetic sent my heart into palpitations who knew what effect it would have on a human heart. I moved the shot glass toward him. "Guess the Council prefers to keep the good stuff for themselves…and guests of course."

"And who am I to argue?" He poured the drink and then corked the bottle and placed it back on the shelf. "That's okay. It amuses me serve it."

My brow furrowed in confusion. "How so?"

He shrugged. "I can always tell when it's a superior batch." As he leaned back against the back counter, he folded his arms in front of him. "Take you for example. Just now you looked like you were in nirvana. You didn't look that way the first time you tried it. You enjoyed it, yes, but something in this batch made your blood sing."

Anthony was definitely right about that. My blood had sung, and I enjoyed every second of it. "Do you have any idea what gave this batch such a kick?"

He laughed and shook his head. "That my friend is

a well-guarded secret. I assume it is like most alcohol. Each batch is affected by a variety of factors, and dependent on the combination of those factors you get a different outcome."

That seemed to make sense. "Gotcha."

I downed the second shot and eased my way through the effects with relish. I could see the allure.

"Where's your partner in crime?"

My eyes flew open as I turned my head to see who'd spoken. My eyes narrowed as I recognized Vinny. "Most likely in our suite. At least that's where he seemed to be headed when I took a detour."

Vinny slid onto the stool next to me. "Ah. Okay." His lips pursed as he seemed to be trying to find something else to say.

Placing the shot glass on the counter, I sat back. "Is there something you need?"

"Well…" Vinny looked uncomfortable as he fiddled with a napkin lying on the bar. "I just…"

"Spit it out. What's happened?"

"I heard a rumor you were involved in an altercation with a human."

I rolled my eyes, leaned forward, and motioned for Anthony to fill up the shot glass one more time. "Good news travels fast, I see."

Vinny frowned. "Not good news."

I cocked a half-smile in sour humor. "Yeah, I know."

"No, you misunderstand." He stood up. "Would you mind stopping by security when you're done here? I have something I need to show you."

I paused in lifting the shot glass to my lips and glanced over at him, my eyebrow rising in curiosity. "You find out something more about Karina or the hacker?"

He cast a surreptitious glance toward the bartender and then leaned over a bit. "Not here. Come to security and we'll discuss things."

What was it with the Alimentatori in this country? Why did they all behave like everything was a matter of national security?

I shrugged silently to myself and downed the last shot. Once the effects mellowed, it left me in a relaxed state. I sighed contentedly. Whatever Vinny wanted, at least I'd be in a more amiable frame of mind.

"Lead the way, Vinman."

Several minutes later, we entered the security office.

This time I was greeted with no craziness. No one barking orders. No one running from console to console in panic. Just calm, quiet, steady work being done. As it should be.

I followed Vinny across the room and into the office I took from Karina.

He closed the door behind us and then crossed to the desk.

"If the Council knew about this, I'd probably be fired. Or worse."

My brow rose again as I stared at him from across the room.

Dropping to a knee, he opened the bottom right hand drawer. "When I gave Alcie a copy of the footage...." he bent over and reached back into the drawer. He seemed to struggle for a moment, then his hand emerged. "I didn't think they were going to use it against you."

He held up a shiny, silver disc which had tape across its surface.

Quickly closing the gap between us, I took the disc from him. "What's on it?"

Vinny shrugged. "It's footage from the interior and exterior cameras of Eros from last night. I made a copy before sending it down to Alcie, so she could give it to the Great Council."

I scowled. "Why the hell would you send the footage to them to begin with? It's not like anything happened."

He rose to meet my stare head on. "I had no choice, signore. They asked for it."

How had the Great Council known to request the footage?

A memory of Adrien talking to Alcie triggered a sudden realization. That's why she'd been so standoffish and afraid of our anger turning on her. She'd probably been the first to see the wanted poster, recognized me, and then had no choice but to inform the Council about the previous night's confrontation.

It would explain everything.

The poor girl had been caught between a rock and fucking hard place and did the only thing she could. She ratted us out.

I would have to confirm it the next time I saw her. For now, I had bigger fish to fry. My eyes narrowed suspiciously. "And you just decided to make a copy for your own amusement?"

"No. I was curious as to what they were looking for, so I viewed it first. Then when I saw it, I realized you needed to see it as well. So, I made a copy."

"Alright, then. Let's take a look at it shall we?" Pulling out the office chair, I paused. "Do you have a spare pair of glasses? Mine are in my room."

Vinny grabbed his glasses from the inside pocket of his sports coat. "You can use mine."

As the computer whirred to life, I donned the glasses and waited. Before long, I was in the midst of the first file. The interior footage showed exactly what I remembered. The woman striking out, nearly hitting me, the man, and my confrontation, his being escorted out. Really nothing of note.

The next file however, was the footage outside of Eros. The door of Eros opened, and I exited. Then several moments later Adrien exited at a run and joined me at the car. I watched our exchange seeing nothing alarming at all. Then, as the car pulled away from the curb, the human rushed out of the crowd and dashed toward where our car had just been. He stood, back to the camera, watching after us and then waved to a taxi. In excitement he shouted at the driver and pointed in the direction our car had gone, climbed in, and then was gone.

He'd followed us? A feeling of unease grew within me. *Why?*

I sat back staring off into space, considering the possible ramifications of the footage.

It was no wonder the Council suspected I'd done something to the man. He was last seen chasing after us. If I'd been investigating a disappearance of someone, I'd start with the people he'd pissed off and then followed as well. It was only logical.

But, there was one problem. I was innocent.

Sure, I had a whole slew of Cambiare who could attest to my whereabouts after driving away from Eros.

Of course, why hadn't I seen it sooner?

If the human had followed us all the way to Assisi in the hopes of getting even with me for humiliating him at Eros, he could have walked right into the same trap I had, but he wouldn't have had anyone to pull his ass out of the fire. The likelihood of him walking away, like I had, was non-existent, especially if he'd heard the exchange between me and the Cambiare.

Talking the glasses off, I folded them carefully and handed them back to Vinny. "Thank you, Vinny. I appreciate your loyalty."

He grasped the glasses and stuffed them back into his inner pocket. "What are you going to do, signore? The Great Council is sure to think you are responsible."

I groaned. "I'm sure you already know they requested my presence a couple hours ago."

"Si. I let you in through the door myself. I was hoping it wasn't about this." Vinny leaned back against the edge of the desk.

"Unfortunately, it was. And you're right. They do suspect me." I rubbed my jaw with a hand.

"You didn't, did you?" Vinny's whisper seemed to

echo in the room.

"Of course not," I snapped, tired of being accused of something I hadn't done. "I didn't even know he was following us."

"Did Adrien? I mean, would he have done something to the man if he thought you were in danger?"

Of course, under normal circumstances that was a completely logical question. But Vinny didn't know the whole story of where we'd ended up that night. He had no way of knowing I suspected Cambiare involvement. Nor could he, as that would require me to admit that I'd ventured into their territory without Council sanction. "I have no doubt Adrien would do whatever it took to protect me if he truly thought I was in danger." *Hell I had almost daily proof on that account.* "If he'd done something to the man, then he would have had a reason for it." I paused for effect. "However, I can't imagine Adrien would have had any need to do so. After all the man was merely a human. What possible danger could he have posed to me?"

Vinny's brow crinkled. "Did you not read the documentation I sent with Adrien about the Vuote?"

I snorted. "Oh, come on, Vinny. You can't seriously believe the Vuote have sent an assassin after me, in the heart of Alimentatori territory?"

His chin rose a touch as he appeared offended by the question. "You laugh at the suggestion, but you do not know them like I do. With the recent computer hacking, is it really that farfetched?"

He was right of course. I didn't know much about

the Vuote. However, I did know one thing for sure. "The Vuote like to use methods that keep their hands clean. They use high powered riffles and explosives. Nowhere in the footage did that man have a high-powered riffle, and my car didn't explode. Wouldn't you think that if he was out to assassinate me, it would have been easier for him to place a bomb in the car and then simply wait for me to come out of Eros and get in?"

Vinny thought for several moments and then nodded. "I see your point, signore. It is unlikely the Vuote would change procedures in order to go after someone who isn't important." As he realized he insulted me, his eyes grew wide, and he rushed on, "Oh, that's not to say that you're unimportant, signore. I just meant—"

I stood and held my hand up to stem the flow of apologetic words. "It's okay, Vinny. I know what you meant. And you're right. In the grand scheme of things, I am wholly unimportant. Hell, I'm not even a blip on the Vuote's radar, so they have no reason to be out to kill me and even less to be after Adrien." I extended my hand to him, and he gripped it in a strong handshake. "Thank you for allowing me the opportunity to see what you gave the Council. I know you didn't have to, and your loyalty is very much appreciated. At least now I understand why the Great Council suspects me."

Chapter Twenty-Two

Several minutes later I opened the door to the suite. Though I expected to find Adrien sitting on the couch, the room was empty. Glancing toward his end of the suite, it took a moment to realize why. His door was shut against any intrusion, and an empty dinner tray sat on the table just to the left of it.

Figures he'd chose to brood in his room. Guess I would be eating dinner alone tonight. Crossing to the phone, I let the door swing closed behind me.

I punched in the number for the butler's station and waited.

"Buona sera, signore. What can I do for you?" The older gentleman's aloof voice came over the handset. Why did he always take himself so seriously?

"Hey, Belvedere."

"Sir, I would appreciate it if you would cease calling me that ridiculous name. If you insist upon calling me by name, then I am Orsino."

It never failed. He always sounded as if he believed I was one of his master's redneck Kin. And boy did I enjoy tweaking him. "Orsino? Then why did you tell me your name was Belvedere?"

"But, signore, I never—"

"Never mind, it's not important." I interrupted him before

he could tell me he'd never told me his name and I'd just assumed it was Belvedere. I chuckled as I adopted an equally arrogant tone. "Call yourself whatever you want, Belvedere. You're not going to fool me. Now, bring me a dinner tray. I'm hungry." I hung up the phone before he had a chance to respond.

"You really enjoy giving that man grief, don't you?"

I turned around to find Adrien leaning against the doorframe of his room.

Shrugging, I crossed to the couch and then plopped down onto the soft surface. "I thought you weren't talking to me."

He joined me, taking a seat in the overstuffed chair opposite me. "Jacen, I—"

"No. Wait. Before you say anything, I have something I need to say." I paused, allowing myself a moment to think through what I wanted to tell him. "First off, I want to thank you for defending me to the Council. I know you had reason not to."

Adrien extended his legs out in front of him and crossed them at the ankles, while folding his arms over his chest. "No need to thank me. I did what any Second worth his salt would do for his Padrone."

"Be that as it may, I appreciated it. The Gods know I don't deserve it." I shifted uncomfortably under Adrien's hard stare. "Which leads me to my next point, I'm sorry about questioning your loyalty. I never should have done that. It's just...you have to understand how hard this is for me."

Adrien sighed as if he was exhausted by the sheer weight of the responsibility resting on his shoulders. Several minutes passed before he spoke. "Did you know Jules once told me you were meant for great things?"

I gave a snort of laughter and shook my head. "Yeah, right."

"No. Don't laugh. I mean it." He sat up, an intense look on his face. "Jules was my best friend and my Padrone, Jace. He was a good man—"

"He was a great man." I rushed to interrupt him before he finished his thought.

Adrien held up a hand to return the favor. "Yes, I know. But, he was a great man who believed in you." He leaned forward and propped a hand on his knee. "He always told me you had the potential to be a great leader."

I shook my head sadly and leaned back into the cushions of the couch. "Unfortunately, Julian always had a blind spot when it came to me."

He leaned back against the chair and folded his hands over his stomach. "Yeah, well I believed that too. In fact, I always thought you were spoiled, egotistical, and wouldn't know an honest day's work if it bit you in the ass."

My lips twisted into a severe frown. "Thanks for the vote of confidence."

He chuckled. "No problem."

"Is that it? That's all you wanted to tell me? That my brother believed in me, but you think I'm a lazy, egomaniacal prick?" *That's what I fucking get for apologizing. It never fails.*

Before he could answer a knock on the door interrupted our conversation.

Rising, I crossed to the door and ripped it open. Belvedere…Orsino entered with a tray laden with food, coffee, and a can of cola. He placed it on the table, turned and walked out without a word. Sitting down at the table, I cracked open the soda and poured it into the waiting glass. *No ice. Damn Italians.*

A moment later, Adrien joined me. I busied myself with my dinner, doing my best to ignore his presence.

For several minutes the only sound in the room was the clinking and scraping of utensils against the china plate. Then, Adrien spoke. "You didn't let me finish."

I swallowed the piece of steak I'd been chewing and took a sip of the cola. "I think you've said quite enough."

"Well, I respectfully disagree. You missed the point of what I was saying." He perched his folded arms on the table and leaned over them, his intense glare penetrating my attempts to further ignore him. "I said I *believed* those things. I didn't mean to imply that I still do."

I sat back to look him in the eye. "So, you don't think I'm an egotistical prick?"

"I never said you were a prick. That was your term." He met my glare straight on. "As far as egotistical, I was wrong. What I initially believed was ego I now understand is internal fortitude and pride. It's these same traits which get you into trouble. They make you believe you are invincible and must do everything alone." He paused. His gaze penetrated me as if willing me to pay particular attention to what he was saying. "You aren't indestructible, and you don't have to be alone, Jacen. Let me be here for you. Allow me to make things right in the only way I know how."

His tone wrapped around me, choking me with its sincerity. *Make things right? Not in this lifetime.* "I've got news for you, Adrien. Nothing you can do will ever make this right." I paused as bitterness rose within me. "You failed my brother. Why should I give you the chance to fail me as well?"

Adrien pulled back and sucked in a breath. I think I couldn't have hurt him more if I'd physically struck him. It didn't matter. I wanted him to hurt. I wanted him to feel the pain that I lived with every time I thought of Julian.

"So, that's what you think of me then? That I will fail you when the time comes?"

I didn't respond, just sat there stoically.

A look of sheer torment reflected in his eyes, before he raised a hand to rake it through his hair. "Jacen, I don't know how many times or in how many ways I can apologize for losing your brother. If you think for one moment I wouldn't go back to that night and sacrifice myself in his stead, then you don't know me at all." He paused shaking his head, fighting whatever emotions were running through him. "Perhaps that's the true issue here. You don't understand how the loss of Julian torments me."

My anger and bitterness overrode any compassion I might have otherwise felt. "Good. It should. You had one job to do and you failed. How am I supposed to forgive you for that?"

Once again he recoiled as if I'd struck him. Sorrow etched

his features as he stood up. "Then I will no longer ask for your forgiveness, Jacen."

He turned to walk back toward his room, but then paused and turned back toward me. "There is something you should know. I presented myself for consideration as your Second for a reason. I did it for Julian. Some time ago he extracted a promise from me that if something ever happened to him, I would protect you no matter what the consequences. And I did what I had to do to keep that promise."

"Bullshit. You didn't even know I was going to be Padrone when you jumped up to offer your services."

"Didn't I?" A strangled bark of astonished laughter erupted from him. "Who else would they have chosen, Jacen? Who else would the clan look to in their darkest hour? Of course, I knew. So, did Julian. We talked about it on numerous occasions. On one such occasion he extracted that promise from me."

In stunned silence I stared at Adrien. He'd known all along I'd be named Padrone and spoke up to claim the position of Second before I could appoint another? "You had to have known I wouldn't be pleased with you as a Second. In fact, I accepted you because it was easier than going through the drawn-out process of selecting another."

"Yes, I knew that. I realized if I spoke up in front of the clan and offered my service, you had little choice but to consider me. To do anything else would have publicly ostracized me. It was a risk. Certainly, one I was willing to take to see my oath to your brother through. I counted on your impatience to be on your way to drive you to accept my bid. I was hoping if you took me as your Second then you and I could avenge your brother's death together. What I didn't count on was your stubbornness. I expected anger, bitterness, maybe even a bit of resentment. I willingly accepted those as the consequences of my own failure. Only I never expected you to throw caution to the wind like you had nothing left to live for."

I dropped the fork to the table and pushed myself back. "And what have I to live for beyond revenge, Adrien?"

Adrien's face reddened with anger as he glared at me.

"Foolishness with your own life is intolerable, and I will no longer stand for it. Every time you run off on your own you risk not just your life but the life of *our* Padrone. You need to remember there is more at stake than just whether you come home, Jacen. When I said you were not alone, I didn't mean just me. You have a clan awaiting your return. They need a strong, capable leader. Which brings me right back to my initial point, you are that leader, even if you can't see it quite yet. Julian believed in you. So, do I."

With that he turned and exited the room, closing the bedroom door quietly behind him.

*****

You are that leader. Julian believed in you. So, do I.

Those were words I'd never imagined hearing, especially not from Adrien.

I closed the door of my room and stood in quiet contemplation.

What was I supposed to do with that? I hadn't asked for any of this and had none of the requisite skills to embrace their faith in me.

The thought of the clan awaiting my return...Nathanial, Magda, even Eustis deserved a leader they could look to for guidance and strength. In my impatience I accepted the position of Padrone without thought. The fact was, I never really thought about anything except how Julian's death had affected me. I had been selfish and completely unwilling to think beyond my own need for vengeance.

Bah! If I had any hope of seeing this through, I needed to stay focused on the task at hand and not get bogged down in the responsibility of what might come next.

Chapter Twenty-Three

Easier said than done.

I walked out on to the veranda and crossed to the railing. The smell of moisture lay heavy in the air as the approaching storm blacked out the moon. Occasional wisps of moonlight peeked out from behind the angry clouds in a desperate battle to illuminate the water below.

I leaned against the railing, gazing out at the dark choppy waves of the lake as they rolled and churned to shore. Lightening ripped across the sky. I stuffed my hands into the pockets of my black jeans.

Lake Bracciano's stormy mood reflected my own turmoil.

The past hour I'd pondered what came next and came to a difficult decision.

Movement beside me warned that I was no longer alone. Sensing the familiar presence, I didn't need to look to know Adrien had joined me.

"You're right, you know." My whisper was muffed by the thunder which had finally arrived.

"About what?"

Keeping my eyes on the horizon, I gripped the railing as if to let go would cause me to stumble. "I've been contemplating our conversation. And you're right. The clan deserves a leader they can look to for guidance, but that leader is not me. I should never have agreed to step into my brother's shoes. Not when I did so only as means to an end. It dishonors his memory and everything he worked so hard for." I turned toward him to meet his gaze. "If I survive tonight, I plan to resign my position, which will in turn release you from your oath to me and void the contract I signed with the Great Council."

Adrien's disappointed frown said it all. "Why? Why would you even suggest that Jace?"

"Because it's the only honest way to honor my brother's memory. To pretend that I can be him is disrespectful. It's better if the clan appoints someone who can be the leader they need."

"You're wrong, Jacen. The honest way to honor your brother's memory is for you to rise to the occasion and be the person he believed you to be. Running away from your responsibilities and pretending it's for the greater good is just more of the same selfish bullshit you've always relied on. Don't you think it's about time for you to grow the fuck up and realize that the only one who thinks you can't do this is you?"

I cast a glare out to the stormy lake, looking for solace but finding none. "That's just it. I don't want to be the person everyone looks to. I don't *want* to be Julian."

"No one is asking you to be Julian. We are asking that you accept who you are and who you are destined to be."

"And who is that, Adrien?" I glared at him knowing even he didn't have the answer to that question.

He spoke softly with a confidence I wish I held. "The leader of our clan. *Our* Padrone."

In that moment I saw it, that special something Julian had always known resided within this man. "No wonder Julian liked you. You don't pull your punches and you say exactly what you mean even if it's not popular."

"Yes, well those traits have gotten me into more scrapes than I care to remember, and Julian liked me because I reminded him of you. He couldn't have you as a Second, so he took me instead."

I blinked several times. The revelation mystified me. "Really?"

"Yes, really. You were too young to become a Second and you were his brother. He couldn't risk your life just to have you with him all the time."

"I...I never knew that." I glanced away feeling suddenly vulnerable. I took a deep breath. The moist air filled my lungs as I studied the play of seagulls darting away from the gathering storm clouds, searching out a safe haven for the rest of the night. "It seems there is still so much I didn't know about him."

"You knew what mattered. He was your brother, and he loved you. What else is there to know?"

Normally I would have agreed with that assessment, but then, there was something Adrien hadn't been told.

The faintest sound of thunder rolled across the land as the storm moved ever closer.

"We didn't smell alike, Adrien."

"What the fuck are you talking about?" Adrien moved to my side and nudged my arm with his elbow in what I could only guess was an attempt at camaraderie.

I met his gaze. "It seems we were not brothers after all. Brothers share a similar scent and we, Julian and I, did not."

"That's absurd. Who told you that?" Adrien's angry voice vehemently denied what I'd already come to accept.

"Nix."

"Who the fuck is Nix and what business is it of his?" Adrien's enraged tone spoke clearly of what he thought about the person who'd put those thoughts in to my head.

"Nix is the Cambiare woman, the one I've played cat and mouse with since arriving."

"And you believed her?" His incredulous response made me question my own sanity. "Come on, Jacen. She's just trying to rattle your cage."

I shrugged and glanced up at the sky as the first rain drops hit the top of my head. "Possibly, but who cares? Julian and I were brothers in every way that truly mattered." Adrien followed me as I walked back through the French doors. As the rain began to fall in earnest, I closed the portal. "Now, if you don't mind, I have to go."

Adrien's eyes narrowed. "Where are you going this late at night?"

I considered making something up to keep him from tagging along, and then thought better of it. There had been enough feuding over me leaving him behind without causing more issues. "I am meeting Nix about an hour north of here at the Park of the Monsters."

"Were you planning on telling me about this meeting?" His eyebrow rose as he awaited my answer with interest.

"Not initially. However, I've since come to realize it's not so bad having you hanging around."

He chuckled at that. "About time."

"There is one catch though…"

His humor faded as quickly as it had emerged. "And that is?"

"You have to stay with the driver in the car."

Adrien's frown intensified. "No. I'm sorry, but no, I won't do that."

"You don't have a choice. I told Nix to come alone. It is only fair that I do so as well." I crossed the room to the desk and picked up the necklace she dropped and then stuffed it into the pocket of my jeans. "If you want to come along, then those are my terms."

"Fine. Have your phone open and your finger on speed dial. That way if she's not alone, I can—"

"Yes, I know. Then you can swoop in and save the day." I frowned as if angry over the slight. Surprisingly, I didn't really mind the jab. "And who says I have your number on speed dial anyway?"

Adrien grinned. "Does Lois Lane have Superman on speed dial?"

"I'm Lois Lane in this scenario?"

"Hey, if the pencil skirt fits."

"You see, now I'm torn. Should I be more appalled at being referred to as a damsel in distress or by the fact that you know what Lois Lane wore?"

Chapter Twenty-Four

As we approached the village of Bomarzo, Adrien and I discussed a strategy for the night's encounter.

I glanced down at the map Alcie had sent up to me. It was a colored illustration…not at all to scale, though well enough drawn for me to have a good understanding of the layout of the park. "Here's what I'm thinking, you wait here." I pointed to an area outside the entrance of the park. "I have to go all the way in…," my index finger followed the line of the path until it reached the picture of the statue, "to here. She's supposed to be waiting for me at the mouth of Orcus."

The divider between the front seat and the back slid down interrupting our discussion momentarily. "We should be there in about ten minutes, signore." The driver spoke over his shoulder as he guided the car along the highway.

"Very good. Thank you, Sergio." I turned my attention back to the map.

Adrien sat back shaking his head. "I don't like it, Jace. Where you want me to wait is hell and gone from where you're going to be. The parking lot is too far away from Orcus for me to be of any help if you need me."

"Well, I don't see that we have much choice. The statue is

where it is and that's at the back of the park."

"Then I will go with you into the park. You can leave me…," he leaned forward and pointed to the drawing indicating the Pegasus fountain, "right here. I'll wait by the fountain."

"No. You can't accompany me into the park. If she knows I didn't come alone she'll bolt, and I'll be damned if I'll let her escape again." My tone was stilted and unmoving.

"Might I make a suggestion, signore?" Sergio's question once again drew my attention away from planning.

My gaze met his in the rear-view mirror for a moment. "Yes. What is it?"

"Perhaps it is not my place to interfere, but don't you think going in through the front gate might be a bit…obvious?"

I screwed up my mouth in consideration. "I suppose so. I intended to stick to the forest as much as possible and reveal myself once I'm sure she's alone."

"Ah, very good signore. But…" It was obvious he had more to say.

"But what, Serg? Do you have another idea?" I was open to any suggestion that didn't require Adrien to tag along or have me walking into a trap.

"Si, signore. There's another road. It runs along the southwestern side of the park. Most people don't go that way. It's very secluded. I believe if we park there, you can slip into the park with less difficulty and completely unseen."

I thought about it for a moment. Glancing down at the map, I considered his suggestion. "If we were to do this, where would it bring me out?"

"There is a wide field between the road and the park. If you cross the field, at the other end sits the Temple. From there it is not far to the Ogre."

"Am I to assume that the Ogre and Orcus are the same?"

He chuckled. "Si, signore. Some call it Orcus. Some call it Ogre. I've even heard it referenced as the la bocca dell'inferno."

The Mouth of Hell. Perfect. I'd be sure to cast her into it then.

Once again perusing the map, I located the Temple and then found where Orcus sat in reference to it. It certainly seemed a much shorter route than trekking through the middle of the park. It would cut down on time. Even more beneficial was the fact that my arrival from an unexpected direction might buy me the element of surprise.

Confident that Sergio's suggestion was the best way in I folded the map and set it aside. "Okay. Sounds perfect. Let's do it."

My fingers tapped against the walking stick lying across my lap as I stared out the tinted window.

Several minutes later Sergio pulled the car over on the side of the road.

This was it. In a matter of moments, I would be face to face with Julian's killer and only one of us would walk away.

I reached for the door handle and then paused as Adrien's hand shot out and grabbed my arm. His gaze fluttered to the front compartment of the car as our driver opened his door and got out. His door closed quietly, and Adrien returned his attention to me. He leaned over and spoke in hushed tones, "Are you sure about this? I really have a bad feeling about you going in alone."

I cocked a half smile. "Relax. I've got this. Before you know it, I'll be back, and we can go home."

He released me and sat back against the seat. "Fine, but if you're not back in an hour, I'm coming looking for you."

I'd be back well before the hour mark. After all, how long could it take to skin a cat? I shrugged. "Suit yourself."

Sergio's feet ground the gravel as he circled the car to my door. Opening it for me, he waited for me to emerge. I climbed out and moved away from the car to the edge of the field. A moment later he joined me. He pointed out across the darkness. "If you head that direction you'll come to the boundary of Parco dei Mostri. Just after that the Temple."

The moon shone brightly so there would be little cover until I reached the park which shouldn't pose much of an issue as Nix would be waiting within the park and wouldn't expect him from this direction. "Okay, got it. Thanks, Serge."

Several minutes later, I landed with a soft thud on the opposite side of the boarder wall. *So far, so good. No sign of anyone.*

Remaining in a crouch, I froze in position and studied the darkness surrounding me. My head cocked to the side as I listened for any unusual sounds. Nothing but night sounds and no unusual movements in the shadows. The large black mass which rose ahead of me was obviously the Temple. Rising, I inched my way forward. In a matter of minutes, I'd crossed the divide between the boundary and the Temple.

A few more minutes and I'd be staring at the mouth of hell and seconds away from extracting my revenge. My fingers flexed on the walking stick ready for action, as grim determination gripped me. I nimbly released the catch on the hidden dagger and eased it from the sheath. Better to be prepared just in case the element of surprise was somehow compromised.

At a slow, stealthy pace I kept to the shadows. As I neared the area where I thought the statue would be, I paused to listen again. A slight stirring to the right caught my attention. Glancing in the direction where the sound had originated, I trained my eyes on the darkness. *Nothing.* Perhaps it had been a small animal of some kind. Dismissing it, I continued my trek forward knife in hand, ready for battle.

A few yards further and another huge black shadow sprang from the Earth. My eyes focused on it and separated it from the darkness around it. The great stone face loomed over the path like a giant, evil demon, its mouth gaping open to devour any unlucky visitor. The sight sent a chill coursing down my spine. *Orcus, the mouth of hell.*

Hesitant to emerge from the deep shadows two great trees cast as they blocked the moonlight, I hung back and scanned the area for even the smallest of movements. As I watched a shadow on the stairs, just at the base of the mouth, shifted.

Nix.

She lounged on the middle step with her legs extended outward, crossed at the ankles and her arms pitched backward holding her up. She seemed so relaxed and blissfully unaware of being watched that I had to wonder if she knew something I didn't.

No matter. In her current position it would take her too long to react to an attack. Inching my way forward, I reveled in the knowledge that the moment was finally upon me. She'd be dead before she knew what happened.

I raised the knife and moved forward.

Her laughter broke the silence, and I froze in place.

"Are you truly so ignorant of my species, Aliment? Do you not realize I can smell your presence? Not to mention my eyesight is better than yours. So, if you can see me. I can most assuredly see you."

Angry at the thwarted attempt at ambush, I rose to my full height and pushed my way forward through the low hanging branches. "Just making sure you were alone."

She chuckled again. "I do not have to read your thoughts, Jacen of Samsaveel, to know what you were about. Did I not promise to come alone?"

"And I was to trust the word of a Cambiare? I think not."

She brought her knees up and leaned forward, her golden eyes reflective like those of a wild animal peering at me from the darkness. "I would never have allowed you to get close enough. I smelled your scent on the breeze and knew you were here, even before you appeared near the path." She studied me from her relaxed position for a moment. "You should know that if I wanted you dead, it would have been an easy matter many times over. I believe you know this. I didn't kill you when I stood over your bed while you slept. Nor did I follow you out of Eros that first night and corner you in an alley like a rat. Perhaps you should ask yourself why we did not kill you when you strayed into our territory. If we are such cold-blooded killers, why do you still breathe?" She paused and cocked her head as if listening carefully. In a fraction of a second her manner turned from relaxed to alert. Lifting her nose into the air, she hissed at something unseen.

Perfect. Something had distracted her. *Time to make my move.* I ran full bore across the paved pathway. In response, Nix shot to her feet. In the blink of an eye she turned and fled up the stairs then disappeared in the darkness to the right of Orcus. I leapt up the stairs effortlessly and turned in the direction she'd taken. A sound at the opposite end of the clearing caught my attention, causing me to pause. An instant later, something whizzed past my face, narrowly missing me, and ricocheting off the stone edifice of Orcus. As a second muffled gunshot sounded from the same direction I dove for cover…into the mouth of hell.

It took a second to realize what was happening. When I did anger ignited. I'd been ambushed yet again and this time they seemed intent on killing me. *Gods damned lying bitch.*

I clung to the wall of the opening and peered around the edge of the mouth. Another shot ricocheted far too close for comfort and I pulled back further into the hole.

Fucking great! She has me pinned down with absolutely nowhere to go.

There was only one option, call in the cavalry. I sheathed the dagger and pulled out my phone. Before I could hit speed dial, a loud ruckus erupted several yards away. The sound of a man's scream echoed against the stone surrounding me. I inched my way to the opening and cautiously peered out. No bullets careened toward me. Nothing ricocheted nearby, just the sounds of scuffling in the bushes.

Suddenly, the man's weapon hurtled through the night, striking the stone steps with such violence the impact shattered the stock and bent the barrel.

A satisfied smirk spread over my face. Apparently, the cavalry was already here. Leave it to Adrien to disobey my order to stay in the car. Frankly, I was glad he had.

I bolted out of the hell mouth and was about to head into the fray, when a terrified scream pierced the air. Next thing I knew the would-be assassin was unceremoniously and forcefully ejected from the bushes. He crumpled in a heap at the base of the stairs. His moans indicated that he was still alive, which was good because I needed him breathing.

Jogging down the last couple of stairs, I sidestepped the broken weapon and came to a stop next to the writhing man. Thrashing in the bushes alerted me to the fact that my Second was emerging so I glanced up to greet him. "Nice work, Adri—"

My words trailed off as the bushes parted and Nix emerged. Her eyes flashed with fury as she made a beeline for the injured man. "Figlio di puttana! Fottuto vuote anime."

Wait, what? My mind reeled. This didn't make sense. Why would she save my life if she truly wanted me dead?

"I told you, Jacen. We are not your enemies. He and his kind are."

"Humans?"

"Anime Vuote. They usually work alone. So, I'm confident he's the only one out there. At least for now."

Stunned for a moment my brow knit together. Vuote was after me? Why? What had I done to place myself on their hit list?

Nix knelt and ripped off the night vision goggles the human wore, leaving him temporarily blind while his sight adjusted to the change. Grabbing the injured man by the hair, she turned his face toward me, she asked, "He was following you the other night as well. Do you know him?"

Though his face was bleeding and puffy, I immediately recognized him. "Yes, unfortunately, I do. He was in Eros the other night. I had him escorted out."

The man growled and then spit blood and saliva in my direction, obviously meaning it as an insult. "Fucking, Aliment scum."

I raised my leg and gave him a swift kick to the ribs. "Shut the fuck up. No one was talking to you."

He grunted in response, remaining defiant, eyeing me with hatred.

Nix let his head go and it smacked down onto the stone path. "I say we kill him and leave him in the countryside to rot."

I chuckled at the barbaric thought, amused by her blood lust as it seemed to match my own. "As much as I would love to do so, I can't."

Nix rose and glared at me as if I'd fallen short of her

expectations somehow. "Afraid of human retaliation?"

I raised my chin and straightened my back, offended by the suggestion. "Not in the least. Unfortunately, he's caused me too much trouble already, and his death would just make matters worse." Dropping to a knee, I flipped him to his back and then looked up at her. "You wouldn't happen to have something to bind his hands, would you?"

She frowned at me obviously put out by my refusal to kill the human. Reaching back to the pony tail in her hair, she extracted the black ribbon she'd used to tie it back and handed it to me. "Are you planning on taking him with you?"

"Yes. Unfortunately, I need him alive to be able to clear my name with local authorities. So, I'm going to turn him over to the Great Council and let them deal with it from there. Once they see he's still alive, and relatively unharmed, they can turn him over to our contact in the local police department. What they do with him from there, I don't give a shit. As long as I'm cleared of his disappearance."

"Fine. Do what you must." She crossed over to sit down again. "If he'd been shooting at me, he'd already be dead."

After the man's hands were securely tied behind his back, I joined her on the steps. Leaving a wide gap between us, I took a seat next to here.

We sat in tense silence for several moments, neither of us knowing what to say next. My fingers toyed with the catch on the walking stick as my mind wandered. Was it possible that all this time we'd been wrong in assuming the Cambiare's guilt? From day one we'd been so certain, but now I was no longer sure—about anything. If it wasn't her or any other Cambiare, then who was it? A severe frown spread over my features. *Damn it. All this time wasted on a wild goose chase.* I was back at square one and none too pleased about it.

"Are you still going to kill me?"

Her softly spoken words startled me. I'd nearly forgotten she sat next to me. Straightening my back, I extended one leg out in front of me and brought the other up in a casual position. Crooking an arm over the bent knee, I looked over at her to find her studying my features. "Hardly seems neighborly after you just saved my life." Her brow scrunched together as she stared at me, apparently unsure what I'd meant. "No. Not at present."

"Good, because I would defend myself, and I don't want you to get hurt."

That brought a chuckle from me. "And you think you could take me?"

Her bright eyes blinked as a look of innocent sincerity came over her. "Of course. Did I not just toss a man from there," she pointed to the bushes she'd emerged from and then to the man lying at our feet, "to here?"

"Ah, yes, but he is merely human."

She shrugged. "Human or Aliment, what does it matter. You both fly efficiently when given incentive."

"Hey, now, I thought we were trying to be nice to each other."

She laughed as she leaned back in the same manner she'd been when I'd come upon her. As her long neck extended and her head tilted upward, thick hair, freed from any binding, cascaded like a luxurious river of ebony down her back brushing the stone steps. "I thought I was being nice. After all, I said I didn't want to hurt you."

I watched her for a moment, curious about the woman whom I'd believed was a beast. Moonlight touched her features setting her eyes on fire like the mysterious twinkling stars she watched, and I could find nothing within her countenance to affirm my previous belief. But, then again, her kind was dangerous in a whole different way. With eyes like liquid gold she was a dangerous beauty, able to devour a man whole. The phrase rushed through me as if carried on the wind. A shiver coursed down my spine.

Was she truly not guilty of Julian's murder? Nothing she'd done thus far spoke of someone willing to kill for the sheer joy of doing so Had Julian been attracted to her as well? Had Julian done something to set her off, like the human at our feet? I couldn't imagine that would be the case.

"He was my friend, you know." Her quiet words broke through my thoughts.

"What? Who was?"

"Julian." She pulled up her knees and wrapped her arms around them, pulling them tight against her chest.

She'd done it again, entered my mind without me even knowing she was there. How the hell did she do that? I shot to my feet and paced for a moment, anger welling up in me again. "You'll have to excuse me if I don't believe you. Everything I've been told says otherwise."

"Then what you have been told is not the truth." Her gaze met mine head on, unflinching. "Julian and I met at Eros. He was kind and understanding. He was going to help me…" Her voice trailed off as her gaze shot passed me to the forest where I'd first emerged. "Someone's coming." She rose and looked at me accusatorily. "You aren't alone."

I put my hands up in innocence. "It's probably my Second. I told him to wait in the car, but I've been gone awhile, and he worries like an old woman."

She nodded relaxing. "He wishes to protect you."

"Yes. He does." I walked over to her and turned to face the woods, awaiting Adrien's arrival. "He and Julian were very close."

"Then I should go. He will want me dead too and I have no desire to explain myself yet again." She turned from me and darted away.

I reached out and grabbed her by the wrist. "Wait."

She paused, staring up at me with the most beautiful eyes I'd ever seen. Her scent enveloped me like it had outside of the basilica. Somewhere in the back of my mind I knew I was being foolish, trusting her because she'd slayed my dragon, but I couldn't help myself. I leaned in until her lips were a mere hairsbreadth from mine. As our lips touched, passion ignited within me. I pulled her toward me. Her left breast pressed against my chest and her hip brushed against me setting fire to my blood. I swallowed, mesmerized by the contact of our bodies, her breath against my lips, drowning in her scent.

Then suddenly the contact was broken as she pushed away from me. Her hand went to her lips and her eyes questioned me. Breaking free from my grasp she turned on a heel and ran into the darkness. In the next instance the night swallowed her whole leaving no trace behind.

I stood there for a moment, stunned by what I'd just done. It was surreal. I'd come her to kill her and ended up kissing her. What in the hell was wrong with me? Had I completely lost my mind?

"Jace?" Adrien's urgent whisper broke my concentration.

I turned back to the task at hand and waited for Adrien to appear. "Yeah. I'm here."

"Thank Aita. I thought something had happened to…" His gaze came to rest on the human laying on the ground. "What the hell happened?"

"Adrien, meet…" I glanced down at the man trussed up like a holiday turkey. "I'm sorry I didn't get your name. Never mind it's not important." I grinned at Adrien. "He's Vuote and he tried to kill me."

"What?" The question exploded from him as he rushed forward.

I stepped between the two to stop Adrien from taking his anger out on the vulnerable man. "Take it easy. I've handled it."

A snort came from the man at our feet. "You've handle it? I dare say *she* handled it while you cowered in the mouth of a statue." I kicked backwards landing the blow on the other side of his ribs. He huffed yet managed a laugh at the same time. "I know. Shut the fuck up."

Adrien's eyebrow rose in curiosity. "She?"

"Yeah. It's a long story. I'll tell you on the ride home if you'll help me get him back to the car." I moved aside to let him assess the situation.

His brow crinkled in confusion. "And just what are we going to do with him?"

"I figured we'd present him to the Great Council as a gift. He's already wearing a ribbon."

When we crossed the open field heading back to where we'd left Sergio, I noticed right away that he'd managed to turn the limo around in anticipation of our leaving. *Excellent.* The quicker we could be on the road and heading back to the villa, the better I'd feel about the evening.

As we approached the road, Sergio moved to hold the door of the back open. He stopped just short of doing so when he noticed we had a human in tow. Crossing the road, I shoved the man ahead of us and addressed the driver, "Put him in the trunk."

The Brit turned his head to glare at me. I simply raised an eyebrow, daring him to say a word.

"In the trunk, signore? But why?"

My teeth ground together in vexation. How many times was I going to have to say the same thing tonight? "He's Vuote, and he tried to kill me."

The look on Sergio's face changed immediately. Doing as requested, he preceded to pop open the trunk and waited.

Figuring Adrien would be more than happy to deal with the Vuote bastard I opened the door and climbed into the backseat.

The car dipped as the human was shoved into the trunk, and the door slammed shut.

A moment later Adrien climbed in the opposite side, and the driver took his seat up front.

"Serge, call ahead and have security meet our car. I want to turn over that Vuote bastard as soon as we arrive."

He glanced in the rearview mirror and acknowledged my request with a nod. "Si, signore."

Within minutes we were on the road. My head dropped back to lie on the headrest and I expelled a tired breath. It had been a crazy night and not in the way I'd expected.

"So, you want to explain to me what happened back there?"

I motioned for him to hold on for a second and leaned forward to speak to the driver, "Hey, Serge, would you mind putting up the divider? I need to talk to my Second in private."

In response the driver reached over and pushed the button

sending the divider sliding upward.

I relaxed back into the seat. "Thank you."

"Siete benvenuti."

Once the divider was in place, I turned to look Adrien in the eye.

When Nix told me that she and Julian were friends, the shock I felt was twofold. First, of course was wondering why. Why had he befriended someone who was an enemy to the Aliments? Second, my thoughts had flown to Adrien. How could Julian and Nix possibly have been friends without Adrien knowing anything about it? It just wasn't possible, was it?

"Before I tell you the whole sordid story, I need you to answer a question I have."

"Shoot. I'm an open book." Adrien turned his body to lean against the door.

I screwed up my mouth. There was just no easy way to do this. "Adrien, I need to know the truth about Julian's relationship with the Cambiare."

Adrien shifted in his seat. "What do you mean? What relationship?"

I took a deep breath, preparing myself for confronting him with my next statement. "Nix told me that Julian was her friend." I paused to let the information sink in, then continued, "Can you tell me how that is even possible?"

"It's not."

My fingers wrapped around the walking stick as I ignored the urge to question him more aggressively. "She said they met at Eros."

"Again, not possible. He was completely faithful to Magda. In fact, he only ever met one woman at Eros that even interested him, and she was…" He seemed to get lost in thought. Then his hands balled into a fist and he glared out the window. "Oh fuck."

Obviously, he'd remembered something crucial. "What?"

"It didn't dawn on me until just now." He shook his head, still stunned by whatever memory he'd just experienced.

Impatience was starting to take hold. "What is it?"

"That night you ran out of Eros and I was left standing there, I thought I recognized the woman standing next to you and now I know why."

"She was the woman Julian took home."

"Yes and no. She was the woman, but Julian never slept with her." For some reason his answer pleased me. At least until he followed it with a disclaimer. "Or at least he didn't that night."

Brushing aside any emotion, I redirected the conversation. "So, it's possible the two of them were friends."

"No, that's still pretty improbable. He was with his mentor most of the time, and during his spare time he was with me."

Frustrated by the answer, I grumbled, "There wasn't any time he ventured off by himself?"

Adrien chuckled. "No, Jace. He wasn't you. He actually enjoyed having me around."

I gave him a cool smile. "Yes, well, you're growing on me."

He laughed again then said, "I don't know whether to be flattered or afraid."

"Jackass." I chuckled then sobered. "But seriously, wasn't there any time he had to himself? Did he ever disappear for long walks around the grounds or make time for mysterious meetings? Anything?"

He thought for several minutes and then shook his head. "No. He really didn't. He was just not into venturing off on his own. If he left the villa, I was with him."

I racked my brain for...*for what? A reason to believe her?* It hardly seemed possible that this morning my first thought was slitting her throat and tonight I was looking for reasons not to.

"There is really no way they could have been friends, Jace. Truthfully the only time he was ever alone was when he retired for the night."

I closed my eyes as enlightenment dawned. "She knew exactly how to get in."

"Get in where?" Adrien's response startled me.

Glancing over at him I shrugged. "Sorry. I was talking to myself."

"Anything important?"

I nodded, lost in thought. "Yeah. Maybe."

"Okay. Mind sharing?"

Shaking myself out of the daze, I glanced over at him. "Remember that night she was in my room?" He nodded in response. "She knew exactly how to get in undetected. I now realize it's because she had done it before. My bedroom was Adrien's room. I think they were secretly meeting at night." For some reason that last bit really pissed me off. "There is no other explanation."

"Or there's always the possibility that she's lying." Adrien stuck to his guns. "I don't understand why you're so quick to believe her, Jacen."

"Because it no longer makes sense to me, Adrien. When I came over here, everything you told me, everything Gino read to me—it all fit together in a nice, neat little package. After meeting her face to face, I don't know. She saved my life tonight and she didn't have to. He was gunning for me, had me pinned down with no way out, and she could have left, but she didn't. If it weren't for her, I might very well be dead."

The muscle in Adrien's jaw ticked as he worked through the information I'd just imparted. When he spoke, it was slow and deliberate. "I should have been there."

"Don't." I stopped him from any further speech. "Don't even go there. You did exactly what I told you to do, and I was literally a second away from calling you when she intervened."

He shook his head. "Doesn't matter. My place was with you."

"And what would you have done. Adrien? Taken a bullet for me?" My tone expressed how absurd the thought was.

"Absolutely. If it came down to putting myself between you and an assassin's bullet, yes. Unequivocally."

Adrien's quick forceful response took me aback. It wasn't every day someone told you they valued your life over their own and meant it. "You'd really do that?"

"Of course. It's what I've been trying to tell you all along.

I'm your Second and I take my duty seriously. I failed your brother. I will *not* fail you."

I stared at him in stunned silence. Somehow all those times he told me he would have given his life to save Julian, I'd doubted it. Down deep inside, I had believed the worst of him and never gave him a chance to prove himself to me. His reaction tonight forced me to take another look. "Well, then I am glad I made you stay in the car, because both of us managed to live out the day."

"Yeah, well don't ever ask me to do that again, because next time you might not have Nix to come to your rescue."

I held my hands up in surrender. "I know, and I won't. Like I said, you're growing on me."

"About fucking time. You really made me work for it, didn't you?"

I laughed. "Hey, you know what they say, if it's worth having, it's worth working for. And I can tell you, I'm completely worth it."

"Oh no conceit in that statement at all."

"Nope, none."

Chapter Twenty-Five

The next morning, as I descended the stairs to the first level, I noticed Gino sitting on the bottom riser. Stopping on the step next to him, I nudged him with a foot. "Hey Gino, how're you doing?"

He glanced up at me with a frown. "Buon pomeriggio, signore. Mi sto annoiando e tu?"

"I'm doing well. Thank you for asking." I took a seat next to him on the stair.

"Very good. You are learning Italiano already."

I chuckled at the boy's exuberance over my understanding of the simple phrase. "Si. Who knows? Maybe one day soon I will be able to read from those dusty old books by myself." I winked at Gino, making him laugh.

When Adrien came down a few seconds later, he stopped and leaned against the banister. Ignoring the impatient look he wore; I gave Gino my full attention. "So, nothing to do this morning? Shouldn't you be in school or playing with friends?"

The boy shrugged in a bored manner. "It's Saturday and all my friends are at a party. I wanted to stay home so I could go with them, but Papà wouldn't let me. He and Mama have much to do today and wanted me left here where I would be safe." He rolled his eyes expressing his opinion on the matter clearly.

"I see. Missing a party is never fun."

He nodded and put his chin on his knees in abject misery. "I'm to stay out of trouble while they are gone."

"Do you get into trouble a lot?"

His demeanor changed as he turned his head to look up at me with an impish grin. "Sì, signore. Too much trouble. Papà calls me furberia coniglio." The name was said with pride as if it were a badge of honor.

"Cunning rabbit?"

His grin grew even wider. "Sì, signore."

"Well, I am sorry you weren't able to be with your friends today. Maybe you can find something fun to do around here to keep you busy until your parents return for you."

He shrugged, returning his chin to his knees, and adopting the look of a bored twelve-year-old again.

"I know you said Leo has much to do, but do you know when your father will return for you?"

"Not for many hours."

"Alright, I will have to talk to him when he gets back." I grasped the railing and pulled myself to my feet. Turning, I glanced down at Gino's dejected face. Reaching down I ruffled his hair. "It was nice to see you again, Gino. Please tell your father I'd like to speak with him either when he returns tonight or sometime tomorrow morning."

Adrien straightened, realizing I was ready to move on. Before he could join me, Gino stood up and reclaimed my attention. "Signore, why do you need to talk to Papà? Is it important? I can call him."

I paused with a hand on the railing and turned to look back at him. He wore a look of eager anticipation as if I had just given him something on which to focus. A slight smile tugged at the corners of my lips. Poor kid was desperate for something to do. Unfortunately, calling his dad wouldn't help his situation...or mine. "Oh no. Don't disturb him. He can't do anything for me over the phone. I was just hoping to be able to get into the archives either today or tomorrow to do a little more studying.

Why don't you and your Papa discuss it and let me know what time is better for the both of you." The eagerness in his eyes faded as he realized I had no immediate solution for his boredom. "After all, I know there is much I have yet to learn about the Cambiare, and your offer to read me the good stories has me intrigued."

The eager gleam returned to his eye as his lips broaden conspiratorially. "I will read only the best stories to you."

"Excellent. I look forward to it." I proceeded down the stairs and sensed Adrien do the same. "Have your father contact me when he gets back, and we will make plans. Perhaps tomorrow would be best for all of—"

"No."

I stopped as Gino's emphatic tone gave me pause. Turning back toward the boy, I realized a stubborn looked had replaced his eagerness. "No? You won't ask your father to contact me?"

Gino crossed his arms and raised his chin. "There is no need. I will read your stories to you right now."

My eyes narrowed as I gazed over at him. "What do you mean right now?"

"I know Papà's code. I'm not supposed to, but I watch him go in and out of the archive room all the time."

I shook my head. "Ah, I see. Then you also know that a code is merely part of the problem. You would need a key to get passed the lock on the door."

"Hmm, I forgot about that." He looked stumped.

"It's okay. I appreciate you wanting to read to me, but I wouldn't ask you to do something like that even if you had the key."

The boys jaw jutted out stubbornly as he exhaled noisily in exaggerated frustration. "You did not ask. My father did. He said I should read to you. He did not say only while he was present."

The boy had a point, but our inability to get passed a locked door made it moot.

"Be that as it may, there is still the problem of no key for the deadbolt on the door."

Then, as if the light of inspiration ignited within him, Gino smiled from ear to ear. A gleeful kind of giggle escaped him. "Oh! I've got it. Wait in the library. I will be back in a few minutes."

As the boy bounded down the hall toward the back of the villa, I couldn't help but feel like I'd unleashed a monster. Leaning a forearm on the banister, I shook my head. Where he was going I hadn't a clue, but he seemed like a man on a mission so who was I to argue.

A moment later I joined Adrien at the bottom of the stairs.

Adrien's eyebrows rose as he cocked his head sideways. "Seriously? You're going to allow that child to get himself in trouble, just so you can hear another story?"

Finally, he was talking to me. Nonetheless, his tone of censure made me frown. "Of course not. The boy doesn't have a key for the dead bolt on the door. He'll never be able to get us in there." I thought about it for a minute as genuine good humor split my lips and I actually bared teeth. I truly like that boy. "What's the harm? He thinks he's helping. Besides, if by some miracle he returns with a key, what else do we have to do this afternoon? Exploring the archives without Leo watching over our shoulders might prove interesting."

Adrien, obviously not impressed with my argument, shrugged it off. "Whatever you say, Jace. You're the boss."

"Yes. Yes, I am."

We waited in the Library as requested for nearly twenty minutes before Gino joined us.

He rushed over to me, pride beaming from his face like rays of sunshine. "I got it," he whispered and held the key up in front of his face. "See?"

Surprised by his revelation, I took the key from him. "How did you get it? I mean, I thought you said your father wasn't here."

"Yes, he's in town. Alcie keeps a spare in case he forgets the key or loses it."

"And you just walked up to Alcie and asked for it?"

"No, of course not. She wouldn't give it to me to use. I told her Papà forgot his key again and sent me to fetch it."

As the head of security my first thought was to fire Alcie. As someone wanting information out of that room, I thanked the Gods for the tiny little slip up. I ruffled the boy's hair and chuckled. "Cunning little rabbit. Now I understand the name."

The boy beamed as if I'd just given him the best compliment in the world. "Come, let's read some adventures."

Adrien followed us into the vaults. Once the door was secured behind us I jogged down the stairs after Gino. He turned to look up at me, pride at his accomplishment showing in his face. "I'll get the other book. The one I told you about."

"Okay." I paused at the bottom landing. "Would you mind if we look around a bit while you're finding it?"

He looked at me for a moment as if knowing that allowing me to look around unsupervised was wrong.

There was simply one way to assure him that his father's treasures would be safe in my hands. "I promise we won't mess around with anything. I'm just so amazed by everything here I'd like to take a closer look."

My answer seemed to mollify him. "Okay but be careful. Papà would be very angry if something happened to one of his prized possessions."

"Will do, Champ." I winked at him garnering another broad smile.

He ran to a hook next to his father's desk and grabbed another key hanging there. A moment later he crossed to a door I'd not previously noticed before. Unlocking it, he disappeared inside.

A locked room inside a vault? Interesting.

Adrien stepped up next to me and spoke in hushed tones, "We should not be in here. This is wrong."

"I would think you'd be less uptight." I rolled my eyes and shook my head. "Where's your sense of adventure?"

"Are you kidding me? After last night and then being called to the Council chambers I've had more than enough of your brand of adventure." He paused and glanced around the archives. "And this…this could end us right back in front of the Great Council."

"Oh relax, will you? We will be out of here before his father even knows we were here." I perused the volumes of handwritten books containing the histories of our people ignoring his pleas. Running a hand down spine after spine I went from shelf to shelf in amazement.

"Just what are we looking for?" Adrien's urgent whisper seemed irritated, although resigned.

"I don't know but I'll tell you if I find it," I responded absently. I truly didn't know why I was compelled to search the stacks. "Do you think they have records of all the Alimentatori births here?"

Adrien crossed to another section, something catching his eye. "I don't know. Maybe. Why would you want to see birth records?"

I shrugged. "No reason in particular. Just curious."

Several minutes later, I glanced over as Adrien whispered my name.

"What?"

"You've got to see this." He walked toward me as he stared at a scroll he'd unrolled. The brittle yellowed parchment was obviously aged from being left in the open and it occurred to me that the hidden room where Gino had disappeared might be a clean room, where all the truly ancient works resided. That seemed to make sense. With as long as the records had been kept, they couldn't keep everything out in the open or time and age would degrade them.

"What's that?" I asked, crossing to his side.

He tilted the paper, so I could see what he was looking at and I froze for a second. "It's the symbol. The one from Julian's missing ring.

I stared at the image scrawled across the top. "Holy shit." My whisper seemed to echo in the silence of the room. My mind raced as I swallowed the information. "Yes. Yes, it is."

"Do you know what it says? Can you read it?" His urgent whisper hissed next to my ear.

I glanced over the rest of the document. Failing to comprehend the flourishes and curves of the language, I scowled. "No. I can't. Maybe Gino will translate it before we get to story time."

As if on cue, the door across the room opened and the boy emerged laboring under the weight of a hefty book. His little hands were encased in oversized white gloves and he handled the book with the utmost care. "This is from Papà's private collection. No one is supposed to know about it. You won't tell him, will you?"

"Don't worry. We won't tell." I assured the boy as I carefully rolled the parchment up. "Your secret is safe with us."

Adrien moved to help him with the heavy book, but the boy shook his head. "No, you can't touch it without gloves."

My Second put his hands up and side-stepped out of the boy's way. "Just trying to help."

The boy ignored him as he placed the book on the table where we'd sat last time. "Come. Sit. I will find the part where my grandfather first meets the Cambiare."

As Gino took a seat and opened the pages of the book, he turned each one carefully.

"Before we start, can you do me a favor?" I slid into the seat across from him and waited for the boy's attention to shift back to me. When he looked up, his curious gaze met mine. I held out the scrolled document. "Can you read this for me?"

Gino reached out and took the parchment. Unrolling the scroll, he scrutinized it carefully. "Where did you get this?"

I sat forward, sensing the documents importance.

"Adrien found it on a shelf over there." I motioned to the location we'd found it.

"It should not have been left out. It's not like my Papà to be so careless." He rolled the parchment back up and set it aside and went back to finding the section he was looking for. "Oh well, I will put it back after we are done."

I sat back as I realized the boy had no intention of reading the document to me. "What's wrong? Why won't you translate it for me?"

He looked up at me with a serious look on his face. "Because that is part of the forbidden treasures. We are not allowed to read them or show them to anyone."

I blew out a breath in frustration. *Damn it.* Now I really wanted to know what the document said. Regrettably, I sensed pushing the boy would result in him shutting me down completely. It would have to wait. "Can you at least tell me what the symbol at the top means? My brother had a ring with that symbol on it and we never knew what the symbol meant."

Gino's eyes grew wide as he stared at me. "A ring with *that* symbol? Impossible."

"No, it's completely possible and completely true. Adrien can vouch for me. He's seen it as well." Adrien nodded as the boy looked between us in confusion.

"That's the symbol of the royal house."

My confusion compounded. "The house of Armaros?"

The boy shook his head vehemently. "No, the old royal house. The one that no longer exists."

I stared at the boy unable to comprehend what he was telling me. How in the hell had Julian ended up with a ring that belonged to a royal house? "Wait, you're confusing me. Are you saying that the symbol on that parchment, the same one that matches the ring my brother owned, is a symbol for a royal house which is now dead and gone?"

Gino nodded. "Si that is exactly what I am saying. You must never mention it to Papà. He would not be happy if he knew I talked about it at all."

A mix of feelings rushed through me, confusion, curiosity, wonder. But what could I do? The boy, completely unaware of the impact his words had on me had already gone back to leafing through the ancient book.

Did he have any idea how badly I wanted to know more about the *forbidden treasures*? Probably not. However, Adrien was right. It wasn't fair to put the boy into that position. Maybe if I could find the ring to prove our connection to the symbol Leo would allow me access to the things that would explain how it had come into the possession of the house of Samsaveel and ultimately on to the hand of Julian.

Yes, once I find the ring, I'll confront Leo and demand to know what he knew. If anyone would have the answers it would be the archivist. In his absence and without the ring I was just going to have to bide my time.

Realizing the boy was ready to begin, I settled back against the chair. In a manner reminiscent of the first time he'd read to me, Gino's proud, young voice rose in crisp, precise English.

"Thirtieth day of the fifth month in the four hundred and sixteenth year of our king, Gustav Semjaza the Good." He paused to look up at me, obviously remembering my previous trouble with the year. "That's May thirtieth, fourteen thirty-one."

I nodded in understanding. "Got it. Thanks. Wait, this happened the same day as the first book you read from?"

"Si, signore. But that book was just stories. This is history.

Chapter Twenty-Six

1431 A.D. Rouen, France

Black smoke rose up, churning like some great dark beast against the brilliant blue of an early summer sky. As the putrid stench permeated my senses and her agonized screams echoed through the town square, a spasm of disgust shot through me. Knots of angry tension twisted at my gut, filling me with fury. When I came to France so long ago to right a wrong, I hadn't envisioned the sweet child I'd befriended would meet this horrific end. She should have been a hero. Once again, I'd underestimated the barbarity of humankind.

Stepping away from my vantage point at the second story window of a local Inn, I closed my eyes against the sight, cupped hands over ears and leaned against the sill. By all rights, I should be watching, scribing notes for posterity and living the history I so loved to record.

Opening my eyes, I flung my hands away from my ears and shook my head. *I could not do it this time.* At a full out run I propelled my way down the hall to the back stairs. Normally we moved only at night, sticking to the shadows, being careful not to be seen. But, today the need to punish myself for the young girl's suffering caused a recklessness I'd never experienced before.

Pushing hard against the door, I burst through it and into the sunlight. Squinting against the brightness of the day, I held a hand up to shield my light sensitive eyes from the harshness of the afternoon rays. Scanning the alley from one end to the other, I stood for a moment numbed by what I'd witnessed, unsure of where to go. It didn't matter where I went. The sight of her tiny writhing body, blackened by the irrepressible smoke of the executioner's flame would follow. I couldn't stay here. I needed to get as far away from these monsters as possible, or I just might do something that would see us hunted by every human across Europe. Throwing caution aside like the edges of my lightweight cloak, I bared my wings for the entire world to see. With a rolling push of the shoulder blades, a great expanse of feathers extended out behind me, their tips nearly brushing the buildings on either side of the alleyway. The dark feathers, blue-black in the sunlight, rippled as the slightest breeze caught their edges urging me to take flight. Very glad to heed their call, I inhaled and pumped my wing blades once, twice, thrice, each time pushing harder as my body lifted, readying for flight. Bending at the knee, gently pushing off the ground, I eased into the air as naturally as a falcon lifting from a branch. My wings worked hard against the air, lifting me further and further until I rose above the rooftops. Once clear, a sudden gust forced the wing blades to turn, snapping them into position for flight. In response I flapped hard, the wings spread out to my sides. Within seconds I soared free above the dinghy rooftops of the square and looked down upon the horrific sights below. Tears of sorrow and anger slipped down my cheeks. Rising higher, reveling in the ability to escape the bonds of the earthly realm, if only for a short time, I angled west and left the atrocities of man behind. The cool wind rushing past dried the trails of unheeded tears. Nothing, not even distance could erase the sound of her cries within my mind.

Extending my wings to their fullest, I glided along the breeze and let my mind wander.

I'd met Jehanne in the field outside of her family home near Domrémy when she'd been no more than a babe. She'd been singing and gathering wildflowers, blissfully unaware of the turmoil brewing around her. When I landed before her for the first time, I didn't know what to expect. Any other human child of her age would cower in fear at the sight of a man with wings, but not Jehanne. She'd been different from the start. The sight hadn't frightened her in the least. Instead, the experience seemed to ignite something within her. When I introduced myself, she gave me a knowing look and stated, "You're an angel, aren't you?" I smiled but kept silent, intentionally not denying her statement. How does one explain the existence of my kind to one so young? Better she thinks me an angel than a perversion of nature. We sat together amongst the wildflowers and spoke for hours. She impressed me with her knowledge as she spoke with authority and the bearing of one twice her age. When I left, we parted as friends.

Sadness overtook my thoughts as reality struck home. If I had known where that friendship would lead, would I have gone back?

My lip curled in self-reproach. *Yes, I would have.* I knew early on what the Council expected of me. The child was a pawn in a game played by kings, and I might as well have been her executioner. I did everything I was told to do. It should never have come to this. I hadn't believed humans were such fickle creatures. *How could they turn on one of their own like rabid beasts? She was to be the hero of a grateful kingdom not a martyr on the burning pyre of their deceit. How? How could I have known?*

Unwilling to face the reality of my own betrayal, I pushed my body to its limits, testing my ability to stay aloft for as long as possible. When I thought I could go no farther, I forced my tired extremities to labor harder still, keeping a punishing pace, groaning as I met each gust of wind with an equal force of thrust.

When a sudden burst of rain forced me to take heed of the changing weather, I growled, cursing the angry clouds gathering overhead. A jagged bolt of lightning cut a path across the sky electrifying the air around me, warning me of imminent danger. Not caring if I lived or died, I darted through the gathering storm. Somewhere in the back of my mind a little girl's voice whispered, *you're an angel, aren't you,* and I cried out in guilt, "No, Jehanne. I'm not. I'm not an angel. I used you to change the world, and you paid for my sins."

As my words trailed off, a blinding flash of light illuminated the world around me and searing pain ripped through me. A faint contentment drifted across my features, as the world darkened.

Peace at last.

*****

After what seemed like seconds, I opened my eyes and gazed into a great nothingness.

Attempting to sit up, I groaned aloud with the effort. I realized quickly that my sense of sight was not the only thing I had lost. I heard nothing, not even the sound of my own breathing. It was as if I dropped from the sky and into sealed a cask. I saw nothing. I heard nothing. Far more alarming than being robbed of sight and sound, was the realization that my body hadn't moved. Trying again to summon motion from my limbs, I cried out internally, struggling to subdue the rising panic within me.

I was dead, my soul trapped within the confines of a useless shell. A moment of sorrow overwhelmed me. Was this to be my fate then? To lie here hungering for The Release that would never come?

Calming myself, I thought through what I knew of the situation.

What happened? I struggled to remember what had led to this end. My headlong dash into the sky, struggling against the strengthening winds, a light so bright I had been blinded by its brilliance, the searing pain, and then...nothing.

The birth of understanding dawned, flowering forth like the first breath of spring.

I supposed I deserved this. Every Aliment knew to vacate the sky when a storm approached. I foolishly spat in the eye of the Gods and then was surprised when they struck me down.

The true irony was of course the realization that I spent the last several years of my life manipulating and playing with the lives of humans as if they were chess pieces on the board of the Gods. Now, I found myself on the receiving end of their wrath. Or perhaps it had been her God who'd dealt the fatal blow, taking out his own vengeance on the one responsible for her demise. It seemed the more likely reason. Guilt washed over me once again as I nodded in agreement with my own conclusion.

Wait. Had my head just moved? I tried again and realized I could indeed feel the movement. The meaning of the small movement struck me in an instant, and relief temporarily replaced the smothering guilt.

By all that is holy, I'm alive! An irrational laughter bubbled up within me, further confirmation that I'd somehow managed to survive both the lightning strike and the fall. Little by little my senses returned to me, first ringing within my ears, which started low, becoming louder with every passing moment, and then the darkness ebbed, giving way to the shadows around me. A strange metallic tang filled my mouth, and I swallowed to rid myself of the taste. Within moments, little shock waves of sensation ignited every nerve ending in my body as they awoke to the pain. As quickly as it descended upon me, all semblance of joy fled my pain-racked body, and suddenly I knew—the Gods had allowed me to survive the fall so I might suffer this agony before crossing over.

Whatever the reason, it did not matter. I was alive, and as long as I had breath in my body, I would fight to keep it that way.

With grim determination, I pushed myself up from the ground sucking in a breath as my world teetered on the edge of a black abyss. Fighting to keep myself from passing out, I cried out as pain shot through the entirety of my body. Nausea washed over me, and I knew I was only seconds away from losing the fight. As I rose to my feet, a wave of dizziness struck with the force of a hundred thundering horses. I pitched forward and knew the battle was lost. Instead of landing face down on the wet ground, my naked body crashed against something more delicate. Something that smelled of a sweet spice reminiscent of something I experienced while in the Far East. A soft feminine voice soothed in lilting French, "Il est bien. Je vous ai. Vous êtes sûr maintenant."

As the darkness overcame me, her words echoed through my mind...*It's all right. I've got you. You're safe now.*

*****

The endless shivering, which wracked my body, stilled as a vague sense of warmth enveloped me. The softly uttered words of a little French angel sang within me. Had she been real or was she a creation of a fever-soaked mind? I didn't know. Either way, the scent along with her sweet voice haunted my dreams, teasing me. Would that I could stay within the realm of dreams and forever be in her embrace. Alas, even now, the pull of reality broke through, tugging on my eyelids urging me to awaken.

The scent of fresh straw and smoke from a fire replaced the tantalizing spice I so enjoyed in my dreams. The pummeling rain had disappeared, and her voice faded into memory leaving only silence, broken by the occasional crackling of a burning log, and the sound of lapping water, coming from somewhere nearby. Slowly becoming aware of the changes in my surroundings, I opened my eyes. I lay on my stomach, naked as the day I was born. My one protection against the makeshift bed of straw on which I lay was the rough woolen blanket beneath me. Confused by the unfamiliar surroundings, it took several moments for the memories of recent events to surface.

Remembering the pain which had sent me spiraling back into unconsciousness, I lifted my head, gingerly testing my range of movement. The pain which had been so excruciating moments ago seemed to have eased a great deal, though the throbbing seemed to worsen as I elevated my head. Moving from side to side, I tested for any damage to my neck and sucked in a breath when my muscles twinged as I twisted to the right. Pain shot down my right side. It didn't seem to be originating from my neck or head. Curious, I pushed myself further, moving slowly into a sitting position. As I moved, another burst of pain shot through me. Brushing my fingers gingerly along my ribs, I found one source of pain: at least three broken ribs, but such a minor thing could hardly be responsible for so much pain. Not satisfied, I continued the assessment. Extending my wings, I cried out in agony and immediately knew its source. Sweat broke out on my forehead as my breath came in tiny gasps. Breathing through the pain, I sat immobile, afraid to move.

Damn it. I won't be flying anywhere anytime soon.

When the pain subsided, I moved slowly, careful not to disturb my injured wing. Unfortunately, even the smallest movements caused excruciating pain to shoot through me. *How was I going to get home?* It could be months before my wing would heal enough to support flight, and without an Aliment doctor to set it properly…

The thought was too horrific to finish. An Alimentatori without wings could hardly be considered respectable.

Disgust tinged my voice as I spoke to the empty cave, "I might as well be human."

"Why would you wish that upon yourself?" An amused and strangely familiar voice came from a darkened corner of the chamber.

Peering into the darkness beyond the firelight, I realized my first impression was incorrect. I was not alone. At the farthest side of the large chamber, a glistening pool of water disappeared beneath the stone wall, and swimming within its gently lapping surface was my little French angel. The water rippled around her neck, her black hair slicked back against her head, and the strangest golden eyes stared back at me. Her full lips parted seductively as she walked toward me. The water descended lower and lower, revealing first bare shoulders and then the tops of her naked breasts. Silently I urged her forward, out of the water and into full view. Regrettably, she thwarted my efforts, stopping just shy of revealing the secrets the water kept hidden. I swallowed, unable to draw my eyes away as the water played about her pale breasts, her steady breathing pushing their tips within a hair's breadth from the water's surface.

A moment passed as her amused voice broke the silence. "Have you had quite a good look, Monsieur?"

Having the good sense to look ashamed, I cast my gaze downward and away from the vision she presented. "My apologies, Mademoiselle. I didn't mean to offend."

"No need, Monsieur. I am not shamed by your attentions."

My brow furrowed as I considered her response and countered with my own. "Regardless, Mademoiselle, it is not in my nature to be so bold, and I apologize for forgetting myself momentarily. Your presence here surprised me, and to find you in an unclothed state..." My throat tightened as the image of water lapping at milky white breasts teased my mind.

Her chuckle echoed in the confines of the cave and seemed to mock my serious tone. "Well, is it not fair that you should see a glimpse of me? After all, I've been tending to your nakedness for the past three hours."

Her words brought heat to my cheeks. I had forgotten my own nakedness when confronted by hers. Her statement brought the full realization home. Reaching for the edge of the blanket, I tucked it around me and did my best to ignore her as the water lapped harder against the sides of the pool. A few seconds later the lapping stilled, and I knew she must have left the water, which meant one thing.

I resisted the urge to gaze in her direction, knowing that to steal even one small glance would make it much harder to resist her. The soft patter of her feet against the dirt surface could barely be heard in the silence of the chamber, yet it seemed to pull at me, coaxing me to glance up at her.

Once again, her bubbling amusement echoed in the chamber as she spoke from a few meters away. "Are all men with wings this easily embarrassed or are the others made of sterner stuff than you?"

The question, though she teased me, smacked of insult. I glared at her. "Modesty is not a weakness, damsel. It is the mark of a well-bred man, with or without wings." My left brow rose in challenge. "It is true that men of all kinds appreciate the naked form of a beautiful woman. Nevertheless, that does not mean we must exhibit our baser needs like animals in rut. Perhaps that kind of behavior is acceptable among your kind. It is not among mine." The comment elicited an angry gasp from the woman and I scowled. "Though I appreciate your kindness in caring for me while I slept, I am awake now and can fend for myself."

It was a lie. I knew it to be, and I sensed she did as well, though she didn't give any outward indication of even hearing me. In fact, she didn't move at all, just stood there glaring at me as if I were the one to start throwing insults.

A low growl filled the room, sending a chill racing up my spine. I considered the woman standing mere footsteps away. Her golden gaze bored into me, and I suddenly understood how a rabbit must feel when being stalked by a wolf. The hair on the back of my neck rose as an overwhelming sense of danger ricocheted through me, setting my nerves on edge as it went. Determined not to show weakness in the face of her wrath, my gaze met hers. I could not stop the rush of air as a gasp expelled the oxygen from my lungs. The wildness reflected within the depths of her eyes intensified, and a deep throaty growl rumbled low in her throat. What the hell was she? More than human— obviously. But, what else?

As if in answer to my unspoken question, her body twisted, and she screamed, dropping to her knees. The spicy, cinnamon musk thickened around her, and she shook her head in a silent plea. Glancing up at me, her eyes flashed with an unearthly glow. Whatever was happening, it didn't appear that she had any control over it. She seemed afraid. Even as the thought slipped through my brain, I knew somehow it was wrong. Perhaps it was my own fear of what was taking place which tainted my perception of her feelings. She breathed deeply and gritted her teeth as if in pain, yet she didn't cry out. For several moments she closed her eyes and ignored my presence as if lost in whatever internal battle she was fighting. Then the woman was gone, and in her place stood a large black cat with the same beautiful golden eyes. My breathing slowed as I stared at her in wonder. How could this be? The Aliments had kept detailed records for centuries on every known beast, yet here stood a creature we could never have even imagined into existence. The same size as the woman who disappeared, the cat had gleaming slick black fur, and I moved forward cautiously, astounded by the creature's beauty. Reaching out, I touched the slick coat unsure if what I saw was real. She growled in warning, and I withdrew my hand, whispering, "What are you?"

She stared at me with the same wise, gentle eyes, which had moments ago piqued my interest when she was human standing in the pool of water.

Though she did not speak, her familiar voice echoed within my mind. *Though you may think me a beast to be tamed and brought to heel, I can assure you I am descended from a proud and noble line of ancient kings.*

As her voice whispered into silence, I looked on. Her transformation reversed, and within seconds the tawny-skinned beauty stood tall before me once again. Shaking my head, I stared up at her in awe. "How…"

"My name is Adara of Aberffraw. I am a priestess of the Cath Boblogi."

Cath Boblogi? I searched the languages I knew and came up with no answer.

As if understanding my confusion, she smiled and continued. "Nella vostra lingua forse? Siamo la gente che cambia in gatti?"

In your language perhaps? We are the people who change into cats.

Stunned by her fluent use of my mother tongue, my eyes widened in interest. Answering in kind, I couldn't help but marvel at the uniqueness of the woman standing before me. "You speak Italian as well?"

"Si. Und Deutsch."

I chuckled, shaking my head, astounded by yet another language. "Amazing."

She stepped forward and knelt before me, her musky scent filling my senses, igniting a desire I didn't even know existed within me. A fine sheen of perspiration caused her naked body to shimmer in the dancing firelight. Lifting my hand, I weaved my fingers through her draped hair, mystified by the sensations racing through my body. What power did this creature, this woman have over me? She leaned forward, snaking her hands around my shoulders until her fingers threaded through my hair. I groaned in response, knowing that resisting the urges within me would be futile. I let go. My fingers found the back of her head and pulled her face toward mine. Our lips met, the taste of her as sweet as the musky scent enveloping me...

Chapter Twenty-Seven

"Cosa diavolo sta succedendo qui?"

Angry Italian broke the spell the story had woven around me and shook me back to reality. I glanced up to find a very irate Leo standing on the bottom stair glaring at us. Gino shrunk down in his seat as if trying to disappear. I knew he would not hear the end of this.

"Leo, your son was kind enough to read me another bit of the Cambiare history." I spoke up in the child's defense hoping to redirect the man's anger toward me. "He didn't want to. I insisted."

The older man's glare shifted from the back of his son's head to me. "What is the meaning of this? You come down here without permission and talk a young, impressionable boy into reading from a book that should not be seen in the light of day? Do you have any idea how dangerous this is?"

Leo's answer seemed odd. "Dangerous? Why should reading from a history book be dangerous? And for that matter, why are there two versions of the same story in two different books?"

The archivist flushed. Crossing the room in an angry huff, he dragged the boy from his chair and pushed him toward the stairs. "Vai al piano di sopra. Tua madre è in attesa."

Gino removed the gloves and handed them to Leo and then ran to the stairs.

"Please, don't be angry with him. It's not his fault. I'll take the blame for all of this."

Leo waited until his son had exited the room before turning on me. "You most certainly will. The Council will not stand for this."

"If you go to the Great Council, then I guess I will have to tell them about how Gino took a key from Alcie on your behalf to get me into this room. And how you have a secure, locked room within the vault where so called dangerous documents are held." My tone, deathly serious, conveyed every bit of animosity I felt for the tiny weasel of a man. "How do you think they will react to knowing your son not only knows about those documents, but willingly read to us from one of them?"

The man swallowed as fear lit his eyes. "No, you mustn't. If they ever find out the originals weren't destroyed...," he sat with a thud on the chair Gino had recently vacated. His hand moved lovingly to caress the pages of the book and in his distress forgetting his own rule of never touching them with bare hands. "They must never know about these."

"Then tell me what they are and why they are hidden."

Sadness overtook him as a deep sigh escaped, and he looked away. "These are my grandfather's original writings, the true history of the interaction between Aliment and Cambiare. If anyone knew they still existed, my life, my family's lives would be forfeit." He glared up at me, a look of fierce protectiveness on his face. "You understand? No one can ever know this exists, or the Great Council will raid the archive room, take everything we've kept hidden for generations, set fire to them, and make me watch as years of our history, years of truth turn to ash. And only after the smoke has cleared will they be satisfied."

"Why would they do such a thing?" Adrien's puzzled tone mimicked my own confusion.

Leo glanced at Adrien with sadness filling his eyes. "Because, the Cambiare are our enemies though for many generations they were our friends and allies. As you know from this tale, my grandfather fell in love with one. She was killed when their kind were rounded up for slaughter by the church. My grandfather was responsible for their removal from France. He brought them here where they would be safe."

I sat back, stunned by the revelation. The Cambiare and Aliments were once allies? "If that's the case, then what the hell happened? Why are they our enemies now?"

The archivist, shrugged. "All I can tell you is that it happened when I was just a child. The Cambiare stood up against a rising regime and fell with the old one."

My eyes narrowed, and I glanced to the scroll laying unnoticed at the book's edge. "You're talking about the old royal house, the one which no longer exists."

Leo's intake of breath was audible and his surprise unhidden. "How do you know about them?"

I nodded to the parchment to the right of his hand. "We found that among the stacks and asked Gino about the symbol." Anger caused Leo's features to contort although he remained silent. "Don't get your knickers in a bunch. Gino wouldn't translate the document. He did tell me that the symbol stood for the old royal house, not the one who currently runs things around here."

Leo relaxed a bit, although his glare pinned me to my seat. "You shouldn't know about them. No one should. They are a long-buried secret that only the elders remember. Most of those who supported the old king died at the hands of the new regime. If they were very lucky, they escaped and fled to the corners of the world."

"So, you and your family support the new regime?"

He sat forward and jammed his index finger onto the pages of the book emphasizing each point. "My family did what we had to do to survive. We keep the records." He spread his fingers and laid his hand on the pages. "We hold the secrets and truths within the palms of our hands. It is our burden to carry through the ages. Only when the time comes, will we be able bring the truth into the light. Until that time, we must keep its secrets."

I sat back in equal parts of amazement and skepticism. "And when will the time come for this great revelation of truth?"

He gently closed the pages of the book, almost symbolically closing down the conversation. "I don't know. However, when the time comes, I and my family will be ready." He rubbed the worn leather cover of the book with a faraway look in his eye. A moment later the look was gone, and he stood up. "Anyway, those are problems for another day and another hero." He drew on the white gloves his son left behind and picked up the parchment. "None of it has anything to do with you and your issues with the Cambiare. As I believe you've garnered far more information than you should have, this will be the last time I will help you on this matter. If you need further assistance, I would suggest you find another source." Placing the parchment on top of the closed book, he picked up the lot and walked back toward the closed room.

"Wait, Leo."

He paused to look at me, raising an eyebrow in question. "Yes?"

I stumbled over what to say. Should I ask about the ring or should I leave it for another time? Would there be another time? Not likely if Leo wouldn't speak to me again. "What about the symbol? The one on the parchment."

Leo frowned. "What are you asking?"

"Well, is it really the symbol of the old royal house?"

My eagerness must have come through in my tone, because Leo's frown deepened. "What does it matter now?"

I scowled. "It matters to me."

Seeing that I would not let go of the issue, he relented. "I don't know why it's important to you or how you even know about it, but yes, it was the insignia of the extinct House of Semjaza. No one has seen it since the downfall of the old king."

I glanced briefly over at Adrien and could tell he was thinking the same thing.

We have.

"Was there ever a piece of jewelry or anything with that

symbol on it?" I knew the answer of course. I just needed to know if I could trust what Leo was saying.

The archivist paused to place the book on his desk and then turned around and took off the gloves. His brow knitted in thought. "Si. As you know, every house has a ring." He nodded toward my hand where the House of Samsaveel was duly represented. "If memory serves, I believe it disappeared a very long time ago."

"Disappeared? No one knows what happened to it?" I hedged around the question hoping I didn't sound too eager.

His eyes narrowed. "There are some who speculate."

"What do they think happened to it?" I pushed a little more. If he shut me down, at least I wouldn't go away empty handed.

Leo's frown intensified. "Why are you asking all these questions about a ring that disappeared two hundred and some odd years ago? What interest could you possibly have in an ancient, long dead family?"

I shrugged, hoping it would seem nonchalant. "I find history fascinating. It astounds me that there is so much Aliment history buried down here. I like the idea of knowing the hidden history as well as that which is widely known." Sitting forward, my gaze captured the older man's. "On that note, what happened to the House of Semjaza?"

Leo looked away as if deciding whether to say anything more. Then, his gaze found mine. His hard, pointed stare bored into me, unnerving in its intensity. "You have no understanding of how truly dangerous those questions are. The history of the old and current royal lines is volatile. There are things that cannot be known, cannot be thought, or uttered in the presence of those who wish all knowledge of our past to be forgotten. I hide what I can to be sure our true history survives. The knowledge you seek is dangerous for you and me." He glanced toward Adrien and then back at me. "And to anyone we care about as well."

Adrien leaned forward, apparently wanting to be part of the conversation. "Don't worry about me. I can take care of myself.

Just give him the information, so we can get the hell out of your hair."

Leo met Adrien's amused gaze and seemed to think it over. Then he sat down across from me with an annoyed *humph.* "Fine, but this is the last time I will help you."

I almost chuckled but though better of it. "And I promise this will be the last time I bother you...unless it's a matter of life and death."

Leo waved away the promise in disgust. "Promises mean nothing unless you trust the person making them."

I chuckled and mocked his seriousness. "Aw, Leo. That hurt a little."

His irritated sigh said he'd had enough and was losing patience. "Are you quite through?"

I straightened up and curbed my humor. "Yes, quite."

"Good." He settled back against the chair. "The House of Semjaza led our kind since the beginning of time, sometimes benevolently, sometimes not, but always with the good of the race in mind. There were those who tested the patience of the king and, well, it was the 1800s so bloody wars and coups were commonplace. Anyway, the king was killed by his enemies, and his wife, heavy with child, was injured. Though they managed to escape, her lifeless body was found in the hut of a local midwife. The child was gone. Some speculate that the child was secreted away and kept safe from those who would do him, or her, harm. Others believe that a local villager took him and raised him as their own."

I nodded even though I wasn't quite satisfied. "And what do you believe?"

Leo's eyebrow rose. "Me? I think it's all just wishful thinking." He shrugged and folded his hands together on the table. "Like I said, it was commonplace to kill a ruler and his family in order to gain power for oneself. The old king, his lady, and his child died at the hands of a bloody coup, and the rest is history."

"So, you don't think there is any possibility that the child survived?" I sat on the edge of my seat eagerly awaiting his response. Why the answer to that question was so important to me, I didn't know.

Leo shook his head then paused. "I suppose anything's possible, though I doubt a human family would have survived taking the child in. The new king's enemies would have killed anyone found in possession of the heir, and then the child would have been killed as well. If the child survived birth and was secreted away, then the likelihood of him being found is lessened. But still, it is my understanding that the king's troops were relentless. They tore apart an entire village looking for any newborn Aliment children."

"Wouldn't that mean they believed the child had survived?"

Leo seemed to go over the facts in his mind as he sat, legs and arms crossed in front of him. "It could mean that, or it could have just been par for the course during that time period. They were an invading army after all. Besides, I don't have any records of the child's birth let alone survival."

"But you wouldn't necessarily have any records if the child was born outside of the palace and then secreted away, would you?"

Leo took a deep breath as he considered my statement. "No, that is true. Our records show the births of those born within the confines of their respective Houses. If anyone was born outside, then they would technically not exist within our records."

A sense of satisfaction rushed over me. *I knew it.* We could trace Julian's and my births back to our parents and prove Julian and I were brothers, despite any difference in scent.

"Leo, I have a favor to ask." His co-operation was imperative. "Can you look up Julian's birth records and let me know what you find?"

Confusion was apparent on both Leo and Adrien's faces. "Why would you need me to do that?"

"I'm just trying to confirm something for myself."

Leo thought on it for a long moment and then nodded. Taking a notepad from the pocket of his sports jacket, he placed it on the table and then reached for a pen. Pen poised for used, he glanced up at me. "Okay. I already know his house. I will need your parents' names, and his date and place of birth. It may take some time. The birth records are stacked to the ceiling back there."

"That's fine." I recited the information he'd requested by rote memory. I knew it as well as I knew my own.

Once he'd finished scribbling his notes, he slipped the notepad back into his pocket. "Alright, signore. I will call you when I have confirmed Julian's information."

Rising, I held out my hand to him. "Thank you, Leo. You are a good man, and I'm sorry for misjudging you."

Leo's stern features broke with genuine happiness as he rose. Gripping my hand in a firm handshake he looked up into my eyes. "And perhaps I have misjudged you as well."

Chapter Twenty-Eight

As we climbed the stairs, Leo disappeared through the door of the inner vault to tuck his contraband safely away. This whole situation was about as far away from what I'd expected as it could get.

Adrien followed closely as we emerged once again into the Library.

When he spoke, his curious tone seemed overly loud in the relative quiet of the room. "What was all the interest in the original royal house?"

I glanced over to where Anthony usually stood. Someone else stood in his place, serving drinks to the few patrons sat at the bar. They seemed to be less interested in our conversation than in the story the bartender was relating, which worked to our benefit. The last thing I needed was to have the Great Council learn that I began poking my nose in where it clearly did not belong. In a stern whisper I responded, "Not here. We'll talk about it later."

His whispered retort held the same note as mine had, "I have a feeling I'm not going to like what you're thinking."

Truer words had never been spoken. Adrien was not going to like anything I had to say on the subject of Julian's birth.

"Probably not."

He followed me across the room and out the double doors of the Library. As we emerged into the hall, he grabbed my arm. "Jace, this whole thing has me really worried. I saw the look in your eye when Leo was talking about the ring." He paused as his gaze found mine. "You think Julian was that baby, don't you?"

I cast a wary eye down each side of the hall before answering. "Adrien, trust me, this is not the place to have this conversation. This afternoon we will find someplace where the walls don't have eyes and ears, and I will tell you everything."

"Fine, but we *will* talk about it."

I chuckled at his adamancy. "Yes. We will. I promise. However, right now, I need to deal with the Vuote goon from last night. I have some questions I want to ask him before the Great Council gets their hands on him."

He nodded and fell into step beside me. "Fine by me. I'll enjoy seeing that cocky little bastard sitting in a cell."

We preceded to the second floor Security office.

The door opened before we had a chance to knock, and Vinny stood there looking rather formidable. "Good morning, signore. I hear that last night was rather exciting for you."

I nodded as I walked into the room. "You could say that. How's our guest doing?"

The security officer shrugged. "I, personally, have not been down to check on him yet this morning. We sent him breakfast about a half hour ago. He was reported to be in good health."

"Good to know. Can you have him brought up to my office? I want to ask him a few questions before we give him an audience with the Great Council."

"Certainly, signore. I will have him delivered to you immediately." Vinny closed the door behind us and left Adrien and I on our own for the moment.

A few moments later, I sat behind the desk, and Adrien lounged, his head leaned back against the soft brown leather of the chair as he stared at the ceiling lost in thought. His voice broke the silence and drew my attention. "I'm thinking about asking Alcie out. Not now. But when this is all over, it would be nice."

I looked up from the papers I had been perusing. "I think that is an excellent idea. In fact, why wait? You deserve a night on the town."

"Do you think I'm too old for her?" His question spoke to his uncertainty regarding the young woman's interest in him.

"Nope. Not at all." I went back to looking over the service order for the new cameras that were finally going in this afternoon. "I think she would be lucky to have you."

He sat up and screwed up his mouth. "It's been years since anyone has lit my fire like that little lady does. What if she turns me down?"

I laughed. "Relax, Adrien. You're asking her out on a date, not to marry you."

A smile broke his lips as he chuckled. "Yeah, well you never know."

My brow furrowed as his words seemed contrary to everything I thought I knew about him. As dedicated as Adrien was to his duties and as fond as he was of proclaiming himself a lifelong bachelor, the thought of him looking favorably on marriage seemed far-fetched. Then again, with the way he looked at Alcie, I could see it. All he needed was a little encouragement. "I suspected there was something special growing between the two of you."

"And what about you? Any thoughts to what's ahead for you after all of this?"

Adrien's inquiry took me by surprise. "To be honest, I haven't thought past the end of the day, let alone what will happen a week from now."

My Second nodded in understanding. "There is always Magda."

My gaze flew to his and my jaw set. "What about Magda?"

He flushed crimson as he must have realized how that sounded. "I...what I meant was that she would make a good wife for you. She was prepared to take on the duties of a

Padrone's wife."

"She may be prepared for such an outcome, but I am not. Besides, I will not set Angel aside. She is my il Scelto."

Adrien inhaled deeply. "I realize you have an attachment to Angel, but you must consider your future. You are now the leader of our clan."

"Becoming Padrone has no bearing on Angel's status."

"That is true. However, unless a loophole miraculously appears, you will also be taking the house seat within the Great Council. It would be logical for you to find a wife to share the responsibility. Magda could run things with the Clan when you are not around to do so, and Angel is…"

My teeth ground together in suppressed ire. "Angel is what?"

"Human."

The one word said it all. It was the one thing that had always held us apart, which was fine by me. As much as I enjoyed her company, I had no desire to tie myself to her for life, even if her life was exponentially shorter than mine. As things were now, she had no claim on me. I could come and go as I pleased and be with whomever I chose. To elevate her to wife? A shiver of revulsion raced through me.

No way.

Marriage was one institution I had no intention of ever embracing. I had more than enough demands on my time. Who needed a wife to muck things up? How my brother had stayed the course, I didn't know. Then again, he was always the better man.

A little whispering taunt snaked through my mind, *was he?*

And for the first time I questioned. Had Julian been the better man? Did his trysts with Nix take away from who I knew him to be? Never in my wildest dreams would I have suspected my elder brother of cheating on Magda. It had been love at first sight for him, and he never indicated otherwise. So, why would he do this to her?

My jaw clenched as a vivid memory of Nix's lips touching mine clouded my mind. She had been so hard to resist. Had Julian experienced the same thing? An inability to keep her at arm's length?

Irrational anger leapt to life within me. Damn her and her fucking scent!

She had probably used Julian, seduced him as easily as she drew me to her and he had been helpless to resist. That was a secret I would take to my grave. Magda and the clan would never know.

"Jace?"

Adrien's voice jarred me out of my thoughts. "Hmm, what?"

"I mentioned the unfortunate disadvantage of Angel's birth, and you disappeared. What were you thinking about?"

"Nothing. Don't worry. You're right. It would not do to marry a human, and I have absolutely zero desire to do so. In fact, I will proudly step into your soon-to-be-vacant-confirmed-bachelor shoes."

"Hey now, don't go shoving me out the door yet. Alcie and I haven't even been on one date. We could be completely incompatible."

I chuckled. "True enough."

The phone on the desk rang and I glared at it. *Someone looking for Karina, no doubt.* Reaching out, I picked up the receiver fully prepared to give whoever it was the bad news.

"Ciao?"

"Ciao, signore. It's Vincenzo." Vinny's familiar voice sounded strained.

"Oh, hi Vinman. What's up?"

"Signore, can you please come down here? We have a problem."

I sat forward and propped my elbow on the desk. "What's wrong? Did our prisoner escape?"

"No. Not exactly."

"Then what is it?"

Vinny's voice elevated as his stress level rose. "I think you better come down here and see for yourself."

I took a deep breath, exasperated by the security officer's hesitancy. Yet, in the end, agreed to his request. Hanging up the phone, my stomach churned. Glancing over at Adrien, a frown pinched my lips together. "We need to head downstairs."

Adrien stood immediately. "What's happened?"

"Nothing good."

*****

Several minutes later, we stepped through the secret door which led to the underground portion of the headquarters. At the base of the stairs we turned left and took the hall which led the opposite direction of the one we'd take to the Council chambers.

As we approached, Vinny's angry voice echoed in the close-knit space. "Vi spiegherà l'incompetenza al Signore Jacen immediatamente!"

One of the guards shifted under Vincenzo's stern look, obviously the higher ranking of the two officers. The two men stood ramrod straight with a look of sheer terror on their faces. Something was seriously wrong.

As we neared, I noticed the door between the guards stood open.

Peering over his shoulder and into the room, I understood.

"What happened?"

Vinny turned his head to look at me over his shoulder. He wore a sour look on his face. "He's dead."

I pushed past him and rushed into the room. "How?"

"I'm not sure how it happened, he…si suicido."

"Committed suicide? What the hell?" As my gaze travelled around the room, it came to rest on the bed along the opposite wall. Our would-be assassin lay at an awkward angle, one arm thrust up behind him as if he'd been leaning back when he collapsed. The other arm dangled off its edge giving him the appearance of sleeping. However, the purplish tinged fingertips brushing the floorboards said otherwise.

Closing the distance, I squatted down to examine the body. Eyes, clouded over in death, stared blankly at the ceiling. His mouth gaped open, making it obvious that he'd spent his last moments gasping for breath. A small amount of foamy spittle trailed down the side of his cheek. Gingerly lifting his chin, I examined his neck.

No ligature marks, so he wasn't strangled. So, what had killed him?

My eyes narrowed as a suspicion arose. I leaned forward to sniff his mouth and was rewarded with the almost imperceptible scent of bitter almonds. I rose and crossed my arms, glaring down at the dead human. "He's ingested Cyanide."

Adrien joined me by the bedside. "How?"

"A self-administered tablet, maybe?" My gaze swept the sparse space in intense scrutiny. A tray sat on the small table next to the bedside. On it sat a white plate, which looked to have the remnants of eggs, toast, and bacon. Next to the plate a tall glass of orange juice had been emptied and abandoned. "Or possibly..."

I reached out and picked up the plate. Taking a deep sniff, I placed it back on the tray then did the same with the glass. Immediately I identified the contents and handed it to Adrien.

Adrien's eyes widened as he too smelled the almond scent. "That's cyanide?"

I nodded and took the glass from him, and then set it down on the tray.

Vinny joined the discussion. "Are you suggesting this wasn't suicide? That someone intentionally slipped poison into his drink? That's absurd."

I looked up at the man with a frown. "Is it? Why?"

Vinny's cheeks reddened as his frown grew intense. "Because...well, I think...the guards would have..."

"Noticed?" I stepped back and met Vinny's confused, defensive glare. "Not likely. Unless they are in the habit of smelling or tasting a prisoner's food, I don't see that there would have been any way for them to know."

Remaining silent, he folded his arms over his chest. From the relieved look on his face my explanation appeased him. He probably didn't want to take the blame for the loss of such a valuable prisoner. No matter. His issues were the least of my concerns. Whether the poisoning was self-inflicted or administered without his knowledge, the man was still dead, and I no longer had a Vuote assassin to gift to the Great Council.

Adrien glanced between us and then intervened. "No one is saying that the guards were lax; however, it is feasible that something slipped past them." He paused to look past Vinny to the two guards who stood just outside the door. "Do we know who delivered his breakfast?"

Vinny's shoulders rose in triumph. He finally had something he could help with. "I will check with the guards." Directing his attention to the two at the door, he shouted, "Chi ha trasportato il vassoio questa mattina?"

The higher-ranking officer, answered, "Alcie portato il vassoio giù. Allora lo ho preso e lo ho dato lui."

My brow crinkled as a frown creased my features. I didn't understand everything. I caught enough to know Alcie was the one who delivered the tray.

Turning back to us, Vinny gave us a quick translation, "He says Alcie brought it, but he delivered it to the prisoner."

Adrien shifted his weight and cleared his throat. "Well we know she had nothing to do with this."

"Do we?" I questioned, unwilling to rule anyone out.

"Yes," Adrien's stern voice reflected his belief in the object of his affection, "we do."

Vinny nodded. "I agree. Alcie would never do this."

"Then we need to start with her, so we can rule her out as a suspect." My tone was equally stern, brooking no disagreement from either of them.

Vinny, in his infinite wisdom spoke up, "I believe this is a suicide. Vuote do not get captured. When they do," he made a slicing movement at his neck, "they do not live to tell tales." He slapped his hands together in a motion meant to indicate finality. "Ha commesso il suicide. Rifinito!"

I shook my head. "Not rifinito until I say it's rifinito."

Vinny's disgruntled frown said he disagreed.

Continuing my thought, I said, "Now, as we need to investigate this under the radar, I say we declare it a suicide but investigate it like a murder. If someone did do this, the last thing we want to do is alert them to the fact that we suspect foul play. If it was self-administered, then someone here had to have given him the means, and we need to find out whom. Agreed?"

Vinny's arms dropped to his sides as his defensive posturing eased. "He could not have brought something with him? Like a spy in the movies?"

I shook my head both in disagreement and astonishment. Hollywood had fans everywhere. "Not likely. If he had it available to him the moment he arrived, I doubt he would have waited until morning to use it."

Adrien interjected, "The driver and I searched him before shoving him in the trunk. He was clean. We even made him take off his socks and shoes to verify nothing was being hidden in the heels of his boots."

"Ah, I see. Then, I guess...yes, I agree."

Adrien turned to me and nodded. "I can live with that. But, I want to deal with Alcie. Not you and certainly not security. Is that understood?"

The stubborn tilt to Adrien's chin indicated clearly that arguing would be futile. Instead, I allowed him to take the lead. "Fine."

"Good. Now, I would suggest we get the coroner down here and explain the situation. We will need him if this is going to work."

I cast a quick glance at the security officer. "Vinny, make the call, and make sure you tell him we want this kept quiet."

"Certainly." He stepped away from us and withdrew his phone from his pocket.

Adrien frowned at the body on the bed. "You don't really think Alcie had anything to do with this, do you?"

I sighed. "All I know is that nothing here has been as it seems. It would behoove us to count nothing and no one out."

He seemed to mull that over as he turned his back to me for a few seconds before answering. "I agree, but I still don't believe Alcie's capable of this. The woman practically cried when she thought we might be angry with her over her telling the Council about our excursion to Eros and the altercation with the human."

My eyebrow rose as I looked at my Second. "You mean *this* human. The same human who'd inexplicitly shown up at Eros and started a fight? The very same night we saw Alcie at Eros as well?" Adrien scowled. I proceeded with my argument. "Listen, I'm not saying she's guilty. Simply that there are questions which need to be answered, and Alcie is going to have to provide them."

My stern-faced Second looked back at the dead human and frowned. "I see your point. Rest assured, if she did have anything to do with this, I will find out."

I relaxed, knowing we were finally on the same page where Alcie was concerned. "Good. Glad to hear it."

Chapter Twenty-Nine

$\mathcal{A}$ couple hours later, the body had been dually processed and then packed into a body bag for transport to the morgue. The coroner had come and gone having agreed to "suicide by poison" as the cause of death until we could provide any proof to the contrary. Vinny might be inclined to believe it would stay that way. I was not.

I took a seat at the table in our room lost in contemplation.

Every instinct I had told me this was an inside job and unfortunately for Adrien, Alcie seemed to fast become the prime suspect.

As of right now, she was the only one we knew of who had means, absolutely no motive, though. That was the solitary thing keeping me from going back on my promise to Adrien. If I thought it was a slam dunk, nothing would have stopped me from marching directly into her office and dragging her in for questioning, never mind the effect such a rash action would have on my relationship with Adrien. If it turned out she was the culprit, then my Second would just have to fucking deal.

Several minutes later Adrien entered the room, having stayed a few minutes longer to get some information from the guards before they were released. He crossed to the buffet where a fresh pot of coffee awaited and grabbed a cup from a small stack of clean ones.

"This was at the very least assisted by someone here. Worst case scenario an Aliment perpetrated it. I just don't know why. What would any Aliment have to gain from killing a Vuote assassin who's already in custody?"

Adrien shrugged. "Only they know that for sure. I suspect if it is an Aliment, he or she might be the same one who fed the Vuote our passcodes, giving them the ability to lock us out of our satellite systems." He paused as a thought occurred to him. "They could be working with the Vuote to bring down the current regime."

"I suppose it's possible." My brow knit as I played with the corner of a napkin, which had been left on the table. "Doesn't it seem strange that this particular Vuote went after me? I mean, who am I to them? I shouldn't even be on their radar."

Adrien carried his steaming mug over to join me at the table. "It's obvious he followed us out there, and unfortunately, we didn't get to question him this morning on the why of it."

My frown deepened. "Maybe that's why he was killed."

Adrien sipped some coffee then set the cup on the wooden surface of the table. "That would be a logical assumption. There are also a few humans who work here as well. We will need to start with them."

"The butler did it." I sat back with a chuckle. "Nah, just kidding. If Belvedere was going to poison someone, I have no doubt it would be me."

My Second laughed as well. "No doubt. Seriously though, I'll start looking at all the humans who work for the villa. As far as I'm concerned, anyone who was here between the hours of his arrival and when he died is suspect."

"My money is on someone from the kitchen staff. They had access to his meal. Let's start there first."

Adrien paused in another sip of his coffee, as he peered down at the steamy liquid in the cup. "If there is a Vuote agent working in the kitchens, why haven't they poisoned the lot of us?"

I couldn't hide the slight upturn of the corners of my mouth as he placed the cup down on the table and pushed it away. "That is something *you* will have to figure out over the next few days."

"*I* will have to?" His eyes snapped upward to find me staring at him. "What the…"

I interrupted him, "You don't expect me to set aside the investigation into Julian's death for some dead human, do you?"

His face reddened. "Of course not. I had thought we would interview suspects together. You are the head of security after all."

I relaxed back against the chair and folded my hands over my belly. "And as head of security, I am delegating my authority to you. I am completely confident in your ability to hunt down the culprit on your own. Once you're done, then you can join me in my search." His mouth scrunched up as if he were getting ready to take me to task once again for leaving him behind. I held up a hand to stop him from doing so. "There is no use arguing over this. We have two unsolved murders on our hands. Vinny seems to be a good man. Honestly though, the longer I'm here, the less I trust anyone…except you. *You*, Adrien, are the only one I can entrust with this investigation. Before I can do that, I need you to believe that I can handle myself without a bodyguard constantly looking over my shoulder."

He exhaled as he considered my words. "Fine, but do me a favor? Stick to the villa or stay with Nix as much as possible. Also, if it looks like you are heading into danger, call me first. I don't want to find out after the fact that you went off and did something stupid, something I could have prevented. I can't go through that again, Jacen."

My lips spread in a grim smile. That was simpler than I thought. "You've got it. I will let you know anytime I leave headquarters, and I will always be just a phone call away if I need you."

"Great, because the less I have to worry about where you are and if you're in danger, the more I'll be able to focus on finding whoever slipped the Vuote a deadly mickey." He leaned forward on his elbows, resting his chin on his knuckles. "Speaking of our original reason for being here, where are you going to start?"

I shrugged. "I wish I knew. When I came over here, everything was straight forward. Kill the Cambiare responsible for my brother's death. Now, things are a jumble of secret truths and unknown histories. How can I possibly know what the right course of action is if everything I'm being told is a lie?" I glanced in Adrien's direction, "Where do you think I should go from here?"

He sat back with a satisfied grin as I asked his advice for the first time. "Well, I think the objective is still the same. We need to start over at the beginning as if we were given everything for the first time. We'll re-evaluate all of the information we've been given, toss out what we know is false, and see what's left over."

I considered his words for a moment. "Sounds good. For whatever reason, we were led to believe the Cambiare were responsible. If we take them out of the equation…" I screwed up my mouth and shook my head. What was left? "Where does that leave us?"

"Well, let's start back at the beginning. What facts do we have?"

I thought for a moment and then spoke, "Julian left the party with Nix. That we know for sure."

"Right, but she did save your life. She also claims she and Julian were friends." He leaned over on his elbows again and looked me in the eye. "Do you believe her?"

I nodded hesitantly. "Yes, I do. However, I'm still not sure if I can trust her." I rose and crossed to where Adrien acquired the coffee. Grabbing a mug, I poured a cup for myself. Preferring it strong and black, I chose not to add anything to it. Continuing the conversation, I spoke over my shoulder, "I think she is hiding something. Maybe I'm wrong, but there was definitely something about the way she said they were friends. It was like there had been something more between them." Turning around, I leaned back on the buffet and took a tentative sip of the hot brew. I stared off into space for a moment as I recalled her sitting on the steps of Orcus, her glowing eyes downcast as if she lost herself in a memory. No, there had been something special between Julian and Nix. What it was I wasn't sure. I guess I was going to have to find out. "I think we should pin her down on what exactly their relationship entailed. We also need to know what she expected from him in return."

Adrien rose. Picking up his coffee mug, he crossed to where I stood. A moment later, he placed the mug on the tray someone had left for our dirty dishes. Mimicking my stance, he too turned to lean against the buffet's edge. "Easily accomplished with another meeting between the two of you. I say we concentrate our efforts on piecing together what happened that night. As far as we know Nix was the last one to see him alive. I think all the answers must lie with her which means heading back to Assisi." Adrien was nothing if not wise. He boiled it down to an exact course of action, but his unenthused grumble spoke clearly. He didn't like the thought of me taking another jaunt into the heart of Cambiare territory alone.

A snarky response came to mind. Instead I ignored his discomfort. "You know what I just don't get? The fact that the Great Council seems to want to vilify the Cambiare when according to Nix and the histories Gino read, we have been allies for centuries. I mean, what happened to cause the Council to want to wipe the history between us away? Why are they our enemies?"

Adrien shrugged. "Does it matter? It's totally irrelevant to why we're here. Before long, we'll be home and can forget Nix and her kind even exist. So, as far as I'm concerned, if the Great Council choses to treat the Cambiare as enemies, then who am I to question them? "

My mouth screwed up as my eyes narrowed. *Not a satisfying answer.* I turned to face him. "If we don't question it, who will?"

He rolled his eyes, lifted his hand, and rubbed at his eyes in frustration. "Okay, fine. But can we please tackle one problem at a time? We've already got way more on our plate than we planned for. It could take us weeks to get to the bottom of a centuries-old cover-up that no one even cares about."

My brows rose. "I care about it."

It was weird. Originally when I told Leo I was interested in the histories of our people, I said it to get what I wanted from him, but now, thinking about Nix and Julian and what might have been between them, I realized I needed the tales to be true. If they weren't, then it meant Julian had been a traitor to his own people, and that thought made my stomach churn.

"Well, care about it a little less…at least until after we find the bastard who killed Julian and send him to Aita." He pushed himself up from the edge of the buffet and rose to his full height. "Then, I promise, we will follow every little twisty, turny tangent you want to follow including the whole Julian was a long-lost prince thing." A bark of laughter escaped him as a look of surprise crossed my features. "Oh, you thought maybe I'd forgotten about that? Not a chance. When my Padrone starts to believe in conspiracy theories, I'm going to sit up and take notice."

Conspiracy theories? "I never thought about it that way. You have to admit, it does seem like every time we turn around someone is lying to us."

Adrien nodded, folding his arms over his chest. "Sure, we've been lied to. But, that doesn't mean we have to start seeing demons where there aren't any."

I growled. I was done trying to make him see what I saw around us. "You know as well as I do that seeing demons or angels all depends upon your perspective." Pushing myself off the furniture, I shrugged. "For now, I'll ease up on the crazy conspiracy theories. However, once we deal with Julian's murder and the Vuote killing, I'm going to make you keep that promise."

Chapter Thirty

A while later, after Adrien left for security to commence the interviews of the human staff, I readied myself for a trip into Assisi. Since it was the middle of the afternoon, there was no need to change into the black attire I worn for my previous excursion into Cambiare territory. In fact, doing so on a bright spring day would cause me to stick out like an emo chick at a debutant ball.

Nope, the blue jeans and white button down I had been wearing all day were fine for this little outing.

Turning on a heel, I crossed to the desk and picked up the silver locket. I turned it over in my palm. The shiny silver glinted with the movement. Popping it open I looked over the features of the woman who sat smiling up at me. It looked as though she might have been Nix's age when it was taken, most likely with one of the first cameras in existence at the time. The resemblance to Nix and Alegra was uncanny. Long ebony hair pulled up into a style which must have been popular in the 1800s. In the image the woman had light-colored eyes, which I could only assume were like Nix's, warm, honeyed, amber. Stunning. Like mother like daughter. If not her mother, then she had to be another close female relative, and someone of importance in Nix's life. Why else would she carry her image everywhere she went? The locket was a treasured item, and she would want it back. Snapping the lid of the locket closed, I stuffed the necklace into the front pocket of my jeans and moved to pick up the walking stick.

Best to be prepared for any outcome...just in case.

"Going somewhere?" Her voice purred through me like the low rumbling of thunder.

Glancing up, intense interest replaced surprised confusion.

The curtains billowed in the spring breeze and the sun illuminated Nix for the first time since we'd meet. Her long ebony hair, tied back in a ponytail like it had been last night, draped over one shoulder. The soft pink tank top, unusually feminine for the woman I'd come to consider a formidable presence, bared her tanned shoulders and well-toned arms. The scoop neck line of the garment revealed the tops of ample breasts and the deep crevice between. I drew my eyes away from her...assets and met her gaze. Surprise registered as I realized her golden eyes were no longer golden. They'd been replaced by dark brown. *Contacts perhaps?* I wouldn't blame her. Her eyes would only serve to draw unwanted attention to her while out in public. Though I was curious, a different question formed on my lips, "What are you doing here?"

"I came to see you."

"Then you are either incredibly brave or exceptionally stupid." I paused to raise an eyebrow and cross my arms leaning back against the desk. I studied her as if puzzling over an enigma. "I just haven't figured out which it is...yet."

She gave an unladylike snort and sashayed forward like she owned the place. Most likely because she had been here many times over when Julian was in residence. Pulling the doors closed behind her, she leaned back against her hands still resting on the handles. "Why? Because I dare to come to your room during the daylight hours?"

I watched her closely, intrigued by her disregard for the danger of the situation. "Yes, for one. It takes a lot of courage to walk into the Alimentatori stronghold in the middle of the day."

Stepping away from the doors, she shrugged as if the feat was nothing special, and shoved her hands into the back pockets of her pants. Like me, she wore dark blue jeans, but if mine hugged my body like hers caressed her curves I'd be singing soprano.

"Middle of the day. Middle of the night. It matters not. Your people have not even come close to capturing me."

Her overconfident attitude almost elicited an overly sarcastic response. I refrained preferring to keep things civil for the moment. "Did you visit Julian here as well?"

"Yes, on occasion. When we had no other choice."

My curiosity burned until I could no longer withhold my questions. "Did you love him, Nix? Is that the secret you're hiding from me?"

Her head snapped back toward me. Those strange brown eyes grew wide in shocked surprise. "Don't be absurd. I could never love a Feeder. He was a means to an end."

Stunned by her adamant denial, I pushed myself away from the desk and snarled, "A means to an end? That's all he was to you?"

She looked away again as her cheeks reddened. "At first, yes."

I steadied my breathing as the anger subsided enough to allow me a chance to listen without judgment. "What do you mean, at first?"

"I...," she paused and withdrew her hands from her pockets. Like a caged lioness she paced the small expanse in front of the French doors. "You have to understand. I was sent to him to seek his help. He was not from here and didn't have the same loyalties that those born into power here have."

"Are you saying you were trying to turn him, into a double agent?" My mouth turned down in a severe frown. "You used him?"

She stopped and dropped her eyes to the ground. Her whisper was strained. "Yes, though it wasn't what you think. We never meant for him to get hurt."

Anger licked to life again burning through me like a wildfire. "What was so fucking important that it was worth risking my brother's life?"

She turned toward me, her hands outstretched as she pleaded for understanding. "You do not understand. He had been accepted into the deepest darkest parts of Aliment society. We needed him to be able to investigate the increasing disappearances of our people. He was our last hope." Her gaze found mine as her jaw set. "Until you arrived. Now, that hope rests on you."

My eyes grew wide. *Astounding.* As if I would help those whose actions resulted in Julian's death. "Then you have no hope."

Her shoulders fell as she stared at me. She inhaled and exhaled as if frustrated. "Please, do not—"

"Do not what? Tell you to go to hell?" I growled as I crossed the room and towered over her, glaring down at her. "You and your kind may not have had a direct hand in killing him, but by dragging him into your problems you might as well have. I won't be making the same mistake, so unless you plan on ending up like Julian, get the fuck out of my room and leave me alone." Retreating from her, I jammed my hand into the front pocket of my jeans. My fingers curled around the warm bit of metal within the pocket. I withdrew my hand and thrust the locket and chain toward her. "And take this with you when you go. I want no part of you left here as an excuse for you to come back."

The stunned, almost hurt look on her face was quickly disguised by a rush of anger. The becoming pinkish blush she'd had moments ago turned to a more vibrant hue. Ripping the necklace from my fingers she glared up at me. "Testa di cazzo! You think I wanted Julian to pay for our recruitment of him? I would have gladly given up my life to save his." Angry tears formed in her eyes, unheeded. Her hand balled into a fist around the locket, her fingers clenched down on the small metal oval as if restraining the urge to do me physical harm. She paced again, addressing me over her shoulder as she did so. "Julian and I...we may not have been lovers, but he was special to me and my people. He held the future of our people, and yours, in his hands. We approached him because we needed someone we could trust. And you know what, he proved worthy of our trust. He died keeping our secrets. To my knowledge, he never breathed a word of his involvement with us."

Incredulous, I shouted, "If it weren't for his involvement with your people he'd be alive today."

She paused in her pacing with her back to me. Her shoulders rose as a heavy sigh escaped her. The clenching of her fist eased as her whispered tone sliced through the tension, "I know, And I'm sorry. I liked Julian. Like I said before, we'd become friends. And his death has weighed heavily on me. I...," her head dropped as her sorrowful tone spoke of remorse, "I left him there by himself. He was supposed to go home. I didn't know he'd not made it until the next morning when the news..." Her shoulders trembled a little, a minute outward sign of her inner turmoil. "If I could go back, I would have stayed with him— made sure he got back here safely."

The emotions she tried so hard to stuff down and keep hidden flowed from her like a river of shame, guilt, and anger.

And amazingly it touched me. Where Adrien's guilt had never been able to melt my anger, hers pulled at my heart, which made me uncomfortable. The hard edge to my tone softened. "Why did you need him, Nix? What made Julian so special that he was your only hope?"

Before turning, she reached up and wiped away any evidence of her momentary slip obviously not wanting to seem weak. Turning to face me, she met my gaze. "I told you. He wasn't Italian born aristocracy. We needed someone who would understand our plight and be willing to feed us information."

A severe frown creased my brow. The idea of Julian committing such a treasonous act did not sit well. "And did he?"

"He was going to. Unfortunately, he was killed before he could do much of anything. That night, he called me. He wanted to meet but he couldn't get away. So, I went to him. I knew it was risky, but it couldn't wait."

"I see. And you thought you could waltz in and out of the event without being noticed?"

She shook her head as she toyed with a strand of hair. "No. It's never been that easy. I had help."

"Of course, you did." I thought on it for a moment, then asked, "Karina?"

"Si."

That did little to shake the frown from my features. "If you had Karina in your pocket, why did you pursue Julian? Couldn't she have provided the information you needed?"

Again, she shook her head, this time more adamantly. "You Americans. Always assuming things only get done in foreign countries with bribery." She paused to let the insult rest solidly on my shoulders then continued, "Karina wasn't in our pockets. We never paid her. We didn't have to. She's Dante's cousin."

Stunned surprise sucked the air from my lungs. "Whoa, wait. Karina is a half-breed?"

That explained so much. Why she'd left the cameras on the roof in disrepair. Why she covered up the footage of Julian leaving with Nix. Why she was afraid to leave with the guards. No wonder she had been desperate to escape. Being held in an Alimentatori prison as a half-breed wouldn't be pleasant.

Nix scowled, obviously angered by something I'd said. Her tone confirmed her anger as she recaptured my attention, "Not half-breeds. Di due anime."

"Of two souls?" At her nod, I gave a cool smile. "Interesting."

"Calling someone a half-breed is derogatory. Being *di due anime* is a gift and should not be punished." She held up two fingers. "Two worlds. Two parts to their soul...," then brought her hands up and clasped them together, "one body to contain them." I nodded in response. When it was obvious I was not going to say anything further, she continued her explanation. "Anyway, to answer your question, no, Karina could not provide anything more. She'd given us everything she could. She suspected the Great Council might be watching her. Your replacement of her says she was right. Besides, what we really needed was someone with access to the Council, someone who could find others in power who might be sympathetic to our cause."

"Which led you to Julian?"

"Yes. We'd cultivated his friendship for months." A haunted look entered her eyes as she suddenly looked away. "Funny thing is, I found that I enjoyed his company, and the cultivated friendship became real…to both of us." She shrugged off the melancholy feelings enveloping her and looked back at me. "Anyway, most who have Ascended were brought up in the life. They are part of the system. Your brother was not. Once he ascended, then he would be one of them. Even so, he would never be as firm in his beliefs as those who'd been raised to not question. We'd hoped with his direct access to the Council members he would be able to gain their trust and maybe even convince a few others to help. So, you see, we had great reason to want him alive. We were finally going to be able to infiltrate the Great Council, find out who we can trust, who is involved, and where those who have disappeared are being held."

"And what makes you think the Alimentatori are responsible for your missing?"

She paused and cocked her head to the side. "Everyone who has disappeared did so after visiting Eros."

That made no sense. "But you've been to Eros and are still here. That reminds me, how are you able to get in and out of Eros? It's an invitation only club."

"The club didn't used to be exclusively Aliment. In fact, it was founded by one of our servant's families. They wanted a place where the Aliments and Cambiare could interact with humans without pretending to be human. However, when things turned ugly between us, he chose self-preservation for himself and his family. They now cater almost exclusively to the Alimentatori." Casting me a sly look, she said, "I believe you've met him."

"I have?" At her slow nod, I thought about it for a moment, and then it dawned on me. It could be only one person. The man who owned Eros…*Alrigo Gattoli.* "Of course." I rolled my eyes and chuckled. "Why didn't I see it? His name translates to cat, doesn't it?"

Her eyebrow rose wickedly. "Alrigo is a personal favorite. He's very good at giving the Alimentatori what they want, while remaining loyal to Dante. No one bothers him because his family is of Dante's house. Something happens to him, and Dante goes on the war path."

With a sideways glance at the door she said, "Sounds like you've got company."

I turned to face the door. I'd not heard anything. Still, if she said someone was about to enter, then someone was about to enter. Using my body to shield her from the direct line of sight of whoever was about to burst through the bedroom door, I spoke over my shoulder, "I'll handle this."

As the door swung inward, Adrien rushed through the portal. "Jace, we've got him."

"Got who?"

Pride puffed up his chest and raised his shoulders. "The guy who poisoned the Vuote."

"Great. I'll be there in a second. I just have to have to finish up things here first." I turned to the side to allow Adrien to see past me.

Confusion replaced the smile he wore. "Um, okay. What are you doing?"

"We were just talking." I responded, stuffing my hands in my pockets.

"We who?" Adrien responded, obviously further confused by my response.

Startled, I turned. The French door behind me stood ajar, though Nix had vanished. "Uh, never mind. I'll be right there. Give me a second, okay?"

"Sure. I'll wait in the living room." He closed the door behind him, leaving me alone.

Opening the patio door, I exited on to the balcony expecting to find Nix waiting. Regrettably, she was gone. Crossing my arms over my chest, I gazed out over the water. All this new information helped the puzzle pieces slide into place.

At Eros Nix was able to come and go as she pleased because of her connection to Dante. That was where she'd met Julian. She recruited him to aid in her cause. They needed him to take his seat at the Great Council in order for their plan to work. As such, it was now obvious the Cambiare would not have done anything to put him in danger. To do so would jeopardize whatever they were working toward.

So, if that was the case, had someone in power figured out what they were up to? If so, why hadn't they just put a stop to it by arresting him for treason or outing him to the Council to stop his ascension? Why kill him and frame the Cambiare? It was opportunistic and underhanded, which spoke of a hidden agenda.

The whispering of a thought coursed through my mind, *because the murder had nothing to do with the Cambiare.*

Laying the blame at the Cambiare's feet may have been *because* of Julian's relationship with Nix. Who better to frame? There was an established, traceable connection between the two. Someone had known what I would find if I dug into the details. They had only to point me in the right direction.

It was now readily apparent. I was not looking for someone within her ranks. I was looking for someone within my own.

Chapter Thirty-One

I entered the living room to find Adrien leaning against the buffet, talking on his cell phone. He saw me and nodded.

"Yeah, we're working on it." He nodded as if the person on the other end had said something he agreed with. "Yes, I know. Things here are kind of a mess right now. It's been more difficult than we first envisioned. We will be home as soon as we can." He paused as the voice on the other end spoke again. "Listen, Jace is ready. I've got to go." One more pause as the conversation closed. "Okay. Yes. Take care of yourself, Magda. We'll be home soon."

My brow knit together as Adrien crossed to join me. "What did Magda want?"

"Just touching base. She called to see if we'd made any progress and to let you know the ceremony for Julian was completed just after he arrived home."

I chewed on the side of my cheek as the unwanted reminder of why I'd come to Italy lay like a lump in the pit of my stomach. "Good. At least his body is at rest, and the clan can begin to heal."

"Agreed."

Anxious to finish up with the Vuote murder, I moved the

conversation along. "So, give me the details. What are we looking at?"

Adrien smiled, obviously looking forward to doing so. "Why don't we walk to the security office, and I'll give you a run down." I nodded and fell into step beside him. As he held open the door for me, he continued, "I started with the kitchen staff, figuring they provided everything on the tray. Turns out, they don't even keep orange juice in the kitchens because, as you know, it's too acidic for the Aliment system."

Stepping through the portal and into the hall, I waited for him to close and lock the suite door. I nodded, "Of course. That makes sense. So that led you to?"

He chuckled as if about to spring a surprise on me. "The Library. The bartenders use it for mixing drinks. I checked with Alcie and the person scheduled to work the bar this morning showed up, and then went home 'sick'. That person was…," he paused to build my anticipation, "Anthony."

"Anthony. The man who recommended Eros? That Anthony?" My surprise was genuine. He was the last person I would have suspected of murder. I had to admit though that posing as a bartender in the Library might be the perfect position for a Vuote spy. You'd see the comings and goings of everyone through the Library. It was where I was shown the first day I arrived. Not to mention conversations are easily overheard. No one pays attention to the one serving when they're busy drinking. And the ones who do are usually spilling their guts about relationships or work.

"Yes. That Anthony." He paused to swipe his key card in the reader, and the door clicked in response. Pushing open the door, he held it for me. "I've had him brought in. He's waiting in your office."

I stepped through, and my gaze immediately sought the enclosed glass office. Two armed guards stood to either side of the door, in much the same manner as the ones had stood guard over the Vuote. For Anthony's sake, I was hoping for a better outcome. It would be nice to be able to question the man before someone got the chance to put him in the grave.

As we approached, I glanced in through the glass window. It appeared Anthony had settled himself in one of the leather chairs across from the desk. From what I could tell, he had nerves of steel. Despite being brought to security and locked in a guarded room, the man seemed relaxed.

I nodded toward the office and addressed Adrien, "Have you questioned him?"

"Not yet. Once I had word he was on his way in, I came to get you."

I paused and turned to Adrien with a frown. "So, he's not admitted to it, and you don't actually have anything on him yet."

"Well no. But I thought you might want to be the one to take him down."

Realizing there was little I could do about it now, I responded. "I see. And you're confident he's the one?"

Adrien frowned, obviously not happy about being questioned. "I am."

"All right, then let's do this." I continued my trek across the room. Showing my badge to the guards, I stated, "Open it up."

A moment later, the guard held the door open for us to enter. As I stepped into the room Anthony made to rise. Waving him back into his seat, I proceeded to the other side of the desk. "Sit. We just have a few questions for you."

"Did I do something wrong?" Though his manner seemed to state he was relaxed, the slightest tremor in his voice indicated a touch of nervousness.

"I don't know." I placed my hands on the desktop and leaned over. One brow rose as I glared down at him. "Did you?"

"I...," he looked from me to barrel-chested Adrien who stood at the end of the desk, muscled arms folded, looking altogether like the right-hand man to a mafia kingpin. "I don't...think so."

My gaze met his, and for a briefest of seconds I read fear in his eyes. "Anthony, where were you this morning?"

"I was downstairs, working."

I rapped my fingers on the desk. "Alcie stated you went

home early. Can you tell me what happened?"

He glanced back at me and absently picked at the arm of the chair. "About nine o'clock I started feeling off, like something wasn't right with my stomach. I called Alcie, and she told me to check out and go home, that she'd bring someone in to watch the Library."

With his pasty, peaked complexion I almost believed his story…almost. "Watch the Library? You mean tend bar?"

"Yes and no. We weren't hired just to tend bar. We watch the door to the archive room and log any unusual activity."

"I see." And I did for the first time. Our unsanctioned trip to the archives wasn't as secret as I'd hoped. Good thing they weren't privy to what was being said behind that closed door, or Leo and his family might just find themselves in hot water. "And who do those logs go to?"

Anthony clasped his hands over his belly and sat back. "Alcie, of course."

I nodded as if that was information I already had. "Of course."

"Is that why I'm here? Did I make a mistake on the logs?"

A tolerant smile spread my lips. "Not that I know of."

He looked confused as he picked at the chair again. "Then why am I here?"

"Someone poisoned a human we were holding downstairs."

His incredulous voice rang in the quiet of the room. "And you think I had something to do with it?"

My gaze bored into him. "The thought has crossed our minds. Did you pour a glass of orange juice which was to be served to a prisoner?"

Anthony's hands gripped the arms of the chair as he responded adamantly, "I poured several glasses of orange juice this morning. I do every morning. Some are for humans who work in the villa. Others are for guests. I have no idea if one of the glasses I poured this morning went to your prisoner."

"How many glasses do you normally pour in the morning?"

"Depends on the morning. This morning I poured three

glasses. I had a glass when I got in because I felt fuzzy this morning, and figured I needed the vitamin C. Then the butler came in and requested a glass for his breakfast. And the last one was for the kitchen. They were fixing a tray for a...guest?" His voice trailed off as he realized he'd just incriminated himself. "There was nothing in it. I swear. Just orange juice."

I nodded. "I see. And who did you give the glass to?"

"I gave it to Alcie to deliver to the kitchen."

My curiosity peaked. "Alcie? Why Alcie?"

He shrugged. "She was the one who came for it."

My eyes narrowed as Alcie re-emerged as a suspect. "Is that normal?"

"No. Not really. Normally she doesn't bother with it. She came upstairs because she wanted to check on me. When I told her, the glass was for the kitchen, she volunteered to take it for me, so I could go home."

I sighed heavily. This wasn't boding well. Everything seemed to come full circle to Alcie. "I would really like to believe you, Anthony, but you must realize that you are in serious trouble here. If it's proven you slipped something into that drink and then gave it to Alcie to deliver, we will have no choice. You will be brought before the Great Council."

"But I didn't. Isn't there any way you will believe me? A lie detector test or something?"

I bit the inside of my cheek in thought. There was one way to be sure he told the truth. "There is a way, but I will need your permission."

Anthony's desire to clear his name motivated him quickly. "Yes. My answer is yes. Whatever it is."

"Okay. Have you ever heard of *collegamento di mente*?"

He nodded. "Of course, signore. It is the connecting of minds. What your people do to place visions into the minds of others."

"Yes, it is. We can also use it to extract a memory, to view it as if we were you. We do not like to use the ability as it has long been a taboo. Entering the minds of another to enhance their pleasure or give them something in return for what they give us, is one thing. Perusing through the private thoughts and memories of others is quite frankly an invasion. However, with your permission I am willing to take that step to see what you saw, hear what you heard. It's better than any lie detector test I could make you take. No one can hide the truth from their own mind. If you are in fact innocent I will know in a matter of minutes."

Anthony hesitated a moment before nodding. "Si, I agree, signore. Do what you must."

I glanced up at Adrien. "Adrien, would you mind getting the blinds on the windows?"

"Jace, are you sure about this? If something goes wrong…"

"We will cross that bridge when we come to it. Now, get the blinds." I rose to walk around the desk. Moving behind Anthony, I waited until Adrien had dropped the blinds into place. Once the last one fell, I knelt beside his chair and looked up into the young bartender's eyes. "What I want you to do is close your eyes and simply think about this morning, remember what happened, and when the time comes, allow me into your memories of the events."

He nodded and laid his head back on the chair and then closed his eyes. By doing so, I knew he was not guilty. Anyone who was willing to submit to *collegamento di mente* had nothing to hide.

I rose and thrust a hand through my hair. "You're free to go."

His eyes shot open. "But collegamento di mente…"

I shook my head. "There is no need. You wouldn't have allowed me to proceed if you were guilty. You would have been terrified of what I would find." Stepping back, I waved a hand toward the door. "So, go. Get some rest. You look terrible."

He looked up at me and then at Adrien. As my Second turned his back to us, relief flooded the human's face. "Oh my God. Thank you, signore. You won't regret this."

I crossed my arms over my chest with a stern look on my face. "Make sure I don't."

Anthony stood. Walking toward the door, he paused halfway across the room. Turning back to face me, he asked, "signore, if you don't mind my asking. Who was the man who died, and what did he do?"

I ignored his question for a moment as I walked back to my chair. As I pulled it under me and sat down, I shrugged. "He was a Vuote sniper. Adrien and I brought him in last night, and as far as I'm concerned whoever hastened his demise did me a favor. One less Vuote in the world can only make it a better place."

"A Vuote?" The man's curiosity was obviously peaked. "What did he do?"

Sitting back, I tilted the chair back and draped my right arm across the desk. "Does it matter? He's Vuote."

He crossed back to stand behind the chair in which he had been sitting. Leaning over, he placed his hands on the chair back and spoke urgently, "It matters. There is much history between the Alimentatori and the Vuote. The Vuote target not only your kind, but those who work for you. All of the humans who work in the villa could be in danger if they have come to Italy again."

Weighing his concern against the need to keep the incident from being blown out of proportion, I realized perhaps it was unfair to keep this particular incident quiet. If others could be in danger, then they should be made aware. "It was a failed attempt on my life. He tracked me down last night but with the help of…a friend he was thwarted."

Anthony looked over at Adrien. "And he stopped him before he—"

I recaptured the bartender's attention by interrupting him, "No, the man got off several shots before he was stopped."

The man's brows knit together in concern. "But that can't be, signore."

I sighed and drummed my fingers against the surface of the desk bored with his curiosity. "While I appreciate your concern, I am alive and well. There is no need to be melodramatic."

"No.," the bartender shook his head sternly, "No, you mistake my meaning." He came around the chair and placed himself directly in front of me. "The Vuote are renowned for their marksmanship. If they take aim and you're in the crosshairs, you do not walk away. They do not miss."

My fingers stopped drumming as I looked up at the man. "What are you saying?"

"Signore, I don't know who you captured last night, but I highly doubt he was Vuote."

Stunned, I eased back in the chair. "That's one man's opinion."

"You want another man's opinion? Call Vincenzo in here. I have no doubt he'll tell you the same thing."

I stared at the man across from me, studying his every move. He seemed confident in what he was saying, though I found it hard to believe. Without looking away, I spoke to Adrien. "It seems Anthony thinks he knows better than we do. Call Vinny in here and lets just see what he has to say."

Without responding, Adrien moved to the door. Opening it, he spoke to one of the guards, who immediately went across the room to where Vinny was helping another security officer. Within seconds Vincenzo stood in front of me.

"Yes, signore? Can I be of help?"

I glanced up at him. Whether or not I was doing this to prove myself right or Anthony wrong didn't matter. Both ways, I would win the argument, and we could dispense with this conversation. "Vincenzo, this gentleman seems to be under the impression that the Vuote are somehow superhuman. It seems Anthony believes that once a Vuote sights his target, he never misses. What is your opinion?"

Vinny shifted his weight from one foot to the other. "I would not say superhuman, but extremely accurate."

My eyes narrowed but I was confident of the security officer's impending support. "Accurate. But they do miss?"

He clasped his hands together in front of him. "There are currently no accounts of anyone surviving a sniper attack." He looked down at me and gave a slight incline of the head as if to acknowledge my narrow escape. "Until now, of course."

I studied the man who first brought the Vuote to my attention. Was he supporting me to save face? By Aita, I didn't need a yes man. I needed the truth. "Vinny, I know I never thought to ask, but I'm asking you now. Was the man we brought in Vuote?"

Vincenzo looked to Adrien and then back at me as if deciding what was best to say. "Though he was dressed as Vuote, his inaccuracy as proven by your continued existence seems to suggest that he was not."

That was not what I expected to hear. I sat back against the chair, dumbfounded. "How certain are you of that?"

Pride lifted the man's shoulders. "I'm very confident, signore. No one here knows the Vuote like I do."

"Then why in the hell did you let me keep on believing the man was Vuote?"

The security officer's gaze met mine head on, not shirking from the guilt of withholding information. "As you said, signore, you did not ask. You assumed. Had I been asked my opinion it would have been given regardless of the Great Council's misinformation."

I had the good sense to look ashamed. "Is this why you were so insistent that the man killed himself and there was no foul play?"

"Yes and no. It is widely known that the Vuote do not allow their people to be taken prisoner. It made sense that if someone meant him to look like Vuote they would instruct him to take his own life if captured. It is what a Vuote would do."

I mulled over his answer. He could be right. If I had taken a moment to ask, I would not be making a fool out of myself in front of the human. Arrogance had its price, and I believe I just paid it. "Thank you, Vinny. I will make it a point from here on out to bring my questions about the Vuote to you."

Vincenzo flushed but remained stoic. "Is there anything else, signore?"

My response was flat and unenthusiastic. "No, you can go."

He bowed and turned toward the door. Moments later he'd exited the room.

As the door closed, I turned my attention back to the one who started me down this uncomfortable path of self-discovery. I stood up and held out my hand to him. "Well, it does seem that I owe you a debt of gratitude. I appreciate your input."

The bartender grasped my hand and pumped his arm enthusiastically. "I'm glad I could help, signore."

"It also appears that you and your friends have nothing to fear at this time."

Alarm lit Anthony's eyes as he dropped his hand. "But it appears you do, signore. If the man was not Vuote, then he was specifically after you."

The man wasn't wrong. Why I'd been the target of an assassination attempt puzzled me. "It appears so."

Anthony stepped back; his eyes wary. "Be careful, signore. There may be others."

I nodded. "I will. Thank you for your concern."

The man shrugged. "It would be a tragedy for you to fall...like your brother."

My brows knit. The man turned and walked out of the room leaving Adrien and me alone.

Adrien scowled as he took the seat the other had vacated. "So now we have a hired gun instead of a Vuote assassin?"

"It would seem."

"Which means someone specifically paid him to take you out."

I nodded, lost in thought. This was not random. Someone wanted me dead, and they had gone to great lengths to make it seem like I was on a Vuote hit list. But, why? Was someone afraid of what I would find while investigating my brother's death? It seemed the only logical explanation. "Adrien, I think it's time we pull out all the stops. We need to stop looking at the humans involved and start looking at the Aliments. I want phone and bank records, surveillance video, anything, and everything we can find on every Aliment even remotely involved in the deaths of both men, starting with Alcie."

At first, I thought he was going to argue, but then he stood up. "Fine. I'll investigate Alcie's office tonight after she leaves. I can riffle through her desk, her files, even tap her phone. Whatever it takes, Jacen."

"Sounds good. In the meantime, do whatever you can to clear as many others as possible. If it comes to taking down Alcie, I want no stone unturned. The Great Council will have my head on a pike if we fuck this up."

"Understood."

"I'm going back to the room. Call me if you need anything."

As I rose and walked toward the door, Adrien's hand grabbed my arm. Glancing over at him, my gaze met his hard eyes.

"Jacen, I'll find whoever is behind this. I promise."

I nodded and gave him a reassuring smile. "I know you will. I trust you."

Chapter Thirty-Two

I pulled back a sheer curtain and gazed out at the night. The daytime staff had retreated to their homes hours ago, and Adrien left to check out Alcie's office to see what he could find. He insisted I stay behind, something about plausible deniability if he was caught. Whatever. The time alone had given me ample opportunity to plan my next course of action. When Adrien returned, we were going looking for Nix. I had a deal for her she wouldn't refuse. She wanted my help, then she was going to have to work for it. I wanted every detail she could remember from that night, every sound, smell, sight. I missed something, and she might be the key to figuring out what.

The door across the room opened quietly and without looking, I knew it was Adrien. I turned just in time to catch him yawning. "Long day?"

He didn't say anything. Just dropped onto the couch and stretched his legs out in front of him.

I turned back to the window. "Did you find anything?"

"Apparently, she's not overly cautious about access to her computer." He stifled another yawn. "I was able to get into the office without an issue, and the computer wasn't very well protected. She had her access code and passwords written down on a sheet of paper taped to her keyboard drawer."

I turned around. Walking forward, I took a seat across from him. "Most likely because she's in the bowels of the headquarters and is afforded the protection of the Great Council. Who in their right mind is going to break into her office and steal something off her computer?"

He chuckled. "No one ever accused me of being in my right mind."

Nodding, I smiled. "Right mind or not, were you able to find anything of value?"

He sat forward and draped his arms over his knees. "I scoured every personnel record I could find. A couple warrant further investigation. I checked out Vinny. Something's strange about his appointment as Karina's assistant." He rubbed a hand over his eyes, as if the last couple hours had worn on him. "He took the job a few weeks before Julian's murder."

It was appearing as if Adrien had sidetracked himself with Vinny, instead of checking out Alcie. "Okay. So, he was new at his job. What does that matter?"

"It wasn't the fact that he was new to security. It was the fact that Morbius himself signed the man's reassignment papers."

Confused, my brow furrowed. "I guess I'm missing your point."

He sighed and sat back, running a frustrated hand through his blond hair. "My point is, as far as I can tell from his file he's a highly trained undercover operative who also happens to be a member of the *Venatori*."

Confused, I frowned. "And that is?"

Adrien shrugged. "Unfortunately, I couldn't get into any of the referenced case files."

"You tried?"

"Of course, but I got an 'access denied' every time. I don't think Alcie is privy to any information dealing with them."

"That still doesn't answer the question about who they are."

"I know, and I'm sorry I don't have more for you. I can quietly ask around and see if anyone is willing to clue me in on what the Venatori does."

I nodded. "Fine but be careful. There is no telling what will come of tipping over that can of worms." A thought occurred to me as I mulled over this new information. Vinny was loyal to the Great Council, that much was obvious. So, what had prompted his transfer to the less prestigious Security office?

My Second's stare intensified as he expounded on his search. "It makes no sense. I went through every other security officer's file. None of them are Venatori. And not one of them had Morbius's signature on their paperwork."

A sigh escaped me as a reason for Morbius's attention dawned. The image of Karina's outrage at being caught came to mind. Nix had said that Karina had believed the Council was on to her. She must have been right.

I sat back and met his gaze. "I think I know why." His eyes met mine in curiosity. "There's something I haven't told you." The sour look on his face as he rolled his eyes and pushed himself off the couch spurred me forward with an explanation. "Not that I wasn't going to tell you, I just hadn't had a chance."

His shoulders fell in disappointment. "And here I thought we'd gotten past this."

"It's not like that." An exasperated sigh slipped out. "I didn't intentionally keep anything from you. I just didn't think to fill you in on the details. Earlier, when you barreled into my room...without knocking I might add, Nix was here."

"Well, yeah. I kind of figured you weren't talking to yourself." His sarcastic tone said clearly that he had been waiting for me to confess. "Are you going to fill me in on the details or make me guess?"

"She was here to talk..."

*****

For the next several minutes I recapped the conversation Nix and I'd had. From the dumbfounded look he wore, Adrien had not expected it any more than I had.

"So, you're telling me Karina was the mole." His scowl intensified as he rose and swore under his breath. "Why the fuck didn't you tell me this before I wasted my time piecing together a whole lot of nothing?"

"I'm sorry. I would have told you sooner, but the whole conversation kind of got lost in the shuffle when you rushed in with your news about Anthony."

He slapped a hand across his eyes and turned his back on me. "Fuck! This changes everything."

I stood and held my hands up. "It changes nothing. It only gives us a reason for the Council's acute interest in the daily running of Security."

He stopped his pacing and turned on me. "You don't get it do you?"

Anger leapt to life quickly. "There's nothing to get."

Stunned by my defensive response, he scowled, heaved an exasperated sigh, and he shook his head. "Don't you see, Jacen? The Council already had a man on the inside. Why go to all the trouble of insisting you take the position as Head of Security? Why not just unseat Karina and replace her with Vinny?"

And for the first time I understood. I turned away and dropped my chin to my chest. Staring at the floor, I studied the intricate pattern of fibers in the carpet. *He was right.* There was only one explanation. They used the job to distract me, to keep me preoccupied with something other than Julian's murder. *And I let them.* I closed my eyes in an attempt to block out my own stupidity. "Why?"

Misunderstanding my question, Adrien responded, "Because it's better to keep you busy, then to have you find out they are protecting Julian's killer."

I rubbed a hand along the back of my neck to ease the sudden tension filling my body. This was crazy. What we were talking about was treasonous. My voice dropped to a mere whisper, "You think it is someone on the Council?"

"I hate to say it, but at this point, it's the only thing that makes sense. Why else would they lead us down the wrong path and put obstacles in the way?"

I had to admit, he had a point. The Council had been less than helpful and seemed to know everything and nothing all at the same time. I swallowed but it didn't alleviate the growing dryness of my mouth. "True. If it wasn't one of them, then it was someone close to them."

He nodded. "Yes, and who knows how deep that rabbit hole goes, Jacen? Maybe it's better if we allow Julian's murder to remain unsolved. We should go home...while we still can."

His words sliced through me like a blade. Everything within me rebelled against the thought of giving up. Leave Julian's murderer to walk the Earth while Julian's ashes were scattered to the wind? *I don't think so.* "No. If you choose to go home, then so be it. But I will do exactly what I came here to do. No more distractions. No more worrying over justice for that human filth. For all we know, he was hired by the same person who had Julian killed." My jaw set, and I cast my Second a steely eyed glare. "No. Julian's murderer will die by my hand, even if it's the last thing I do in this realm."

Adrien's chin lifted, and the muscle in his jaw flexed. "If you're staying, I'm staying. We'll take down the bastard together."

I gave a curt nod. "I was hoping you would say that."

He crossed his arms over his barrel chest and gave me a serious look. "So, where do we start?"

Turning away, I propped my hands on my hips and crossed the floor back to the windows. Where did one start when every road was designed to lead nowhere? The only place one could start. "Back at the beginning."

"Which means?"

I looked over at him. "The footage of the night Julian died. I went over it a dozen times, but I had a single-minded purpose. Maybe there was something else there, someone else leaving I didn't pay attention to."

"You want to go back over it one more time."

"No. I want you to go back over it."

His brows drew together in concern. "Where are you going?"

"I'm going looking for Nix."

"Why?" His unenthused tone said he didn't approve.

It didn't matter. I was doing it anyway. "Because, Adrien, she wants my help, and with the way things are heading, we might just need hers."

Chapter Thirty-Three

⏁n my way out, I left Adrien at Security and headed down the stairs. As my foot hit the bottom step, the hair stood up on the back of my neck. Glancing around, I saw no one, but the reaction didn't ease.

Every synapse in my brain fired warning shots through me. *Someone is watching.*

Peering up at the camera which sat in the corner of the foyer I realized it was currently trained on the base of the stairs. Apparently, the knowledge that someone on the Council might be responsible for my brother's death had wheedled its way into my consciousness and made me jumpy. I shrugged it off and shook my head at my own foolishness. Giving a quick wave to whoever sat behind the monitor, I continued out the front door.

Alrigo would have a way of contacting Nix, so I needed to find my way to Eros. Unfortunately, with everything I knew, I couldn't trust an Alimentatori driver. Glancing around in the hope of finding a car I could hotwire, my eyes lit on a taxi which sat idling in a small parking area off the left side of the villa. A smile spread my lips. *Perfect. Just when I needed a ride.*

I sprinted to the side of the building. Crossing the short expanse to where the cab waited, I collided with someone, nearly knocking them to the ground. Reaching out, I grabbed the gentleman by the arms and steadied him. "Whoa there, you okay?"

My concern dropped when I realized who it was. "Belvedere? What are you doing here? I thought you went home hours ago."

The man brushed at his suit jacket as if my touch had mussed him. "Don't be ridiculous, signore. I'm the first to arrive in the morning and the last to go home at night."

My eyebrows rose, but I refrained from giving him a snarky response. "Then it seems luck is with me. I just happen to need a ride into Eros."

His eyes narrowed suspiciously. "Where's your driver?"

"Gave him the night off, but now I want to go out." His exasperated frown said he didn't care. "If you would be so kind as to let me share your cab, I will pay the fare."

He sighed as if heavily put upon. "I will allow it." I smiled, but my joy was short lived as he held up a finger and continued, "Under one condition."

"Anything. You name it and it's yours."

"Stop calling me Belvedere. My name is Orsino."

I laughed and slapped him on the back. "I know. You just kind of seemed like a Belvedere to me. But, I promise, Orsino it is."

The barest hint of a smile briefly appeared but was quickly replaced with his stern business-like manner. Stepping to the side, he opened the car door and held it, just as he would for someone arriving or departing the villa. Instead of sliding into the car, I stepped away from the opening and motioned with my arm. "After you."

A confused but wary look crossed his face. "But...I...are you sure, signore?"

I nodded and made the motion again. "Of course. You hold the door for me during the day, but you, my friend, are off duty."

He grinned, timidly at first, but then he beamed as if I just handed him a trophy. "Thank you, signore.

"My pleasure, Orsino and feel free to call me Jacen."

*****

The ride was filled with small talk. I asked questions, and Orsino answered. He had a family. His wife was named Lucia and they had three boys and a girl. They had a niece serving a family in America, whom I promised to look up when I got back. Not that I was into poaching servants, but it was the thought that counted anyway. Overall, nothing of import. Just all the little things one learns if one just thinks to ask.

"So, do you work this late every night?"

"Not usually, signore. I leave when I am dismissed for the day. If the Council has need of me, then I stay."

"That must be difficult on your family."

He looked away from me and wistfully looked out the window into the darkness. "Sometimes."

"Have you ever thought of leaving and finding a job that doesn't require such long hours?"

Orsino chuckled. "Where would I go? I was born into this life. It's all I know."

My eyebrows drew together as I studied the back of the other man's head. Until that moment I did not realize how trapped a human could feel.

Turning away from him, I stared straight ahead, and for the first time in quite some time I thought about Angel. Did she ever feel trapped like Orsino? If she did, then I would do the only thing I could to make it right. She was never going to feel that way again.

As the car pulled up in front of Eros, I sat for a moment, unsure of what to say to the man at whom I had taken great pleasure in poking fun. It was hard to reconcile this quiet, soft spoken man with the arrogant, stiff-upper-lipped butler he was at work. Who knew he had a personality? Reaching for my wallet, I pulled out a few Euros and handed them to him. "Thanks for the ride. I really appreciate it."

Orsino nodded but refused the money. "You're welcome. Keep your money."

I blinked at him, confused by his refusal to take the cash. "But we had a deal."

He smiled. "Si. And you kept your end of the bargain."

"I told you I would pay the fare."

"Sì Sì, but I never said I would accept it. Now, go on. I've got a family waiting for me."

I stuffed the bills back into the wallet. "Fine. But I'll owe you one." Opening the door, I stepped out onto the sidewalk. Turning, I bent down to peer into the car. "Thanks again. Have a good night."

"Buona notte, signore."

A few minutes later, I walked into Eros. Scouting the room, I spied the man for whom I came looking. Alrigo stood near the bar, talking animatedly with a few patrons. Laughter erupted from them as he spoke. I hope he doesn't lose his sense of humor when he finds out why I'm here.

When I came up behind him, I clapped a hand down lightly on his shoulder.

He turned to look up at me. The smile he shared with the others didn't fade. "Signore Trudeau. It is a pleasure to see you again."

"It is good to see you as well, Signore Gattoli."

"Please. You must call me Rigo. Everyone calls me Rigo."

His exuberant laugh made me chuckle. "Very well."

"Now, what can I get for you? Limoncello like before, eh?"

I shook my head. "Not tonight. I didn't come here to drink."

His smile dimmed as suspicion entered his eyes. "If not to drink, then what can I do for you?"

I met his stare head on. "I need a favor. I'm looking to get a message to someone, and I think you are just the person to deliver it."

The suspicion fled as his smile returned. "Of course, of course." He looked around the club knowingly. "Which young woman is lucky enough to have caught your eye?"

"Not that kind of message, Rigo. The young woman I want you to contact is...*special*." I leaned in and met his eye, "Nix."

Looking suddenly nervous, he shifted his weight from one foot to the other. He glanced around to see if anyone else had heard my request. Appearing relieved that our conversation had not been overheard, he relaxed. "Not here. Come to my office."

I followed him through the throng of club goers. At the back of the club we passed through a swinging door and entered a back hall. The dimly lit corridor ran back toward the bathrooms. A few seconds later, he ushered me through a door marked "Solo il Personale" – personnel only. The door closed behind us, and the slightest click of the lock denoted his concern for privacy.

Walking around the edge of his desk, he took a seat. Glaring up at me, he demanded, "How do you know about Nix?"

His accusatory tone and defensive manner indicated that our relationship had changed.

"Why? Am I not supposed to know that your family is still loyal to the Cambiare?"

The blood drained from his cheeks. "Who told you that?"

"Relax. I'm not here to cause trouble for you." I moved forward and dropped my hands to the back of a chair. "Nix told me about your family. She said you could be trusted. That's why I'm here."

He stared at me as if assessing the threat, I might pose to his little world. "Forgive me, signore, if I am skeptical. Nix is very dear to me. It would not sit well with me if you were to use me to harm her."

I studied the man intently. "I understand your hesitation. It's not every day that an Aliment walks into your establishment and asks you to use your connections to contact a Cambiare."

He gave a curt nod. "Indeed. So, you will also understand if I decline to aid you."

My jaw clamped down. Taking a moment to ease back on the throttle of my rising anger, my fingers clenched the chair, digging into the soft velveteen surface. I stifled a rude response in favor of remaining civil. "And you will understand if I don't take no for an answer."

His eyes widened. "Is that a threat, signore?"

A grim smile lifted the corners of my lips. "I do not issue threats, Rigo. Rest assured, if I wanted to hurt you or Nix, I would have already gone to the Council with what I know. I'm sure they would love to know that the one place Aliments go for a night out is owned by a man still loyal to the Cambiare."

He shot to his feet, anger cascading from him in waves. "Il mio dio! Non!"

My brows rose in humor. "Sit down. I said if I wanted to hurt you, which I do not. All I want is for Nix to meet with me. We can do so here if you feel the need to supervise."

He stood for several minutes staring at me as if trying to decide what to do. Then, he sat and picked up the phone. Waving me into the chair on which I was leaning, he scowled. "This will only take a minute."

He dialed a number on the phone and waited.

A few seconds later, he spoke, "Ciao bella."

Hello beautiful? Why did it not surprise me that the man had Nix's direct number?

"Spiacente per essere una seccatura, ma io abbia qualcuno qui chi desidera parlare con voi." He laughed in response to something Nix said. Probably an endearment of some kind. Did the Cambiare take il scelto? Did he belong to her? Regardless, the human's easy manner and good humor with her irritated me. "Si. Come lo sapevate?" He nodded as she spoke. "Certamente. Un attimo per favore." He held the receiver out to me all humor gone from his face. "She wants to talk to you."

I took the phone and sat back. "Hello?"

"Ciao, Jacen. I did not give you the information about Rigo to have you track me down through him."

I cocked a half smile as her familiar voice purred in my ear. "Yes, well...if you hadn't disappeared without leaving me a way to contact you, I wouldn't have had to track you down this way."

I could almost hear her smiling as she responded, "I do believe you told me to leave. That you wanted nothing more to do with me."

"That was before we came to an understanding."

"And have we, signore?"

"I believe we have. We now have something to talk about. Can you meet me?"

"Si. Give me an hour. I will meet you there." She paused, apparently doing something at the other end of the phone. "You can buy me a drink."

"Alright. I'll be waiting." The other end of the line clicked, and she was gone. Not even a goodbye. Handing the receiver back to the night club owner, I gave him a superior look. "Thank you. Your help was much appreciated."

Chapter Thirty-Four

𝒜lert to even the smallest of unusual activity, I stared at the entrance, waiting for Nix to put in an appearance.

An hour had come and gone. Aggravated I fended off yet another offer from a drunken human vessel.

A moment later, the waitress sidled up with a drink placed it in front of me. Agitated by its arrival, I waved it away, "I didn't order that, Dani."

Indifferent, she dropped her tray to her side, resting her weight on her back leg. She looked world-weary. "I know, signore." She nodded toward the bar. "She did."

Glancing in the direction she indicated, a smirk spread my lips. Nix stood, elbows propped up behind her as she leaned casually against the bar. She had somehow entered without me noticing. *But, hey…she was finally here.* Picking up the glass I sniffed at the amber liquid. *Whiskey. Not my favorite, but it would do in a pinch.*

Holding it up in a mock toast, I spoke to Dani. "Tell the lady thank you and ask her to join me."

The waitress' eyebrows rose in surprise, most likely because I' sent back every other drink she brought over. "As you wish, signore."

A pleasant heat coursed through me as the first sip of liquid slipped down my throat. Smooth, refined, not a cheap blend. At least she had good taste.

My eyes met Nix's over the head of the server. Once again, a deep brown had replaced their golden color. She leaned down to listen to what the smaller woman said without losing eye contact with me. A second later she turned, scribbled something onto a napkin and then handed it to the waitress.

As Dani approached me on Nix's behalf, I downed the last of the whiskey. Dani stopped next to me, temporarily blocking my view of Nix.

"The lady declines your invitation, signore, preferring that you join her elsewhere." She slid the napkin across the table until it sat in front of me. She tapped a finger on the napkin.

Picking up the napkin, I read the inscription. *Rigo's office.*

I stood and pulled my wallet from my back pocket. Handing Dani several Euros, I met her eye. "Thank you, Dani."

Without looking at the money, she pocketed it. "Thank you, signore."

Leaving the table behind, I headed off and maneuvered my way to the back hallway. In a blink, I was down the hall and pushing open the office door. Nix lounged behind Rigo's desk, her black-booted feet propped up as she kicked back and leafed through a magazine.

She didn't bother glancing up from the colorful pages but spoke as I closed the door behind me, "You wanted to see me?"

Control. That's what it was all about with her. What would she do if she ever lost it? "I thought I was the one buying the drinks."

At first, I thought she was intent on ignoring me. But then she shrugged and tossed the magazine on the desk. Dropping her feet to the floor, she finally looked over at me. "Maybe later." After resting her arms on the surface of the desk, she leaned over them. Humorless eyes gazed up at me. "Why am I here?"

No idle chit-chat seemed to be the way she wanted to play

this. Fine, I was good at direct and to the point. "I've decided to help you."

Her brow rose, but she gave no further indication that my words made any impact. "And to what do I owe the sudden spirit of co-operation?"

I pulled back the same chair which I had sat in during my previous visit and turned it around. Straddling it, I leaned against the back. "It appears Karina was correct. There are a lot of dirty deeds being perpetrated at the behest of someone within the highest ranks of our Kin. I believe whoever it is, is also behind Julian's death. I don't know why, but that is something Adrien and I are working on. Anyway, in my zeal to extract my vengeance, I foolhardily signed an agreement with the Great Council. Once Julian's killer is dead, I will have no choice but to ascend and take my house seat. I would walk away, but the ensuing dishonor would unfortunately taint my clan as well. Now, I wouldn't give a shit if it were just me, but no one in my clan deserves to be ostracized by the community because of me."

"Very noble of you." Her brow furrowed. "Why are you telling me this?"

I ignored her sarcastic tone in an effort to remain on task. "Not noble, just practical. I want you to understand. I am not looking to betray my people."

"Then what are you seeking, Jacen?"

"Justice. For my clan. For me. But, most of all for Julian. If I can help you in the process, then I see no harm in doing so."

"But you wish me to do something for you as well." Her eyes narrowed in suspicion. "I will not sleep with you, if that is what you want."

Taken aback, by her accusatory tone, I struck back, "Sweet Aita. Why in the hell would I want that?"

Before she could hide her reaction behind a mask of indifference her mouth gapped open like an outraged guppy. Fire crackled behind her eyes negating the hard, icy tone of her voice. "Why indeed, signore?"

There was no doubt. My unintended insult had hit the mark.

Not the purported outcome for this conversation. "That didn't come out right. What I meant to say was I'm not bartering for sex."

Her pinched expression eased. Though her mask was firmly back in place, I knew the anger lay simmering just under the surface. She was a storm cloud just waiting for an excuse to let loose on an unsuspecting parade. "As long as we understand each other."

"I assure you; we do."

"Then what *do* you want?"

The muscles in my jaw flexed as I stared at her. "First, the truth."

"About what?"

"About Julian. I believe you were the last one to see him alive."

She rapped nails against her arms in impatience. "Second to last. His murderer was the last."

"Semantics." I propped up a foot onto the rung of the chair. "I need you to tell me anything you remember about that night, like, did anything seem out of place or strange to you when you saw him?"

She chewed on her bottom lip. "That is easily accomplished. But, before I answer questions, I want to know what else you require."

I took a deep breath, exhaling slowly. This was the true reason I had come. If she expected my help, then I was going to make sure we had an understanding first. "It has become clear that I do not understand what is going on behind the doors of the Great Council. I do not know whom to trust. I need someone outside of Sede di Alimentazione, someone who has no interest in keeping the status quo. What I need from you is the support of your people."

She sat back and hugged her arms to her chest. For several minutes she didn't speak, and just sat staring at me assessing my proposal. When she did speak, her tone was flat. "Are you suggesting we stand with you while you take on the Great

Council?"

"Yes."

Her eyes meet mine across the desk. "And how do you know I can be trusted?"

"I don't." My eyes narrowed. "But you saved my life when you didn't have to. That was enough to earn you a fair amount of trust. I'm willing to balance on that for now."

The corners of her mouth turned a tad upward. "Say we agree to this. Do I have your word you will then help us?"

I nodded. "After I deal with the person who killed Julian, we will work out the details."

Nix hesitated for a second before speaking. "Then we have an accord."

"Excellent." I stood up and turned the chair back around. Glancing down at my watch I realized the evening was still quite young. Holding out my hand, I smiled. "Shall we go get you that drink now?"

*****

A short time later, we shared a table in a corner of the club. I waved a waiter over. "The lady will have…" I looked to Nix to fill in the blank.

"Van Gogh Blue straight up."

The waiter gave a quick nod. "Excellent choice, signorina." He then looked to me. "And for you?"

"I'll have a shot of Grand Patron."

"Platinum or Burdeos?"

"Burdeos."

He nodded. "Very good, signore. I will be back shortly with your drinks."

I waved him off, impatiently.

Apparently annoyed by my treatment of the waiter, Nix called after him, "Thank you, Carlo."

He rewarded her with a warm, genuine grin. "Un piacere come sempre."

The boy was obviously smitten with her. Irritated by the

exchange, I glowered. "He seems to be quite taken with you. Does he know what you are?"

She gave me a cool arch of an eyebrow, which was quite the opposite of what the human had garnered. "I'm fairly certain he knows I'm a woman."

I gave a derisive snort. "No one could miss that." I leaned in as if sharing a deep, dark secret. "I meant that you're Cambiare."

She rolled her eyes and groaned, showing her disdain. "The only one here who knows *that* secret is Rigo. Like you with those you cannot trust, I keep that knowledge to myself. When they see me with Dante, they believe I am his human."

"How is that possible?"

Nix toyed absently with a discarded cocktail napkin as if deciding how much to tell me. Then, appearing to have made a decision, she met my gaze. "When I frequent Eros or any place I might be discovered, I wear a specialized camouflaging body spray. A few spritzes, and a pair of brown contacts do a lot to keep the truth hidden. It allows me to come and go without being noticed."

"I hate to tell you this, but I don't think you've been applying it properly." I paused as the waiter brought our drinks.

"Is there anything else I can get for you, signore?" He asked me but didn't take his eyes off Nix.

My mouth twisted into an annoyed grimace. "No, *we* are fine. You can go."

The man had the good sense to look embarrassed before turning on his heel and walking away. When he'd cleared earshot, Nix spoke, "You don't like humans do you?"

"I don't dislike them. I just prefer keeping them at a distance."

"Is that because of your parents?"

Surprised, my eyes grew wide. "What do you know about my parents?"

She picked up her drink, warming it with her hands. "Only what Julian told me."

Picking up the shot of high-end Tequila, I killed it off as if it were water. Slamming the glass down on the table, I slid it away from me. My voice took on a hard edge. "My parents are none of your fucking business. And for the record, there is yet to be a time when I didn't recognize your scent. It practically strangles me every time I get near you."

She scowled. Somewhere in the distance I heard the rumble of thunder. I cocked my head, or was she actually growling at me? "I'm sorry my fragrance is so offensive to you."

"Your scent isn't offensive as much as it is distracting." My brow scrunched as I waved a hand past my temple. "It makes it hard to think."

Taking a sip of her vodka, she looked anywhere but at me. A becoming pink tinged her cheeks, whether from anger or embarrassment, I wasn't sure. "Oh?"

I toyed with the empty shot glass, staring absently at it as if its clear, smooth surface was infinitely more interesting than she. This was not how I imagined this going. Where moments ago, easy conversation flowed between us, a pregnant pause now filled the empty space. When the silence overwhelmed me, I spoke, my tone hard and unforgiving, "I didn't realize you knew Julian well enough to exchange childhood sob stories."

Nix shrugged. Downing the rest of her vodka, her eyes flashed with repressed anger. "That's because every time I try to talk to you, you're either trying to kill me or telling me to shut the hell up and get out." She set her glass down with a decisive thud. Rising, she shoved her hands into the front pockets of her jeans. Withdrawing several Euros, she tossed them onto the table.

"I said I got this."

She stuffed the remaining bills back into her pocket. "Don't do me any favors, testa di cazzo."

Now, that insult I recognized. Julian had picked it up on one of his many trips over here. Grabbing her wrist, I stopped her. "I'm not trying to be a dickhead. And you're not leaving."

"I get the feeling you don't have to try. It seems to come naturally to you." Her eyebrows rose arrogantly as she attempted to shake off my hand. "Now, if you don't mind, I have better things to do than sit around exchanging insults with you."

Tightening my grip, my glare met hers head on. "Well, now, there's the rub. I do mind."

We stared at each other in a silent battle of wills. This was one battle I had no intention of losing.

Without so much as a flinch, she brought her free hand up and wrapped her fingers around my wrist. Her eyes narrowed. "Last chance, Jacen. Let go."

Not impressed with her bristling warning, I retorted, "Not until you agree to sit back down."

Suddenly, searing pain gripped me. My jaw clenched. *What the fuck?* Releasing her, I pulled back my injured appendage. Glancing down, an angry growl rumbled within me. Four evenly spaced scratches ran along the top of the wrist. They weren't deep, just enough to burn. "Gods damn it, Nix."

She glared at me. "You were warned."

With that, she turned and walked off, leaving me staring after her.

Amazingly, in a matter of seconds she was halfway across the club. Another few seconds she'd be out the door.

Unwilling to leave well enough alone, I charged after her. Just as she stepped out the double doors and into the night, I caught her by the shoulder.

She whipped around, fully prepared to go another round. "Get your hands off me."

I released her, holding my hand up. "I don't want to fight with you."

"Good. Then don't," She stormed off again. Heading for the parking lot, keys miraculously materialized in her hand.

"Nix, wait." She ignored me. Rubbing at the raw marks on my wrist, it occurred to me pushing her buttons was perhaps not the most prudent of actions. I stopped my pursuit, unwilling to make a fool out of myself in the parking lot of Eros.

As she unlocked the door of a newer model Fiat, I realized we'd not talked about anything other than the initial agreement.

Damn it. I couldn't just let her walk away. I had yet to get anything from her other than attitude.

Breaking into a brisk trot, I crossed the expanse between us swiftly. In less time than it took her to unlock the car and open the door I had reached the other side. Just as she slid behind the wheel, I opened the opposite door. Sliding into the passenger seat, I closed the door behind me.

"Che cazzo pensi che stai facendo?"

With a tolerant tone, I stated, "English please."

If looks could kill, I'd not survive the night. "I said what the fuck do you think you're doing?"

Ignoring her outburst, I reached for the safety belt. Once it was secure, I glance over at her. "Where are we going?"

"*We* are not going anywhere. *I* am going home."

"Home it is then. You can drop me off at the Sede on your way. In the meantime, you can give me a rundown of what happened the night Julian died."

From the way she continued to scowl at me she was contemplating my demise. Several minutes passed as we stared at each other, neither giving an inch. But then, in a huff she threw her hands into the air. "Figlio di puttana."

A few seconds later she wrenched the key in the ignition, as if attempting to break the key off.

I chuckled. "Careful what you say about my mother. She's not her to defend herself."

Nix threw me a quick scowl before shoving the car into reverse. Pulling out of the parking spot, she kicked the little car into drive. A few seconds later, tires squealed as she gunned the engine forcing the Fiat into the sparse traffic.

I swallowed hard as we narrowly missed a car parked in the middle of the street. "Gods damn it, Nix. Take it easy. You're going to get us killed." Bracing a hand against the dash, my heart dropped as a Ferrari pulled out in front of us. If I thought Nix was driving crazily, the owner of the sports car had her beat tenfold.

Taking a sharp left at a speed normally reserved for a straightaway, she retorted, "You're welcome to walk." Her foot pressed down on the accelerator a smidgen more. "I promise to slow down to let you out."

The scenery sped by, passing lights, mere flickers beyond the windows. "No, I'll be fine. Just don't want you to take out your issues with me on your little car."

A bark of laughter filled the interior of the car. "Please, signore. Don't flatter yourself." The car darted between two more cars. "This is how I always drive." She turned the wheel again taking a side street. "We all do."

Trying to relax, I loosened my grip on the dash. Maybe it had been sitting in the back seat or perhaps having a distraction on previous rides that had kept me from noticing the insane speeds and crazy maneuvers Italian drivers used while navigating. But whatever *it* was, it was not present at this moment. I cringed as a pedestrian shot across the street ahead of us. Nix hit the brakes while cursing under her breath. The moment the person to made it out of the middle of the road, she slammed her foot on to the accelerator and we were off again.

When we reached the outskirts of the busy village the traffic eased into a more normal albeit speedy pace. Letting my grip on the dash board drop, I breathed a sigh of relief. "What the hell is wrong with you people?"

Nix snorted. "Don't be so…American."

I gave her a wry smile. "Then don't be so Italian."

She chuckled but slowed her rocketing speed. "I will try if you will."

"Deal." I adjusted the seat belt to loosen it against my chest. "Speaking of, will you tell me what happened that night?"

Obviously uncomfortable with the turn in the conversation, she kept her eyes straight ahead blinking on occasion. Just when I thought she wasn't going to say anything, she sighed. "I wasn't supposed to go back to the Sede that night. It had become too dangerous for Karina. Remember when I told you she suspected the Council was watching her?" I nodded. "Well, she'd discovered that someone close to her was actually a Council spy. Apparently, he had been sending secret reports to someone on the Council."

"That fits with what Adrien and I found out. Vinny was appointed to security, though he was a high-ranking and well-respected officer of a specialized guard or something."

Nix's face turned ashen. "The Venatori?"

"Yes." I watched the play of emotion on her face. Disbelief, fear, anger, all rolled around within her at once. "What's wrong?"

"You don't know who they are, do you?" She glanced over at me with a befuddled, almost incredulous look. Then, her jaw set as she looked back to the road. "If you did, you wouldn't need to ask me that."

I didn't appreciate the look. Perhaps it was the reminder of how truly foreign the Italian Alimentatori were to me. "Apparently you do."

She gave a curt nod. "Yes."

I glared at her as my answer came out in a flat, defensive tone. "Mind sharing?"

"The Venatori are the King's secret guard. They are used for any job from which the members of the Great Council wish to separate themselves. "

"Like what?"

She shrugged and maneuvered the car onto an empty thoroughfare. "I don't know exactly. What we have on them is mostly rumor. We do believe they are the ones responsible for the disappearances from within our own community." As we approached a slower car, she swung to the left. We zipped past the other vehicle and back into the lane. "I can tell you if you have a Venatori within your ranks, you can bet there is something far more sinister behind it." She paused as a thought occurred to her. "Was this person working under Karina?"

"Yes. He was brought in about three weeks before Julian's death."

Confidence crossed her features when I confirmed her suspicions. "That must have been what Karina found out, why she was so afraid." She rolled her eyes to the ceiling as something dawned on her. Slamming a hand against the steering wheel, she swore, "Porca vacca! That's why Dante forbade any more trips to the Sede. He knew. He was afraid for his cousin." She sighed heavily. "Cazzo. E io li trade per andare a Julian."

I blinked at her quick change of language. "English if you please."

She turned to look over at me. The regret in her eyes faded as she straightened her back. "Scusi. I just said I betrayed Dante and Karina to go to Julian. No wonder Dante has yet to forgive me." Her eyes focused on the road again.

Intrigued, I asked, "Why did you?"

She glanced in the rearview mirror. "He needed me."

My eyebrows drew together. "Explain."

"He wanted to meet with me, but he couldn't get away because of the festivities that were scheduled for the night. So, I went to him instead. By the time I arrived, his Ascension had already occurred, and the party was underway..." The cell phone in my pocket rang, interrupting her. Her brow rose as she cast me an impatient look. "Are you going to get that?"

I fumbled with retrieving the offending object. Glancing at the screen, I apologized, "Sorry. It's Adrien. This will only take a minute."

She shrugged. "Take your time."

Touching the screen, I answered. "Hello."

"Jacen, it's Adrien."

"Yeah, I know. What's up?"

"Where are you?" His voice held a mixture of excitement and anxiousness.

"I'm with Nix. Where are you?"

"At Vinny's."

His answer sent alarm racing through me. "What are you doing there?

He lowered his voice conspiratorially. "I was going back through the footage like you asked me too. I noticed that right after Julian left the party, Vinny followed him out. It made me curious, so I fast forwarded a few minutes. Turns out, Vincenzo's car left the front gate shortly after Julian and Nix disappeared. Who knows? It might just be a coincidence but…"

"You think he might be responsible for Julian."

The signal broke up, as he responded, "when he came into the office to pick something up…invited me over for a drink. I couldn't pass up the opportunity to do some up close and personal sleuthing."

"Adrien, be careful. You have no idea how potentially dangerous he is."

"Don't worry. I'll watch my back." He paused as if interrupted, then whispered, "I'll call you if I find out anything."

The line dropped leaving me staring at my cell phone.

"What's going on?"

Nix's question, drew my gaze back to her. "Adrien's taken it upon himself to become Sherlock Holmes. He's at Vinny's house hoping to find something to tie the man to Julian's murder."

Nix's eyes grew wide as she looked at me. "Jacen, you have to stop him. He's going to get himself killed."

"Adrien can take care of himself." I shoved the phone back in my pocket. "Anyway, you were saying?"

"If you say so." She looked back to the road and took a sudden left. As the road veered off, she maneuvered the car to the side of the road. She blew out an exhausted breath as she put it in park and turned off the engine. Then she turned to stare out the driver's side window.

Following her gaze, I realized we stopped along a strip of road running by the beach. My brow furrowed as I glanced over at her. "Why are we stopping?"

"It was here. *This* was the last place I saw Julian." Her tone sounded haunted as if the events of that night dogged her every step.

I once again glanced past her and into the darkness beyond the glass.

As her whisper filled the tiny space, pain and regret lined every word. "I wasn't supposed to go back to the Sede, but I did anyway…"

Chapter Thirty-Five

Sede di Alimentazione
Night of Julian's Ascension

Music and loud exuberant talking echoed into the night. An occasional bout of laughter emanated from the glowing downstairs windows. I hugged the wall as I dashed through the shadows, pausing only long enough to assure the guards weren't early for their rounds. When sure no one waited for me around the corner, I eased into the shadows next to a darkened window. Inching my way toward one of the ostentatiously trimmed topiaries, I froze as the side door swung open and bathed the walkway with artificial light. *So much for becoming one with the shadows.* Holding stock still, unwilling to even breathe, I willed the door to close. Instead, two men dressed in identical red jackets stepped out. One paused to flip on the outside light and then close the door. The other strode across to the edge of the steps. He lit a cigarette and inhaled deeply.

Definitely a human.

The Alimentatori, like the Cambiare didn't tend to smoke. It damaged our sense of smell, which made us more vulnerable. For the Aliments? I didn't know, and I didn't particularly care what their reasoning was. Until recently, I wouldn't have cared one whit if an Aliment lived or died, and I certainly wouldn't have come running at one's beck and call. But then I met Julian. He was different than any Aliment I had ever known. Most carried their conceit like a designer handbag, proudly displaying it for the entire world to see. From what I knew of him, Julian was the complete opposite, more like what I imagined his ancestors might have been, quiet, reserved, a watcher of events rather than an instigator. So, when he called, I knew it had to be important.

As the man who closed the door approached the edge, his friend offered him a cigarette. He took one from the pack his friend held and then lit it. Blowing out, he squinted through the smoke snaking out from his lips. "You worked one of these before?"

His companion stuck the pack back into his pocket. "Sure."

"Is it always like this?"

The other man took a long drag on the butt and then shrugged. "Nothing like this. Usually, it's a lot quieter. With the way they're hitting the booze, you'd think someone just got married."

"Yeah, they sure know how to throw a party." The younger man studied the glowing end of his cigarette for a moment. "Do you know what it's for?"

The older gentleman shook his head. "That's not something we worry about. Serve the drinks and mind your own business if you ever want to work another one."

He took a puff. "No problem. The money's too good to ask questions."

The other laughed softly. "Good boy."

He motioned to his head, indicating a hood. "Who's the guy in the cloak?"

The other shook his head. "Uh uh, no questions."

"But, haven't you ever wondered what kind of crazy shit goes on out here? I mean, looking at him sitting there overseeing the party like some king on a throne."

The older man looked impatient as he checked his watch.

"Look, I don't get paid to wonder, and neither do you." He took one last drag on the butt and then leaned on the pillar next to him. Reaching down, he tamped out the burning ember on the underside of his shoe and pocketed the butt. "I'm going back in. You coming?"

The younger of the two blew out a weaving tendril. "In a minute. Just want to finish this first."

"Fine, don't be late, and don't leave your butt out here. They don't like it. And once you're back in there, remember to keep your head down and don't ask questions."

As the older man entered the villa, a wry smile crossed my lips. Time for plan B. No shimming up the topiaries tonight. I was going in the front door…well, side door.

Standing, I dropped the loose skirt of my deep blue evening gown back into place. Patting the dirt off it with my palms I frowned as one stubborn stain didn't want to come off. Giving up, I straightened. Oh well, it was going to have to do. Pushing my shoulders back and hoping to give the appearance of a guest arriving, I sauntered into the light. "Ciao."

The young human, probably no more than twenty-three stared openly at me as I emerged as if by magic before his eyes. "Where did you come from?"

"Just over there." I waved toward a limo sitting at one end of the parking lot. "I forgot my lipstick in the car. A girl can't look her best without having her favorite shade with her." His eyes followed my every move.

"Why didn't you send someone for it, signorina? We would have retrieved it for you."

If our scent worked on humans, I'd just employ it to wheedle my way inside, but unfortunately, their sense of smell was too weak to pick up on it. So, instead I was going to have to rely on a far more conventional method. As if my skin needed cooling, I dabbed a handkerchief between my breasts purposely drawing it along each curve of the low-cut dress. My nose wrinkled. I didn't have to be near him to know he was aroused. Young human men were far too easy to manipulate. He leered at me as

I approached. "I didn't mind. I needed some fresh air anyway."

He swallowed. The hand holding the cigarette dropped to his side unnoticed. "Can I get you something cool to drink?"

My lids lowered as I bit my lower lip feigning attraction. His eyes warmed as, I placed a hand on his arm. "If it's not too much trouble, I would love a glass of champagne."

Did Aliments drink champagne? The wayward thought sent alarm through me. If they didn't, then I had to hope this kid didn't know about it.

Dropping the butt to the ground, he stepped on it and then patted my hand in reassurance. "No trouble at all. Anything for you, beautiful."

Bluhck, he was so easy, and I was so disgusted. But I suppose it was a small price to pay to be walked right into the party. I gave an obligatory twitter of embarrassment. "Aren't you sweet? Would you mind escorting me in?"

His face beamed as he pulled my hand into the crook of his arm. "Not at all."

A few minutes later, I was through the door and navigating through a short maze of halls leading from the foyer to the back of the house. The sunken living room area was full to capacity with Alimentatori. My nerves leapt to life fairly singing with anticipation. My gaze travelled around the room, assessing any dangers which might lurk in the shadows. If any one of them made a move for me, I would be ready. At the opposite side of the room, large plate glass windows stood open, allowing guests to move freely between the inside and outside pool area. A stone railing ran the length of the outdoor patio. I knew from experience, balancing on a similar railing a story up, that all that awaited on the other side was a sheer drop to jagged rocks below.

Turning my attention back to the man by my side, I looked up at him. "Thank you so much. I'll take that champagne now."

Eager to please, he bowed. "I will bring you a glass immediately."

Plastering a simpering smile on my face, I gazed adoringly at the young man. "Take your time. I'm not going anywhere."

He gave a quick nod of the head then headed out of the room. Relieved to be free of the man's encumbrance, I made quick work of locating Julian. I watched him from my vantage point. I had to admit, he looked rather dashing in his tuxedo, with his short sandy blonde hair slicked back against his head. His ready smile crinkled the corners of his eyes as he laughed at something someone said. All in all, he wasn't half bad to look at, if you were into his kind, which I most definitely was not. The silent denial did little to brush off the slight flutter I experienced when he smiled.

His bodyguard, Adrien, was not far from him as they talked animatedly with another of their kind. Maneuvering my way through the jovial crowd, I was suddenly very thankful for the maker of the camouflaging body spray and dark brown contacts I wore. If not for them I'd have drawn Aliment attention like a *prostituta* striding into a black-tie affair.

Regardless, I needed to be in and out as quickly as possible. The longer I prolonged this visit, the stronger were the chances of discovery.

I slowly circled around the area where Julian stood awaiting an opportunity to approach him. Several minutes passed. Then the other man left, and his watch dog leaned over and spoke in his ear. Julian laughed and shook his head.

"If you want coffee, get it for yourself. I'm fine." The slight slur to Julian's words seemed to indicate that he had had a bit more to drink than was his habit.

Adrien frowned. "I'll bring two anyway."

He retreated, finally leaving his charge alone. Seizing upon the opportunity, I crossed to Julian's side.

"You needed to see me?"

Startled, Julian nearly spilled what was left of his drink. "Damn it, Nix." His urgent whisper sounded angry, but the relief in his eyes said otherwise. "What are you doing here?"

"You called. I came."

He looked down at me, concerned brown eyes emphasizing the worry on his handsome features. "You should have waited for me in my room." He cast a furtive look around us. "Or better yet at Eros. I would have come to you after all of this."

"Your call frightened me. I thought something awful might have happened."

A touch of tenderness entered his eyes as he gazed down at me. "I'm fine. But thank you for worrying."

I shrugged, suddenly uncomfortable with admitting what I felt toward him. "What did you need, Julian?"

He glanced around once more. Taking me by the elbow he guided me through the crowd. "We can't talk here."

He looked backward over his shoulder. His pace quickened, urgency intensifying his movements. "Do you have your car?"

"Of course."

"Good. Let's go."

Curious, I glanced back in the direction he looked. A large blonde, military-type watched our every move from across the room. His eyes burned into me, dissecting me, as if searching the recesses of his mind for who I might be. Then they narrowed knowingly. He turned and walked to where a group of high-ranking Aliments sat. Why did I get the feeling he knew exactly what I was? "Who's that?"

The corners of Julian's mouth turned downward giving him a grim look. "No one. Just keep walking."

"But won't you be missed?"

"The only person in that room who will miss me is Adrien, and I plan to be back before he notices I'm gone. The rest can..." He seemed visibly upset.

I allowed him to escort me out the front door. Once we were clear of the veranda, I took charge. Ducking into the shadows by the topiaries, I instructed, "Keep close. The guards come at fifteen-minute intervals, and I have no idea where they are in their sweep."

Hiking up my skirt, I held it around my waist, just as I had done while coming onto the property.

Julian chuckled. "Do you always wear tight leather pants under your skirts?"

I glanced down. Scowling, I shoved his shoulder. "It's really none of your business what I wear under my skirts, but no. I did this, so I could move around but drop the skirt if I needed to do exactly what I did—mingle."

He leaned forward and whispered, "Well, it works for you."

Several minutes later I landed on the outside of the border wall, with Julian close behind me. Dropping my skirt back into place, I lead the way from the wall to where I left my car.

"So that's how you manage to get in and out without being seen."

Glancing over my shoulder at him, I teased, "Only when I don't have my cloak of invisibility with me."

He chuckled. "Ah, what I wouldn't do for one of those."

"Play your cards right and I might share."

"Thank you, Nix."

The tender look returned to his eyes, and I looked away, both flattered and uncomfortable. "For what?"

He reached out and touched my arm, sending a chill through me. "For caring enough to drop everything and come to my rescue."

I laughed nervously. "What else was I to do?"

"You could have told me to deal with my own problems, but you didn't. I want you to know how much I appreciate that."

Concerned, I turned to him. "What's wrong, Julian? Why are you talking like this?"

His gaze met mine. For a long moment we just stared at each other. Then he turned away as if embarrassed and walked toward my parked car. "No reason. I just wanted you to know."

When we reached my car, I pulled the key out of hiding and opened the passenger door for him. "Mind telling me where we are going?"

"Anywhere. I just want to be able to talk to you without the eyes and ears of the Alimentatori on us."

He slid into the car and waited for me to get in.

Once settled behind the wheel, I turned the key in the ignition. "How about down at the beach...the one near the ruins?"

He reached for his safety belt. "Sounds good. The sooner we're out of here, the better."

We rode in comfortable silence, two friends enjoying each other's company. A short time later we pulled to a stop along the road.

I shifted until my back was up against the door, so I could look over at him. "Alright, we're here. Now tell me, what tied you up in knots?"

He stared out the front window, still apparently hesitant.

Following his gaze, I watched choppy waves rolling in. The sound never failed to sooth frayed nerves. "You know, my parents used to bring me down here at night."

He turned to look at me. "My parents…" Troubled by some inner thought, he struggled to speak. Finally, after several seconds he continued, "My parents gave their lives to save my brother. I was Just a boy, but I will never forget that day." He glanced down at his hand with a bitter grimace. "When I came home from school, I found them. My mother was dead. My father, near death's door, clung to my unconscious brother as if to let go were to give up all hope." Rubbing at the ring on his right hand he seemed lost in the memory.

I reached out and touched his hand. "That must have been horrible for you."

"It was." Julian exhaled as if the weight of the world was on his shoulders. "He died in my arms." He balled up his hand and held it up. "But not before giving me this."

The glinting metal caught my eye. The symbol on it seemed vaguely familiar though I couldn't place where I'd seen it before. "A family heirloom?"

He rotated his fist, letting the moonlight glint against the ring's pock-marked surface. "At first I thought so. Then I found out it was nothing more than a useless piece of archaic jewelry." He dropped his hand. Shifting to stare out the front window, he shook his head. "It's not even really mine."

I studied him carefully. "If not yours then who does it belong to?"

"It's not important." He frowned.

What did any of this have to do with why he'd dragged me out in the middle of the night? "You didn't call me to talk about the ring though, did you?"

Opening the door, he stepped out of the car.

Afraid I offended him, I watched as he walked down the beach. This melancholy mood Julian had sunk into wasn't like him. Something serious must have happened to dampen his spirits this seriously. As his friend, I couldn't let him slip any further. Reaching for the door handle, I popped the lever. Within seconds I overtook him and grabbed his arm, effectively stopping him. "Julian, talk to me. What's wrong?"

"Have you ever been so excited about something only to find out what you got was not what you expected?"

"Sure, who hasn't?"

He shoved his hands into the pockets of his slacks. "That's what this whole trip has been like for me. I came over here ready to take my rightful place within the Great Council, only to find out that they are not who I thought they were."

Believing I understood his meaning, I nodded. "I tried to warn you."

A sad smile spread his lips. "I know you did. Unfortunately, I didn't listen."

"It's not too late, Julian. Walk away. Leave Italy and never come back."

He gave a self-deprecating laugh. "If only I could, Nix. But I can't. To do so would endanger every member of the clan, especially Jace. I didn't nurse him back to health when we were children to lead him into danger as an adult."

"Why would he be in danger? Why would any of them? You are all Aliments and I thought your laws protect you from such things."

Julian looked earnestly at me. "They're meant to. Regrettably, I fear there are members of the Great Council who believe themselves above our laws." A vacant look entered his eyes. "The reason I called you, Nix is because...," his voice trailed off as he seemed hesitant to speak. His gaze found mine. The muscle in his jaw flexed in repressed anger. "I found out why your people are disappearing."

Shock ricocheted through me. "What? Why?"

"Because they are using them for their Adrena."

I blinked, not understanding. "I...what does that mean?"

His gaze hardened. "It means they are holding them captive, torturing them, to harvest their adrenaline."

My chest constricted, making it hard to breathe. I closed my eyes to shut out the world, which was spinning out of control around me. "How? How do you know this?"

He looked out to the rolling waves. "I was in the back room of the Council chambers preparing for my Ascension when two men came in. They didn't see me or didn't care that I was there. Maybe they thought I didn't speak Italian. Whatever their reasoning they spoke freely." He paused as if considering carefully what he was about to say. "Unfortunately, I understood every word. He was expounding on his sexual prowess. That he'd tasted some sweet Cambiare ass the night he'd brought her in." I flinched. "Sorry, his words, not mine."

Drawing my gaze up to his, the sympathy I saw reflected there shook me to the core. *This was all real.* Small tremors seized my body, making my stomach heave. Forcing myself to ignore the pain, I motioned for him to proceed. "It's okay. Continue."

"Are you sure?"

I nodded. "Si."

"Alright." He paused a second before launching into his tale. "The other man—I had seen him before. He was the one watching us as we left." I nodded, knowing exactly to whom he referred. "He seemed angry, like he'd had enough of the other man's bragging. He told him he wanted nothing more to do with the whole situation, which is why he transferred out, so he could forget about what he'd helped them do."

Anxious, yet terrified of what would come next, I coaxed him into telling me more. "Go on."

"The first man started berating him, telling him that what they were doing was for the good of the race. Capturing the Cambiare and handing them over to the *Collettore* was their duty.

He shouted that it was all worth it for just a small taste of the newest girl."

I closed my eyes, as my mind reeled. *The newest girl...my baby sister. What torture had she already endured at the hands of these monsters?*

Anger burned within me. "Do you know where they are?"

"No, but I will work on finding out."

I stared blankly ahead, in an attempt to compartmentalize my feelings. "Good."

Capturing my gaze, he looked me in the eye. "I'm sorry, Nix. I know this is a shock."

I blinked at him. "A shock? You just told me your people are capturing, torturing, and feeding from my relatives. How else should I react?"

My question was met with silence. I realized the play of emotions clouding his features reflected my own, varying between barely restrained anger, outright worry, and anxious disbelief. Tears welled up in my eyes, as my chin trembled. Willing them away, I presented my back to him. Tears were a sign of weakness. I'd be damned if any *Feeder* would see me cry...even Julian.

He stepped up behind me, his hands gently rubbing my upper arms. Leaning down, Julian touched his chin to the top of my head. "I know what it's like to feel helpless while your loved ones suffer. But, please, remember I'm on your side."

I swallowed the anguish his words brought. Wiping at the few tears that had managed to fall, I hung my head. "I know, Julian. I just need some time..."

Dropping his hands, he stepped back. "Take all the time you need. I'll be ready to move forward whenever you are."

Chapter Thirty-Six

"Oh, sweet Aita, Nix. I had no idea." The need to comfort her overwhelmed me. Reaching out, I touched her shoulder. "We will find your sister and anyone else they are holding. I promise."

Nix ripped her gaze away from the beach and met my gaze. "Your brother made a similar promise and then I left him there, Jacen." Her fingers tightened ruthlessly on the wheel until her knuckles were pale in comparison to her fingers. In what could only be interpreted as shame, she cast her gaze downward and back to where her hands strangled the steering wheel. "I couldn't bear to look at him, but now...now I can't help but think that if I'd just taken him back to the Sede, he would still be alive."

"Not to assign blame, Nix but why didn't you? I mean, it's not your fault. You couldn't have known what would happen. But, why did you leave him at the beach alone."

"I don't know. I was just so angry. I wasn't thinking clearly. Then I got a phone call from Dante. He'd found out about my excursion to the Sede. I assured him there was a good reason for it, but, he ordered me home immediately. Julian said I should go. He told me he wanted to call you to talk about everything he discovered. So, I left him there. He was going to call for a cab once he finished with you."

"He never called. Wait…a cab, that's right, you said you drove him to the beach." My shoulders tensed. *How could that be?* "I just remembered I was told he was found several feet away from his car, that he'd apparently been dragged from it and mauled to death."

She looked at me her eyes growing wide. "Julian didn't take his car. It would have been impossible for him to be found dead near it when it was sitting in the parking lot of the Sede. I saw it when I pointed to the limo."

"Which leads me to believe someone followed you in Julian's car, picked him up after you left and killed him."

"Who would have had access to his keys?"

"Adrien, of course, but there is no way he had anything to do with it. When we first arrived, I thought maybe he had, but I've since realized he'd have done anything to protect my brother. Hell, he's so guilt ridden over Julian's loss, he doesn't want to let me out of his sight. I've had to sneak around in order to pursue the investigation alone."

"What about the Venatori you mentioned?"

I shook my head. "He was my next choice, but I'm afraid your story actually vindicated him."

"How?"

"That blonde military-type who transferred to forget about what was going on with the Cambiare? Yeah, that sounds an awful lot like Vincenzo. It's obvious he knows what's going on but doesn't approve. He's apparently taken great pains to separate himself from the acts of the others, even at the cost of his own career. To be honest, I'm beginning to think he makes personal honor an art form."

"So, you don't think he transferred in to be the Great Council's eyes and ears in security?"

"At this point, no."

A genuine smile adorned her lips as her tension eased and she reached up to wipe beneath her eyes with a chuckle. "Karina will be glad to hear that."

My eyebrows rose in curiosity. "You know where she is?"

"Of course. She's with us."

"The Cambiare took in an Aliment fugitive? Figures."

She scoffed at that as she turned the key in the ignition and pulled onto the road. "Do you think Dante would let his cousin disappear into an Aliment dungeon?"

I laughed. "I see your point."

Reaching up, she tapped a willowy finger against her chin. "So, if not me, Adrien, or the Venatori. Who else is there?"

I shrugged. "My only other suspect is Alcie."

"Motive?"

"Hmm, good question. As far as I can tell Alcie knows pretty much everything that goes on at the Sede. Maybe one of the men mentioned seeing Julian in the chambers during their conversation. She could have alerted the *Collettore,* whoever that is. That would definitely have put him on their radar."

"But why kill him? Why not attempt to recruit him first?"

Her question was a valid one. Why, indeed? "I guess, they could have tried, and he turned them down."

She shook her head. "No, not likely. If they'd recruited him, Julian would have allowed it. It was the only way he was going to be able to locate where my people have been taken."

"Damn it. I hadn't thought of that." My lips narrowed. *Fuck. No matter how I try, nothing seems to add up.*

As if sensing my frustration, she reached out and touched my hand. "Don't worry. We'll figure it out."

The corner of my mouth rose in a smirk. "We'll?"

She glanced over at me, her golden eyes warming. "We're partners now, are we not? I help you, and then you help me?"

I bit my tongue on a sarcastic response and replied, "Ah, yes. I guess you're right."

The miles passed quickly as we relaxed into friendly banter. Before I knew it, the gates of our estate loomed before us. She pulled up in front of them and shoved the car into park. A shadow clouded her eyes, as concern etched deep lines at the corners of her mouth. "Just for the record, I was going to tell you about all of this even if we did not come to an agreement. Tonight, just gave me an opening. I've always believed you needed to know."

"I appreciate that."

"Julian was a good man, Jacen. He deserves to be avenged."

I nodded, finally understanding why Julian would consider her a friend. "That has always been my intention."

"I did not say this before, but I would be glad of the chance to help. If you have a need, feel free to contact me."

If I doubted her words, the earnest look on her face would have done much to convince me. "Thank you, Nix."

She nodded to the door. "Now, you better get going. I can't hang out at the entrance of the gate too long before someone gets curious."

Grabbing the door handle, I popped the door open. Climbing out, I slammed the door closed behind me. Just as she was about to pull away, I knocked on the window. Once she lowered the glass, "I forgot to get a number where you can be reached."

A wicked look crossed her features. "I already programed it into your phone."

"When?"

"The night you were sleeping. I checked to see who you had in your phone, mostly checking for Julian. When I found him, I put myself in anticipating our future cooperation." She put the car into gear and laughed. "You've had it all along…just didn't know it."

As she pulled away her laughter echoed into the night. I couldn't help but chuckle. She was nothing if not unpredictable.

Chapter Thirty-Seven

Several minutes later I flipped on the light in the suite. Crossing to Adrien's room, I knocked. Waiting several seconds then knocking one more time, I listened for any movement inside the room.

He must still be with Vinny. I should probably let him know what I found out.

Pulling out my cell phone, I dialed his number. A moment later my Second picked up the other end.

"Hey Jace."

Turning on my heel, I made my way to my room. "Hi, how goes your night? Still with Vincenzo?"

"Nope, left a little while ago. I'm heading back to the villa right now."

"Good. How did the investigation go?" Closing the door behind me, I traversed the darkness like a nocturnal predator.

"I didn't find any link to either Julian or the assassin's death."

"Didn't think you would. Nix told me tonight that Julian overheard a conversation between Vinny and someone else. I think it might be what got him killed."

"Really? Why wouldn't Julian have mentioned it to me?" Adrien's voice sounded suspicious.

"Maybe he didn't have a chance. It happened the night of his ascension while he was in the Council chambers."

"Ah, that would be why. They kept me busy that night preparing myself for becoming the Second of a Great Council member. I didn't see Julian until the party afterward. He was in great demand, so even that was short lived. Then, he disappeared with Nix." He paused as if remembering the last time, he'd seen Julian. "What was the conversation about?"

"They were talking about...," remembering what Nix mentioned about Julian fearing his phone had been tapped, I stopped. "Never mind. I'll go into detail once you get here. Suffice it to say, I don't think we have anything to worry about from Vinny."

"That was my conclusion as well." Adrien sounded disappointed. Who could blame him? So was I.

Curious, I asked, "What brought you to that conclusion?"

"I had a conversation with him about Karina and the missing security footage. Turns out, he was the one who deleted the footage, not Karina. He saw Julian leaving with Nix. Apparently, he recognized her from Eros and knew she frequented Dante's table. Afraid Julian might be under duress, he set out to follow them. It didn't take long before he suspected Julian had left of his own free will, so he returned to the villa. Once he got back, he verified the footage and then deleted it. He wouldn't tell me why other than to protect Julian."

It was all starting to make sense. The footage disappeared to protect a newly ascended Council member, not the Cambiare he was sneaking off to spend time with. What I still didn't understand was, why hadn't Vinny come forward immediately? "I understand, but why did he let Karina go down for something he did?"

"Can you really blame him? You were gunning for whoever was responsible. When you called him in to the office, you only asked him to escort Karina out. He didn't know why and did as he was told. He wasn't there when you accused her of tampering with the files. So, the reason for Karina's dismissal took him by surprise. He said he never meant for it to come back on her. Karina wasn't even there that night. He used her code because he didn't yet have access to the office where the footage was compiling." He paused to pay the taxi driver. "Anyway, I'm here. I'll be up there in a minute."

"Fine. We'll continue our conversation when you get here."

I hung up and tossed the phone onto the bed.

Shit. Figures I'd even had that wrong. I apparently had no business running security. I would have to make sure to remedy the situation as soon as possible. "Well, that's one puzzle down. A half dozen or so to go."

Stripping my shirt off, I tossed it onto a chair. Sitting on the side of the bed, I pulled off my shoes. A flicker of movement near the French doors caught my attention. The curtains blew inward, on a breeze.

Standing, I walked toward the doors. My eyes narrowed. Reaching out, I touched the open door. Drawing it open, I peered out onto the empty veranda.

Stepping back, I closed the door firmly and shook my head. Maybe I left it open. Padding my way back to the bed, I froze when the light by the bedside flickered on.

Blinking as my eyes adjusted to the sudden light, I growled. "What the fuck?"

A sleepy voice came from the bed. "Oh Jace. You're back."

Surprised alarm shot to life within me. "Alcie, what the hell are you doing here?"

"I came by to see if you wanted to go out for a late dinner." She yawned. "I guess I fell asleep waiting. What time is it?"

"It's nearly eleven thirty." My fingers balled into fists. "How long have you been awake?"

"Not long. I heard you tell someone on the phone about Karina going down on someone or something."

I chuckled, at her sleepy reply. "Listen, Alcie, as much as I appreciate your invitation, you can't just let yourself into my room."

"I'm sorry. I just thought...the other day we seemed to have a connection." She rose, tripping over the edge of a sheet only to catch herself on the bedside table.

I shook my head. She could hardly get herself out of bed without stumbling over her own two feet. Clumsy, saccharine sweet, embarrassingly awkward. Was there really any possibility that beneath that exterior lurked the heart of a killer?

I almost laughed. I doubted the woman had it in here to kill a spider. She might scream for someone else to do it, but to do the act herself? *Not a fucking chance.*

Time to let her down easy. "I'm sorry if I mislead you. You're sweet, have a Judy Garland-esque thing going on and I have no doubt you will make some guy very lucky. But, hun, I'm not that guy." Her chin quivered as her eyes shimmered. Oh Gods, please don't cry. "But you know who is?" I paused long enough to see her interest peak. "Adrien."

Her eyes widened. "Adrien?"

"Yes, believe it or not, the old man's got a thing for you."

A pretty pink blush spread up her neck and into her cheeks. "I had no idea."

I chuckled. "Sometimes it's difficult to see something that's right in front of us." Stepping forward, I motioned for her to join me. "Come on. Let's get you out of my room before he gets up here."

She walked around the end of the bed. Placing a hand on the small of her back, I ushered her to the door. As we entered the main room, the smile on my face froze when the door to the suite opened.

Shit. Here we go again.

Adrien stopped halfway through the door. His face fell as the sight of Alcie and I standing in the door of my bedroom hit him square in the chest.

A dark, angry scowl etched his hardened features. "How could you, Jace? You knew. You knew how I felt about her."

"Adrien, it's not what you think…"

Furious, his eyes bored into my naked chest. I could almost feel the burn as they passed over me in disgust. "It sure looks like you two are coming out of your room. It sure looks like you're half naked. It sure looks like Alcie's been sleeping."

"Well, those things are all true, but I wasn't sleeping with her."

His brow rose. "I'm sure sleeping was the furthest thing from your mind."

A strangled sound came from Alcie as she stepped away from me. Leaning against the door frame, I crossed my arms and watched the scene unfold.

"Sleeping was the furthest thing from my mind, but Jace is innocent. I fell asleep waiting for him to come back. He didn't even know I was in the room until I turned the light on." Adrien's gaze softened as she left me to walk to him. "He told me he had no interest in me, but that you did." She put her hand on his chest. "Is that true?"

A flush warmed Adrien's cheeks as he stumbled over a response. "I...um...yes."

Alcie giggled. "Why didn't you tell me, Tesoro?"

Caressing her arms, his tone softened, "I didn't think you'd have any interest in someone like me."

"Quello è solo insensato."

"It's not nonsense, mia cara. You're young, beautiful, and have every chance of making a prudent life match."

"Bah, there is nothing wrong with you a woman's touch couldn't fix."

His eyes danced. My stomach turned. "Enough. Why don't you two love birds go somewhere else and do that."

Adrien laughed. "He's just jealous. Missing Angel, Jace?"

"Not at all. Just trying to keep my dinner down."

Alcie put a hand over her mouth to stifle a giggle. "Come on. Let's go to my house. I'll make you a late dinner."

My Second grinned from ear to ear. "Wonderful." Looking over at me, he said, "Don't wait up. We'll continue our conversation in the morning."

With a shake of a head, I laughed. "I have no intentions of waiting up. You two kids have fun. I'm going to bed."

Staring after them as they left the suite, I exhaled a contented sigh. At least one of us was going to come out of this night better off.

*****

Two thirty came and went, as I stared at the darkened ceiling of my room. Sleep seemed to be avoiding me. Frustrated, I shoved the thin white sheet aside. Dropping my feet to the floor, I rose and stretched upward. Padding my way to the bathroom, I flipped on the light. As the light illuminated the little room, my image in the mirror caught my attention. Gods, I looked horrible. Darkened circles under bloodshot pale grey eyes were proof of lack of sleep. My face looked gaunt, as if the stress of daily life had taken a harsh toll on me. I looked much older than my two hundred and sixty-five years. Guess death and vengeance tended to do that to a person.

Turning on the faucet, the soothing sound of running water filled the quiet. I grabbed a glass and filled it. As I turned off the water, I took a sip of the cool liquid. Just as I flipped off the light the feeling I'd had earlier at the base of the stairs returned in full force. I shuddered as a cold chill snaked down my spine.

My eyes narrowed, taking in the recesses of the darkened room. Someone stood in shadow near the doors.

"Nix?"

A low growl emanated from the creature, as it hunched down. Light glinting off four metal blades amidst the blackness drew my eyes. "Your pussy can't save you now, race traitor."

Alarm raced through me, but I gave no outward indication. "So, do you think to frighten me with hateful words?"

"On the contrary, I intend to kill you with...," the bladed tool rose in the darkness, "this."

I remained calm, knowing my best chance was to distract him, get as close as possible, and then attack before he had a chance to use whatever that weapon was. "Why? What have I done to warrant death?"

"I know not, and I care not. I live to strike down race traitors like you...and your brother."

This, this was the one who'd killed Julian. *Finally*. I inched forward, placing my glass on the desk. "So, you are the one who killed Julian."

"Si. He deserved nothing less." The silvery metal glistened in the pale moonlight, streaming in through the sheer curtains as each claw-like blade moved individually. "On the very night he Ascended, I was sent for him. I found him betraying his office with that Cambiare slut. I followed them, waited for her to leave. I couldn't wait to slice him. A race traitor deserves no better than to have their hearts cut from their bodies."

A shudder ran through me at the thought of what Julian had endured at this psycho's hands. Inching closer still, I stated, "Are you Venatori?"

Hesitation came from the darkness. The shadow shifted. His eyes bored into me mercilessly. "It matters not."

"I'll take that as a yes." As I neared the door to the outer room, I reached out and grabbed Julian's walking stick. Sliding the catch, I didn't take my eyes off the shadowy figure. "Who gave the order to kill Julian?"

A sinister chuckle emanated from him. "You should concern yourself with the here and now."

"Fine, then who gave the order to kill me?" A moment more and I'd be within easy range of my prey. Silently sliding the dagger from its hiding place, I held it in front of me, ready to split the man from pelvis to sternum. "I want to know who to kill next."

"There is only one who gives orders to the Venatori, but you will never live to see him dead."

Fuck it. By the time I was done with him, he'd be begging to give me the man's name.

In a split second, I lunged for him. Unfortunately, his larger size and superior training allowed him to brush off the surprise attack as easily as he would a fly. "Come now, you're going to have to do better than that if you want to survive the night."

Fury shot through me with the taunt. Flying into action, I brandished the weapon, thrusting it forward over and over. He thwarted every effort, until I'd pressed him back into the corner.

Finally, the blade sliced along his side, drawing first blood. As I drew back to thrust again, his fist landed a perfectly timed left hook, exploding inside my head like fireworks on a starless night. Stumbling, the breath caught in my lungs as he shoved me backward. My head reeled as I landed precariously against the side of the bed. *I was not going down like this.* Blinking once, twice, I fought to remain conscious. In seconds he hovered above me. As he rushed forward, I caught him square in the chest with both feet and shoved. The force of the blow pitched him backward. He crashed into the closed French doors sending glass and wood splintering outward. Having overturned the bistro table and one of the chairs, the Venatori came to a rest near the banister. Rolling to my feet, I was through the shattered opening in a flash. Recovering quickly, he was on his feet and facing me before I'd exited the doors.

In the seconds it took for him to raise his arm, I realized why it was widely believed the Cambiare were responsible for Julian's death. The weapon looked as if it had been purposefully made to produce claw like injuries.

Four sharp, curved blades, strangely resembling cat's claws, protruded wickedly from suede-like material which was bound tightly into place with leather straps along his forearm. By the darkened stains along the knuckles, the weapon seemed well used.

Free from the restriction of the corner, he swiped downward with the weapon. I screamed as the blades ripped at my t-shirt, clawing four evenly spaced marks across the skin of my chest. Stunned by the sudden pain, I tripped over debris on the floor causing me to falter.

He advanced on me methodically, obviously gauging my actions as weakness. "You will die by my hand, just as your brother did. And I will spit on your race traitor corpse."

Just as he raised his arm again, I thrust upward with the dagger, catching him in the side. He yelped and fell back just as the door to the outer suite crashed inward.

Adrien's voices rose in alarm. "On my Gods, Jacen! Are you

all right?"

My attacker, having wisely decided to retreat, scrambled up on to the railing and disappeared onto the roof.

"Don't worry, Jace. He won't get away." Karina flew past me giving chase.

I sucked in a breath as a burning sensation spread through the wound. Rising despite the pain, I shrugged off Adrien's concerns. "I'll be fine as soon as I kill this prick." Calling after Karina, I said, "I'm right behind you, Karina."

Sparing a glance to Adrien, I realized for the first time that he was hurt. Blood oozed from a large gash along his side. "Sweet Aita, Adrien. What happened to you?"

Walking to my side, his face was a mask of pain. "Pretty much the same thing that happened to you. If it weren't for Karina, Alcie and I would be dead. But I'll explain later. Let's get this bastard."

Giving a curt nod, I turned and darted through the ravaged opening. In seconds I was on the banister. Adrien stumbled through the door. "I'll take the stairs to make sure he doesn't come back through. Meet you up there."

Springing upward, I grabbed the edge of the roof. What should have been a simple task sent pain shooting through me as the torn flesh on my chest gapped and blood soaked the front of my t-shirt and tops of my pants. I cried out but stuffed the agony down. Trying my best to ignore it, I pulled myself the rest of the way up, cringing as the wound scraped along the concrete edge. Finally gaining the top, I sat for a moment to catch a labored breath. My vision blurred momentarily, as though the loss of blood already affected my ability to focus. I shook my head to clear the fog settling into place over my brain slowing my thoughts. *What the hell was wrong with me?*

Refusing to allow the wound to slow me down, I fought back against the tunnel vision, narrowing my concentration to the one responsible for Julian's death. Finding my target, I rose.

Karina struggled with the much larger man. She darted to the side, nimbly avoiding the hack and slash motion the assassin utilized. Apparently Cambiare speed held some benefits against an Aliment attacker, for she was quicker than anyone I had ever seen, with the possible exception of Nix.

Just after a she successfully avoided a powerful blow, she went on the attack, throwing a right hook at his jaw. Unfortunately, he easily blocked the direct assault and grabbed Karina by the arm, chuckling at her meager attempt to harm him. His right arm reared back to deal what would surely be a fatal blow to her stomach.

Rushing forward I joined the fray. Extending my left arm, I blocked his weapon from making contact by grabbing his wrist and pinning to his side.

"Why don't you fucking pick on someone your own size, asshole?"

Stepping in, I thrust the knife forward. He slipped my grip and grasped my right wrist. Releasing her, his left hand chopped down on my wrist knocking the dagger from my hand. With his foot he sent it skittering across the rooftop. Shrugging it off, I didn't worry over the loss. I didn't need a weapon. Tearing him apart with my bare hands would be just as satisfying.

"Nice to have you join us, Jacen. But his size doesn't matter." I gave a quick look in her direction. Karina's appearance caused a double take. Her teeth, more like fangs now, her finger's sporting claw-like nails. Her eyes glowed as if someone had flipped on a switch within her. Though not a complete transformation, like the one spoken of in the ancient texts, she changed from woman to beast without a sound.

A growl rumbled low in her throat.

The Venatori's startled fear-filled whisper brought my attention back to him, "Che cosa la scopata? Siete uno di loro?"

My mind translated his surprised response easily this time. *What the fuck? Are you one of them?* A sinister bark of laughter welled up inside me. Squelching it, I drew his attention to me. "Yes, she is, and I'd rather have her at my side than someone like you." I followed my words with a shot to his kidney.

The taunt hit its mark. Rage lit his features. Momentarily forgetting Karina, he snarled, "Then you shall die together."

S.J. WOLFF

Lowering his shoulder, he rammed into me sending me backwards.

Before he could lunge for me, she was upon him. Like a wild cat, she bit and clawed at his face and shoulders.

In the fury of the battle, he fought to hold her arms at bay, but failed miserably. Just when I thought she would defeat the man on her own, a powerful blow from his left fist connected with her jawbone. Dazed, she stumbled. Taking advantage of the opening he shoved her backward. Before she was able to recover, he grabbed her by the throat. Air hissed out from between her lips as she struggled against his superior strength.

Drawing his arm back for another strike, I saw my opening. Intercepting the blow with my right arm, I twisted around to bring my left arm up underneath locking his arm to my chest.

"Let's see how bad ass you are without your little toy to play with." Grabbing the leather sheath of the weapon with my right hand, I ripped it from his arm and tossed it across the roof. It landed several feet away. As the blades struck the surface, a metallic clang echoed in the night and little droplets of blood sprinkled over the white tiles.

With a loud roar, he tossed Karina's limp body aside. She groaned as she slammed against the ground, but at least she was still alive. For a second relief replaced all other emotion, but it was short lived.

The man turned on me with a vengeance. He barreled into me, planting a shoulder in my already injured chest, breaking the hold I had on his arm while shoving me backwards. Following through with a right punch I deflected it with my left hand.

Ramming a fist into his stomach, I began a frenzy of punches. Stomach, side, stomach, side. Over and over again I landed blow after blow, pummeling him with every ounce of my rage. I would punish his body for every strike the man had dealt Julian.

As the blood pumped through my veins, the burning within my wounds intensified. My fists slowed as the fog settled into my brain.

Sensing my weakening control over my body, he chuckled.

352

He wrapped his arms around me to still my fury.

With a violent growl, he reared his head back. An instant later his forehead slammed into mine, sending stars shooting through my already foggy brain. When he released me, I stumbled unable to bring my eyes back into focus. The sound of something slamming against a hard surface somewhere in the distance caused me to turn in that direction. The darkness closed in around me. Falling to my knees, my head swam. His fingers wrapped through my hair as he bent down to whisper into my ear. "The poison works its way into your blood and soon you will be unable to move. Before it claims your life, I will take my time flaying the flesh from your body."

For a second, he disappeared. Then out of nowhere, his foot struck between my shoulder blades sending me sprawling onto the ground.

I tried to push myself up in a meager attempt to rise, but my arms shook, and the burning in my blood intensified. My assailant's fist landed hard against the back of my neck, thwarting any further effort to stand. Falling forward against the cold surface of the tiled roof, the shock drew a sucking breath from me. The ragged, torn skin of my chest burned despite the chill. I rolled to my side. My gaze focused on Karina who lay unconscious several yards away. Blood trickled from the side of her mouth, bright against the pale skin of her face.

A small inkling of a memory tickled my mind.

It unfolded in my mind like a bud of a flower opening to the sun. So many years ago—my mother lying just as Karina did now, bloody and beaten. The glint of metal in the sunlight streaming through an open window, catching my eye as my father threw himself in front of me, protecting me. Four curved blades winking at me as the man slashed downward and into my father's chest.

The memories my child's mind had hidden from me for so long came rushing back, stealing the breath from my lungs, and plunging me into the experience once again, reliving every moment as if it were happening before my eyes.

I swallowed the anguish and sorrow the memories brought as suddenly, I understood.

The Great Council had sent that man to kill my parents.

They'd sent this man for Julian and me.

What possible threat had any of us posed to them which could justify our deaths? Or was it possibly an ancient vendetta against my family which spurred them to go to such lengths to rid the world of the house of Samsaveel?

I coughed. My fingers brushed my lips, cold against the warm, soft skin. At the feel of warm, sticky liquid against their surface, I withdrew my hand and glanced at the tips. A shiver ran through me. *Blood.* Warm, bright crimson against the cool tips of pale fingers meant only one thing. *I'm dying.* A self-deprecating chuckle passed my lips but slipped away, buried beneath a violent bout of coughing.

I never imagined my life ending like this. In fact, I never really imagined my life ending at all. Why would I? Yet, here I was, dying just the same.

Never in all of my years had I wished for redemption as much as I did now, in this moment.

But I was no fool.

I long ago accepted reality. There would be no benevolent god waiting on the other side to spare *my* immortal soul. I'm not the kind of creature a god wastes time on. Whatever hell I was about to cross into would be one of my own making. And that was just fine by me. It was no more than right. I'd lived my life among the shadows, why ask for light now? Redemption was not for me.

My breath came out in a wheeze. The bitter taste of bile mixed with blood tainted my saliva causing me to gag and my stomach to churn.

The gashes oozed onto the ground beside me. A crimson stain spread like flood waters across the alabastrine tiles, resulting in a pool which shimmered, glistening like rubies in the moonlight.

Attempting to roll to my back, I stopped short as searing pain shot through my chest. Clenching my teeth and pinching my eyes closed, I silenced a desperate cry.

What the fuck?

I'd never felt anything burn like this before.

The weakness, the burning pain, the inability to think clearly, harkened back to the story of Giovanni. In the false version the Cambiare priestess attacked him resulting in poison spreading throughout his body. I closed my eyes as understanding dawned. They'd used the story to spread fear and lies allowing the Venatori free reign. How many had they killed and blamed the Cambiare?

A shadow crossed above me and I gazed up into the eyes of my assailant. He'd retrieved his weapon. Moving forward, stalking me like a predator, he glared down at me, hatred lighting his eyes.

My lip curled in a grimace as another stabbing pain stole the breath from my lungs. A whisper of a thought echoed through me. *You escaped fate once. You can do it again. Fight, damn it!*

Panting to catch my breath, unwilling to show my attacker any weakness I set my jaw and glared up in defiance. I would regret nothing and go out the way I'd come in, proud, strong, and fighting for every last breath. "Finish it already."

Raising his arm, he paused as the sound of splintering wood echoed through the night. Distracted, he cast a glance over his shoulder.

At the same time, something slid against the tiles coming to a stop nearby. Turning my head, I saw Karina nodded to where the dagger now sat, well within arm's reach. A grim smile snuck across my face.

Before I could act, pounding footsteps came rushing toward us. In the next instant, Adrien threw himself against the other man, sending them both flying over top of me. They landed with a heavy thud several feet away from me. They rolled around, each pressing for the advantage until the man was on top of Adrien. In a flash, he straddled my Second and plunged the four-pronged weapon deep into Adrien's stomach.

Gods damn it!

Ignoring my own pain, I grabbed the dagger and pushed myself up. I rose.

The Venatori stood with his back toward me. Shuffling my way forward, I grasped the jeweled handle of the dagger. It slipped in my hand which was wet with blood.

The man glared down at Adrien's writhing body. "You protect a man who sleeps with animals? Not once, but twice. How can you call yourself a proper Alimentatori and condone such behavior?" He spat at Adrien and kicked him in the ribs. "You disgust me."

He must have caught my movement out of the corner of his eye because he turned. Unfortunately, it was too late for him.

Meeting his eyes, I drove the dagger up through his rib cage and straight into his heart. His arm dropped lifeless to his side, as his head lolled on his neck. Falling forward onto his knees, he slid off my dagger. His mouth opened and closed as he gasped for air. My lip curled as he collapsed onto the ground. I growled. "Rot in hell, mother fucker."

My hand shook as muscle strength waned. I moved to Adrien's side and dropped down beside him. Setting the dagger down, I placed a hand on his shoulder. I swallowed the anxiety attempting to rise within me. Grasping his shoulder, I made him look up at me. "Adrien...Adrien, look at me."

His eyes flickered open weakly. "Jacen?"

"Yes, it's me. Hold on. We'll get you help." Directing my attention to Karina, who was slowly rising, I shouted, "Get someone. Find help."

Striping off my shirt, I shoved it into his gut to stem the flow of blood from the wound.

Adrien reached up and grasped my arm. He coughed, spewing blood mixed with spittle. "It's...not important. You're...alive."

I glared down at him. "Shut up old man. We're going to get you through this, but you've got to fight."

He chuckled, but it erupted into a bout of coughing. "Who...are you calling...old?"

"That's the spirit. Now, just rest. We'll find someone who

can help you. You just have to hold on." My vision blurred for a moment as my own strength waned.

He shook his head. "I'm fine. I don't feel anything anymore."

His fingers tightened on my arm. "Promise me...you'll release me. You...won't let me rot in my corpse."

Blackness around the edges of my vision began to draw inward. I shook my head to fend it off. I had to stay conscious. Adrien needed help. "Stop it. You're going to be alright."

"Please, Jacen. Promise...me. I've got no one else." His frantic whisper prompted me to meet his eyes.

"Yes, of course. I promise. When it's your time I will make sure you are released properly. But, that time is not today. I still need you."

"Who knew it would take me dying to make you realize you need someone in your life." His arm dropped, and his fingers wrapped around my wrist. "Jacen, whatever comes...you can handle it. You're stronger than your brother ever was." A sad smile touched his lips as his eyes glazed over. "I'll tell Julian...when I see him..."

Adrien's shallow breathing quieted as his fingers fell away from my wrist stilled by death. The life left his eyes, his soul retreating into the darkest recesses of his body awaiting release.

My fingers tightened in the wet material of the shirt as a tremor shook my shoulders. "No, Adrien. Please. Please don't leave me. I'm sorry for not listening to you." Tears ran down my cheeks freely. "We'll go home...together."

Karina's warm hand brushed my bare shoulder. "Jacen, you need help. We have to go."

I rolled my shoulder to cast off her compassionate touch. Anger bit into me. "No, he wouldn't leave me. I'm not going to leave him."

She knelt beside me, her other hand coming to rest on my cheek. Gently she pulled my face to look over at her. "It's too late. No one can help him now, but we can help you."

Ignoring her urging, desperate to hold on to the one person in my life I had left, I stared down at his lifeless face. "Adrien,

I'm so sorry. All of this is my fault. I should never have accepted your petition to become my Second."

Karina gripped my shoulder, her voice harsh with urgency. "Jacen, you have to listen to me. The poison the Venatori use works slowly, but once it's in the system it does damage to the internal organs. If we don't get you help, you're going to end up like Adrien."

My eyes fluttered as her words penetrated my sorrow. "What does it matter? I've killed Julian and Adrien's killer. But, the Great Council still wants me dead."

She rose, grabbing me by the underarms and hefting upward. "All the more reason to get your ass up and stop feeling sorry for yourself. Adrien is gone. There is nothing more you can do for him."

I shoved her away, angry over her callous words. "Yes, there is. I made him a promise, and by Aita, I will see it done."

Karina's eyes softened. "Il Rilascio."

I nodded, setting my jaw in anticipation of an argument.

"I understand. You will not be able to see that through unless we get you help. Come with me now and I will have someone else retrieve Adrien. He will be waiting for you, when you are strong enough to make good on your promise."

I hesitated several moments, staring down at my Second. Dropping to my knees again, I glared at Karina as she tried to stop me. Bending over, I placed a hand over Adrien's eyes and moved his eyelids down to cover his vacant stare. "I promise, I'll be back for you Adrien. I won't let you live an eternity within a shattered body. Your soul will fly among the ancestors." As Karina stepped up next to me, I sat back on my haunches. I glanced up at her. "Let's go."

Reluctantly I allowed her to help me to my feet and leaned on her for support. She wrapped her arms around my waist to assist me to the stairs. As we made our way through the shattered door which led to the stairwell, she said, "Don't worry about, Adrien. He will be well cared for until you see him again."

I didn't respond, just navigated the steep stairs as best I could.

"I'm sorry I didn't tell you what was going on from the first, Jacen. When you showed up in my office out-of-the blue and sent me packing, I thought you were working for the Council. I didn't know if I could trust you not to turn me over to them. And well, then you tried."

I grabbed at the hand rail as a sudden bout of dizziness made me trip. "Yeah, I didn't exactly make the best first impression."

She paused to open the door at the base of the stairs. "No matter. You did what needed to be done when it really mattered." She poked her head out of the door way. Once she was sure no one loitered in the hall, she dragged me with her. "And once you feel better, we will have a lot of house cleaning to do."

I resisted her pulling, allowing my arm to drop from about her shoulders. "No."

Her confused stare turned on me. "What do you mean no?"

"I mean no. My parents are dead. Julian is dead. Adrien is dead. I'm two steps from death's door. All because we went up against the Great Council. Well, I'm done. I'm going home. Get someone else to conduct your private war."

"There is no one else, Jacen. *You* are the one we've been waiting two centuries for." She grabbed my arm and wrapped it back around her shoulders. Coaxing me down the hall, she held on as if letting go would mean the end of the world. "Now, let's get you out of here."

Chapter Thirty-Eight

The trip to Assisi had been the longest car ride I'd ever experienced, even though Karina nearly broke the sound barrier to get me here as fast as she could.

When we opened the door of a suite in a cheery little hotel, my heart dropped to my feet.

Just inside the door, Dante waited. As Karina half dragged half carried me through the doorway her urgency bled over into her tone, "Dante, did you bring what I asked for?"

Dante's deep voice rumbled from across the room, "I did. It's in the bag next to the bed."

"Good. We need to administer it as quickly as possible. Help him to the bed."

At her request Dante rushed to us and grabbed my other arm. Hefting it around his broad shoulders, he took my weight so Karina could step away.

Intense pain ricocheted through me as if it were a live thing swallowing me whole from the outside in. Knees buckling for the umpteenth time, an agonized whimper filled the room.

Holy fuck? Was that me? I sounded like a sick child calling for its mother. How pathetic.

"Whoa. I've got you." The confidence in his voice was

reassuring.

The leader of the Cambiare held me firmly against his side as if my weight were nothing to him. As he crouched to allow my feet to touch the ground, it occurred to me that in the alley that night I'd grossly underestimated his size. Perhaps it had been a good thing Adrien stopped me from doing something foolish.

Released from crutch duty, Karina flew into action. "I'll get the rubbing alcohol and supplies to sew his wounds closed."

"Dai! I brought everything we'll need. Alegra is on her way from the hospital as well. She's bringing anything else she feels is necessary."

"Alegra is coming...here?" The tone of her voice had changed from confident dictator to unsure follower.

"Of course. She is our doctor." Dante eased me to the edge of the bed then continued, "You didn't think *I* was going to sew him up, did you?"

A long pause silenced the room. Then Karina's hesitant voice drew my gaze. "No, but...do you think that is wise? I mean, what if Nix comes too?"

A frustrated growl rumbled in the man's chest as he inched me toward the bed. "It is my understanding from her sister the two have worked out their differences. If you still question it, ask him."

Karina bit the corner of her lip obviously still unsure.

I sucked in a breath as Dante helped me raise my legs to the bed. "No worries, Karina. Nix and I may not be the best of friends, but it's not like I'm in any condition to do her harm."

A sour look turned her hesitant smile into a slight frown. Under her breath she said, "I wasn't worried about you doing her harm." then louder, she finished, "Look at you, trying to reassure me when you should be concentrating on not dying."

As if eager to remind me of my current, feeble position, my vision tunneled, and a wave of dizziness swept through me. I closed my eyes to combat the sensation. Dante's firm hand eased me back onto the waiting pillows.

"You need to rest. All of this movement is causing the poison to work faster." Dante glanced over his shoulder toward Karina. "Grab some towels. I'll get the alcohol."

At Karina's return, Dante handed her the bottle.

Her eyes widened as she gripped the towels to her chest. "You want me to do it?"

A serious frown turned the corners of his lips downward. "You aren't strong enough to hold him down."

Before I could react, Dante's hands were on my shoulders pushing me back into the cushiony surface. I gazed up at him, his golden eyes serious with intent, his square jaw set in firm resolution. Somewhere in the back on my mind a thought whispered...

You are vulnerable, at the mercy of a Cambiare.

At one time that would have been disturbing. Now, as I stared up into his intensely amber eyes, trusting him with my life, it seemed the safest place to be.

Intent on voicing this new revelation, I opened my mouth. Instead a pained scream ripped from me as cold liquid fire burned my chest. Stings like a million fire ant bites rippled through each and every scratch, gash, and cut on my chest. I reared up against Dante's hands, struggling to free myself from the torture. The fight was futile, his strength ten times mine at this moment.

Casting Karina a wild-eyed accusatory glare, I growled between gnashing teeth as the searing encompassed my mind. Fortunately, she busied herself dabbing gingerly at the wound and missed the look which I was certain would have stopped her heart.

Her pinched features and downcast eyes seemed to broadcast her guilt over the infliction of pain. Finally, she looked up at me. Even the tunnel vision I was currently experiencing couldn't hide the concern in her eyes. "I'm sorry, Jacen. But, there is really nothing I can do to make this easier on you."

My lips pinched together as I breathed heavily through the nose. In, out. In, out, concentrating on controlling my reaction to the pain. The burning eased. I forced a grin out of the grimace and gazed up at Karina. "It's okay, Karina. Do what you must.

I'll survive it."

Famous last words full of bravado—that's what those were.

Emboldened by my encouragement, Karina doused the wounds again, and I gave up the façade. Just as the pain reached its pinnacle, blessed darkness came to claim me.

*****

Buzz. Buzz. Buzz.

My eyelids were so…heavy. Why couldn't I muster enough strength to draw them open?

Buzz. Buzz. Buzz.

The sound persisted like the infernal buzzing of pesky fly far too close to my ear.

Buzz. Buzz. Buzz.

Sweet Aita! Shut up. Instinctively, I reached out to bat it away.

"Careful, Jacen. You'll pull out your IV."

Familiar, feminine…

A cool, damp sensation ran along my brow. Why was she doing that? I brushed her away.

Finally, my lids lifted, but my brow furrowed as the room's walls reverberated around me, heaving as if they breathed. Rushing in my ears temporarily blocked the sound around me. I tried to speak, but nothing would respond to my commands. Sweat sprung from every pore as heavy bouts of shivering coursed through my body.

Her voice sang to me again.

"Jacen? Jacen, stop. We have to get your fever down."

I turned my head toward her and blinked. Long sable hair framed worried liquid gold eyes. The curve of her jaw beckoned a soft touch. Reaching out, I ran a finger along her cheek. My eyebrows came together in confusion as the image morphed into that of my favorite red-head with warm brown sensual eyes…but she was so cold.

She pulled back, her eyes narrowing.

"Angel?" The reverent word slipped from my lips on a sigh. I dropped my hand back to my side, a wistful smile touching my lips. "Turn off the alarm and come back to bed."

Another woman's voice floated to me from somewhere in the netherworld. "Nix, why would he say that? You haven't—"

Nix? But, I thought…

The image cleared, and Nix sat before me.

"No, of course not, Alegra. He obviously thinks I'm someone else."

Dante's concerned voice joined the conversation. "He's hallucinating?"

A bark of laughter interrupted their discussion. All eyes scrutinized me.

"Is this normal?"

Concern bled from Karina's tone and into my fog-like dream state. *Normal? What was she talking about?*

The buzzing began again, distracting me from the question.

A second later the annoying sound stopped mid-buzz followed by an exasperated, "Cazzo!"

Karina's voice demanded, "What is it, Dante?"

"By the Gods, they just won't let him be."

Nix appeared like magic from nowhere. "The Great Council again?" *How did she get so close without me seeing her?* Dante nodded still scowling at the phone. "Well, if they want him, they'll have to go through me."

Nix's conviction amused me. If I had had the ability, I might have even given a cheeky response.

Violent shivers wracked my body. The sheets, wet with sweat, twisted around my naked form. *Sweat? Why was I…?* "Aliments don't sweat."

A cool soft hand brushed my shoulder. "Jacen, can you hear me?" A moment's pause, gentle prodding at the shoulder, blessed silence.

"Jacen, if you can hear me," Opening my eyes a crack, I gazed up at Alegra's anxious face. "The antidote in combination with the high fever is causing hallucinations. We are working on countering this. But, if you don't stop thrashing around, you're going to pull out your IV and tear your stitches."

My lids grew heavy, but I fought being dragged into the abyss yet again. Finally exhausted by the effort, I took a deep breath and let go. *Fuck it. Too tired...*

*****

Sunlight bounced off walls painted a happy jonquil yellow. I squinted, turning away from the overwhelming brightness.

A shadow fell across me, mercifully blocking out the light, albeit temporarily.

"Where...am I?" My tongue seemed unnaturally thick and too big for my mouth.

"You're awake. That's a good sign." Karina smiled down at me. "You're in my hotel room in Assisi."

"Your hotel room?"

Karina nodded. "Yes. Do you remember anything?"

It hadn't been some horrible nightmare. Adrien really was dead, and someone on the Great Council was to blame. "I...remember."

Struggling to sit more upright, I cringed as the skin on my chest stretched with the awkward movements.

Her warm hand touched my bare shoulder as she gently pushed me downward. "Don't. Just lie still. It's too soon for you to be getting up."

I shook my head. "I'll be fine. I have to take care of Adrien."

"I told you we would take care of Adrien. As soon as I had you safely away, I called Leo. He's already taken care of everything. He petitioned the Council to send Adrien home. His flight is scheduled for tomorrow, late afternoon. Then, he'll be safely in the hands of your clan."

I relaxed back against the pillows relieved to know Adrien was secure. The barest amount of saliva touched my swollen tongue reminding me of my own state. A throat, so dry I could have spit dirt, beckoned for relief. I swallowed convulsively but it didn't help. "Can I get a glass of water?"

"Si." Karina rose and crossed to the dresser. A moment later she returned with a tall glass. Sitting gingerly on the side of the bed, she put a hand behind my head. With her help I gulped down over half the glass and then dropped back to the pillows. "I feel like someone dragged me behind a pickup truck for ten miles. How long have I been here?"

Her brow knit as she looked down at me with understanding. "I brought you here three nights ago. Dante helped me clean your wounds, and then Alegra administered the antidote for the poison. Apparently, you had a reaction to the serum. You lost consciousness. You were mostly in and out for a while. At one point you were even hallucinating."

"Alegra?" I searched patchy memories in the hopes of filling in the blanks.

"Yes. We thought we'd lost you there for a second, but Alegra got you back. She patched you up as well. With the efficiency of your species' healing, the bandages should be able to come off in a few days."

I looked away from Karina, lost in my own thoughts. Finally, I turned back to face her curious eyes. "What happened before?"

"Before what?" Here dark chocolate eyes searched my features for guidance.

"Before all hell broke loose. How did you end up with Adrien? He was going to fill me in, but…" I trailed off, unable to finish the sentence.

She sighed heavily and rose. Walking across the room, she crossed her arms and then turned back toward me. "After you and the guards chased me out of the villa I fled to Assisi. I told Dante what had happened, and he took this room." Her gaze flew briefly around the space to indicate where we were, and she continued. "It is for me to hide out in. Then the other day he came to warn me that a Venatori had come to town looking for me."

"How did he know the man was Venatori?"

She nudged her toe into the carpet. "Dante has his ways. I don't question them, especially when his instincts benefit me."

I took the hint and didn't ask anything more. "Go on then."

"Anyway, he told me where I could find the man. However, when I came across him, he was in the middle of a phone call." She shrugged. A look of wry humor lit her features. "One benefit of being half Cambiare, my hearing is superior in every way."

"You were able to hear his conversation?"

"Not all of it, but enough to know he had accepted a job to take out someone important. Intrigued, I followed him." She crossed over to the dresser and poured a second glass of water. Taking a sip, she gazed at me over the rim.

Humor followed closely on the heels of disbelief. "You were stalking a Venatori? And he didn't know it?" The chuckle which started low in the chest transformed midstream into a full-on belly laugh but was cut violently short as pain ripped through my newly stitched wounds. "I'll bet he was as surprised as I was when you showed up."

"Careful. You'll rip your stitches." Karina's genuine concern lit her eyes. "Anyway, yes. You could say that."

Before long, her smile faded, and the moment was gone. She set the glass down again and looked away from me. "When he pulled up in front of Alcie's home, I had no idea Adrien was there. I thought the assassin had been contracted to kill her. Hell, for that matter, even after Adrien and I had managed to take him down, I still thought the man was after Alcie."

What happened to her? Is Alcie okay?"

Karina's frown deepened. "I don't know. When I arrived, Alcie had already been struck down. She was on the ground in the kitchen. I don't know if she was dead. She looked dead." She rubbed her hands along her arms in a self-comforting movement, her eyes appearing haunted. A sad smile touched her lips. "He must have loved her a great deal. He put himself between her and the Venatori just as he did for you. I just don't know if she was lucky enough to survive the ordeal."

"Why didn't you stay with her?"

"I wanted to, but Adrien insisted we go to you. He was afraid with his injury he wouldn't be able to protect you on his own. So, in the end, we both chose your life over Alcie's." Her gaze moved to her feet as she shifted her weight. "Maybe if I'd been there just a few seconds earlier the choice wouldn't have been necessary. I might have prevented both Adrien's and Alcie's deaths."

Empathy. That's what that strange softening of my heart was. Lost for a moment, I searched for something to say. "Don't, Karina. Beating yourself up over something you couldn't have stopped gets you nowhere. Trust me. I speak from experience. Every person I've ever truly loved or trusted has ended up dead."

As I said the words, the reality that was my life struck me full force in the face. *Was I cursed? Were all those I took in to my inner circle doomed to violent ends?* It was certainly beginning to feel that way. I gazed up into Karina's bright eyes. "If there is one thing I can tell you, Karina, it's that no one, no matter how strong, has the power to stave off death when it comes for you."

Her eyes, intense, met my gaze. "No, but we can fight tooth and nail to make sure death is good and bruised when he finally succeeds in taking us."

I chuckled. "Yes, we can."

"Jacen?" Her voice held a hint of hesitation.

"Yes?"

"Did you mean it when you said you were leaving?"

I stared up into her curious eyes. For several moments we said nothing, each assessing the other as if we'd just met. In truth, it was as though we had. Until three nights ago, our dealings had been anything but cordial. However, everything had changed. "I did."

She peered at the ground. "I understand."

No one could have mistaken the disappointment in her tone. Awkward silence filled the room.

Unable to stand it another moment, I shifted in the bed and groaned as my hand slipped on the sheet jarring the wounds on my chest. "Fuck those hurt."

Forgetting her disappointment, she rushed to my side.

Wrapping her arm around my back, she helped me straighten up and eased me back against the pillows. "Are you okay?"

I swallowed, as her breath caressed my ear. Turning toward her, our faces inches apart I looked deep into her soft brown eyes. "Why did you do it, Karina?"

She blinked at me, surprised by the question. "You needed help."

"No. I mean, after how I treated you, why did you try to intercede with the Venatori? You could have been killed."

A genuine grin split her face like an atom exploding into a chain reaction of good humor. "Because, despite your asinine assumptions, Jacen of Samsaveel, I know you have a good heart. You came over here for the right reasons, and you accomplished what you set out to do. There's a lot to be said for someone with that kind of drive. Now, if you choose to stay, it will be because you are the person I believe you to be. But, that is your choice to make and no one else's."

I blinked at her, amazed by her well thought out answer. "And that was enough for you? The hope that I might stay to help the Cambiare?"

As she gazed down at me, her eyes held a youthful self-assurance. Something in that look reminded me of Julian, and I couldn't help but smile.

"Jace, sometimes faith in others and hope for a better future is all we need to see us through. And just so you don't misunderstand me, my hope is not just for the Cambiare. It is also for the Alimentatori. We could use someone like you to lead us."

I shifted uncomfortably on the bed. *Lead the Aliments? Was she crazy? I nearly died trying to mind my own business.* I couldn't imagine what sticking my nose in the Great Council's business would get me. "Karina, I appreciate your faith in me. For some reason, which escapes me right now, there seems to be a lot of that going around lately. Nevertheless, I'm tired and I just want to take Adrien home."

Her face fell in disappointment, a look with which I was

becoming all too familiar. She sighed, all her arguments apparently exhausted. "I understand, Jacen. I will talk to Leo and have him arrange for you to accompany Adrien's body home." Sadness dropped her shoulders as she crossed to the door. "If you change your mind, we'll be waiting for you."

"Thank you, Karina, for everything you've done for me." A lump formed in my throat as I watched her leave.

Chapter Thirty-Nine

Assisi, Italy
Three hours before departure.

It had been days since I'd last seen the streets of Assisi. When we'd arrived, it had been the dead of night and I barely conscious. Now, as the early summer sun made a slow arch across the sky, the sidewalks buzzed with activity. As I neared the Basilica of San Francesco d'Assisi the crowd thickened. I merged with the tourists walking toward the Basilica Superiore.

Hands clasped behind my back; I followed the hedge-lined sidewalk just as I had the night I'd first met Nix. A brief smile touched my lips as the memories enveloped me. She'd lead me on a merry chase that night. Perhaps if I'd known where she was heading I would have thought twice about chasing her through the darkened alleyways. I laughed under my breath when the memory of dropping down amidst a whole cadre of Cambiare reminded me of my own foolishness. *Or…perhaps not. If not for Adrien I might have…*

Haunting memories of the man who'd sacrificed all to save my life swirled around me like a sad melody, his last moments dancing within my mind. The less pleasing images stole the wistful thoughts from me.

Casting my gaze downward, I shoved my hands into the pockets of my blue jeans. I'd been lucky to call him friend. Too bad he'd not been able to say the same of me.

I inhaled deeply.

Would I ever be able to think about my Second without being railroaded by guilt? A voice resembling that of Adrien's whispered, *it's what you deserve.*

I couldn't help but agree.

Arriving at the midpoint directly in front of the Basilica, I stopped and turned. I stood for a few moments to gaze at the antediluvian monastery. In daylight, it was even grander than I'd imagined. Stark white walls lovingly framed by celestial blue skies, rose like a monolithic monument from just beyond a field of emerald grass.

A straw-hatted tourist paused next to me to snap pictures with a smartphone and then shouted to her husband who was meandering slowly along the path.

"Hurry up, Al. I want a picture in front before the bus leaves."

The old man waved a hand of dismissal. "Hold your horses, Helen. We've got plenty of time."

In the next instant she turned to me and smiled. "Would you mind taking a picture for us?"

I rolled my eyes. *Don't you people have better things to do with your lives than stand around snapping pictures of old buildings?* The bitter thought, evidence of my growing irritation with humankind suggested the necessity of finding my way out of Italy and back home where I belonged as quickly as possible. Sidestepping her attempt at handing me her smartphone, I frowned. "Yes, I would mind."

Ignoring the woman's squeak of indignation, I turned on a heel, walked several feet away and resumed my wait.

Home. Now that was a pleasant thought indeed.

Sure, telling the clan of Adrien's heroic death would be difficult, but knowing Angel waited for me...

The image of the beautiful redhead lying naked and

inviting in my bed chased away the blackened thoughts of death. Her presence always served as a pleasant escape which eased the strain of the world. This time would be no different.

Glancing down at my watch, my mouth twisted into a half frown.

Almost noon. The message I'd received an hour ago said to meet her at the spot we'd first come face to face. I was at that spot. But, where was she? My gaze scoured the undulating herd of humans.

Not seeing her familiar ebony hair in the crowd, I turned back to the Basilica. I had just under two hours to get to the hanger. The Council's private jet was scheduled to leave at two p.m. So, if she wanted to talk, she better hurry. Adrien's ceremonial casket would already be waiting in the hold, as should my own belongings. There was no way I was going to miss my one-way ticket home.

One-way ticket? Yeah, right. The Great Council had agreed to a temporary stay of execution—eh, Ascension—not a permanent one. Their letter was quite clear on that point.

You have been granted a temporary release from your contract. You may accompany your Second's body home. As requested, your belongings will be delivered to the hanger where they will await your arrival. The Great Council will expect you to return posthaste. Contact our assistant so that you might take your position as novitiate immediately upon your return.

Novitiate. That sounded exciting. I crossed my arms over my chest. *I couldn't fucking wait.* I doubted they'd released me for my benefit anyway. More likely they were pulling back and regrouping after their Venatori lapdogs bungled the assassination attempt. That was fine. I needed some time too. Time to figure out what my next move was. I couldn't take the Council head on. I would need to reassess the information I had and probably...

"Jacen?"

Not surprised, I glanced over my shoulder. Nix had a way of appearing out of thin air. Not hard to do, I suppose, when you have the stealth of a Cambiare. What did surprise me was the accusatory golden gaze shimmering in the sunlight. *Was she crazy?* Why wasn't she wearing her contacts or sunglasses? There were far too many tourists around for her to be safe like that. "Why aren't your eyes covered?"

She ignored my question as she frowned. "I'm glad you came."

I gave her a sly smile and raised an eyebrow. "Come to give me a proper goodbye?"

She crossed her arms, keeping her distance from me. "Always the playboy Americano, eh?"

"Only with you, Nix. Only with you." As expected, she rolled her eyes. I genuinely smiled. "If not to see me off properly then why did you request this meeting?"

"Because I need to know why."

Lost for a moment, I shot her a puzzled look. "Why what?"

"Why are you leaving?"

Irritated by the accusation in her voice, I met her scowl with an exasperated frown of my own. "Because I made a promise to Adrien?"

"You made a promise to me and to my people." Her fingers gripped her arms so tightly it appeared she was trying to keep from doing me harm.

I heaved a frustrated sigh. "Nix, you don't understand…"

"I believe I understand perfectly well. You come over here, make promises you never intend to keep, and then run away."

She had a right to be angry. I'd made her a promise. I was breaking that promise. She had a lot riding on me and it must appear like I was running out on her, leaving her to fend for herself. "I'm not running away. I'm going home."

Those glistening almost animalistic eyes bored into me as her fingers dug deeper into her upper arms in restraint.

Then, suddenly, she gave an outraged shriek, threw her hands into the air in exasperation and shouted, "Poi si va. Non ho bisogno del tuo aiuto. Cazzo codardo americano."

Stunned by the outburst, I stared at her in silent contemplation. *Had she really just called me a fucking American coward?*

Me? A coward? *Fuck her.* My teeth ground together as my finger nails bit into the soft palms of my hands. If I were any less a gentleman, she'd have been picking up her teeth. "You may call me many things, but coward is not among them."

"No? Why else would you run back to America when you promised to find my sister? I trusted you. I went to my people and told them you would help. Now," her anger intensified, "what am I supposed to tell them?"

In suppressed anger, I raised a shaky hand and raked it mercilessly through my hair. An exasperated and pained growl escaped as I cringed. The pain shot through my chest like a locomotive on fire, reminding me that the wounds the Venatori had inflicted were still very raw. Dropping my arm back to my side, I forced myself to take a slow, calming breath. When the pain subsided, I met her earnest stare. *What could I say that would make any of this better?* Her gaze said it all. *Not a gods damn thing.* Tired of the argument and frankly exhausted by the effort, my shoulders slumped. I stepped to the edge of the road and hailed a passing taxi. "You know what, tell them whatever you'd like. I'm done."

As the car pulled up alongside me, I grabbed the handle and opened the door intent upon escaping her presence.

I paused, feeling her eyes watching my every move. Without turning, I heaved a weary sigh. "What?"

"Is that all the answer I'm to expect? You're done, and I'm dismissed?"

Frustrated, I slammed the car door closed then turned on her with a vengeance. "Sweet Aita, Nix. You could try the

S.J. WOLFF

patience of The Watchers, themselves."

Her eyebrow arched as she met my anger head on, unflinching. "Why because I demand answers you don't want to give?"

Propping my hands on my hips, I stared at the ground for several seconds. "I've given you an answer. It is not my fault if you don't like the one I've given you."

"I just don't understand, Jacen. Why is your promise to a dead man so much more important than saving my sister's life?" Her tone softened perceptively and suddenly I understood.

She was hurt. She believed I never intended to help her...that I'd used her to get what I wanted and was content to walk away without living up to my side of the agreement.

"Listen Nix, I came over here for one reason and one reason only, to see Julian's killer put in his grave, which I've done." I swallowed, as the thought of Adrien pleading for release haunted me. "When I promised you help, I had every intention of following through. I could never have predicted the death of my Second. Adrien sacrificed everything to save me. Giving him his due and performing The Release is the very least I can do for him. I'm not asking you to like it, but my promise to him supersedes anything I said to you. It must. If this makes me a coward in your eyes, then so be it. There is nothing I can say or do to change your opinion about it."

Surprisingly, her eyes softened. She screwed up her mouth and then looked away from me as if seriously contemplating my answer.

After several moments, the taxi driver, growing impatient, honked, startling both of us. I motioned for the driver to wait then turned back to Nix.

Her eyes sought mine, a curious look on her face. "I do understand your commitment to your Second. I, too, am committed to the one's I love. My younger sister, Aria..." she glanced away suddenly uncomfortable with the conversation, "she is testarda...um, headstrong. Dante warned us that Cambiare were disappearing. We tried to protect her as best we could, but she would not listen. She snuck out many times to go to Eros, even though both Alegra and I had forbidden her going alone." She took a deep breath and shrugged, "The last time I saw her, we fought. She and her friends were playing a very dangerous game. Sneaking into Eros was part of it. I told her no, that if she wanted to go to Eros she needed to wait. I would take her once I'd completed an errand for Dante."

Curious, I studied her. "Julian?"

"Yes. I was with Julian the night Aria disappeared." Her chin tilted upward at a prideful slant. "I tell you this, not to garner sympathy, only to show you that I too have an obligation. I must find my sister. I must bring her home." The corners of her mouth edged downward as she met my gaze once again. "It would be infinitely easier with your help."

I gave a curt nod, understanding her better than I had before.

"Will you consider coming back…after you've seen to Adrien?" She shifted from one foot to the other. Her ever amber eyes bored into me, as if they could somehow force an answer from me.

Finally, I shrugged. "Are you sure you want the help of a coward?"

"I…," She flushed and for the first time in our brief acquaintance, she actually looked chagrined. "I didn't…really mean that."

I chuckled, a husky warm utterance I rarely allowed. "Good to know."

"So, will you?"

I studied her, knowing to answer honestly would send her straight into a rage. Instead, I lied. "I will consider it."

A hesitant, grateful smile crossed her features

"That's all I can ask." She turned to walk away. A pang of regret settled into the pit of my stomach. As she paused for a moment as if deep in thought, then looked back at me in question. In that moment, I wondered what it would be like to be worthy of such a woman. A soft smile touched her lips as her gaze sought mine one last time.

Squelching the uncomfortable thoughts, I returned her smile. This would be how I remembered her, standing just steps away, her honeyed eyes twinkling in the sun, the breeze toying with her hair.

So, lost in my own thoughts, it took me a moment to realize she'd spoken my name.

"Yes?" My voice was barely audible to me, so there was no telling if she'd heard me.

Before I knew what was happening, she'd crossed the short span between us. Lifting her hand, she stroked a finger down my cheek. Her touch was electric, burning a path along the jawline. As she leaned in her breasts brushed against my chest. Desire I'd never quite experienced before dwarfed the pain of the fresh wounds. The breath caught in my throat. In that moment she was Delilah, wanton sex kitten and the bringer of men to their knees. Her scent overwhelmed the pleasure centers of my brain. *Rule number two - Don't let her scent get to you.* The corners of my lips twitched in humor. *Too late.*

Her warm, sweet lips hovered above mine. I swallowed, knowing I was about to break the last and final rule, stay the hell away from her...lips.

It didn't matter. Those rules were stupid anyway. What did it matter if I kissed her again? I'd probably never see her...

Her hand snaked up my neck startling the breath from me. In a rough, possessive motion, willowy fingers curled into my hair. Then, without warning her tongue darted out to caress my lips. With the slightest stroke of her tongue, I was lost. My arms slid around her, fingers spreading wide across her back pulling her toward me only to convulsively curl into her blouse as her length caressed the lines of my body. I breathed in her scent, which served to heighten my own pleasure in raw, primal—unimaginable ways. Was this what humans felt when I used my skills against them? If so, I envied every one of them.

Sweet Aita it was exquisite.

With a slight pressure, she pulled my head downward, until our lips merged. My heartbeat raced to a fevered pitch.

The ferocity of a sudden summer torrent could never equal the shocking intensity surging through my blood. But then, as quickly as the kiss had begun it ended leaving me breathlessly wanting.

Her warm breath tickled my lips as she whispered, "Something to remember me by."

Casting me a wicked smile, her amber eyes twinkling with mischief, she pushed out of my arms, turned on a heel and disappeared into the crowd of pleasure-seeking tourists.

Slowly the fog lifted from my brain as the last remnants of her allure drifted away, leaving me shaken. A shiver ran down my back. She was dangerous on a whole other level, one which I'd never considered before.

My cheeks burned as I glanced around. The old couple stood not far away. 'Helen' smirked, her eyes knowing. I turned away, embarrassed.

As I climbed into the taxi, her whispered words taunted me, *something to remember me by*. I gave a snort of disbelief. *As if I could ever forget*. The whole encounter was imprudence at its finest.

But, one thing was for certain, whether or not I ever came back here I would not let *that* happen again.

Chapter Forty

The car came to a stop just outside the hanger. I straightened in the seat and stared at the shiny white plane sitting just inside the open doorway. It sat at the ready just as it had the day of Julian's release but this time there was no ceremonial burial box waiting. The crew would have already tucked it into the cargo hold in preparation for the trip home. An all too familiar ache rose within me. The warm air in the confines of the car grew thick, the dregs of sorrow bitter on my tongue.

Don't worry, Adrien. I made you a promise. Once we're home, I'll see your soul freed from its confines to soar with the ancestors once again.

Not waiting for the driver to open the door, I stepped out into the bright sunlight.

Moving quickly away from the car to the open stairs of the jet, I heard the taxi's engine rev as he pulled away.

I climbed the steps, and then paused when I reached the landing at the top. Glancing out past the open hanger doors, I took a last look.

This was it. My last moments in Italy. For a second, I would have sworn something tugged at my heart, but I ignored the sensation preferring to believe it was nothing more than relief.

I stepped through the hatch and planted my feet in the rich

maroon carpet lining the floor of the plane. The interior of jet was far superior to anything I could have imagined. It was as squeaky clean as the exterior, with plush white leather seats and legroom galore. Maybe if I had flown to Italy in this, I wouldn't have come off the plane relieved to be alive and on the ground again.

The cockpit door opened, and a male voice spoke behind me. "Good afternoon, signore. It is my pleasure to have you aboard. I am Capitano Bové. If you will please take a seat, we will take off momentarily."

"Thank you, Captain. I look forward to getting into the air."

He smiled and nodded. "Your suitcases were delivered earlier. I took the liberty of placing your laptop bag over there. The rest is in the hold. I hope this is okay."

I glanced over to where he motioned and spied my black leather bag. As good a place as any. "That's fine."

"Donella will be taking care of you during your flight. So, if you need anything, feel free to simply ask her."

This royal treatment was very different from what I expected when I accepted the Council's offer to fly Adrien and me home "Thank you, again, Captain. I will be fine."

With a smile and a tip of his hat, he went back into the cockpit.

I maneuvered my way to the seat, careful not to jostle the bandages across my chest.

Grabbing the handle of the bag, I dropped it to the floor of the cabin and then collapsed onto the seat's cool leather surface.

Maybe it was sheer exhaustion or maybe I'd outgrown the fear, but for the first time, the thought of flying didn't terrify me. In fact, I couldn't wait to put this Gods forsaken place behind me. I closed my eyes and laid my head back against the seat cushion, relaxing for the first time in what seemed like an eternity.

An image of Nix, her eyes glowing in the moonlight while she gazed up at me, danced through my mind. She was unusual, foreign, yet familiar, all at the same time. It would have been interesting to see where the attraction led. Her fingers caressing my skin as her scent overwhelmed me. The breath caught in my throat. A wistful smile touched my lips. *Yes, it would have been very interesting indeed.*

The sound of the doors closing alerted me to the fact we were readying for takeoff. Opening my eyes, I glanced up just in time to capture a flash of a woman's drab gray skirt, white blouse, and brightly colored neckerchief disappearing into the service area of the plane.

Donella, I presume.

I turned to gaze out the window as we taxied out of the garage and then onto the runway. A minute later, the phone embedded into the wall next to me rang. Intrigued, I picked it up. "Hello?"

"Hello, signore. It's the Capitano speaking. We are awaiting clearance for takeoff and will be in the air shortly. We are due to arrive in Albany at around ten a.m. I will do my best to avoid turbulence. So, sit back, buckle up, and enjoy your flight."

"I would appreciate that, Captain. Thank you."

"My pleasure, signore."

I hung up the phone and leaned an arm against the wall. Peering out the window, I watched the ground roll by beneath me. Slowly at first, then quickly. I had to shut my eyes to keep the dizziness at bay.

I sat back, content to let the land fall away without bearing witness to our ascent. Then suddenly we were in the air and free of the bounds of gravity.

I exhaled. *Finally.*

Even now as Italy became a distant memory beneath me, I couldn't squash the guilt Karina managed to invoke.

There was the look in her eyes when we said goodbye. Add that to the niggling guilt of leaving Nix and her people in the lurch…

Like Adrien and possibly Julian, they both expected far more than I was willing to give. They saw something in me I was afraid to acknowledge. What made them think I could change things? It was insane.

I glared at the white fluffy clouds streaming past the window.

It would never happen. I was going home, and that was all there was to it. Then, I would see Adrien laid to rest and my Clan steeled against future attack.

Besides, guilt would never drive me to foolishness. I couldn't allow it. My Clan didn't need the Great Council in their lives any more than I needed to sit amongst those who killed everyone I loved. In fact, with everything that had transpired, I would be a fool to ever leave New York again.

That would cause some serious anger issues with both women. But, realistically, what could Karina and Nix do? Fly to the United States and drag me back to Italy?

I gave a snort of derision. *I'd love to see them try.*

An image of the two women dragging me through the airport just to be stopped by security made me chuckle.

"Sir, are these two beautiful ladies kidnapping you?"

"Why yes officer. They are."

Of course, instead of stopping them he'd just say, *"Well done, sir. Carry on ladies,"* tip his hat and allow Nix and Karin—

"Hello, Jacen."

The familiar voice next to me stopped me mid-thought.

Confused, I glanced up. I couldn't stop the slack-jawed amazement her appearance caused. "Karina? What in the hell are you doing here?"

She plopped down into the seat across from me. Crossing her legs, she tucked a wayward auburn curl back into a bobby pin. Taking a moment to smooth her updo, she gave a half smile. "You didn't really think I'd let you travel all the way back to America alone, did you?"

My gaze met hers further confused. "But, how?"

She crossed her hands over her waist and shrugged. "A girl has to use a little magic now and again." Giving me a knowing look, her lips twitched with suppressed humor. "No, actually, Leo smuggled me on." She held out her hand as if set to shake mine. "Meet Donella, flight attendant extraordinaire."

Suspicious of the reason for her new persona, I extended my

hand and took hers. As her fingers wrapped around my hand, our eyes met. "Donella, eh?" My grip on her hand tightened perceptibly. "Why the alias?"

Her gaze wavered as she grew uncomfortable under my scrutiny. She released my hand and tugged hers out of my grip. A grim frown darkened her features. She sat for several moments as if contemplating her next sentence. Then finally, she sat back. "Do you think the Great Council would allow me anywhere near you under my real name?"

I sat back, considering what she said. Watching her closely, I realized she was probably right. But, then the Council had to know she saved my life. "I suppose that makes sense, but I would guess they already know pretty much everything that happened between us."

"Yes, but that doesn't mean they would have allowed me on this plane. So, Leo changed the manifest and stuck me in as a flight attendant. The real Donella is in Greece visiting relatives."

"Ah, I see." I did, but I didn't. None of that explained what she was doing here. "Mind explaining to me why any of this is necessary?"

She shrugged. "All you need to know is that we felt it was necessary to protect you."

"Protect me from what? The Great Council released me from service and arranged for this flight. I'd say they are well-satisfied with this outcome. They send me home, tail between my legs, and I am no longer a threat to any of them."

Her eyebrow rose in question. "And you really believe this? That you are no threat to them?"

I gave a firm nod.

"And you are content? Ending things this way?"

I frowned and cast a glare out the window. "It doesn't matter."

"But, it does, Jacen. What of Nix and the captured Cambiare? Will you not fulfill your promise to them?"

I shifted in my seat, uncomfortable under her pointed stare. Angry over her attempts to shame me, I glared at her with an intensity meant to cow her. "Don't think for a moment that any of your attempts to guilt me into returning to Italy will work. If I choose to go back it will be for my reasons and mine alone."

Her eyes narrowed, and her chin rose. She was not intimidated. "Jacen, do you have any idea how important you are?"

The change of topic threw me for a second.

"What the fuck are you talking about?"

"Without you, the Cambiare who were taken prisoner may be lost forever. How can you be so callous as to condemn them to a life of outright torture?" Her answer was snide, almost disgusted as she wrapped her arms over her chest.

"So, they are the ones who truly sent you." The muscle in my jaw flexed as I turned from her. She didn't rush to deny it, which was enough of a confirmation for me. Under my breath I mumbled, "And Leo is obviously sympathetic to their cause."

"Of course, he is. His grandfather was in love with a Cambiare woman. He lives in the past and likes it that way."

I nodded, understanding. "Well, you can tell Leo you were too late. The plane has taken off and there is no way in hell that I'm having the captain turn us around."

Her eyebrow rose as she tapped her fingers against her arms. "No one is asking you to."

"Good. And you can return to Italy with the plane after we land."

Her features hardened, obviously not appreciating my dismissal. The grim frown turned even more severe. Rage emanated off her in waves. She glared out the window on her side. "Perhaps I will."

We sat in silence for several minutes, each stewing in our own anger. I felt her eyes shift as she turned her stare on me. "Forgive me, Jacen. I didn't come her to fight with you."

Taken aback by the gentling of her words, my gaze met hers. I did little more than stare at her for several moments. Finally, I spoke. "Why are you *really* here, Karina?"

Dropping her arms, she grabbed her purse from the seat next to her. She opened the clasp and peered into the dark confines of the bag. A second later, she pulled out something cream colored. Closing the purse, she dropped it back onto the seat and met my gaze. "I'm here to deliver this…"

She leaned over and held out the item. My gaze sought what she held.

Reaching out, I took it from her and glanced up at her confused. "What's this?"

Karina's gaze met mine, unflinching. When she spoke, her tone held a hard edge, as though the secret the envelope held was of great import. "Something that will change life as you know it."

COME PLAY WITH ME

WHERE THE CAMBIARE
RULE THE NIGHT

Look for book two in the Aita saga coming soon!
Find me on Facebook: @Wolffs.Realm
Or Visit my website: sjwolff.com